To my good friend Bort

Scott Sk[ipper]

4/30/14

FAMILY
TRAITS

SCOTT SKIPPER

D1737987

3

ALSO BY SCOTT SKIPPER

Family Traits
The story of the arrival of the Skipper clan
In the New World
And the negative impact they had

Face of the Angel
The Auschwitz Angel of Death
Josef Mengele's
Forty-year exile in South America

The Hundred Years Farce
Alternative American History
What if we'd annexed México in 1846?

A Death in Carolina
An account of the murder of Deputy Sheriff Isaac
Skipper in 1914
Only available as an eBook

CONTENTS

PROLOGUE

The Indians lived at the fork of the river. They had been there longer than anyone could remember and the rivers were such a part of them that they defined themselves as "The People of the Fork in River"—Cheroenhaka. The game was plentiful and the soil was good for corn and squash. The rivers teemed with fish and it was a short journey to the sea for salt and shellfish. The warriors were many and were feared by their enemies.

Gahuntee Ohunwitstag had spent the day tending a fire that was the tribe's habit to start at the end of summer for clearing the undergrowth. As was usual he was smeared with bear fat, and soot from the fire had settled on him and clung to the fat. He was tall, broad shouldered, and handsome having an aquiline profile and high prominent cheekbones painted with red suns. Darkness had fallen and with him on the buffalo hide was a girl named Cheeta Newisha who was sweet faced and of exuberant form. In the cool air she was dressed in her beaver skin jacket and Gahuntee Ohunwitstag had the idea that it would be a fine thing to put his hand through one its many vents to stroke her breast. Not seeing it coming, the touch made her start and she pulled away from his hand. Relaxing she smiled and said, "A good man would try again."

A sudden light flared. Motion to their right startled them and they looked to see a bright red streak in the sky. At zenith the head of it shattered and so many pieces arced earthward they could not count them before they disappeared behind the tree line. It was over in the time it took the frightened girl to throw her arms around his chest. "What was it?" she whispered.

He thought for a time, baffled but not wanting to admit it. "Surely it is an omen. Your father will know better. We can ask him later."

"Why don't we ask him now?"

He could feel her heart beating against his chest. "It can wait," he said and laid her onto the mat. He took her advice and tried again for the breast which was firm and smooth. Then he put the other hand between her legs and was enthralled by the warmth and texture he found there. Her beaver coat fell away from her shoulders as she arched her back against the pressure of his palm. It was all the consent he needed.

When they were spent and their breathing slowed they fell asleep and he dreamed of the meteor until the chill in the air woke them. The moon was high when they returned to their respective houses to finish the night. In the morning Gahuntee Ohunwitstag reflected that the pyrotechnics in the sky had paled to the fire in Cheeta Newisha's loins, but his thoughts would not let it go.

Cheeta Newisha's father was a shaman. He assembled the chiefs and told them, "Brothers, Otkum is angry and hurled great fiery stones at the earth. It is a sign of much evil to come." The people were afraid and offered tobacco on the *quioccosan* while they chanted and drummed.

Gahuntee Ohunwitstag became obsessed with the idea of finding one of the burning stones. "Surely it will be a magical thing with great power," he told his father, the *werrowance*, who found the notion of trying to recover burning rocks thrown by the devil somewhat foolish but knew that every boy must answer the call of adventure.

He smiled indulgently and said, "Don't be gone long."

Cheeta Newisha's reaction to his announcement was: "It's an evil thing. You should leave it alone." She gave him a look that said if he stayed there with her he was more likely to find something magical with great power.

"But it must be a thing of importance. Besides, I have yet to fulfill my vision quest. It's something a warrior must do."

She thought it was something a fool must do and was irritated at seeming less important to him than a demon stone but she checked her pique and told him, "Don't be gone long. If I get lonely I might have to let Sariyoka Huse amuse me."

He scowled at the threat but promised to hurry. With his bow, quiver and staff he left the village heading toward the place he thought a burning stone had fallen. While he walked he survived mostly on *okeepenauk* which he dug from the ground with his staff. On the third day he shot a duck and carried it until dark when he roasted it over his camp fire. On the seventh day he recognized the form of a man moving through the trees at the far edge of a clearing. With a jolt of fear he pulled his bow from his shoulder and nocked an arrow thinking he was concealed. The stranger dashed that conceit by stepping calmly into the open with both hands raised—one holding his bow and one his pipe. With relief Gahuntee Ohunwitstag raised the hand with palm outward that indicated a preference for the pipe. The stranger smiled and beckoned toward some rocks shaded by an old long straw pine where he sat and began to fill the bowl of the pipe. After the wild tobacco brought its dreams both were lulled into an extended silence punctuated only by the odd grunt of approval and sigh of satisfaction. Eventually the man spoke. He said his name and the name of his people. Gahuntee Ohunwitstag could understand him, though imperfectly.

"I am Gahuntee Ohunwitstag, warrior of the Cheroenhaka," he replied in turn. "I am on a vision quest to the place where a red star fell from the sky seven nights ago."

"Well, brother, we meet by providence for we are on the same quest." The older man's use of the traveling language that allowed diverse people to communicate was not exactly Gahuntee Ohunwitstag's dialect and he spoke with an accent that made even familiar words require some effort but with the aid of signs they managed. The stranger continued, "Yesterday and today I discovered three places where it touched the earth, but it vanished without leaving a clue of its nature. Has your vision revealed it to you?"

"I haven't had a vision yet. Maybe if I saw the place where it fell the visions would come. Can you take me to it?"

"Yes," he said, "I have been away long enough and I do not think there is anything more to be learned by going farther. If you walk with me for a day I will show a place where the fireball gouged a great hole in the earth."

Gahuntee Ohunwitstag eagerly assented. When shafts of sun slanted acutely through the forest Gahuntee Ohunwitstag felt his head begin to clear and set himself to start a fire for the coming of night. The older man watched bemused and when the kindling was aflame he took a burning twig which he used to light his newly filled pipe. Gahuntee Ohunwitstag shrugged and sitting accepted the proffered pipe.

The old man began to talk of his tribe. "My people are called the Winyah," he explained. "Our village is at the edge of a broad bay of the sea which is rich with fish and mussels, and the woods have uncountable deer and turkeys. There is little warfare unless we seek it but we have little need since so much is divinely provided."

Gahuntee Ohunwitstag told his people's story but was

eager to return to talk of the fireball. "From where I saw it, it was in the southern sky and came from the east. I saw it break into many pieces. Our shaman says it is an evil thing but I am still anxious to find it for it must have great power."

"From my perspective it passed directly over head and the pieces fell to the north and the south and the west. I was anxious to find it too, for I am also a shaman, and it is not thought well of a shaman if he cannot explain frightening lights in the sky, but after seeing the places it struck I do not think it can be found. I saw it arrive from across the sea. Surely it is an omen of evil to come from there."

"The shaman of the Cheroenhaka said Otkum is angry and is throwing burning stones at us. What could we have done to anger him so?"

"When your vision comes and you are in the dream time, you will see that Otkum is always angry. Only Quakerhunte can shield us from his caprices. This is why we must make offerings," the Winyah said loftily.

The two relapsed into silence. Each ate what food he carried and soon they drifted to sleep. Later when he woke and stepped away to relieve himself Gahuntee Ohunwitstag began to think more of Cheeta Newisha than otherworldly rocks. In his mind he relived their last night together which aroused him and made it difficult to sleep. He lay staring at the dense clouds of stars and listened to the crickets and wished if he reached his hand he could fondle the girl and not the old Winyah.

Late in the afternoon of the next day they came to the place. Sandy gray dirt was torn from the earth. Trees to the east were broken at varying heights, and the trees to the opposite end of the oblong crater were flattened in a fan pattern.

Gahuntee Ohunwitstag was awed to gaping silence. On recovering somewhat he said, "There was fire."

"Yes, you see now that it true, the rocks were burning."

"Burning rocks? But where are the rocks?"

"Consumed by the fire."

"When rocks are put into the fire they may break, but they aren't consumed."

The Winyah did not appreciate his shamanic insight being questioned by a stripling, but he held his tongue then said, "The stones of the spirit world are among many things that cannot be explained, but look, there is still another thing beyond our understanding—the hole is filling with water. When I saw it two days past some fire was still smoldering in the bottom. Now it is partly filled with water."

The sound of a breaking stick startled them to silence. Three deer stepped tentatively through the fallen trees browsing on bits of charcoal. The two Indians acted from instinct in unison in spite of the heavenly mystery before them. Their arrows felled the smallest of the three does. That night the shaman made the fire with a bow and spindle while Gahuntee Ohunwitstag crudely butchered the carcass with his flint knife. They feasted on the back straps and roasted a haunch for each of them to take when they left in the morning.

At sunrise the air was cool and sweet and the woods were raucous with bird sounds. The hawks screamed and ravens carked while a songbird repeated the same two monotonous notes. The shaman went to the edge of the crater and looked quizzically across it. "You know," he said to Gahuntee Ohunwitstag pointing to the ragged curve of its outline, "its shape is similar to the shape of the great bay of the Winyah but in miniature. Perhaps this is not so evil. It may only be the way the Creator makes bays for us to have fish and mussels."

"I'm not sure. I've never seen a bay but it looks evil to me. I wish my vision would come."

"Do you want to see another place where it fell?"

Gahuntee Ohunwitstag thought for a time weighing the possibility of returning with a talisman against returning more quickly to Cheeta Newisha. "No," he said, "there is a task awaiting me at home that I am anxious to undertake."

"As you wish. Know that if your people ever visit the Winyahs, they will be received in peace. I will leave you now for I must tell the people that the fire in the sky was only the birth pangs of bays. Shamans' work ..." He didn't finish the sentence.

Gahuntee Ohunwitstag made better time returning home. Something was goading him. He made his way to Cheeta Newisha, after a cursory visit to his father, and invited her to walk. He told her of his experiences with no effort to spare any drama. "I have seen how Quakerhunte makes bays," he concluded grandly.

She gave him a look that was similar to the one she used when he left. "Burning rocks from the sky seem more like an omen of evil to me than gods digging bays for fish and mussels. Your new friend sounds like a very bad shaman."

They were a short distance into the thick grove of loblolly pine where the air was fragrant and hot and the floor was made spongy by the soft needles. The low light was diffused and concealing. Their eyes met and he reclined her onto the forest floor where she responded to his urgency with equal ardor.

It was many years before the evil arrived from across the sea but the Cheroenhaka were still there—and so were the bays.

SCOTT SKIPPER

CHAPTER ONE

It was cold and the January sun shone weakly through high, thin clouds. Three brothers shifted their weight from foot to foot trying to keep their boots off the frozen ground. The crowd was hushed but now and again a woman sobbed or a baby wailed. The platform that had been erected to the second story window might have seemed part of the building if the Banqueting House at Whitehall had been timber. It looked nothing like a shaky construction scaffold, but seemed ominously permanent. When the headsman stepped though the window the crowd gasped. His hood was tied at the neck and the eye holes were cut large and ghoulish. He kept his axe concealed behind his back. In a moment the king stepped onto the platform with his slim chest looking strangely bulky in his simple white shirt. His hands were free and he clasped them in front while he prayed and delivered a short speech that no one heard save possibly the headsman. He faced the silent mass and ended with his reedy voice not quavering the least, "a subject and Sovereign are clean different things." Then he knelt placing his neck on the block. The axe arced and Charles' head dropped into the basket. To the brothers' senses time dilated while the headsman lifted the king's head by his long hair to show it to the crowd. The jaw was working spasmodically. Women and men both collapsed in horror and some cheered, but the three Skipper brothers hung their heads and walked toward Charing Cross, along the Strand to their townhouse in Chancery Lane.

It was nearly time for the midday meal. They weren't hungry but they sat at the table in the kitchen of the London house and Ann, the servant, brought some bread and meat. A row of tiny square window lights leaked the sickly sunlight into the room. Ann placed a candle on the table but for the brothers, feeling the nearness of death, it did not dispel the gloom.

Francis, middle son, said, "We should each buy an adventure and get to America in the first ship that sails."

"And do you propose that we buy an adventure for the poor frozen corpse of our father and carry him with us?" John, the eldest, rounded on his sibling.

"Well, do we sit here until the spring thaw so that we can give him a decent burial and give Mr. Cromwell's bully-boys ample time to hang us from a gibbet?"

"We can go to the farm and keep our heads down. When the ground thaws we put him in the churchyard and go about our lives like peaceable country gentlemen."

"And why wouldn't the bastards come for us there? They skewered our father for nothing more than looking his part. They just killed the king. Should we expect better treatment? Not bloody well likely!"

"The Old Man's mouth may have had a mite more to do with it than looking the part of a Royalist, but your point is well taken."

"Johnny, you may be willing to shear your head round and tell people you've changed your ways, but I'm with Frank. You don't kill a king and let it end there," George grumbled. He was slouched in his chair with legs extended and did not bother to lift his chin above the high collars of his coat.

"Out of the mouths of babes…" Francis sang. "Look, John, I share your pious need to see the Old Man's bones laid away all proper, but I can't think how he would look upon us in the hereafter if all four of our frozen arses get dumped in the paupers' grave. Suppose we give Edward his papers if he sees to putting him in the ground nice and proper as soon as he can dig a hole. He can spend his time betwixt now and then getting a stone cut."

"And just whose court do you propose we saunter into to get this act recorded?"

"Ah! We can leave it with the Deacon. If there still is a court come the spring, he can act as the agent of three young adventurers late of the parish. We can leave a bit of tithe to remember us by."

"And what of Thiobridge Brassoir? You want to walk away from our ancestral home?"

"What of it, Johnny? You're the eldest. It doesn't mean a fig to Frankie or me unless, of course, you were to meet with a sudden and untimely end."

"I haven't noticed either of you missing a meal or a roof over your heads at the end of the day." John forked a piece of meat and gnawed the corner from his piece of bread. With his mouth full he said, "Ann, bring us a bit of brandy, will you? That's a girl." Then to Francis, "You two get your adventures if you want. I'm not ready to sail away from two-thousand a year in rents for fifty acres full with wild Indians. Better the Devil you know than the Devil you don't."

Ann poured brandy into three cups. George smiled at her and said, "Ann, would you like to come with Francis and me to Virginia?"

"Much as that sounds like an offer from heaven, I'm duty bound to serve Master John now, and if he's of mind to go to the country I can't be running off to Virginia with the likes of you two."

Francis said to her, "You're not bound, girl, but God help you if you keep to the employ of our brother the Roundhead." He drained his cup and sat it down hard.

John raised his clenched fist but smiled when he said, "If you call me that again I'll be raising some knots on *your* head."

Ann winked at John and said to Francis, "Better the Devil you know."

George roused himself from his supine posture so he could reach his cup and a bit of the roast. He filled his mouth with brandy and held it at the back of his throat to feel the burn. It felt comforting but when he swallowed he had to stifle a cough. He closed his eyes to savor the heat of the brandy rising to his cheeks and when he did he saw the severed head of the king with the mouth trying to form a last word without the aid of its windpipe, and he saw the blood that ran from the open veins drip from the ends of his hair; and he saw his father's white dead face when they wrapped him in blankets and put him in the small carriage house not thirty feet from where they sat. His rage flared as it always did when he thought of those things that made him feel contempt for his race. Civil war ranked fairly high on his list, nearly equal to running his father through on the forecourt of Westminster Palace. His jaws were tight and his ears felt warm. He took another swallow to ease his self-consciousness. He was ready to fight. He needed revenge, but there was nothing to fight and he hated the impotent feeling of knowing it.

Francis watched his brother seething. "Georgie's hearing voices again," he said to the room.

George sneered at him thinking that here might be something to fight. "You can all go fuck yourselves— excepting you, Ann." She smiled at him indulgently. "There's nothing for it and you both know it. I've got to leave England if just to get the taste of bile out of my mouth."

"He's got it right, John. I'll be going with him and if

you weren't so damned prideful about becoming lord of the manor, you'd admit that he's right too."

"He may be right but I'm not about to deny the Old Man a decent burial, or to walk away from the rents, or to let the lands get picked to the bones by those vultures in Essex we call our kin, or worse, Cromwell. You two go and I wish you luck. If you tire of the wilderness in a few years, after we get a civilized country back, I'll send you money for your passage home."

Francis was pouring refills for each of them. He called, "Ann, bring a cup for yourself and join us whilst we plan our escape."

"It's not seemly for the help to drink with the family, Master Frank."

"Hell, girl. We grew up with you. You're a mite more than help."

"If you put it that way, but I'll pour it myself and if I don't hear what the plan is I'm sure to be happier for it."

George raised his cup saying, "Then we'll finish the bottle for the sake of the cold and get down to the quays and see when a ship is leaving."

* * *

There was more activity along the Thames than George and Francis expected considering that nine hours earlier the sovereign government of the realm had been overthrown. Before it was quite dark they pulled the latch of the door to the Crown and Wicket and stepped up two steps. Inside was dim and low and fairly quiet. At the bar Francis asked the barman, "Do you plan to change the pub's name?"

"The proprietor says he will consider that necessity in coming weeks."

They asked for two pints and if the place was frequented by ships' agents.

"Aye," he answered, "a few, but there be none here at

the moment. If you lads have a bit of patience I've no doubt one or another will happen in and I'll send him your way. It does seem a tempting to time to go abroad if one were free to do it."

As might have been expected the bar girls arrived before the ships' agents. A redhead in a dress of green, slightly frazzled brocade, with her bodice very fetchingly unlaced smiled brazenly at George and sat beside him. He returned her smile somewhat sheepishly and asked, "May I get you a pint, miss?"

"Great heavens, no! A lady never takes a pint. A half will do nicely." George returned with more pints for himself and Francis and the half for the redhead which she drained with astonishing speed. George was sipping his absently when she elbowed his ribs. "Ain't you going to offer me another?"

"I thought a lady never took a whole pint."

"I didn't say a lady couldn't have two halfs."

When George went for the girl's second half the barman simply pointed to a man with side whiskers who sat alone at a table with a mug and ledger book in front of him. He gave the beer to the girl and told Francis of the agent.

"Ow, now I suppose you're off to do some business and won't have a farthing left for me when you come back."

"Don't fret. We won't be long and hopefully we won't be broke. By the way, you haven't said what your name is."

"Patience."

The man with the whiskers lifted his head from the ledger and said, "You would be the boys wanting passage to Virginia?"

"That's right," Francis told him.

"Have a seat."

They sat on the three legged stools, and George asked, "How soon can we leave?"

The man squinted at him at length before he said, "Not until spring."

George's mouth opened and closed putting Francis in mind of the King's head. "Go on, Frank, we can't wait around 'til spring. We'll have to find somebody else to book passage with."

"I take it you've not been to sea before," the man said. "Once he's got your sterling the ships' owners don't care much if you get to Virginia alive, but to a man they care about their ships getting there in one piece. Look all you like. You'll not find a boat leaving before end of March."

Francis asked, "How much will it cost?"

"Six pounds sterling. As you're not going in bondage, you'll have to provide your own apparel."

"When do you have to have the money?"

"You'll pay me now if you want to be certain you get the first passage."

Francis took the coins from his purse and stacked them on the ledger. The agent withdrew two pieces of printed paper. "Can you sign your names?" They nodded. "Then sign these. They'll get you on board the Albermarle on March the twenty-third coming." The agent signed each passage and added their names to the passenger list in his ledger. He put the coins in his purse indicating there was no further need for discussion.

Feeling slightly disoriented by the abruptness of the transaction, they gravitated blankly to the bar where they leaned for a moment. Patience crept behind George and fondled his arse. Startled momentarily, he turned and saw her. "Oh, sorry Lass, it seems we're broke after all." Squinting with her whole face, she pinched his cheek and walked away. George and Frank left their cups on the bar and left the pub.

In the street Francis said, "Now, I know you've got enough copper in your pocket for the likes her."

"Well, she was a tempting piece, but I think I've had enough excitement for one day. Besides, I think it be not meet carrying the pox to America."

Francis laughed. "Then what do you propose we do for the next two months?"

"I think we join Johnny keeping our heads down in the county."

* * *

Three days later, before they decamped for the country, six soldiers arrived at the house in Chancery Lane and arrested the three of them. Ann watched, terrorized, as the brothers were prodded with halberds and taken from the house without their coats.

It was not a long walk to the Fleet Street Prison. John entered the cell first noting four others already occupied it. The straw on the floor had not been changed in weeks. The only other feature was a bucket that seemed woefully inadequate, but that he hoped would be used assiduously by all present.

"Oh, it's going to take a great long while to get this outta me head," George muttered to himself.

On the second day Ann brought food, and though there was not enough for seven, they shared it with their fellow inmates to keep peace more than from magnanimity. Ann was told the address of a lawyer who had done work for their father. She left immediately to find him.

Sir Anthony Pitt was small, pale and anything but intimidating in appearance. He arrived at the prison and found the constable who told what he knew of the charges then admitted him to the cells. Pitt found them on the first floor. He had to stand on his toes to see through the barred window in the door.

"Gentlemen," he said, "I advise you not to worry. The problem is one of jealousy. Your late father and a man in Chancery Lane were at odds."

George grumbled, "Rolls! The Roundhead bastard."

The lawyer went on, "Aye, Mr. Rolls. Seems he has denounced you as Royalist conspirators strong in support of Charles II."

"Can't think what it was we conspired to do," Francis said gripping the bars between himself and Pitt, "but Charles is the rightful heir."

"Apparently Mr. Cromwell has a different idea. I am afraid you will need to stand for treason."

George looked at him quizzically. "Seems I remember you saying not to worry."

"Yes, and I stand by my advice. I am told that two of you have in your possession Adventures to Virginia. It will be necessary to purchase a third. His lordship, the judge, will be quite satisfied with your departure for America."

"That's bloody noble of his worship."

Pitt's head snapped to George. "You may yet get to dance at the end of a rope if you don't curb your wit, Master Skipper."

"If he ain't got the courtesy to have me hung, drawn and quartered, I'm afraid I shall have to decline his hospitality."

Pitt managed to ignore him. "Now, I am afraid you will have to remain here until the day after tomorrow. Then you will be brought before the judge and we will put the matter to rest."

Ann returned the following day with another basket of food. This time she had enough to feed seven.

It was late in the afternoon before the constable took them from the cell and led them to a room on the top floor. John had instructed his siblings not to speak and strengthened the command with a mortal scowl. In the courtroom the judge, in his robes, on his throne, dominated one end of the chamber. The brothers were left standing in the dock. The clerk rose to read the charge and addressed Rolls, their accuser, asking him to swear to its veracity which he did. Pitt, who had been seated to the right in the midst of a clutch of lawyers all wigged and robed, rose and spoke.

"If it please the court, these young gentlemen, having been loyal subjects contend that there is no treason in vowing support to the rightful sovereign; however, in the light of certain developments, they are of a mind to remove to the colonies, there taking up the art of agriculture whereby becoming contributing members of the realm. Their ship sails at the end of this March."

The judge seemed happy to move on. He said, "Very, well, the constable will hold them until the day of embarkation."

"But, your lordship, there is a problem. Master John Skipper has yet to book his passage."

"Find someone to be surety for his return—ten pounds."

The constable and his deputies took them by the elbows and marched them back to the cell.

When Ann next arrived she had blankets for them. "How did you get these past the guard, girl?" Francis asked.

"A few pennies. Mr. Pitt came by the house this morning to inquire as to who will pay the bond. I gave him the address of your uncle William."

John said, "I suppose he's the best choice. Why in hell did Pitt go to you instead of coming here?"

"He left his bill as well. Perhaps asking for your uncle's address was an afterthought."

George, sitting on the floor with his elbows on his knees, snorted at that.

"Ann, dear, please call upon Mr. Pitt before you go home and ask that he try to find the time to visit with his clients," John said as he touched her cheek through the bars.

Pitt did not arrive until the following afternoon. He began straight away, "I received a most prompt return post from your uncle in Essex. It seems that he is not at all well-disposed toward his late brother's memory. Blames your father's cheek for his undoing. Completely neglected to respond to the issue of being surety."

John stood at the small window while his brothers crowded at his shoulder to see the wren-like lawyer. He said, "Look here, Pitt, why don't you just post it? I'll take you by the house and reimburse you just as soon you spring me."

"Just isn't done that way. They require someone who can be thrown in gaol if you fail to return. Wouldn't do to throw lawyers in gaol, would it?"

"I can't see the harm in it," George quipped.

Pitt ignored it.

John sighed. "The Old Man's best friend on earth is Patrick Arundel. His house is in Milford Lane on Thames. Just be sure he knows I'll bring him the ten pounds as soon as I can get to the house, and you'll get your fee as well."

"All right, then, we'll see how Mr. Arundel is inclined toward the wayward sons of his late friend."

"Wayward?"

"Say, Pitt," Francis pushed his face in front of the opening, "how is it only Johnny gets sprung? I figure Arundel could come up with ten pounds for each of us if he put his mind to it."

"His lordship is not going to risk a couple of firebrands joining forces with Charles II's cause. The Lord Protector would see that in a bad light. Having the two of you here is the best insurance for bringing Master John back."

From beyond Pitt's view George said, "He doesn't know you, Johnny."

Arundel went with Pitt immediately to the clerk of court and posted the ten pounds. He even offered to stand for Francis and George, but was told that that was not an option. When John was released he thanked Arundel profusely and assured him that he would bring the money to his house that evening. Arundel told him that he did not have to do it, but John insisted. Pitt stood at the side with a demeanor that said he would not be adverse to accepting payment that evening.

In the morning it had gotten warm enough to rain. John went down to the quays and found the Albermarle. The ship's agent was on board and happily accepted six pounds for another passage. "Load your baggage in the week before sailing," he counseled.

John left the river and went round to the undertaker's. He paid for a coffin then went home and sent Edward to fetch it. While he waited for his return, he packed a bag. Later he and Edward put his father's body into the coffin and levered it to the top of the carriage. The corpse was still frozen, but he worried that rising temperature would not keep it that way for long. "Put the bags in the coach tonight. Hitch the horses at daybreak. We'll leave as soon as you have them ready," he told the servant.

Ann had his dinner ready when he went inside. "Eat with me," he asked her.

"How are Frank and George?" she asked putting a plate of sausages and potatoes before him then she turned to fill one for herself.

John chuckled grimly. "They're fit to kill. I can't blame them. Two months in that stinking hole is not a happy prospect."

"You don't think you can get them out?"

"Pitt doesn't think so. Maybe I'll try another solicitor."

"How long will you be in country?"

"Not long, maybe a week." He took a long swallow of his beer, then hesitated before saying, "Look, Ann, do you want to go to America with me?"

She met his eyes and replied demurely, "I'm your servant. I'll go if you tell me to."

"I don't mean like that. I was thinking you might marry me."

"Oh! I wasn't ready for that. John, we've never talked of love."

"I guess I didn't think it was proper, but with the Old

Man gone—I mean, you were his servant. He would have tanned my hide if he thought we were carrying on. But it's different now. I don't want you as a servant, and I don't want to leave without you."

She smiled with one side of her mouth. "If that's a proposal, I shall give it proper consideration."

That took him aback. Afraid to say anything in response, he ate in silence. When the plates were empty, she removed them to basin and began to clean them. He approached, touched her shoulder, and turned her toward him. He kissed her and she responded, then he took her hand and led her upstairs. Tentatively he unbuttoned her blouse watching for disapproval. When he touched her nipple she stiffened and he thought it was over, but she moved toward him and touched his cheek meeting his eyes. Without speaking they undressed each other then he guided her onto the bed. The smooth feel of new skin was delightful, more than he had even expected. When it was done the air felt cold. So she pulled the comforter over them and said to his ear, "Now that you know I wasn't a virgin, do you still want to marry me?"

"More than ever and there will be no need to supply a lot of information about that."

"I promise I haven't been a tart. I thought I was in love once."

"Just tell me it wasn't one of my brothers—or my father."

"I assure you, and I accept your proposal, romantic as it was."

"Well, then, I guess you had better pack for the country."

* * *

The rain continued which hampered travel forcing them to stop at Chelmsford. John had to sleep with Edward. Ann was chastely shown to a room at the opposite end of the hall. Fretting over his father's body on the roof of the carriage kept John awake as much as Edward's snoring, but he couldn't think of a better alternative. Even more than the security of the Old Man's carcass, the awful turmoil of his life elicited a wave of panic. The prospects of the sea crossing, the unknown in Virginia, and not to overlook marriage, ran riot through his mind. He willed himself to picture Ann's naked body, which immediately gave him an erection, and that compelled him to move farther away from Edward. It was a long unhappy night.

Breakfast was copious and satisfying. John wondered when he would see kippers again. The road conditions improved the farther into Essex they went, so it was not late when Edward turned the horses into the lane leading to the manor house which belonged to John now, or would after the proving of the will. Trouble was he would be in the middle of the ocean when that happened. It was not the way he had had things planned.

Ann fixed supper of dried cod and cabbage, which was all she could find, and Edward was left with the remainder of the household chores since Ann had acquired new status. Her presence was required upstairs.

In the morning it was dry but overcast. Edward saddled the horse and John left to find the sexton. On the heath he met his cousin William, Jr. "I heard there were lights at your house," he said. "I supposed it would be you. What about Frank and George?"

"Still in the fucking Fleet Street gaol."

"Are they going to make it?"

"It'll be a bloody miracle if all they come out with is the gripe."

"What are you going do?"

"About what? I've got a few balls in the air. Need to get my father's body in the ground, sort out going to America, fret over my worthless brothers, and, oh yes— I'm getting married."

"No. Who to?"

"Ann."

"You evil bastard! How long have you two been carrying on?"

"About two days now."

"Well, that I don't believe, but never mind; I apologize for my father refusing to help."

"It's nothing more than I'd expect. Ride with me to find the sexton. I've got to see about getting a grave dug."

"Sure," William pulled his horse around. "What do you figure to do in America?"

"How the hell should I know? Until a few days ago I never thought about going to America. It's no easy matter to predict how a king getting his head cut off is going to affect you."

William snorted. "What would you say if I told you I had a mind to go with you?"

"I'd say you were out of your fucking mind."

"Well, maybe, but what would be holding me here? I'll not be getting the farm unless I indulge a little fratricide, which might do the soul good, but has a few risks. The old goat's got his mind set on me getting a trade. He's going to fucking put me out like an urchin he can't afford to feed. In America they give you land just for showing up."

"Land crawling with red savages."

"Can't be much worse than round headed savages."

It was John's turn to snort. "Well, cousin, if you've got your mind set, I'm sure we will appreciate your company."

The sexton's cottage abutted the rear of the church. Outside his gate a cow was tethered to a bare apple tree. Some straw lay on the ground for it. The cousins found him in his kitchen with the deacon reading a Latin prayer book. John's recitation of his needs, requests, and proposals seemed to make the deacon's head swim. He was an elderly man with white hair and beard though bald on top. The lower lids of his blue eyes drooped showing their wet red linings. Apparently working through solutions, he said, "Well, after the rain, I think that a proper hole can be dug. Leave twelve pennies for the gravediggers, and bring your father to the church day after tomorrow for the service. We'll talk later about me collecting your rents. As for the wedding, it would be seemly to grieve for a day or two before celebrating a marriage."

"Sure, Father, but might I point out that the Old Man has been dead for nigh two weeks, and I have a boat to catch?"

"Saturday then. I'll conduct the ceremony at noon."

"Fine. I really appreciate it. We'll be back day after tomorrow."

"Ah, don't forget the twelve pence," the sexton said.

John counted the pennies, and he and William left the cottage. The cow had lain on the ground, and was browsing the straw with her chin recumbent.

John followed his cousin home to pay a call on his uncharitable uncle. William's house was half timber with a hall that was almost great. They found him seated at his desk by the window. "So you've managed to get out of Fleet Street."

"Yes, uncle, thank you for your kind assistance."

"You got yourself in trouble. You can get yourself out."

"And, as you can see, I have."

"Don't delude yourself, boy, you haven't begun to see the trouble."

"I don't expect to see it either. I'm going to America, and so are Frank and George."

"America, and whose fine idea is that?"

"For my part, it was the thinking of the magistrate, though my brothers came up with it first."

"So have you come to ask me to buy the estate?"

"No, I've come to invite you to my father's funeral day after the morrow."

"I'll pay my respects, but you'll need me to take charge

of the estate if you're on the other side of the ocean."

"No, I'll let the solicitor deal with the matters of inheritance, and I expect the deacon will collect the rents for a stipend."

"It'll go to ruin."

"Might a little. I don't expect to be gone very many years. As soon as Charles II comes into his own, I'll be back."

"If you're waiting for young Charles, I expect you'll not be coming back at all."

"Don't tell me you've gone over to Cromwell's side."

"Shit! If you were my own son you'd get the back of my hand for that remark. I'll stay exactly on the side I've always been on—my side, and I'll keep my mouth shut on the topic in public, unlike my late brother."

William, who had felt his cheeks redden over his father's recalcitrance, said, "Oh, and I'll being going to America, too."

His father had perfected the sneer. "Now, there's a fine thing," he said with a cadence that resonated on each word. "So go if I've raised such a fool, but don't be writing me a letter in a year begging for passage home."

"See, I knew you'd be heartbroken."

"Get out of my sight, you worthless whelp. It was a dark day your mother brought you to this world. I should have pinched your head off whilst I had the chance."

John said, "I'll get out of your sight too, uncle. See you Thursday—be about noon."

Outside he said to his cousin, "Well, that was awkward enough. I don't know how you put up with him as long as you have. Why don't you stay with us?"

"Thanks, I will, but I've got to get my things together otherwise he'll lock away everything I consider my own, and I'll land in Virginia with the shirt on my back."

John suffered the affliction of unwanted thoughts. The entire ride home his mind replayed the caustic visit with his uncle with no control to stop it. His mental self-torture segued into the scene of the soldiers arresting them, and standing in the hateful light of the magistrate's glare. He was cold to the bone and his jaws ached from clenching when he got to his late father's house. Entering through the kitchen Ann greeted him warmly. Immediately he thought to ask her to go to bed for the balm it would be to his troubled mind, but he felt too distracted and found a decanter of brandy instead. She sat by him at the table and touched his hand while he recounted the events of the day. After he finished telling of his uncle William she poured more brandy into his glass and took the first swallow. "It's nice not having to sip brandy behind the pantry door," she said smiling beguilingly.

* * *

The day of the funeral William drove them to the church with the coffin still perched on the top of the coach. He and the two gravediggers removed it and carried it into the chapel where they set it on the bier in front of the altar. Some Skippers from Brightlingsea had got the news from William's oldest son, Tom. They were seated in the middle pews on the right side of the aisle. John stopped to greet them and to introduce Ann then they continued to take their places in the front pew. Ann whispered in his ear once they seated, "It's interesting that when introduced to a group of Skippers you only need to know their given names. The fact of their being Skippers is as plain as the nose on their face."

"Will we be making nose jokes for the life of the marriage?" he said scowling at her. She just pinched his nose and smirked.

William arrived promptly with Tom and his daughters, Tabitha and Jane. Happily the prominent Skipper trait visited itself mainly on the male gender. Tabitha and Jane were quite comely young women. Tom looked like all the rest of them. William directed his family to sit leaving an empty pew between them. A few minutes later William, Jr. arrived, strode to the front and sat next to Ann. The deacon made his entrance and droned an abbreviated Latin mass, then reverted to cockney to tell all the fine things the deceased had done in his life. John was bored to tears but when it was over his conscience was clear, and he completed his ritual duty by dropping the ceremonial first spade of dirt into the grave. It was actually a chunk of wet clay that thumped loudly onto the pine box. He turned from the grave and each of the small group of mourners shook his hand and patted his shoulder. The two girl cousins kissed his cheek. Even Uncle William shook hands. The Brightlingsea contingent apologized for not being able to stay long enough attend the wedding, but wished them happiness. When it was over and he was alone with his thoughts and the sadness within him, palpable though it was, it was not as deep as he thought it would be. He could not will himself to tears. His feelings were more akin to the relief of the end of an onerous task. In some ways his father had been an onerous task, and Saturday would bring another task. He winced inwardly to feel that way, but he would just as soon it were Saturday night with the ordeal behind him and be lost in the mindless joy of the marriage bed, anticlimactic though it might be.

Saturday broke sunny and still with the cold air slightly damp. The couple played the game of the groom not being able to see the bride before the wedding. Ann fixed herself in private and Edward drove her to the church. John dressed and began to the stable when a movement within him gave pause. Better a few minutes late than to interrupt the ceremony he reasoned, and turned to the privy. During the time of reflection his mood shifted from dull dread to joy at the prospect of the coming event, and he continued to his wedding buoyed with the lightness of a happy evacuation.

All of Uncle William's children attended, but not William himself which was in a sense another happy evacuation. There was no one else. Ann wore her best white dress, but there were no flowers to be had. The deacon again droned as he always did this time he admonished them against sin, and that their only happiness was in Jesus. John let it run through his ears. He was thinking happiness might be found in something a little more secular and Jesus was not invited to participate. Ann had tears when she said, "I will," and she sobbed when he gave her his mother's ring. She didn't know that he had it.

The deacon's servant woman served dinner for the party in the meeting hall. There was some laughter and a toast to the couple, but it was as mercifully brief as spare. The guests left en masse and John settled his affairs with the deacon, paying stipends for the two services and signing a letter authorizing him to collect the rents and keep ten percent. The rest was to be deposited with a goldsmith in Threadneedle Street with whom the Old Man had left his spare plate from time to time. In the coach going home they kissed and fondled and John felt that he was moving forward for the first time since the King lost his head. For the sake of not having preoccupying distractions in the nuptial bed it was just as well that John never would know that the deacon died in his second year of collecting rents, William convinced the tenants, and eventually the court, that he was the only surviving heir, and the goldsmith in Threadneedle street was quite satisfied with the small windfall he then possessed.

* * *

Edward, the household groom, helped George trundle his trunk on board the Albermarle as he had done the previous day for Francis. John and Ann were in the process of packing several trunks, and judging from what he gleaned from eavesdropping, they might have to charter a separate ship for their freight. After stowing the trunk in the hold, Edward departed with only a casual goodbye knowing he'd be back soon with the newlyweds' luggage. George inspected the niche that would be his private space for the crossing; then he found Frank in the common cabin where they played cribbage until the cards became thick and sponge-like from the sea air. By the second week George was so tired of trying to shuffle what felt like damp slices of bread he decided to go ashore to buy a fresh deck.

"Mind the constables on the quays," Frank warned.

"I'll take my chances. Being back in the cage wouldn't be much worse than being stuck in this floating gaol. Fleet Street wasn't that bad after you straightened out the bugger who wanted to bugger—excepting the bucket, of course." With that he walked off the gangplank, along the quay and up a side street to a shop where he bought four decks of cards. He returned to the quays unmolested without seeing constable or soldier, so he decided to drop into the Crown and Wicket for a pint. After his third he continued to the Albermarle in peace.

"Nobody is watching us," he told Frank. "The whole bloody episode was for nothing. They've forgot about us."

John, who had not been admonished by the magistrate to go directly to the ship, checked as to the departure date, but stayed at home. When queried as to the departure, the captain gestured with his pipe and grumbled about the wind and tide. Captain Martindale was built like a stoat. He had an accessible nature that he came to regret. George also harangued him about when they would leave to the extent that he developed the habit of doing an about face when they met on deck. When George trapped him, he would ask, "Why are you afraid to push off from the dock? Everything I've ever seen thrown into the Thames floats down to the sea eventually."

The captain only moaned.

To lessen the tedium of endless days waiting for wind and water to satisfy the exacting needs of Captain Martindale, George took to finding creative ways to kill rats. The number of them was ample to allow him to experiment with many variations. The most satisfying method was to swat them with a stick and when they were stunned to bludgeon their little brains into haggis. It was difficult to get close enough to them to put much of dent in the population, so he inveigled the ship's carpenter to make him a live trap with a story of having been assigned to rodent abatement by the captain. While the carpenter was building the rather artful and clever trap to his specifications, George fashioned a stick like a niblick. The result of all the handiwork was a rat disposal system of satanic dimensions. The trap's door naturally snapped shut instantly when the baited trigger was touched, but the mechanism that opened it was retarded so that George had time to assume the proper stance to loft the escaping creature against the hull with his rat whacking stick. Even Francis thought it was a productive change of pace from marathon cribbage. The carpenter shook his head derisively, but couldn't resist trying it a few times before scuttling back to his shop hoping that the captain hadn't seen him.

Francis eventually believed George's assertion that no one was watching their coming or going, and they developed the nightly habit of visiting the Crown and Wicket where George quickly succumbed to Patience's patience. After multiple flagons she cajoled him to go to her room which was in an alley behind the pub. Inside he asked her, "So, lass, how do I know you're free of the pox?"

"Because I'm a clever girl who insists on inspecting her clients for nasty pustules and vile emissions, including you, though I promise it won't be unpleasant, and you're welcome to inspect for the same. Leave the money by the candle and get out of your breeches."

George had had a few rolls with neighbor girls who were eager but frightened because of their inexperience, but Patience was the consummate professional with a repertoire that aimed for repeat business. Before the ship weighed anchor George had given her half of his money.

On the first of May the wind rose and continued blowing into the evening. When Frank and George started down the gangplank the ship's agent stepped in front of them and said, "Tonight's the night. No time for the pub or your lady friend. Bring your brother and get your arses back on board inside of an hour."

"Ow, I can't just abandon Patience without telling her I'm leaving," George told Frank. "You go on and fetch Johnny and Ann, and I'll just pop into the Crown to say goodbye."

"And you'll miss the boat and end up back in Fleet Street."

"You know me better than that. I'll be along straight away."

Francis shook his head and went for John. When he explained George's recalcitrance to his older brother, John sent their cousin William, who had been staying in the house, with Francis to bodily remove George from Patience. Edward, the soon to be unemployed groom, helped load the trunks onto the carriage and drove to the quays. The agent had stationed himself at the top of the gangway and told John, "The wind is right and the tide is rising. We'll not be waiting for your brother."

Francis knew where Patience lived. They skipped the formality of knocking, and at first sight of the room thought that Patience was alone. When their eyes adjusted to the low light, they realized that three quarters of their quarry was hidden under her skirts. William said as they hauled him to his feet, "At least he's still got his breeches on."

Patience was philosophical since she always got her money up front. "Have a good life in America, Georgie," she said while they marched him through the door.

George took it surprisingly well, but said, "There's not a whit of sense of humor betwixt you."

George was first up the gangway. The agent was still at his post. He groaned, "I'm glad I'm not going," which elicited a guffaw from Francis. William was more inclined to see George's side.

It was a warm night with a stiff breeze following. The flood tide turned at ten and the Albermarle castoff. Tied to the wharf the ship's movement was imperceptible. On the current it was hypnotic, and once the excitement of departing subsided, everyone slept the sleep of the dead. In the harsh light of dawn the first long reach began and those not accustom to sailing opted not for breakfast. When she could no longer see England Ann had an attack of anxiety that frighten John. He wanted to console her but she coldly maintained nothing was wrong. Baffled, he found Frank who could only think to suggest that he loiter in another part of the ship. William and George stood at the rail just to starboard of the bowsprit and were enjoying the wind in their faces. In a week the bowsprit's bulging breasts were more interesting to them than the wind and the waves.

"I think we're going to burst before we get to bloody America," George told William.

"Well, there're a few lassies on board. We just need to get them separate from their masters."

"And get them to a place without twenty onlookers."

"I am sure you're up to that. Just start batting rats in the hold and you'll have all the privacy you need."

George considered the notion then said, "Sure, if I can find a girl who likes rat batting."

The wind dropped by half and the monotonous progress through the sea took faith to perceive. George did not quit watching for a female in a fortuitous situation, but he passed his time by making a fishing line from the sail mender's thread. He made a hook from a whittled piece of oak and a nail, and baited it with a rat. For days he had no result, but on the fourth day he caught a shark. He had an enthusiastic audience while he tried to haul it on board, but its teeth cut the line and it splashed vigorously back into the water. Undaunted, he fashioned a leader from a length of wire and went back to the task. Eventually he caught a tuna. The appreciation at the dinner table was enthusiastic. The captain just shook his head, although he did not refuse a helping of tuna; however, George's capital was rising to the extent that he learned the names of a couple of servant girls who remarked on his cleverness.

The days strung together endlessly. George studied the sea and the sky and the wind, and concluded that sailing was an art not fully understood. When the captain had the misfortune to be confronted by him, George pointed to the rigging and declared, "Surely you could string some more canvas up there."

Martingale prayed for a fair easterly gale. He got some of his wish, but regretted it all because the wind was too strong to be useful and he hove to. All the passengers were sick. George could not bear the hold, though the deck was cold and awash, he clung numbly to the lifeline when poor Captain Martingale passed not realizing who hung his head over the rail.

George recognized the gait. "You see," he said between spasms, "there's plenty of wind, but you shorten the damned sails, and we sit here bobbing like a cork. We're all going to heave our guts out, and you won't risk your precious canvas to get us through."

When they reached the tropics and the heat became oppressive to their English hides, George and William found a great tun empty of its contents. They broke the head from it, and by bucketsful, filled it with sea water. They built a barricade with John and Ann's stuff, and hid the barrel behind it. Next they set about to lure sweating lovelies to their illicit bath. Results were disappointing.

John, in the meantime, was as frustrated as his cousin and brothers because the lack of privacy in the cabins made Ann unwilling to comply with her wifely duties. John insisted he could be quiet. She said, "If I have to be quiet, what's the point."

He offered to show her the point, but she declined.

Louisa was indentured to a humorless London merchant who was going to Virginia to export tobacco. George eventually got her to join him in the cramped barrel when the wind died and the temperature became intolerable before noon. The water in the barrel was on the low end of tepid and tiny barnacles were growing on the sides, both discomforts distracted him to the extent that although he managed to go through the motions, he could not consummate the act. Louisa did, however, use their protracted conjugation to her advantage multiple times. After that George dumped the water into the bilge and suffered the heat. Somehow the merchant discovered the tryst and objected to the captain who protested to John.

"Am I my brother's keeper?"

"One of you needs to be," Captain Martingale insisted.

The sky was red at first light. It was a big sea and fair wind from the east. The crew was aloft setting more canvas than George had seen the entire voyage. He went looking for Captain Martingale to praise his courage, but Martingale was wary. As the sun climbed the wind rose and clouds appeared on the horizon. By noon the storm was overhead and the crew was reefing the sails. George hunted for Martingale to criticize him. Before supper the waves broke across both rails and no one could reach the rigging to do anything with the sails. Everyone lashed themselves in their berths, and wished they could sleep, or it was over, or they were drowned and done with it. When the sun rose it was still. The brothers ventured on deck to see that two masts were gone. The crew was busy securing what gear was still useable. The captain approached without much malice and told them, "We're in the eye. The worst is coming. Get below and secure anything loose you find."

John rushed George below before he could proffer advice to protect the remaining mast.

The trailing side of the hurricane blew through the night. If anyone other than George had a thing to say, it was lost in the howl. It passed as quickly as it came, and the addled, sleepless passengers crept on deck in the relative calm of the wake of the storm. The mizzen was still standing.

The captain stood on the poop to address the passengers. "Get into the hold and move whatever is hefty to the stern," he told them. "Move what is fluff to the bow."

George, standing next to Ann, said to her, "Well, I guess you're going to the bow." She punched him in the ribs.

It was two more days before the captain saw the stars and made a guess as to where they were. The helmsman could not hold an accurate course with all the wind's energy pushing at the stern, and the bow buffeted by the swells. Ann and nearly all the rest of the passengers became frightened. George and William discussed it, and did not see why the mizzen could not be moved to the bow, but when given the suggestion, Martingale lost his temper.

He told them, "I'm the master of this ship, and I'll decide what can and cannot be done, and seeing that we're lucky to be afloat, I'll thank you not to add to my problems."

George lifted his chin, scowling looked him in the eye and said, "My father always told me there are none so blind as those who will not see." William removed him from the area.

Five days after the hurricane the lookout sited Barbados, but the helmsman could not make the ship respond, and ran aground on the rocks on the northeast side of the island. The rock was the size of a tenet's hovel, and the wave had eroded it so that it balanced on a spindly neck which broke under the impact. The ship then became wedged between the jutting neck and the fallen head. It was starting to take water. A party was rowed ashore to find some help in removing the passengers and cargo to Bridgetown. It took several days for the Skippers to gain lodging in an inn. One night they slept in a barn with several families of rats, the next they slept under a mahogany tree with several families of lizards and a great many mosquitoes. Ann said it was a hard choice, but she preferred the mosquitoes. The inn, when they achieved it, sat above the waterfront. They took two rooms, one for John and Ann, and the other for the bachelors. Word of the wreck spread right round the island, and the issue of how to transport the castaways to America was the inspiration of much scheming. Martingale himself seemed not too interested in getting on to Virginia. He was focused on repairing the Albermarle and returning his crew to England. After supper the Skippers held a council.

Frank began. "This island doesn't seem such a bad place. Who says we have to get to Virginia?"

George had been swimming in the afternoon. A sudden squall drove him to shelter under a large tree overhanging the beach. The rain that dripped from the foliage burned his skin, and a fruit, that he contemplated tasting, left blisters on his fingers. "You're not getting me to stay on this island with its poisonous trees," he groused. "There's alligators in the river, too," he added.

"You don't think they have alligators in Virginia?" Frank asked. "For all we know, they may have poisonous trees as well."

"What's Annie like to say? 'Better the devil you don't know yet, than the one that you're headed for.'"

"That's not quite what I said," she murmured.

Sometime between his resignation to emigration and

being beset by a hurricane, John had also resigned himself to the role of patron, "Well, lads, if you can recall, the real reason we want to get to Virginia is the head right. We're sitting here without much money, we've got no prospects on Barbados, and we are apparently going to have to pay again for passage out of here."

"Isn't that a good reason to stay?"

"I'm not living in a place with poisonous trees."

"In Virginia they've got poisonous snakes."

William had listened with detachment until his soliloquy was perfected. "Cousins, I joined your adventure to keep from being put out for a trade. Now, I've engaged a few locals over a pint, and it seems to me there isn't an acre unspoken for on this piece of limestone, so what am I to do here but put myself out for a trade? Virginia at least holds out hope to the freeman. And there's another thing a bit more prescient, it's all those black-a-moors. Now, I'll grant you some of the wenches are comely, but the bucks are more than a mite intimidating. When they rise up, who do you think they are coming after? I'm with Johnny here. We're going to Virginia as soon as we figure out how."

Frank was ready for this. "And Virginia has got the red Indians."

"Yes, and by all accounts the red Indians are tamed and kept under control."

John felt assertive. "Frank, you went with Will to drag George onto the Albermarle. Do you not think we'll drag you as well onto the ship for Virginia, when we find it?"

"Gentlemen, and me lady," said a man approaching with a crockery jug on his finger, "I couldn't help but overhear your discussion. If passage to Virginia is what you need, I think I can be of assistance. Ben Coward's the name, distiller and shipbuilder of renown. May I offer you a libation whilst I explain myself?"

George was the first to respond, "Well, if you need an explanation, I guess a libation is in order."

Coward was tall, well put together, and fair. He poured

rum into six cups, and raised his in toast, "To your safe passage to America." Everyone drank to that. Some sipped, some swallowed mightily the coarse rum burning their throats, Ann gasped slightly, no one else made any sign of complaint. "So, you see, your plight is all but at end. At this very moment I have standing on the beach, the nearly complete hull of a sailing ship that will soon be bound for the coast of Virginia."

William was enthused as much by the rum as the prospect of a ship. "When will it sail?" he asked.

"Ah, just as soon as you four strong lads help me finish it."

Ann groaned and took a bigger swallow of rum.

John met Coward's eye, "I assure you there is not a one of us has the least idea how to build a ship, and if we did help you finish it, we're not near fool enough to go onto the ocean in it."

"No need to fret. I will direct the construction, and you will be perfectly at ease when you see the results; furthermore, free passage will be the fruit of your labor." Coward splashed rum into the men's cups. Ann held her hand over hers. "You see, gents, all that remains is a few items of housekeeping. The hull, the cabins, the helm work, is all but done. Just help to tie off a few loose ends and you're off to Virginia at no cost at all."

"I'd call the sweat on my brow some cost," Frank said across the rim of his cup.

"Aw, what's a little labor when the return is great?"

"We'll need to see this ship of yours," John told him.

"Fair enough. Come round in the morning and inspect her all you need. Then we'll seal our agreement, and the work will be done in no time at all. Now, let's drink to our new found friendship."

When in the course of conversation Coward learned that the brothers had witnessed Charles' execution he was dumbfounded. "This makes you three heroes. This here is a Royalist island, my friends. If there is a roundhead left on Barbados, he best not ever remove his hat. Just this year we shipped a hundred of them off the island, and gave their plantations to loyal Royalists. They are a bit of a rowdy bunch. Myself, I'll be happier when Carlisle's man, Willoughby, gets back and puts things in order."

Ann finished another modest cup of the rum while the men joked and caroused. Coward filled his cup twice to the emptying of the others, but he showed the effect less than any of the Skippers, in fact he showed it hardly at all. John was not behaving as moderately as Ann would have preferred, so when she finished her second rum she tugged at his sleeve with a wink and jerk of her head toward the stairs. The prospect of a bed with no onlookers and only a reasonable number of vermin had a regenerating affect on him. He took her hand, promised to attend the inspection at daybreak, and made his excuses.

Coward told him, "I'm glad to see you've got your priorities in order."

When John and Ann had gone, Coward insisted on a cup draining toast to which there was no dissension. While he refilled their cups, Frank asked, "How many ships do you have?"

"Oh, this is my first. I told you, I'm a distiller. Shipbuilding is my new avocation. Why don't you come around and have a look at the distillery? Got to refill the jug anyway. Then, since the lady is gone, we can pursue some more prurient interests."

Frank went to pay Peevy, the innkeeper, for the pints they had before Coward arrived. He asked him why he let Coward bring his own jug. "He's my rum supplier," the innkeeper said. "He takes good care of me, besides there's simply no stopping him anyway."

They staggered to the distillery in the dark with walls of cane towering above their heads. The jug was empty before they arrived at the still. Heaps of cane crowded the place and the fecund bouquet of fermentation was overwhelming. An old slave fed the fire under the large copper vessel. It was twice the size of the barrel into which the rum was dripping.

"Ain't she a beauty? I had her shipped from England. There may be bigger stills on Barbados, but none as lovely as my Prudence," Coward said while he stroked the condensation spout.

"Prudence?"

"Sure. How could something so sweet be aught but a lady? Come on, now, let's get our jug refilled." He pulled a key from the purse on his belt and unlocked a door at the back of the room. Taking the old slave's lamp, he motioned for the three to follow him into the warehouse. Barrels rested on X shaped racks. One had a bung in it and Coward went to it to fill the jug.

George asked him, "You sell any of this? Or is it for your personal consumption?"

"Oh, I sell a bit, but there's plenty of competition on the island. When I have my boat, I'll be taking it America where I hear there's more thirst than supply, and now that you gentlemen have graciously agreed to complete my enterprise, America will benefit sooner than later."

"I wasn't sure we'd agreed."

"Ah, come now. It's a marriage made in heaven. You supply your skills as shipwrights, I supply the capital then you and the rum get free passage to America. When the colonists realize your part in their salvation, they'll petition the Pope for your sainthood."

"Not much interested in sainthood really."

"Figure of speech it was. Don't worry, the next hour or two should banish any threat of sainthood for you. Get that little bucket, will you?" He pointed to a small wooden pail on the floor.

After locking the door he bade the fairly addled Skippers to follow. The shed that housed the still was situated below the great house, and the slave quarters were in a low area beyond that. A dozen shacks stood in no semblance of order. Fires burned in two or three places amid the cluster of shanties. Coward found the slave he sought. She sat cross legged at the fire with a monster of a man whose huge round face was circled with little peaks of tribal scarring. Coward addressed the woman, "Bina, love, we'll need a bit of privacy, and can you send that boy of yours to fetch Sallie, Emma, and Oma?"

William was unnerved. "Say, Coward, old man, isn't this buck her husband?"

Coward beamed. "Sure," he said, "but they're both my property. If he doesn't want to go away quietly, as he usually does for a pot of rum, he knows there's always the bull whip." He poured rum into the little bucket, handed it to the huge Negro who nodded and left. "Don't forget to send those girls around, Gideon, before you join up with your mates for your heathen jigs."

All three were drunkenly aghast, but George recovered quickly. He sat on the ground next to Bina who regarded him sidelong. She was in her twenties and had clear skin that glowed in the firelight. Coward laughed, "Bina's my personal favorite, but since you're a guest I suppose I could make do with one of the others. Here they are now. Gentlemen, take your pick."

William was past his alarm and picked the youngest of the three girls. Francis was reticent so Coward made his choice. George was tugging at the cord that held the bodice of Bina's dress closed. "Georgie, my new friend," said Coward, "you can take her into her shanty. We may be provincial, but we're civilized enough not to do it front of God and everybody."

"Oh, sorry."

Bina found his eagerness sweet, and he responded to her ministrations with affection, but his urgency was great and he moved directly to get inside her. And that did not last long. "How long it bin, massa George?" she asked when she felt his full weight motionless on her.

"Oh, it's been awhile."

She rolled him from her and squeezed him in her hand.

"Den res' awhile an' maybe you can do it agin. Dis time slow down so I kin do it too."

The girl William chose was newly nubile. Her breasts appeared to have grown large so recently that the skin had not yet stretched their full extent. Their conical nipples, a blacker shade of brown that was difficult to distinguish in low light, conformed to the jutting shape until he touched them, then they contracted to wonderful little points. She was frightened and barely moved under him, and she never said a word. Francis tried his best but the foreignness of the situation unnerved him, and his drunkenness deflated him. After ten minutes of rubbing himself against her with all their clothes intact, he rose suddenly and left the hut to sit by the fire. She went to sleep with a smile on her face.

William joined Francis shortly thereafter, but when he heard the sounds of Bina's gratification during George's second event, he stood at the door listening. "That George surely knows how to ingratiate himself with a whore."

"There's some little difference betwixt a slave and a whore," Francis told him. "A whore gets paid to pretend she likes it, a slave gets beat if she doesn't"

"He may well be beating her, but I can't tell what with."

Bina had her ankles crossed behind the small of George's back and was digging her stubby nails into the skin of his buttocks while she bit the tendon in his left shoulder. She was still thrusting when detumescence caused him to slip from her. She began to slowly massage herself with her left hand, and he studied her breasts with his right. They were round and soft but not yet pendulous—obviously maternal. "Where's your little one?" he asked.

"Sold," she said, and abruptly stopped touching herself.

Surreptitiously George went back the following night and tried to buy Gideon's absence again with rum. "No, suh," he declared, "Youse ain' my massa." George offered him six pence, but he remained intransigent. "Massa jus' take it." Bina stared fixedly into the fire, her profile motionless. She never met his eyes. He shrugged and left.

* * *

The morning after the three were feted by Coward, they went with John and Ann to the beach where the ship was being built. The hull looked complete from the sand. It was newly caulked with hemp cord and pitch, but no one was working, and it was derelict except for two Negroes who eyed the five apprehensively. Rude ladders, actually trunks with notches leaned on the rail, so the three climbed, then Ann with John following to protect her modesty while violating it himself. She kicked at him gently with her bare foot. Each was surprised to find no deck whatsoever, only another ladder. This gave Ann a problem which she solved by pulling the rear hem of her skirt between her legs and tucking it into her belt, then she waddled down the ladder facing forward clutching the hem of her makeshift pantaloons.

The bow pointed to the sea which was where the slaves were perched on the rail looking very much like a pair of ravens who were disinclined to meddle in the white folks business. "Still needs a bit of work," John said to no one.

"Do you think four lads so recently exiled from the gentry are up for the task?" William asked.

George grinned widely, "I hear the Irish build ships. How hard can it be?"

Ann hid an unladylike laugh behind her hand and said, "How would you know where to start?"

"Well, it looks like the seaworthy business is already done. All we need to do is make it snug."

"Well, well, well, I see my new shipwrights are on the job." Coward was climbing down the ladder with a woven sling over one shoulder from the top of which could be seen a jug with a stopper in it. "So you see the job's almost done."

Ann raised an eyebrow. "Me thinks you've already had the cork out of the bottle," she said with theatre.

"Well, lady, the sun is well up, but that's got nothing to do with the price of coals. Now, with my supervision, your ten hands, and the backs of those two boys up there, we'll be afloat in no time at all."

John looked serious and said, "Frankly, Ben, I am not sure our purses will hold out long enough to finish her even if we find the wit to do it."

"Aye, it's probably true if you intend to keep residing at Ye Flying Fish. My old friend Peevy is a larcenous bastard, but there's more the reason you should get on task. As soon as there's a deck overhead, you can move onto the ship. I'll even send a girl around each day with a basket of victuals for your suppers."

"We need to discuss it among ourselves."

"Of course you do. I'll come 'round to the Fish after dinner, and since I know you will come to the right decision, I'll bring the plans to show you."

The midday meal at Ye Flying Fish was barracuda with rice and pineapple. Afterward the men were leaving for a swim. John had tried to cajole Ann into accompanying him, promising that they would go in the opposite direction of the others, but she did not think any of them could be trusted and opted for resting in the room. Before making the street they were confronted by Coward with a rolled parchment in his hand.

"On your way to the ship? Good lads, but I'm sure it will aid you to study the plans with me over a wee dram," he said waving the parchment and patting his ubiquitous jug.

"Well," John groaned, "we did want to see the plans before deciding."

"Wise course. Here we go, let's sit under the window where there's a bit of light," he rambled while unrolling the plan and staking one end with the jug and the other with a salt cellar. "The first thing to do is saw the beams and peg 'em betwixt the ribs. Then planks on the beams, a little pitch, and you've got a deck to live under. My boys'll bring you the tools in the morning. You select the proper trees, they'll cut 'em and bring 'em to you. You shape 'em and fit 'em. Nothing could be simpler."

It was dusk before they made it to the beach. Coward led them into the surf still passing his jug, but they were too drunk to go very far, and made too much noise to avoid attracting the attention of the constable who stopped at the tide line to tell them that if they didn't put their clothes on he would put them in the gaol for the night.

"It'll be dark before we come back out," Coward reasoned to no effect, so they dressed and scattered to their respective sanctuaries. Coward weaving up the hill to his distillery singing something nobody understood. John, who thought he had composed himself adequately, was greeted coolly by Ann, in fact, when he thought about it the following morning he labeled it: "angrily". The other three found themselves back in the common room, after short naps, for pints, the evening breeze, and another dip in the surf.

Work began in the morning when the two slaves arrived riding an oxcart laden with axes, adzes, a crosscut, a whipsaw, chisels, mauls, draw knives, braces, bits, wedges, and cord. "All we need is somebody who's not too hung over to use them," Ann groused.

It was decided that the best use of their time would be to select some nearby trees for the slaves, called Henry and Elyhu, to fell. The first two trees that were dragged by the ox to the beach failed to have enough straight timber to span any part of the beam. "We'll burn them to melt the pitch," John rationalized.

The next tree brought by Elyhu, who was informed by George that he would be called Ely and not one syllable more, seemed long enough, straight enough, but after a full day of sawing slabs from the sides of the log in their hastily constructed saw pit, which flooded and collapsed hourly, the resulting beam was too thin to use.

"Save it for a deck board," John encouraged.

There wasn't a whiff of strength left among them, save in Ann of course, who had spent the day offering wearisome advice, but somehow managed to avoid becoming weary herself. Coward had been true to his word in sending a prepubescent slave girl with salt fish, bread, and fruit, but the unaccustomed effort burned through all that quickly leaving the men ravenous and irritable when John announced the end of the day.

Francis said to them, "We're trying to cut too fine a line. We're going to have to start with really big trunks to get a decent board. I'll take the boys into the woods and blaze a couple for 'em to start on first thing. Then I suggest we use the shit wood we collected today to shore the bloody pit so we don't all drown."

"Suit yourself," George muttered testily.

"He's right, you know," Ann insisted. "Don't snap at him because he has a good idea."

He scowled but began to walk toward town with others while Francis took the slaves into the forest.

Eventually they shaped their wits and their muscles as well as the beams. They caulked the deck, covered the bilge, and divided the hold with sail canvas. Ann swiped some of it to sew ticks which she stuffed with the beards of the bearded figs. It was Ann who had the good sense to suggest that they wait until the newly sealed deck was tested by a decent rain before moving from Ye Flying Fish. After the leaks were plugged, and retested with buckets of sea water, they took residence in the hold. Once again Ann insisted that celibacy was preferred to silent coitus, and once again, John differed, but never stood a chance. To his credit, at least in his own conscience, he turned being sullen into renewed enthusiasm to build cabins. His sudden zeal was so transparent that it became a joke, which evolved into a contest to see who could offer the most outlandish suggestion for the suite of rooms. What finally got built was a private room for the relative newlyweds, a common room for the bachelors, a conjugal chamber in case one was suave enough to bring a wench to his way of thinking, and a pub. All this consumed more of the foredeck than Coward's plans allowed, but he seldom visited, and then only to cheer their progress rhetorically, and offer rum as motivation.

On one of Coward's incentivizing visits George separated him and asked to be allowed to visit Bina again. "Of course, Georgie, anytime. Come 'round tonight." When George arrived later that night Coward was nowhere to be found, and Gideon responded as he had done previously. Bina's gaze remained implacably fixed on the fire.

In the ensuing weeks and months of progress and frustration they built a slightly truncated captain's quarters, rude crew's quarters, and a galley for which they enlisted another of Coward's slaves, who was a fair mason, to build an oven. Days passed, some with satisfaction in the increasing progress, some with the bitterness of utter failure, and not a few with the guilty glee of evading work altogether; often with the inducement of the irrepressible Coward and his rum. Eventually the fact of having to erect the masts could no longer be ignored.

"Let George do it. He was ready to refit the Albermarle before Martindale interfered," was William's suggestion.

John took that under consideration. "We can follow the plan well enough, but how do you stand it up?"

Ann told them, "You'll have to build a scaffold on top of our bedrooms, and lever the mast up."

"I suppose that's how they did it at bloody Stonehenge." Frank was looking toward the cabin when he said it. "

The tree William selected for the mast had a dogleg at

three quarters its height. "You can't use that crooked thing. We'll be the laughing stock of the high seas," George told him.

"What difference will it make? We can shift the yardarm to compensate."

"The damn thing won't sail straight," George insisted.

"You think the wind cares?" William truly did not want to shape another tree.

The four were evenly split and Ann refused to cast the tie breaking vote. They were still arguing when Coward came walking along the beach. He sighted one-eyed down the length of the mast and said, "Turn the crooked part toward the stern. It'll give us a rakish look."

"Now, I've come to tell you two things," he went on. "You've got to install gun ports. Six to a side."

"Gun ports?" John was puzzled. "There are no gun ports on the plans."

"You see, I've just yesterday come into some guns. A gentleman privateer had some extras and wanted to trade them for a little rum. I'll have them brought round so you know how big to make the ports."

"So we're going to be carrying twelve cannons?"

"Not twelve. Only two, but how would it look to French man-o-war if we only showed two gun ports? It just won't do."

"You mean we might be attacked?" Ann's eyes got round when she asked.

"Annie, love, every time we go to sea, we might be attacked. If not by the murderous French, then the Spaniards are even worse, and of course there's the pirates. That's why I wouldn't dream of letting you go without protection."

George cocked an eyebrow to say, "That's why there's no gun ports on the plan?"

"Plans are made to be revised, Georgie."

"What's the other thing you came to tell us?" Francis inquired to keep things from moving toward the inevitable row.

"I've decided on a name for her: The Three Brothers. No offense to you, Will, or you, Annie, but I don't think there's room on the stern to say 'The Three Brothers, Cousin Will and Lady Ann'."

William responded, "That's fine. I won't have my name on a ship with a crooked mast."

"Well, then, with all the problems of the world straightened out, it's time to celebrate," Coward announced and pulled the cork from his jug with his teeth. With that the work day ended.

One day in July of the second year at the task Coward brought a cask of rum which he said was to trade for paint. Francis took it to Bridgetown where he visited Ye Flying Fish to ask where one might be able to barter rum for paint and for a pint for himself after the walk in the rising heat. Peevy was sure John Chandler had paint and plenty of thirst for rum, then he told him, "The uh, gentleman, who sold your friend Coward the guns was here last night. He'd come straight over from London. He says our Lord Protector, Mr. Cromwell, doesn't think well of our loyalty to young Charles. Says he might be sending a ship of the line or two to teach us respect. You and your kin best get that sloop you're building on the water before it gets sunk right on the sand. Governour Willoughby has called a meeting of Commissioners come Saturday in St. James to plan defenses. I know Coward will attend, but you might think to bring your mates so there's a chance one of you will remember what's said."

"Peevy, are you inferring that my kin might suffer from intemperance?"

"Perish the thought."

"Nevertheless, your point is well taken. I'll get them there."

Francis took some red and some white paint back to the ship. George immediately took some of each to mix so he could paint pink the naked breasts and belly of the bowsprit he was carving. William grinned and Ann just shook her head. John said, "Let him be. It gives him an outlet for his baser urges."

When Francis told about the threat of Parliamentarians invading, John erupted, "The filthy bastards will never rest until they've destroyed every part of England, and all she stands for! We'll have to get Coward to buy more guns. I suppose the round headed sods will send their lackeys all the way to Virginia looking for us."

"You flatter us, Johnny," William said, "you think he's coming for us and not that Cavalier band of commissioners?"

"Aw, you know what I mean. Everywhere we look Cromwell's ugly face is keeping us from peace and quiet."

"Yeah, I do know what you mean, and we had better get the Brothers afloat so we can join the fight."

The meeting at The Hole was a disappointment. There were as many calls for moderation as for confrontation. The planters were more concerned with the protection of their property than with taking a stand one way or the other. Willoughby did order the lands of the exiles sequestered to raise money for defense which, prompted Coward to commit his as yet unfinished sloop to the cause. Being new to the island, Willoughby was pleased, but one of the commissioners who knew Coward well said, "We will accept the offer of your somewhat immature vessel on the condition that you are never aboard her."

"No need to fret, your worship, my doughty crew here will man her."

"Coward," said John, "none of us knows how to sail."

Later Coward demanded a relation of outstanding tasks. Sails and rigging were the biggest remaining items. Ann had been sewing sails for weeks, but much remained, and the whole idea of rigging had them scratching their heads. Ultimately it was agreed that everyone would join the sewing of the sails, Coward would hire a captain and some experienced mates, and that he would find a carpenter to build a decent ship's wheel. The Three Brothers floated at high tide one week later.

When Coward discovered the pub he was delighted and stocked it with rum and beer. The captain objected, but Coward mollified him by promising to maintain strict segregation between crew and passengers. He also beamed at the conjugal chamber which again suited his devilish nature. "You boys are bleedin' geniuses," he proclaimed. "Maybe I will go along after all."

By late summer Marten, Willoughby's man in London, was sending ugly dispatches. Parliament had sent a fleet to regulate rebellious colonies, and to enforce the Navigation Act. Its whereabouts was uncertain, so the royalists' ersatz navy patrolled the island's perimeter with the vain hope that should it be discovered, it would consist of modest numbers. The Three Brothers enjoyed its shakedown cruise on this exercise with the Skippers aboard in a role that neither the captain nor John understood clearly. George was more to the point. "We're the publicans," he decided.

The fleet arrived in October with enough ships to blockade the whole island. There was no firing, and Willoughby, who wavered frequently between firebrand Royalist and appeasing Parliamentarian, folded his Declaration of Independence and put it in his pocket. By January Barbados was quietly in the fold of the Lord Protector.

"I'm ready to go," Frank told the others over pottage in The Three Brothers' pub. When it was tied at the quay in Bridgetown The Three Brothers was a popular public house, although no one understood how Coward had persuaded the council to give him a license.

William commented, "Uncle Ben says we're waiting until we have some escorts. He doesn't trust us alone with his rum."

"As well he should not," Ann remarked.

George had enticed some free white women to sully

their reputations by attending the pub. He and the other two unattached were enjoying their increasingly regular company. Ann was a bit irritated by them, and worried that no good could come from their presence. She too was eager to leave, as was John who chafed in his role as peacekeeper. One day two ships loaded with colonists bound for America arrived in port. They were the Carolina and Port Royal, and Coward wasted no time in offering The Three Brothers to join them in their crossing. He loaded the hold with hogsheads and put an agent onboard to take responsibility for the care and sale of them.

"I didn't want to burden you with the chore," he told the Skippers when they expressed disappointment.

The Port Royal and the Carolina needed repairs and supplies. It was three months before they sailed.

One of the women who frequented The Three Brothers public house was the bored daughter of a planter who apparently aspired to be the death of her father. She had joked with George about going to Virginia with him. For his part, George liked the idea of her company during the crossing, but he could think of no way to assure that she would remain on board when the ship returned without him. Her name was Drucilla, and on the morning of the second day at sea she was found stowed away in the hold. Captain Howell, who took the separation of crew and passengers seriously, led her immediately to George. "This is your doing. Keep her in your den of iniquity."

Drucilla was a rebellious daughter, but she was not a slut, and she clung strictly to George, which aggravated Francis and William. She went by Silly and was a bit of a tomboy. She liked to play rough with George who found wrestling with a girl the greatest of diversions. Ann was aghast. "I feel like the proprietress of a bawdy house," she complained to John who could think of nothing to say that would be in his interest. Though George thought he should be worried, he and Silly took residence in the conjugal chamber.

For several days the crossing was pleasant with fair wind and weather. The other passengers crowded the pub, and at night there was much singing and revelry. The Skippers actually found their fortunes increasing by the percentage of the till that Coward had agreed to pay them.

They sailed to the east of the Windwards hoping to avoid Spanish men-o-war departing Cuba, but it didn't work. Two warships were accompanying a treasure ship back to Spain. When they were spotted, one separated from the small fleet and set itself close hulled to intercept them. Coward could not be persuaded to install more cannons, so crewmen moved both of the little guns to the side that would bear the attack if it came. Every passenger who owned a weapon brought it to the rail where they watched for over an hour as the Spanish ship closed with them. The captain used every artifice of his experience to try to outrun the attacker. The sloop was clearly faster, but the vector of the approaching Spaniards was such that it was too soon to guess whether they would cross ahead or astern.

The Spanish had real guns with serious range which they fired as soon as they could. The shots fell short and wide. "Why would they want to shoot us?" Drucilla, who was waving one of the dueling pistols John had brought from the Old Man's estate, asked.

"They probably smell the rum," George told her.

The Carolina and Port Royal were less fleet and soon were receiving fire. The captain of The Three Brothers brought her about and positioned her to harass the Spaniards from abeam. The three inch guns were more of an annoyance than a threat, as was the musket fire from the rail. Spanish soldiers fired back but were not any more accurate than the Englishmen. The respite did give the Carolina and Port Royal some breathing room and the next volley toward them fell short. The galleon came about, evidently intending to give chase. The captain of

The Three Brothers did not think they could out run him, so he came about and made to slide between his companions and the Spaniards.

Drucilla shouted, "He's mad!"

William was standing by her tamping the charge into his musket, and said, "We'll get another chance to pelt them with cricket balls."

The Brothers slid in front of the Spanish ship with scarce two hundred feet to spare, and fired their rather tepid broadside. The respite was enough to allow the other two ships to move out of range. The galleon came about to give chase, and George exhorted the captain to do the same so they could fire another salvo, but he ignored the advice, ran full ahead of the wind and drew steadily away from the warship. Further pursuit was clearly futile and soon the Spanish ship turned back toward its convoy.

At the bar there was much backslapping, breast beating, and denigration of the captain for begrudging them another shot. Francis was feeling frankly randy. He said, "Silly, love, give us a feel," and he slipped an arm around her back and cupped her breast before she could reply.

She punched him square in the left eye then said, "Oh! Now how did I miss that nose?" The blow staggered Frank into one of the adventurers who transferred from the Carolina because the Brothers had better amenities. He spilled his beer on his shirt, and being a boorish lout, shoved Frank into another drinker. The result was a brawl that spilled onto the deck. The seamen came quickly and made peace with battens.

Hearing commotion, the captain stepped from his cabin and bellowed, "If the gentlemen with the prominent proboscises cannot maintain order in their floating brothel, I will put you in irons."

George shouted at him, "We'd have made a prize of that galleon if you hadn't lost your nerve."

"I warn you, I am the captain of this ship, and you, Mr. Devilment, will get the cat-o-nine-tails along with your leg irons. Now, close that rough house, and get out of my sight."

"This ship needs a new Skipper, and as John's been a Skipper longer than anyone else, I nominate him."

John grabbed George by the collar and pulled him into the pub before the mate could seize him.

Frank's knuckles were bleeding, William had a cut lip, John had a bloody nose, and George had been kicked in the ribs. Only Silly was intact. When they were all inside they closed the hatch to the outsiders. Ann hadn't a shred of sympathy in her. She poured herself a cup of rum and took it to her quarters. Silly poured for the rest of them.

George said to her, "I can't take you anywhere, girl."

"I was just defending my honor since it was clear you didn't intend to."

The days dragged and soon the crowd returned the pub for the amusement Silly and her companions offered. The captain groaned and stayed in his cabin.

The storm rose at daybreak as they were approaching Bermuda. The three travelling companions were separated in the rain. They never saw the other two ships again, and they never knew that the Port Royal was wrecked. The Three Brothers was clear of the storm by midnight. The sun rose and the captain set her course on west by south. On the third day they sighted land. Word spread that it was the Virginia coast. The captain made straight for it and dropped anchor inside the mouth of a broad bay. He conferred with the mate and told him, "Bring me the four big nosed goons, under guard."

He found them where he knew he would, stood around the bar eating pottage. The mate found their antics amusing, and even surreptitiously visited the bar when he thought he could get away with it. "Captain requires a word with ye," he said.

"Gentlemen," the captain began, "this body of water is

called Winyah Bay. It is somewhat to the north of Port Royal and south of Virginia. I will be turning north to keep my duty to Mr. Coward. You will be staying here. Bring all your goods to the boat immediately." Then to the mate he said, "Mr. Johnson, do not let them from your sight until they are on the shore."

It took two boats to hold all the trunks. Ann was indignant. George was itching for a fight, but John kept him from rounding on the sailors who loosely pointed pistols at them. Silly was effusive. The mate took her arm when she tried to step into the boat after George. "Not you, missy. Captain says you're going back to your daddy." She had to be taken away by two burly seamen. George thanked his stars. She didn't know yet that she was pregnant.

CHAPTER TWO

"Damn that son of a saggy teated bitch. Why didn't we mutiny when George raised up Johnny. Curse his cowardly hide to Hell by every profane thing in this world. May his balls shrivel like raisins and his member never rise again. May all his issue have clubbed feet, and big round watery heads just like Cromwell's. May the whole of the Spanish Main await him 'round land's end. Damn that sod Coward for hiring him in the first place, and damn the dolt Johnson for kissing his arse." Ann was not happy. John tried to crawl into his collar. Francis and William admired the play of the sunlight shining through the pine needles.

George said, "But he did take Silly off my hands."

She turned chin to chin with him saying, "And if you and that reptile betwixt your legs gets us into one more predicament, I will personally remove it and feed it to you well done on a spit."

"Annie, give us a break. We need to sort this out."

"And just how do you suppose we are going to sort this out? We've got a single box of biscuits, a pail of water, a ton of belongings, no shelter, and no idea where we are."

"That's not true. We're at Winyah Bay, somewhat north of Port Royal."

She made a sound that ought not come from a woman and walked away.

They found a freshwater stream, so they moved the trunks closer to it and used them to build walls then they cut palmettos to make a roof. It was only tall enough to sit, but it got them out of the sun. Francis found clams and mussels where the stream drained to the sea. When it began to get dark they built a fire, not that it was cold, but it was a comfort.

John began thinking out loud, "This Port Royal place must be the nearest settlement. We should consolidate what we need to survive and start walking. Following the coast we can't get lost."

"You're basing our survival on the word of the arsehole who stranded us here," William observed. "For all we really know, Virginia may be closer in the opposite direction, and what we can't carry, which is most everything we own, we ought to attempt to preserve, don't you think?"

"Sure. How do you propose to do that?"

"I don't know."

They spent the following days deciding what was essential for surviving their expedition, and arguing whether succor lay north or south. John even put forth the notion of founding their own colony where they were. Ann found that idea immediately unacceptable, and even more so when George observed that if they remained isolated, it would be necessary for Ann to be shared. On the fourth day of indecision the naked Indian startled them when he stepped from the shadows. Francis was sitting next to Ann and he attempted to push her into the shelter, but only succeeded in falling on top of her.

The Indian raised his empty hand and said, "Greetings, Englishmen."

George recovered from the start sufficiently to ask,

"Do all naked savages speak the King's English?"

"Very few. When I was a boy I was taken to live in Portsmouth by a gentleman sea captain who was a man of peculiar passions which forced me to depart his company, and I learned to prefer London. Eventually it was my good fortune to return to my home by way of Spanish Florida. I am Ocanahonan of the Winyah people. Our town is not far from here and we think that you will be more comfortable there. Come, later I will send men to bring your trunks."

Ann was dumbstruck by the whole situation. All she could think to say was, "Wouldn't you like to borrow some clothes?"

"No thank you."

Then each man took his musket and Ann stuck the ancient pistols into her belt, and they left following the Indian. The strip of land by the beach was thick with marsh grass, screw palm, and scrub oak, but they entered groves of loblolly pine and red and white oak and were amazed to find a total lack of undergrowth. The terrain was park-like and the air cooler. The village of the Winyah was mostly cleared of trees, the houses stood on straight streets with cultivated patches between them. The savages came to stare at the strangers. Some fondled their clothes and a young warrior with designs painted head to toe shoved Frank who turned to fight but the youth made no further sign of aggression. Ocanahonan paid no attention and led them straight to a longhouse in the center of the village.

"You can rest here. I will send food, and some boys to bring the trunks."

About two thirds of the Indians were completely naked. All the children were, but most of the women wore doeskin aprons, some front and back and some only in the front. George was taking stock of this fact while the others observed the accommodations. There were raised cots all around the walls with twine supporting leather mats stuffed with Spanish moss. An area in the center of the building was devoid of furnishings. A circle of charcoal and a hole in the roof indicated a fire pit.

"Did any of you catch our new friend's name?" William asked in general.

"Ot-something," Frank answered. "Love his cockney."

"Ot-something, yeah, I got that much."

"Does any of you think this is a trap?" George asked.

Ann was looking at bric-a-brac hung from the columns. "If it's a trap, we're square in the middle of it."

"Well, if we don't wake with a tomahawk betwixt our eyes I'd say we're safe."

Francis made an observation, "It will be a comfort to dispel the threat of a trap, but allow me to point out we are still surrounded by savages. Did you forget the buck that gave me shove?"

"I thought you handled that well," George poked.

A woman arrived with a jar on her back hung from a tumpline. It was full of water and she left it and a gourd dipper. She returned with corncakes and things that tasted like potatoes. Children peeked through the door, but no one bothered them all the afternoon and evening. At sunset young men and boys arrived with all the baggage which they left inside the longhouse, then departed. Ocanahonan did not return so they made themselves comfortable in their new lodgings. There was chanting and drumming after dark which put the hair on Ann's nape on end, but it stopped soon, and the rest of the night was dead quiet save the calling of owls and the flutter of moths.

Ocanahonan arrived shortly after sunrise with some dried meat. "I hope your night was restful," he beamed.

"Extremely," John told him. "Say would you happen to know how long it will take us to get to Port Royal?"

"You mean the place where the Spanish fort is? Why do you want to go there?"

"Well, we're thinking we could find a ship there bound

to Virginia."

"Not much chance. The fort has been abandoned for longer than I've been alive."

The white faces were crestfallen.

"But if you want to go to Virginia, go to Virginia. It's just up the coast."

"How long a walk is 'just up the coast?'" George asked the Indian who spoke better English than he did.

"A warrior alone could do it in four days. A group such as yours might need a bit longer."

Ann asked the Indian with a noticeable tremor in her voice, "Could we get there without being killed?"

"My good woman, if you were killed, you could not get there at all, but if you think it too dangerous, you are welcome to stay here with us."

"Thank you," she said somewhat tentatively. "We'll have to discuss it amongst ourselves."

Ocanahonan had a son who he had taught some English. His name was Auteur Awwa. He was muscular and taller than his father. When he came to inspect the visitors they appraised him equally deciding that he was roughly sixteen and had not put much effort into learning English. "Come. Watch," he said motioning to follow. The young men of the village were organizing a game which Auteur Awwa joined. It consisted of throwing and catching a ball with a stick having a mesh pocket between a forked end. The ball was a leather bag stuffed with sand. For a time no one could understand the object, and they were shocked by the violence of it. The sticks were as useful for tripping as for catching and throwing, and a generous percentage of follow through landed on some ones back, but the Indians howled with laughter and jeered their bleeding opponents gleefully.

Auteur Awwa ran panting to the place where the white spectators watched. "Come. Play," he urged.

"What the devil are you trying to do?" William asked, but the Indian didn't understand. They all aped and pantomimed the game with shrugs and questions.

"Take ball to stick," their new friend indicated a pole stuck into the ground. Ann forbade John to play but told the others to kill themselves if they liked. The three stripped their shirts and joined the chaos. None of the Englishmen every managed to catch the ball, but they got rather good at tripping the Indians while they were running to the goal. They did not know what signaled the end of the game or who won, but they were as dirty and bloody as any Indian, and either Auteur Awwa had joined their family or they had joined his.

All the players ran to the beach to rinse the blood and dirt from themselves. When they were clean and floating on their backs in the warm water Auteur Awwa said, "I take you Virginia."

It did no good to argue since he didn't understand a word they said. "Maybe Annie will feel better about having a guide," Francis said to the group.

"A teenaged savage guide at that," George replied, then said to Auteur Awwa, "have you ever been to Virginia," but he just grinned and shook his head.

They discussed with Ann the idea of being guided to Virginia by the eager adolescent. She gave a half hearted approval with the codicil that there be no playing heathen games on the way. The men sought Ocanahonan to be sure that he approved of the plan. They found him in the evening sitting at a fire with several men of various ages smoking a huge pipe. When asked if he had heard of Auteur Awwa's proposal, he said, "Oh, yes. It is an excellent idea. If he makes it back he may have become a man." Then the four Englishmen discovered that the Indians' tobacco induced a lethargic dream state which reduced further conversation to monosyllables. A bright moon had risen above the tree tops when they returned to the longhouse. They had been joined by an Indian woman with an infant, and later one of the men from the fire circle arrived and began shaking a rattle to which he and the woman chanted softly. Ann was unnerved and saw to it that John shared her discomfort. The others found it soothing to their ethereal state, and followed the rhythm to a satisfying repose.

Much grief accompanied the selection of baggage to carry and to be left. For the bachelors' part, they traded Ann's tea set for good buckskin rucksacks, and her doilies and tea towels for dried venison which they packed on top of the change of clothes that was their entire load aside from knives, guns, powder and balls, and bed rolls. Ann refused to leave the plate, so John, with a sigh and a shrug, put the serving tray into his rucksack with three dresses, her Bible and his share of the venison. On the morning of departure Auteur Awwa arrived with his bow and a quiver on his back.

"Is he going to be stark naked all the way to Virginia?" Ann wondered aloud. John just shrugged.

"He likes to travel light," George told her. Her distress was palpable. She alternately stared and averted her eyes. The attention gave the boy an erection and everyone expected Ann to swoon.

"Lead the way," she said, pointing to the north while looking at the sky.

The land was usually low and wet, when it wasn't, it was sandy. Under the various oaks, which were generously hung with the grey moss, the ground was generally clear. Though the walking was easy, the oppressive heat and the swarming insects that plagued their eyes and ears kept the trail punctuated with curses and complaints. For diversion, and the hope of convenience, everyone worked to improve their guide's English. Auteur Awwa took to his lessons and was soon combining words in painful attempts at humor, usually to the expense of Ann whose discomfort was readily apparent. "Be more cool naked," he advised her.

"It's already a long way to Virginia," she groaned.

On the second day they shot some turkeys, and Auteur

Awwa was adept at locating starchy roots, some of which were eaten raw, and others wrapped in wet leaves and steamed in the hot coals. Ann had never seen a snake. The first one that she found underfoot sent her dancing loudly in the way that she had come. Auteur Awwa killed it and ate it when they stopped for the night. No one else would try it, and from that night Ann never had another peaceful sleep.

Their guide's English improved rapidly and his jests became ever more grammatically correct. Soon it was not just Ann who regretted that they had verbally armed him. He was also quite deadly with his bow and augmented their diet with much game that they roasted over their nightly campfire, and revisited at breakfast, but then left for the scavengers when the day's hike began. The wanton waste rankled Ann's practical nature. One afternoon the Indian shot a fawn still with white spots.

"You beast!" she exploded. "How could you kill that precious baby?"

He grinned at her. "Be happy. Less waste in the morning."

On the fifth day three Indians calmly walked onto the trail. To the white travelers they were identical to the Winyah. Auteur Awwa hailed them and entered into an animated discussion with much pointing, gesturing and pantomiming.

"Cheroenhaka," Auteur Awwa explained. "More at hunting camp nearby. We are invited to feast tonight."

"Do you know them?" Ann asked suspiciously.

"Hear of them. Cheroenhaka friends of Winyah."

"And they speak the same language as you?" William asked.

"No, Cheroenhaka sound like mouth full of shit. We talk travelling language."

The hunting camp was on an island in a great expanse of swamp with an oval pond in its center, and consisted of a dozen people sharing three rude huts. Four men killed the game, six women jerked it; one woman had an infant, and a crone supervised. The feast began as dusk. It offered fresh meat and fowl plus a dish of corn and beans. The Cheroenhaka were used to Englishmen, though only the warriors and old woman had actually met any. The women were as comfortable with the strangers as the men and the crone. They posed a barrage of questions through Auteur Awwa, who embellished everything. One warrior wondered if they had any whiskey, another wanted to trade a bear skin for a musket, the old woman would trade five rabbits for a steel knife, and another woman, a girl actually, wanted to know Frank's name. "This one wants to have your babies," Auteur Awwa added to his translation.

She moved to the place by him and pointing to herself said, "Howerac Unke," saying it three times before he could repeat it.

"Couldn't I just call you Annie?"

"Frank," she said and squeezed his crotch giggling.

"Ow, that's Frank, all right."

The girl would not relent. When everyone spread their bed rolls she laid her furs next to him and continued to grope and giggle and bite until, admittedly without much real resistance, he succumbed to her advances, then he had to try, to no avail, to keep her quiet. "I'll not hear the end of this," he whispered into her uncomprehending ear.

In the morning when they prepared to depart, Howerac Unke made it clear that she intended to accompany her conquest, but the old crone cuffed her and heatedly told her what she would and would not do. Frank led the party in making their exit quickly while the girl was otherwise occupied.

Auteur Awwa chided him, "Good you no let her follow. No sleep for nobody."

By midday Howerac Unke materialized from a cluster of stickers and fell into step with Francis. She beamed at him, his mouth fell open but no sound emerged. Auteur Awwa touched his elbow and said to him laughing, "Her name mean 'Hairy Belly'."

"I'll just call her Ann."

The original Ann did not seem pleased.

* * *

The first large river sent Auteur Awwa searching for an elm tree. With George's knife and his stone tomahawk he made a serviceable canoe from a large section of bark in a couple hours with the aid of Howerac Unke's skill at stripping cord from oak saplings. Frank was becoming enamored. The party and their baggage were ferried across the current in stages, and John agonized at the thought of lugging the canoe. The Indians found the idea laughable and insisted on leaving it on the river bank.

On the twelfth day, however, they arrived at a river with the opposite bank barely discernable on the horizon. Auteur Awwa told them that he thought this must be the river on whose opposite shore they would find the white settlement. No one could guess in which direction Jamestown might lie, but it was reasoned that the river was more likely to become manageable upstream than downstream. They walked for another whole day before finding white men.

Four men sat beneath a shelter. Two wore uniforms and carried muskets. They watched the seven approach with no indication of interest until one of the men rose and said, "Where the devil did you come from?"

"London," Frank told him curtly.

"London, you say," the man said turning to his associates. "Seems to me that most visitors from London arrive by ship, and rarely in the company of red Indians."

"Yeah," said William, "well, we took a circuitous route."

John interrupted the exchange to inquire how one could find Jamestown.

"It's quite easy," the man assured him, "you step out of

this here boat on the other shore and you're there. It only costs you a penny a head." Then indicating the Indians, he asked, "What d'you intend to do with them?"

Frank answered the question, "He's on his own, but the girl may be here awhile."

"Maybe me too," Auteur Awwa said, "Maybe I like white-devil's village."

"Now, his Excellency, the Governour, might have something to say about that. I don't suppose I'll be handed me head for delivering one boy and one girl savage so long as they behaves themselves. But they're still going to cost you a penny a head."

John found seven pennies in his purse and gave them to the man then they clambered over the gunwale into the boat. The two men manned the oars and the soldiers never rose from their seats. The crossing took a rather long time and the oarsmen were sopped with sweat when they grounded the boat on a low muddy bank covered with tiny crabs and it began to rain.

"Damn the luck," the boatman said, "I suppose Alf and me will have to wait it out at Ollie's tavern."

George wiped the rain from his eyes and said, "Perhaps we could join you."

The people of Jamestown were used to seeing Indians in town, and to some extent, they were used to them being naked, but Ollie, the tavern keeper, would not let them inside. William said to Auteur Awwa, "Sorry, mate, we won't be very long."

"Wait under tree," he grunted.

Frank added, "Keep an eye on my Annie."

The Indian grunted again, she just smiled.

In the tavern the travelers were considered a novelty. Ollie, who was tall and leathery, explained the patch over one eye philosophically, "The Indians are wild. We moved into their land. You got to expect some of them to try to kill you. The bastard that took out my eye probably felt he was just doing what he had to do. I don't even think he

67

held it against me for shooting him clean through the heart. Still, I find it a bit hard to swallow your walking twelve days in the wild without runnin' into any that felt inclined to cleave your skulls."

"Must be our gentrified manners that appealed to them," George remarked.

William contradicted, "Nah, it's Frankie. He's got a special way with them."

Ollie gave Frank an amused look. "Well, you won't be the first here about to take one for a pet."

Frank reddened and hid in his mug. Ann looked uncomfortably toward John who took his cue to change the subject. "Can you direct us to some accommodations?"

"Aye, I can offer you room and board for a shilling a night. The Indians can stay in the room if you want them but they can't take their dinner in the common room. Either in the sleeping room or outside. If you think that's too rich for your purse, there's plenty of folk who'll take you in as servants, probably not all of you together, but most are going to want to bind you for some years."

"We intend to claim our head rights."

"Sure, it's a sensible thing to do, but you've got to eat until the Council grants your patents, and then you've got to bring in a crop."

William offered, "We didn't lose any weight coming here from where that right bastard put us off the ship."

"I don't doubt you'll make good," the publican replied, "but the first year is hardest. You should be prepared."

CHAPTER THREE

That October the weather at Jamestown was exceedingly fine. The resources of the extended family were being depleted at a precipitous rate, and the close quarters of Oliver's sleeping room was grating on the nerves of all but the Indians who seem perfectly comfortable wherever they found themselves. Getting to know their new environment was respite for the rankled new arrivals. Hogsheads of tobacco crowded the little wharf and reeked their seductive stench—black slaves and white servants moved them to the ships. Planters and Gentlemen of Quality coming from the plantations strolled around the dusty triangular fort in wool and velvet coats that were much too warm for the season. Trees had begun to turn, and in the evening, when John and Ann found a quiet spot beyond the bulwark to watch the enormous orange moon rise over the water, they felt the freshness of autumn on the land.

Jamestown was as novel to Francis as was his feral companion, and both the surroundings and the company were novel to her. Wearing a dress was nearly the only concession to English manners she would make. She might dance and chant whenever or wherever. Being in public did not deter her from being amorous. She was enthralled with the more macabre trappings of civilization, and would stand in awe before the whipping post and the gallows. Frank ignored his concern for her fascination with brutality because she inevitably forced him thereafter to any convenient place of repose and vented her savage passions. She had marvelously globular breasts with dark, high set nipples that froze to points whenever Frank's fingers teased them. It was her delight to straddle him, teasing his face with their hardness. "Bite harder!" she insisted until she wailed and he thought he had hurt her, but if he stopped she exhorted him to bite even harder. He became the butt of much envious humor from his male companions, and the object of a worrisome amount of righteous disapproval from the upright members of the community. However embarrassing the girl's behavior might have been, Frank was enthralled by every bawdy minute of it.

* * *

George and William were obsessed with the idea taking revenge on the captain who stranded them. They passed as much time possible in the common room at the tavern trying to ascertain the whereabouts of The Three Brothers. There being exceedingly few unattached women in the colony, carousing was mainly confined to drinking and bantering with their fellow frustrated males. In the early days of November a man came to the common room and asked for whiskey. The fact that a patron was opting for the much more expensive essence of home instead of colonial rum caused a small stir. William scrutinized the man and said to his cousin, "We know that man."

George closed one eye to peer through the murky light. "It's the captain of the Carolina. Maybe he knows where the arsehole is."

He went to his table and respectfully said, "Begging your pardon, sir, but we couldn't help noticing that you bear a resemblance to the captain of the Carolina."

"I am that man, and who would you be?" His eyes fixed George with a suspicious glare.

"We were passengers on The Three Brothers, and we are curious as to how you fared after we got separated."

"Indeed! And I'm as curious as you as to the fate of the Brothers. Have a seat and join in what's likely my last indulgence in the finer things. I've decided to quit the sea and throw my lot in with the likes of you," though the phrase sounded anything thing but praiseful of their likes.

William mounted the three legged stool and said, "Well, as the official welcoming committee of the parish, we are pleased to accept your offer."

The captain of the Carolina was a young man to have such a position. George thought that perhaps he was thirty-five. He extended a hand and said, "Always pleased to make the acquaintance of a skipper. George Skipper at your service, and this would be my cousin, Will Skipper."

The captain was clearly confused. "Eh, Joseph Bayley," he said shaking George's hand and then William's. "Skipper is your family name?"

"Guilty, sir. We are sorry to report that we have been Skippers a bit longer than you have. Not that we profess any knowledge of the art."

"It's a remarkable name. If it were mine, I might not leave the sea, but tell me the fate of the Brothers."

The bottle arrived, George and William drained their mugs of cider, and Bayley poured them each a generous ration of whiskey.

George said, "We don't know. We hoped that you might have heard."

"No, I haven't, but how is it that you don't know?"

William, feeling animated, responded, "Well, it seems that the gentleman who held your position on The Three Brothers, and I might point out that the owner of that vessel chose the name in honor my three cousins, put us ashore in hostile territory."

Bayley slapped his knee and laughed. "Whatever did you do to that curmudgeon to incite him?"

George related the facts as he saw them, "Well, as you may know, Mr. Coward, owner of the ship, put us in charge of his cargo, or at least the dispensing of it, and we were a little too successful for the likes of our captain, Mr. Howell. So blinded was he by his prejudice, that he didn't even appreciate our selfless defense of his ship when those filthy Spaniards attacked us. After the storm tossed us around a good bit, he sighted some *terra incognita* and he beached us there straight away, including our saintly sister-in-law. Thanks be to God, we fell in with friendly savages who, although they stole our belongings, led us safely here."

Bayley smiled and chuckled. "I'm sorry to hear of your rough treatment, but I'm happy that you've weathered it well, and I am sorry to report that I know nothing of Howell or the Brothers. After the storm the Carolina limped into Bermuda for repairs. It just arrived here two days back, and as I said, I've had my fill of water. I think I like the look of this place. Here's to Virginia!" He lifted his mug to the pair.

Bayley proved to be an affable sort who took to George especially. They each were blessed with the gift of impertinence, and a fondness for the camaraderie found in the sharing of a pint or two. Bayley was also possessed of sufficient hard currency to acquire a small plantation on Chappell Creek. Since the seller had cash in hand, he had no problem with Bayley occupying the property during the pendency of the patent. The house was ample; being two stories with whitewashed clapboards and black shutters. Bayley extended an invitation to George and his entourage to stay rent free for their help in opening the place, and providing companionship. There was little debate at Oliver's Tavern.

The Indians migrated to their new lodging with the same serenity they displayed in the single room. English Ann had convinced Indian Ann to wear one of her dresses most of the time. Auteur Awwa condescended to wear a flap of leather across his loins—in the front. Howerac Unke was acquiring sufficient English to refer to Francis as her husband, and to confirm that her name did in truth translate as "hairy belly".

"See, is true," she said lifting the hem of the muslin dress.

Frank gently pushed her hands down saying, "Your name is Ann, dammit. Ann!"

The other Ann had gotten inured to the flagrant immorality of her in-laws, but the incident of the belly showing moved her to find John alone on the verandah and she pulled him aside. "You must convince Frank to marry her, and very soon, or they will both find themselves in the stocks for an early birth." His eyes widened, but he saw the wisdom of his wife's advice.

Frank was dismissive at first, but with Auteur Awwa helping interpret the medical questions, he attempted to quiz the girl. "Ann, dear, before we met did you have a problem with the hairy place every month?"

"My hairy place no problem. Hairy place problem for you?"

"No, no, I'm very fond of it. I meant—"

"He means: do you bleed with the moon?" Auteur Awwa contributed.

"Sure. Each moon since hair grow."

"But you haven't, uh, bled since we met, have you?"

She spoke to Auteur Awwa in the abrupt sounding travelling language. He turned and told Francis laughing, "She going to have your baby."

The next day everyone, including Bayley, hiked to the Middle Plantation where Frank paid twenty shillings for the license and the union was solemnized. Indian Ann wore English Ann's best surviving dress, and Frank admonished her to keep it in situ when in front of the minister.

John clapped him on the back and said, "Welcome to the plight." Ann jabbed her sharp elbow into her husband's ribs.

They retired to the tavern to celebrate, and the barman allowed Auteur Awwa to enter the common room. He considered the new Mrs. Skipper to now be civilized. Frank thought, "*If he only knew.*"

It was here that the young warrior did battle for the first time with the demon rum. It was George who brought him the cup, "Here you are, my friend, in honor of the occasion you must join us in a little fire water."

This seemed to perplex the Indian. "Why you call it that?"

"You'll see."

"Quakerhunte!" he gasped, "it is fire water. Why you like it?"

"You'll see straightaway. Have a bit more," George raised his glass and, having seen the white men toast, the Indian copied the gesture.

"I ever tell you want my name say in English?"

"No, what does it mean? And don't be telling me it means 'him with big manhood'."

He laughed, "No, Indians only give girls funny names. 'Auteur Awwa' mean 'Fire Water'."

"Go on," George really thought he was being mocked.

"I show you." He whistled like the lark which got the bride's attention as surely as if he had sent a waiter with a note card. "Tell George what 'Auteur Awwa' say in English."

She seemed pained in thought, then she told him, "Fire and water."

George shook his head ruefully. "This bodes no good."

* * *

By the time The Council approved their head rights it was December and the Adventurers learned from the Surveyor General, Mr. Theodorick Bland, where they could expect to be given grants. Bland was intrigued by Cheroenhaka Ann, who he pronounced to be a Nottoway. He had encountered her people while surveying on Rowantree Branch. Ann didn't recall his visit, but was incensed at being labeled Nottoway. "He call my people snakes!" she railed to Frank.

"Oh, I'm sure he meant it in the kindest way," Frank attempted to defuse her.

William opened his mouth and immediately wished he hadn't, but he said, "At least snakes ain't hairy."

Frank glowered, Ann chuckled, but Theodorick Bland was simply confused.

They inspected the sites and found parcels that suited them. John and Ann wanted to be as convenient to Jamestown as possible, as did William, but the good parcels were taken, and they ended in Norfolk where they found three parcels stretched along Indian River in Lower Norfolk County about five miles upstream from the tide water. George tried to find fifty acres near to his partner in debauchery, Joseph Bayley, but was forced to settle on land several miles farther upstream. The Worshipful Justices of the Council took their pleas under advisement with little comment, except that George nearly earned a night in the stocks because he tried to claim having transported Auteur Awwa. When the Council convened next, their patents were duly granted.

Although they were warmly ensconced in Bayley's plantation house, the brief period of freezing weather in January and February started Ann to worrying about accommodations in the following winter. Ann told John matter-of-factly that they were all going to cooperate in building their respective shelters, and since he was eldest, his would be first. He dutifully took the message to the others.

"We'll have a babe come summer. You could give that some consideration," Frank argued.

"We built most of a ship, we ought to be able to get two houses finished before winter," John reminded him.

"Anyway, the hairy one is used to the elements," Will said before he thought better of it.

"Listen, you little prick, she's my wife now, and you best show her some respect."

"Damn, cousin, what happened to your sense of humor?"

"Marrying a woman makes a man see her sort of different. Don't it, Johnny?"

John's eyes rolled. "I'll give you that."

William stood for a time with his jaws clamped shut and his fists clenched. His pique did not relent when he said, "You're the patriarch, Johnny, we'll do what you think best, won't we Francis?"

Frank made a dismissive flap of his hand and walked away.

"Pressure of fatherhood is getting to him," George opined to the group.

"Well," John reminded, "even if we don't work together, there's not enough money left for each of us to buy tools. We're going to have to cooperate."

"We don't need convincing, cousin. Even your newlywed brother was only objecting to Annie's commandeering the first project of the new Carpenters' Guild."

John made sure Ann was not in hearing range before he admitted, "We had plans to build the ship from. I wouldn't mind at all if we learned to build houses on Frank's shilling."

The awareness of shillings and their paucity preyed on John when he tried to go to sleep most nights. He had written letters to the deacon, the goldsmith in Threadneedle Street, and to his Uncle William to advise where correspondence and rents could now be forwarded. No responses were ever returned.

* * *

They moved onto the plot and erected tents. After the trees were cleared labor was divided between the sexes. The women planted the garden until the County Collector happened by and informed them that the law forbade white women to work the soil. After that poor Indian Ann was left to the task alone. The men began setting piers. Auteur Awwa, who refused to go home, commented, "Looks foolish to cut down trees and then plant them again."

George found the Indian amusing and was becoming proficient with the language. They would bait the others by making disparaging comments in the travelling language and laughing pointedly. Ann, the Cheroenhaka, would smile knowingly but not intercede.

"We need a horse," Auteur Awwa announced at the end of a workday.

"Yeah, we probably do, but what do you want a horse for?" George inquired.

"You pay the Germans to cart the logs to their mill and to cart the boards back. Pay for a horse very soon."

"Out of the mouths of savages now."

"Not going get this done without horse."

Frank reminded them that a horse was a large investment and the cartage fee was small, if ongoing.

"No difference if you don't have income."

"Christ! The savage's an accountant now."

The Indian did not know what an accountant was, but he continued, "Germans make fire water. Why don't you?"

"Because you'd drink the profits."

"Not all."

Frank reminded them there was a problem with the

idea. "Do you think the Burgesses are going to give you license to make whiskey without some sort of emolument?"

"Best not to tell them." Again, this came from the Indian.

George was intrigued by the notion, but he doubted that he had enough cash to buy a still, and doubted with more certainty that Ann would let John enter into a joint effort. He went to Bayley who jumped at the idea, and offered his plantation as the site for the operation. George did not feel he could absent himself from the housing effort for very long, but he went abroad for a time gathering components. He found a copper vat which he purchased reasonably. Bayley gave him money to commission the fabrication of a coil of copper tube for the condenser and an oaken cover for the vat. He had learned from Coward in Barbados the rudimentary steps of distilling rum, and opted for that formula instead of trying to guess the secrets of whiskey. Bayley bought the molasses and the operation began.

The still was tiny by comparison to Coward's Prudence and it had leaks, but it worked. The first elixir to drip from the tube was impotent and undrinkable. After a second distillation it was passable though raw, but only amounted to enough to entertain George and Bayley for one evening. Nevertheless, production continued while George and Auteur Awwa were gone to work on John's house. When they had two casks nearly full, the Indian disappeared. When he returned he was in the company of a band of Cheroenhaka. One of them was the brother of Howerac Unke who went to Bayley's plantation when she heard of his arrival. Frank was suspicious and angry with Auteur Awwa for revealing her whereabouts thinking he might carry her home, but she assured him, "Just visit and tell *ena* about the baby. Don't worry. I stay with you so long as you get hard."

The Cheroenhaka arrived with two horses. They left

with one horse and two casks of rum. It had prominent ribs and a swayback, but after having it shod, it was able to drag logs to the sawmill and saved much needed money. Even Ann was pleased.

Indian Ann gave birth on July 15, 1653, somewhat less than the usual length of time after their marriage. Frank was concerned about retaliation from the vestries, and insisted the birth be concealed. Ann did not understand. When he insisted that the boy was to be named John she wanted to know what "John" meant. "It doesn't mean anything. It's just a name," he told her.

"Names have to mean something," she insisted.

"Not in this family," he declared.

"Is that why you call me Ann?"

"You'd prefer if I called you Hairy Belly?"

"Well, at least it means something nice."

Motherhood did not dampen her fleshly ardor, but while lactating she did not invite Frank to bite her nipples.

Enough of the house was finished by September to allow them to quit the tents which they sold for nearly what they paid. George and his young Indian friend were frequently absent while tending the production and distribution of rum. So far the entire shipment was acquired by the Cheroenhaka who were paying in furs and hides which were sold in Jamestown for tobaccos. Bayley hired workers who were preparing his land for the growing of tobacco in the coming season. It had previously been used for that crop, as was every plantation in Virginia, so the means to store it were available to the entrepreneurs. George's decreased attendance to the communal construction projects was noted with displeasure by his family members.

"It's about time you started carrying your share of the load around here," John exploded to him when he returned after several days at Bayley's plantation.

"What have you got to complain about? You've got a horse now, thanks to me."

"The horse is very good but we didn't think it would be the last contribution you ever made. You'll be the first one to complain that you're not getting enough help when it's time to build your house."

"You could at least bring some of the rum," Will added.

"That's trade goods, cousin. I don't even drink it myself."

"Sure you don't."

George had ignored his brother, but John was not having that. "If you expect to be part of this family, we expect to see quite a bit more of you here when there's work to be done," he scolded.

"If I expect to be part of the family, is it? Well, I have to think about that." He turned and walked away from his family. He went back to Jamestown where he visited the tavern and paid Ollie with a twist of tobacco for a bottle of good whiskey. He was still too furious to sit still so he paced while he drank. There was a handbill on the wall. It seemed a certain Roger Greene intended to found a new colony some distance south. Something in that intrigued him, but he found that he wasn't enjoying the whiskey so he corked it and left.

In the third week of October the constable arrested George for selling rum to the Indians.

"What's wrong with that?" he protested. "The buggers need a drink as much as the next person."

"The Council and his Lordship, the Governour do not share that opinion," he was told.

The arrest took place in the settlement based on the report of a witness who had been present when George and Auteur Awwa sold furs. Bayley, who stood for George, was not implicated, and the still was not confiscated. It took nearly all the tobacco to cover the bond that got him released. The Quarter Court had just adjourned and would not reconvene until December, so when Roger Greene departed in November for Albermarle

Sound with one-hundred men, George and Auteur Awwa were among them. Bayley bought his untouched parcel of land for hard currency, a little of which he used to buy tools, ammunition and some corn.

Greene had arranged with a slaver returning to England, lightly loaded with the hogsheads of tobacco received in payment for the slaves delivered to Virginia, to transport his colonists to the sound which he had briefly explored and believed to be favorable. A site was selected by a river draining into the north side of the sound, and the hundred began in earnest to erect shelters. It was still November when the hurricane struck. The storm surge flooded the settlement destroying much of the supplies brought from Virginia. Several men drowned. All were miserable when the rain subsided on the third day. Greene was at a loss as to what to do.

George told him, "We might look for some higher ground."

This group of would be colonists was not greater than the sum of their parts. George and Auteur Awwa focused on their own comfort and well being, and to the extent possible, enjoyment. Greene had no motivational skills; consequently men who rightly needed to lend some effort were spectators. Indians began to harass them. A hunting party was ambushed killing one and wounding another. They began sniping at the camp in broad daylight and shooting the odd flaming arrow during the night. Sentries were posted day and night, but George and his tame Indian were skeptical of their reliability.

"Why don't you go into the woods and meet these bastards. Tell them we will soon be supplying them with rum if they don't kill us," George suggested to Auteur Awwa.

"Nansemond. Can't talk sense to them."

"Well, I don't trust our fellow colonists to guard the perimeter whilst we sleep. What makes a Nansemond want to kill white men?"

"They kill red man just a fast. Indians no follow laws. Follow whim."

"Where'd you learn that word?"

"English Ann say it about you."

"I think Mr. Greene's grand scheme won't hold together more than a month or two. What do you think would be the safest place we could go?"

"No place very safe. Closest place we don't lose scalp and you don't end in calaboose be Chounteroute Town. That's Indian Ann's town."

"Excellent idea! I say we don't announce our departure. We'll go hunting and get lost; though I'm damned tired of leaving baggage lying in the woods everywhere I go."

"Good to travel light."

Within six months all of Greene's colonists had either slunk into the woods, been killed by the Nansemond or marched back to Jamestown in frightened clusters. Auteur Awwa led George more or less directly to the Cheroenhaka in five days. The way led though familiar landscape of oak, short straw pine, maple, and circumvented as much as possible the swamps. Other Indians were encountered without conflict by the universal signal of the pipe. On the approach to Chounteroute the underbrush was recently burned and the air smelled acrid from it.

Ann's brother was a *cockarouse* whose name was Hahenu. He had circles of tattooed welts on his cheeks and pectorals. He remembered George from the first trip to trade the horse for rum, and he welcomed the two into their village. "Has my sister's child come to the light?" he asked.

"Yes, she had a boy. Named him John."

"What's that mean?"

George took a deep breath. "English names don't mean something. They are only names," he explained in his best of the travelling language.

"You learn to speak well, but your accent is mushy," Hahenu told him.

The village was much like the Winyahs' having a longhouse in the center of town, a central avenue with the half round topped houses on each side, garden plots usually separated the houses, and at the end of town was a ceremonial center consisting of a ring of poles—with faces carved on them—set in the ground. George thought there might have been twelve-hundred souls living there. The king coincidentally bore the same name as the town. On Hahenu's recommendation he welcomed the two into his community with the passing of the pipe. The narcotic effect silenced the circle putting George in mind of the night in the hunting camp.

"Why does Indian tobacco have so much more wallop than what the Englishmen grow?" he asked the group.

Chounteroute answered, "Different plant. Whiteman's weed just makes a stink. It's a mystery why they love it so. Sometimes we mix other weeds. Call it *kinnikinnick*. Depends on where you want to go."

Most of the Cheroenhaka girls were as feisty as Frank's Ann, and both the newcomers had a fine time availing themselves of their licentiousness. They slept on furs in the longhouse with a girl on either side. In the morning Hahenu invited them to accompany his hunting party. George earned considerable stature by dropping a stag with his musket at fifty yards across a grove of beech.

"Why is the woods so clear of brush?" he wondered aloud.

"We burn it to make shots like that possible," one of the hunters told him.

They skinned the deer, quartered it and each carried a piece back to the village. George was given the antlers, and the girls fought for his attention at the feast that evening. In the trance of the rustic tobacco he and his happy choice staggered to the longhouse to sport on the bearskin. Her name was Genheke which George learned meant Summer. "That's a whole lot better than Hairy Belly," he told her and she bit his ear. Sometime in the aftermath of playful exertion he was struck by an idea that made him smile.

In the morning he sought the king and offered a proposition which was enthusiastically received. That very morning, accompanied by Hahenu, Auteur Awwa and a horse, he left the village. It was a two day walk to where Bayley's plantation stood. He had bought a slave who was beginning to put in his first tobacco crop. Bayley was pleasantly surprised at the sight of them. "So the prodigal son returns," he said embracing George. "How goes the new colony?"

"What new colony? Greene proved to be a bloody fool, and the miscreants he took along could hardly find their arses with both hands. We've taken up residence with the folk of my brother's wife, Hairy Belly, and we are badly in need of the still—if the sheriff hasn't smashed it."

"More likely he'd take it for himself," Bayley said, "but he hasn't been around." He had a servant attend to the horse and he took them into the house where they exchanged their goings on since they had last seen one another.

"Be visiting the family?" Bayley asked.

"No, best not to be seen around. If you have occasion to run into any of them, give them my regards."

"Sure. So you think you might stay with the Indians?"

"Until one of the bloodthirsty savages slits my throat in the middle of the night," he laughed swatting at Fire Water, Hahenu, of course didn't understand.

Auteur Awwa translated and Hahenu replied through him, "His throat is safe if he can make rum."

George thought aloud, "We'll have to find a reliable source of sugar cane."

Bayley said, "I doubt if you can grow it in this latitude."

"We'll find something that ferments. Bloody tobacco leaves if nothing else. You know, you really ought to plant

Indian tobacco."

"It's different?"

"Mightily. Visit us when I get the still fired up, and we'll show you what I mean. Come to think of it, if you recall the spirited nature of my sister-in-law, you might find other reasons to enjoy the visit."

"I'll be sure to do that after I get the crop in the ground."

They had a fine evening. Bayley served a supper of mutton stew with rice, winter squash and Madeira. They stood a log by the fireplace and had an archery competition using the Indians' bows. The Indians won handily, and the servant girl, who was not at all comfortable around the Indians in spite of the bearskins they wore in the winter, stayed out of sight while arrows were flying and the men howled and passed a jug.

The quirky little still was assembled at Chounteroute with great ceremony. George had enough molasses to make a batch of rum, but a new medium needed to be found and of course it was corn. It only took a few experiments to perfect a survivable corn liquor. King Chounteroute considered George a hero and formally adopted him into the tribe as a chief man. Quickly a house was built for his use. Soon it was clear that Chounteroute had a problem holding his liquor so much of the business of running the village was thereafter attended by his primary wife, Eteshe Ena. She gave George the evil eye, but said nothing about him.

George's celebrity made him the goal of numerous female suitors. Each evening found him sybaritically sampling their wares. George was a connoisseur of the female form, and one of his stringent criteria was the geography and expanse of pubic hair. His sister-in-law notwithstanding, the Indians were generally sparse of body hair. Some of the girls that he joyfully rutted were nearly bald in the genital area. Although he was liberal minded in the short term, these candidates could never survive the long run. However, he remained convinced that his brother could not have taken the only hirsute maiden of the Cheroenhaka.

When Bayley came in the spring he was smitten with the place. "I have never seen such a garden of earthly delights," he remarked after his first night in Chounteroute.

"The place does grow on you," George agreed.

"By the way, old man," Bayley said, "I forgot to tell you that I discovered molasses can be made from sorghum, and you can grow that here. I even brought you some seed."

"Clever bastard. Do you suppose it's too late to get a crop in the ground?"

"Only one way to find out."

As it was in the interest of most of the tribe, George enlisted some aid to clear a parcel and plant the seed. Planting was usually considered woman's work, but Eteshe Ena refused to allow the women to participate. The men had no such qualms.

The village of Chounteroute was situated at the fork of two rivers, one was diaphanous and playful, the other muddy and robust. Both branches were well populated with pike, bass, bullheads, sunfish and every now and then an alligator's spiny back was seen floating serenely in the current. Between the village and the vertex of the fork the land was kept in a state that put Bayley in mind of Hyde Park. He delighted in strolling under the oaks and loved reclining beneath the pines on the bed of dry needles while watching the sunlight play through the boughs and sparkle on the water. A certain girl had graced his bed the previous night. She had vanished before the sun rose, but she followed him and watched from concealment. When he was still and seemingly asleep, she crept silently from downwind. A body length from the supine Englishman she launched herself on top of him laughing, whooping and pinning his arms to the ground.

"Jesus! Deeshu, you scared the bloody hell out of me." Getting free from her grip he held her at arm's length studying her, grinning doglike. She was wearing the frontal apron of doeskin with bead work in a celestial motif. "You could give a man his death with a fright like that." She did not understand a word which restarted her laughing fit as she pulled the slip end of the thong that held the apron across her loins. "God, I love this place," he gushed.

Deeshu was as determined to snare Bayley as Howerac Unke had been to bear Frank's children. During his tenure as a ship's captain he had had occasion to cavort with some highly exotic women, but this girl of less than half his age performed on him feats of ecstatic stimulation that he expected to cause permanent damage. Without there being a coherent word exchanged she made it last until the sun's rays slanted beneath the boughs of the pines and illuminated her skin in the tawny light. At the end they both lay on their backs and dozed in the caressing breeze.

A row occurred when Bayley made ready to return to his plantation. Deeshu desperately wanted to go with him. He was seriously conflicted, but the rational him thought it best to leave her with her parents who were equally adamant that she was too young to run away with a white-devil. They finally tied her to her bed so Bayley could make his exit, but he had George assure her that he would come back to her. She was inconsolable.

Throughout the summer George tended the sorghum and tried to keep ahead of the demand for his corn liquor. Early on he realized that if he did not increase his yield he would never be able to age a batch, thus making it gratifying and possibly marketable elsewhere, as opposed to simply intoxicating. The Cheroenhaka were accommodating but they were not fools. They cheerfully provided him with sustenance in barter for his product. Though the system was informal, the value of each others' commodities was clearly understood. In addition, the tribe's supply of corn from the previous harvest was almost gone and the new corn would not be ready for over a month.

The kernel of a plan was germinating in his mind but it was fraught with obstacles. One evening while he and Auteur Awwa sat smoking on the mat in front of their house, the Indian announced the desire to see his family. George put that piece of information in a part of his brain that he hoped would not be erased by the rustic tobacco. In the morning he rummaged through the possessions that he had carried from Albermarle Sound. Among them was the indenture whereby he had sold his head right land to Bayley. It was a concise document with half a page left blank on the back. On it he made a list items that he had been mentally inventorying for the purpose of expanding his industry.

"When are you leaving for Winyah?" he asked Auteur Awwa.

"Not sure. Not decided yet to go."

"You ought to see your dad. What kind of son are you? And why not go by way of the plantations so you can take this letter to Mr. Bayley?"

"Go to Bayley's add four days to trip."

"Yes, but if you take this message to Bayley, by the time you come back we will be able to make four times as much rum."

"Already have more rum than is good."

"There's no such thing. Besides, it will be better rum and we can trade it for—well, we can sell it."

"Sell it for money? What good is money here?"

"Believe me, you'll find some use for it."

Eventually George shamed the young Indian into going to see his father, and to make the detour to Bayley's plantation. He gave him a purse with most of his hard currency, and the deed containing the list of required materials. Auteur Awwa was fairly hazy about the concept of writing and it concerned George that he would not be able to convey the message about reading what came after the end of the deed. When he felt he had made it as clear as he could, he resigned his plan to fate, and went about his daily affairs.

Chounteroute, the *teerheer*, had the largest single family house in the village, only the longhouse was bigger. He was sitting in the shade on a mat with his number two and three wives. Eteshe Ena refused any communion with the co-wives. Their section of the house was separated from hers by hanging skins. Chounteroute preferred the company of the two younger women, whose names were Sunhe and Youhanhu, because they were less domineering and more accommodating. George approached the chief's house and greeted him and his wives formally. He carried a small gourd filled with whiskey which he offered to Chounteroute. "This is the last whiskey that can be made until there is more corn," he told the Indian.

"This is very sad, George." He turned to Sunhe and asked, "Is there not more corn in the larder?" He swallowed a mouthful of the awfully raw liquor and passed the gourd to the women.

She replied, "There has been no corn since the moon was new two times."

"George, what of the new plants your friend, Bayley, brought?"

"If we harvest the sorghum now before it's fully mature, it will yield very little molasses. I see ripe corn in all the gardens, when is it going to be picked?"

"It is forbidden to use the new corn until after the Green Corn Dance. Personally I would make an exception, but Eteshe Ena would heap much abuse on both of us."

"So, let's dance."

"It cannot happen before the New Year. There is much talking to do and much preparation. In two days I go to meet with the other Cheroenhaka and the

Nansemond to begin the work on the pottery. This is always the first thing to be done. You must come with me. It will help you resist temptation to steal corn."

"I thought we were fighting with the Nansemond."

"The New Year is a time of forgiveness. Nansemond aren't so bad once you get used to them. I especially like the way the women arch their backs."

The party that left the village two days hence was in high spirits. Chounteroute took Sunhe and Youhanhu, his oldest son and his wife, and Asunta, the shaman with his entourage. They walked all day through the shaded forests avoiding the full sun as much as possible. The late summer air was dense making it a chore to breath. The women sang most of the time which was as much to keep the bears away as it was entertainment. When they came to a fair river, George was forced to worry about keeping his gun and his powder dry, while the Indians made a game of it. Chounteroute was towed by his rowdy young wives to the center of the current where they ducked him and swam away. His son and his wife relaxed amorously on the verge of a sandbar but the older, unattached women jeered and splashed them with water. The shaman's wife found some mussels that she was daintily feeding him. George attained the opposite bank where he put his burden down and was considering removing his clothes and getting back into the refreshing water when the others, as one, left the river and resumed the march.

The sun was low when they reached the ceremonial center but the air was still oppressive. George was surprised to find a large rectangular earthwork with four shelters built at the cardinal points. He began to walk into the central part of the place when Chounteroute took his arm. "No one can step on the ceremonial area before the ground is solemnized."

"Sorry. Just when does this dance begin?"

"Not until the moon is next full, but there is much to do before then. You will be very busy and time will fly by."

"What do I have to do?"

"Listen."

The Nansemond party was already there and the Cheroenhaka from Tamahiton Town arrived shortly after dark. The men sat around a fire smoking and sharing the dried venison they brought, but the night was deathly still and hot, and no one sat very near the fire so the mosquitoes had free access to them. As always when the pipe was passed, people grew inward and conversation devolved to monosyllables. When the grunting subsided George lay back on his mat and before he closed his grainy eyelids, he looked at the crescent moon and estimated the days until it would be full.

In the morning business was perfunctory. The three leaders agreed to send delegations to make pots. Each group began the slow walk back to their respective village where they dispatched the potters to the ceremonial center with orders to do what potters do. On the fourth day after returning to Chounteroute, the village, Chounteroute, the *teerheer*, advised George that it was time to attend another meeting of the chief men. The following day they marched back to the ceremonial center, this time they inspected the progress of the pottery before passing the pipe and going to sleep. In the night they were brought to sudden alertness by lightening and big peals of thunder, and everyone quickly retired to the shelters. In the morning the air was fresh and gentle. The requisite business was conducted with the same formality and predestination. This time it was agreed to send men to cover the dance platform with fresh soil.

"I thought nobody could set foot out there," George inquired of Chounteroute.

"Don't worry. They will first be purified."

"Naturally."

Again they marched in oppressive heat back to their respective villages, again the bears were vanquished by the women's chanting, and again a work crew was dispatched who had been standing by awaiting orders.

"Chounteroute, there is a lot more walking involved in the Corn Dance than there is dancing."

"These are things that we know we must do."

"Do we know why?"

"No, but we know we must do them."

The heat sweltered unabated, the moon waxed, and George took to going about naked. Bayley arrived one particularly fetid afternoon and could not stop laughing at the spectacle. George told him, "I began to feel right silly being the only person in town with clothes on."

Bayley grinned hugely. "Well, I confess there is something paradisiacal in watching the girls go about their business in the altogether. Normally when one has the good fortune to coax a woman from her clothes it's in a darkened room, and the first chance she gets she covers herself again. This is truly liberating, though one could do without the old men and the crones."

"A man learns to direct his ogle. Do I detect that my humble order has been scrupulously filled?"

"Indeed, and something extra in case your stores are low," he said patting a cask.

"Bless you, sir. The stores are exhausted."

"Barbarous! Well, give us a hand then."

George had caused Bayley to bring to him nearly a whole smithy, although he had spared him the burden of an anvil. The two set themselves to the task of cannibalizing the condensing tube from the old still. They turned a huge iron cauldron into a retort by soldering a cone of hammered copper sheet to its rim. The village watched transfixed as the work progressed, but when they were done, they had nothing to ferment. While the two were greedily inspecting the sorghum George complained, "Bah! There's nothing for it but to get this damned corn dance behind us."

The gibbous moon still required several days to

complete itself. Bayley sported with young Deeshu in any confines that offered the semblance of privacy, and George accepted the willing attentions of the village girls but he remained dissatisfied by the want of perfection in form of foliage.

Chounteroute at last announced that it was time to go to the Green Corn Dance. The two white men overslept. When they stepped outside they found the place empty. They departed in Bayley's wagon but it was late before they caught the stragglers from the village approaching the ceremonial center. The combined populations of the two Cheroenhaka towns and the Nansemond aggregated to more than two-thousand persons. The ceremonial platform was neatly covered with freshly packed gray dirt, though not a soul dared cross it; however, George cynically noted that somebody had crossed it to erect four log piles that defined a smaller square within the larger. Each of the four shelters had a row of newly fired pots aligned in front of them, and the shamans immediately set about to fill them with an evil smelling black brew which they tended fastidiously as it came to a boil. The day waned hot and stifling, but the Indians, counter intuitively, were all wearing clothes. Everyone save the chiefs and shamans, mingled about the periphery of the ceremonial quadrangle. George was astounded to find a few Nansemond who spoke passable English, notably a chief's family, and especially his daughter who introduced herself as Mary.

"I've been baptized," she boasted.

The next day everyone fasted. Deeshu was removed from Bayley by her father. Chounteroute occupied George with explaining what was expected of him, and they passed the time affixing feathers to man-high canes. When that was complete the remaining day was spent sitting cross-legged in silent meditation which put George in mind of interminable Sunday afternoons when he was made to sit in the parlor from the end of church to supper without swinging his feet. Bayley, whose lack of status exempted him from the ordeal, enjoyed a perfect idyll alone in the woods.

When at last it was dark, the moon rose orange above the trees and bats flitted over the ceremonial floor. The women segregated themselves from the men who sat in silent ranks behind the chiefs. The shamans ceased to stir the contents of the pots and extinguished the fires. In turns they commenced to start a new fire with a small bow and spindle. When it kindled firebrands were carried to each of the shelters and very soon new fires burned where old had been. Brands of the new fire were solemnly carried to the piles of wood in the middle of the earthen square. The *werrowance* of the Nansemond spoke to his people followed by Chounteroute telling the Cheroenhaka to maintain themselves pure and to keep the purity of their ancestral customs. Following that all the chief men rose and were handed a gourd of the black viscous contents of the shamans' pots. Chounteroute whispered in George's ear, "Do not swallow it. Hold it in your mouth while you silently say the prayer to the Corn God, then spit it out."

It was the most hideous tasting slime that ever crossed his lips. He mentally chanted the prayer he had learned earlier in half the requisite time, and he was only too happy to spit the concoction at his feet. Had there been anything in his stomach, it would have followed quickly. The awful taste lingered and the lining of his mouth tingled.

Chounteroute was giving instructions to the seated multitudes while others were distributing gourd rattles and receiving the potion. In unison they rose and began a chant that George had no hope of joining. On a signal that he missed from Chounteroute the men began to form a line circling the nearest fire on the dance platform. George followed as best he could but the step was just too alien for his European rhythm. The moon neared zenith. The dance continued endlessly looping around the fire, sometimes faster other times slower. He thought he would drop when on another unseen signal, a whoop rose from the dancers and the entire population ran to the river where they splashed and jostled one another and kept the whooping going the whole time. He expected that the water would revive him, but while others organized less formal and spontaneous dances, he reclined on a mat and took scope of what was happening behind his eyelids. His head seemed to be floating free from his body. Brightly colored shapes floated serenely across his field of vision, three moons separated and coalesced, and the painted faces that darted near, bizarrely illuminated by the firelight, grew huge in his giddy gaze and mocked his befuddlement. The sense of detachment, the improbable visions, the monotonous beat and the feeling that his empty stomach might escape through his mouth persisted until the first trace of dawn at which time he rose to a sitting position and felt profoundly pleased with himself for no discernable reason.

Breakfast was unnecessary due to the stimulant effect of the hallucinogen. Clusters of people were everywhere scattered, some still dancing but most talking and laughing. English speaking Mary walking from the river saw George alone with his thoughts. Sitting cross legged on his mat he noted her hair was wet but her dress was dry and he thought about the opportunity that he had missed. It was a white cloth the texture of good linen and had bright beads sewn in rows across the bodice.

"Did you enjoy the Green Corn Dance?" she asked.

"I'm still enjoying it, but I found the steps a bit challenging," he replied, and blatantly inspected her. She was finely proportioned and slightly fairer than most Indians. "Tell me how you came to speak English."

"My grandfather was an Englishman. He took my grandmother to Jamestown to marry her in the English church, and there she was baptized and given the name Mary. When he was alive he made everyone in his family learn English. Now my brothers don't speak it much and they begin to forget. I am glad to be able to talk to you in English, if you don't mind."

George felt the foundation of connection growing. "Of course I don't mind. Then when did your grandfather die?"

"I was ten years old. The white settlers were moving closer to our village and they killed all the game. Our hunters started killing cattle so we would have enough to eat. A group of settlers raided our village and burned the houses and drove us farther away from their settlement, but when we moved they kept moving closer until all the warriors of the village struck back. My grandfather was killed by his own people while he was trying to kill them."

That wasn't where George had wanted the conversation to go. "Do you hate all Englishmen?" he asked.

"I don't know any Englishmen, that is, until I met you, but people are people. Indians kill Englishmen and Indians kill Indians, just as Englishmen kill Indians as well as each other."

"I'm not sure where that puts me in your thinking."

"The Green Corn Dance is a time to forgive. I forgive you for being English."

"Well, thank you, Mary, and I forgive you for being part English."

That puzzled her. "What's wrong with being part English?"

"Well, nothing. I was thinking it might be beneficial. Why don't we go for a walk and get better acquainted?"

"Better acquainted? What makes you think that I don't already have a husband?"

"Husband? Let's not get ahead of ourselves here—you don't do you?"

"No, I don't, and I think I would very much like to get better acquainted with you," she met his eyes and offered a smile that made the skin of his scrotum tingle, but it might have been due to the elixir.

The woods around the ceremonial center were crowded with people, some wandering ecstatically, some chanting, others coupling. The lingering effect of the black potion still expanded their awareness of the vivid hues of morning and the sensual feel of the air. What inhibitions she may have had were blunted by the fading effects of the hallucinogen, and George never had any. A mound above the river bank was covered with vibrantly green grass and shielded by a wall of sumac beginning to turn to red. George stopped and touched her bare arm. He got the response he had hoped—a sharp intake of breath—but she said teasingly, "Did you forget that I've been baptized?"

"That means you'll be forgiven," he said which made her smile.

Awkwardly he tried to find the way to remove her dress. When he failed she stepped back and pulled it over her head. When the hem rose above her waist but still had her head and shoulders covered George experienced epiphany. She was a good sized girl with broad shoulders and splendidly large breasts having nipples somewhat paler than the full blooded Indians. Her hips were full and round, descending to strong thighs. A faint trail of hair originated between her breasts and grew in a line that broadened and darkened, was bisected by her naval and continued until it erupted into a dense, perfectly proportioned delta of shining black curls. She laid her dress on the grass wrong side out, executing a graceful bow in the process that revealed a beckoning tuft of hair below the exuberant hemispheres of her buttocks. George stared fixedly and felt preternatural depth to his attraction.

"You're making me self conscious," she said.

"Sorry. I've never seen anything quite like you in my life," he said staring.

"You're poking fun at my *niminisisan*."

"No! No, it's the most beautiful thing I've ever seen

although poking fun—well, precisely."

"And you've known so many?"

"Well, not that many. And none that ever compared to you."

"Now you're being silly."

"I'm deadly serious." He stroked the delicate trail from her breasts downward with the back of his knuckles. She drew a sharp breath and began undressing him. He hastily pulled off his breeches and she reclined on his arm.

She pulled the hair on his chest. "You're hairy too. Are all English people hairy?"

"Generally a bit hairier than an Indian."

"But I'm only part English, the rest of me is wild Indian."

"Aye, and that's the part I'm interested in knowing."

* * *

When they approached the ceremonial center a young Nansemond came toward them. He walked rigidly to Mary and spoke angrily to her in their language. She responded sharply in the same dialect, then in English she added, "And speak English! You're being rude to my friend who is Cheroenhaka."

"He's no Cheroenhaka. He's a white Nottoway."

Mary winced at that. "George is English, but he lives at Chounteroute now. George, this is my brother Richard, although he wants to be called Mahkwa." Mahkwa stood as straight as he could and looked George malevolently in the eye. "You will not disgrace my sister, Nottoway."

George tensed to fight and met the Indian's gaze. He said to Mary without looking at her, "What's this Nottoway business?"

"It is what the enemies of the Cheroenhaka call them. It means snake."

"Richard, your sister's a big girl. You need to let her make her own mind," he was sure the Indian would swing on him and never blinked so he didn't see the older man approach who barked at Mahkwa in Nansemond and cuffed him hard on the back of the head. Mahkwa was enraged and argued vehemently.

Mary took part in the very heated family discussion then said to George, "I am going to eat dinner with my family," and she left with father and brother.

George found Bayley's wagon and found Bayley giving teaspoonsful of whiskey to Deeshu. "The girl's a demon without it. I'm half afraid what she might do if she ever got really drunk," he explained. "I noticed that you're one of the tribe now, and sit with the chief—not really a dancer though."

"Do you think you can spare a little of that for me? I've just met my future wife's family, and you know how that goes."

"Sure. Take a long draught. You obviously need to clear your head."

George filled his mouth and let it burn for some seconds before swallowing. It felt like coming home from long stormy travels. "I tell you, this girl is exactly right," he said when he could breathe again.

"Georgie, it's that Indian potion. It made me think crazed ideas as well."

The festival lasted two days more with the activities becoming decreasingly formal and ever more secular. Bayley and Deeshu were inseparable and the casual way that her parents observed her behavior toward the older white man was an item of curious admiration for George. For his part, he and Mary spent time together each day. She made sure that they did not approach the place where her family camped. He asked to visit her in her village after the end of the dance.

"If you come alone, my people will kill you. They are bitter and sworn to take the scalps of all white men. If you come with others, there will be war betwixt our towns. Give me time and I will come to you," she told him.

That did not set well. "Why don't you come with me now?"

"I don't want to leave my family in anger. With time I will convince my father that my decision is good."

George figured he would not live long enough to see that happen, but in the interest of short term gain he said, "Fine. I hope you hurry. Now, let's visit the woods."

The march back to Chounteroute was subdued for all and George had a sense of loss that not even whiskey and the antics of Deeshu and Bayley could lift. Straight away they began to solicit contributions of corn from every family that grew it in their garden plot. Eteshe Ena objected strongly but her husband, having been dry for several weeks, was firm and the corn was collected. At the same time the sorghum was harvested and the vat of the old still was used to convert it to molasses. The first batch of corn liquor was small and aimed at appeasing the customers until they could make a sizeable amount of rum which George hoped would last long enough to distill some corn that could be aged.

Bayley announced his imminent departure when the rum began to brew. His crop would be ready and he naturally wanted to supervise its harvest. Deeshu again insisted on following him. "If we don't tie you to your bed, will you behave yourself?" he tried to reason with her.

Their conversations were then roughly half and half English and Cheroenhaka. She said in English this time, "Tie me or I go," so they tied her to her bed and Bayley made good his departure.

Auteur Awwa returned in the following month and set about helping with the production of trade goods. George and the young Winyah collected barrels, casks, and crockery to store and age their products. They processed and guarded their raw materials with growing husbandry, and the number of their customers grew to include members of neighboring tribes, including the Nansemond. George inquired of that delegation as to the mind of Mary.

"She makes much trouble for her father," was the answer. He could think of no way to get around the problem of being killed, and so he decided to continue to wait for her to come to him. A young girl named Darsunke kept him from pining overly. Some men of the village even brought their daughters to him in lieu of tangible trade goods, but he declined out of some convoluted sense of morality, however he was unable to prevent Auteur Awwa from accepting their submission as payment for his share of the product.

"When you're hungry you'll wish you had traded for something more filling," George warned him.

"I'm hungry now," was his answer.

The two distillers were crushing sorghum stalks when Deeshu arrived. "George," she whined, "take me to Joseph's house. I'll play with your man stick all the way there."

"Deeshu, that's a lovely offer, but what shall I say to Joseph about that?"

"I'll stop when we get there. You don't tell him."

He laughed, "Girl, you need to be tied to the bed all the time."

Auteur Awwa told her, "I know where Joseph lives."

"Maybe so, but you don't have *eniha ocherura.*"

"What do you call this?"

She looked at the proffered appendage and laughed, "Boy stick."

He swung to slap her but she was too quick. George said to her, "Be patient, child, Joseph will come back for you, and when you're older you can go home with him."

"Does he keep a white woman in his house?"

George thought about how best to answer that. "Not like you mean," was the best he could do.

"I don't care. I will be his number two wife. I have to go to him very soon."

"I understand the urge, but you really must find some diversion."

"I have to take his baby to him."

"Good Lord."

George went to Deeshu's father and discussed the situation. He was ambivalent about her pregnancy, but was strongly opposed to her leaving Chounteroute. George had been thinking about going to the plantations to trade the furs he had accumulated so he agreed to take the news to Bayley. He left the following morning with Auteur Awwa accompanying but only after ascertaining that Deeshu was safely tied to her bed. The days were still hot but the air had the feel of changing seasons. When they arrived Bayley was philosophical.

"Well, I suppose it was inevitable," he said. "I can't leave here until the crop is dried and sold. When do you think she is due?"

"She's not showing yet. You have time," George assured him.

There were no problems of a legal nature that George encountered when he entered the town and conducted his business, so he thought it would be right to visit the family. John's gut reaction was pique but Ann hugged him and that had a softening effect on his brother. Ann even went so far as to hug Auteur Awwa who was wearing his frontal apron and a deerskin cape. He grinned but resisted the temptation to do something salacious.

The travelers had found everyone engrossed with finishing touches to the house of Francis. "It's good to see you're still in the realm of the living," William told him while he shook hands and slapped him on the back. Then he raised his guard and pretended he would box with Auteur Awwa. "What's the idea bringing this wild Indian into town?"

"Hah," he laughed, "your brother is wild Indian now too. He has become a chief man of the Cheroenhaka."

That silenced the crowd.

"What's this all about?" John asked sounding concerned for his brother's mortal soul.

"I seem to have found my calling."

"You won't be showing up here naked, will you?" Ann asked in complete earnest.

"Promise I won't, but if you call on me in the heat of the summer you'd best announce your arrival."

"God, Almighty! I never dreamed coming to America would yield so many surprises."

John's face grew serious. "Don't be too forthcoming with that information outside of our own company. I hear tell the House of Burgess has ruled it a flogging offense to approach an Indian town."

George tried to look pained and said, "What's a man to do? The savages love me."

The two houses had come together sufficiently to give shelter to both couples. William was sleeping in the common room of Francis' nearly finished house and was struggling with the art of the yeomanry. George and Auteur Awwa passed several pleasant days with them before beginning the hike to Chounteroute but they first passed through Jamestown where he invested in a pair of breeches, a linen shirt and felt hat. His native companion ridiculed him. "Is this for when Miss Ann come to call?"

"Never know. I might need some new clothes to get married in."

The Indian just shook his head.

Part of his payment for the furs was in tobacco which he spent first, but had a fair amount left, so he left it with Bayley as they passed saying, "If I take it back it'll just get chewed and I'll have nothing to show for my good works. If you can get hard money for it I'd very much appreciate it, but if you can't, just hold it till I come back. It spends as good as sterling in town." Bayley, who was a tobacco planter, tried not to scowl at the lecture.

Walking to Chounteroute was idyllic if uneventful. The season was as fine as George had ever seen with warm nights and fair days. After they left the cultivated fields behind there was an area cluttered with undergrowth before they reached the Indian controlled lands that were cleared by burning. The air was sweet and frequent streams flowed clear and cool. Game was theirs when they needed it, and they did not meet another soul of any color.

On the second day after arriving home George was making a fire under the still when Auteur Awwa came to deliver the news that some Nansemond had arrived in a state of distress. They were waiting in the longhouse to meet with the Cheroenhaka *werrowance*. George, hoping to gain news of Mary, arrived at the longhouse before Chounteroute. Six warriors sat grumpily on the ground. They glowered at the white man and they refused to respond to his questions. When the reason for the visit was explained it was understood that settlers had moved to within arrow shot of the Nansemond's town, and hunters had been fired upon by the farmers. The Nansemond warriors intended to kill the settlers and had come to enlist aid from the Cheroenhaka. Young men, eager to make their first kill, clamored to join the fight, but Chounteroute had proven himself years hence and was no longer a warrior at heart.

"If you kill them, they will send soldiers to take revenge, and you will have to leave your town. Leave it without killing the Englishmen. You can build a new town here with us."

Much arguing ensued but the delegation eventually agreed to pose the offer to their council. George was enthusiastic about the idea and offered to accompany them to Nansemond; however, he was dissuaded by Chounteroute who assured him that the warriors would turn on him as soon as they were out of sight, being still eager to draw some white blood.

"So, what's to prevent them from turning on me when they move in with us?"

"You must learn to sleep with one eye open," the old Indian told him then added, "I do not think that they will be anymore of a threat to you than my wife."

The Nansemond began arriving in a few days. Mary and her family were among the first arrivals. She immediately stole to George's house, and after the heat of their reunion was sated, he began the business of ingratiating himself with her father and, begrudgingly, her brother. All of the Cheroenhaka were engaged in helping to build houses for their new neighbors. George attached himself to the crew that was building Mary's father's house. He called himself Sam Turner and he quickly became fond of his daughter's suitor. When George, after what he considered a suitable period of waiting, approached the subject of marriage, Sam said to him, "I think that you had better do it soon, considering the way you are carrying on."

George actually blushed. "I thought we had been discreet."

"You may be but she isn't."

That evening, after the day's work was over, George dined at the Turners' house. There was no meat in the meal because everyone was too busy building to hunt. Conversation was in English because of the novelty of George's presence, except Richard refused to use English prompting George to ask him why he could not relent his grudge.

He condescended to depart from Nansemond for two words, "You're white."

Sam slapped his son with the back of his hand. "You might as well get over that," he said with an unexpected calmness, "because this white man is going to be your sister's husband."

George was the only one present who looked surprised. He said, "Damn, Sam, I haven't had a chance to ask her."

"That's only a formality. When the shaman gets here we will asked that he solemnize it, and later you can go to Jamestown and be married in an English church."

That never happened. The shaman arrived and somehow in the midst of the upheaval rattling the town time was found to conduct the Nansemond ceremony of union. To George it looked enough like a wedding, but he could not understand a word the shaman recited over them. When it seemed like an appropriate time he said, "I do," and that night Mary simply moved into his house. Auteur Awwa berated him for his foolishness claiming that Mary would stifle their industry. He also showed no intention of leaving the house until George threatened him with violence.

"There is more than enough room for me here," he protested. "I will sit outside when you mount her."

"You can sit in the longhouse."

"The longhouse is full with Nansemond. A Winyah cannot sleep in the same room with Nansemond."

"Then you had best get your arse back to Winyah, because the mistress of this house is a Nansemond."

The glowering young Indian collected his possessions and took them to the longhouse. Before he left Mary said to him, "Come for George in the morning with your bow. We need some meat." That softened him—somewhat.

Before the chaos of the Nansemond relocation was fully subsided, Bayley arrived with his slave, his servant, and a sizeable trunk. Deeshu ran to greet him wearing a smile. Her belly and little breasts were now clearly bulging, and he shook his head saying, "What are we going to do with you?"

"You better do it now before I get too big," she told him.

He and his boy commenced to build a house and later to clear a field as it was his intention to put a crop of tobacco into the ground when planting season arrived. The union of Bayley and Deeshu was solemnized according to the custom of the Cheroenhaka which meant appeasing Eteshe Ena. It was his intention to sell the plantation and transfer his residence to Chounteroute with all his staff, but the servant girl was terrified of the Indians and fled as soon as she got a chance.

Deeshu did not clearly understand the situation. She said, "Now I'm your number one wife."

* * *

William was not adapting to the role of gentleman farmer. He hated working the soil and the idea of planting something that was not going to be of any use for several months struck him as highly unrewarding labor. Then there was the attrition rate of things planted. He was driven mad by the mental repetition of the doggerel he had unfortunately learned from the farmer who sold seed corn:

One for the blackbird
One for the crow
One for the cutworm
And one to let grow

"I've no idea what a bloody cutworm is, and I hope to God I never see one," he ranted when he and his cousins were inspecting the new corn stalks. "There is a mason in the county who wants an apprentice. I think I'll put myself out."

Francis was stunned. "You left England to keep your father from putting you out," he reminded.

"Well, at least I was able to keep him from doing it."

"Are you sure about this?" John asked.

"I'm as sure as I can be. Besides, I really can't face the thought of hoeing another row in the dirt or pulling another damned weed."

"How long is the indenture?"

"Five years."

John Parke was an old man. His drooping jowls and rheumy eyes belied the strength that still resided in his back and arms. He had arrived in the colony some twenty years thence and built a brick kiln before he built a house. The first year in Virginia took his wife and he had lived

107

alone since. The motive that moved him to break his solitude by making the indenture with William was a sense of mortality and the altruistic urge to pass his knowledge onto posterity. Parke was a kindly man and he looked forward to having some companionship. The first task he set to William was to bring a load of clay from the riverbank, and then, logically, to pack it into brick molds. He dug the clay with the sense of having made a very bad mistake, and later remarked to his cousins, "I thought a mason bought his bloody bricks."

In the evenings Parke rambled garrulously about his glory as a Free Mason in England, and charged William with the responsibility of founding a guildhall in America when he became a master mason and had made his fortune. He treated William less like a servant than a son and William had no heart to tell him that so far he hated being a mason as much as being a farmer. During the days he dutifully, if miserably, applied himself to learning to fire bricks and make mortar. He felled the trees to fire the kilns, and continued to fetch clay from the river until the ground froze, then the work next to the kilns became less odious, and each night he smiled and nodded when exhorted to build that guildhall. When Parke had a job he took William to dig foundations and mix mortar. He taught and lectured but guarded his tools and always kept a little something secret. William was fond of the old man and his regret over putting himself out softened with the passing months.

Although Parke was not a pious man he would do no work on the Sabbath. One Sunday William ventured to ask, "Would you consider it a job of work to call on someone who sorely needs a chimney?"

Parke grinned and winked, although his eyelids never quite met. "I suppose we could tell the deacon we're on a social call."

William took him to John's plantation where they were met with much joy. Ann served tea and John went for

Francis. When he arrived he shook hands with the old mason and asked, "Is my cousin's complaining or his incompetence a greater burden to you?"

"Oh, no, your kinsman is becoming a fine mason, and within not so many years will found the first guildhall in these colonies."

William grimaced, but Ann said, "Will, we had no idea you were handy."

Frank hastened to add, "We haven't actually had the pleasure of inspecting his work."

"Indeed," William said, "and that is precisely the reason for our visit, not that I feel it necessary to have a reason to visit my kinfolk, but we are here with a motive. Mr. Parke is willing to offer a very favorable consideration for the construction of a chimney at the end of your house."

The faces of the women brightened, but John spoke before either of them, "Will, I'm sure Mr. Parke is a generous man, but I doubt he is willing to give his service for naught. There's been not a farthing come from the rents, and our crops don't even quite fill our bellies."

"It's just a matter of the bricks," Parke told him. "I'm willing to freely give you your cousin's time and loan him my tools if there's no work for me, but you'll have to find a means to pay for the bricks."

"You're very kind, Mr. Parke. We will accept your generous offer as soon as our fortunes improve," John assured.

When the tea was finished and the conversation began to slow, young John began to fuss. His mother slipped her dress from her shoulders and let him suck. Parke and William took their leave. Service was over when they crossed the churchyard. A deacon separated himself from the congregation and strode quickly through the graves toward the two. "I did not note the two of you at the service just over." He put William in mind of a mantis.

"You know I'm not part of your congregation, Bridger," Parke told him.

"I haven't heard that you're part of any congregation, Mr. Parke. It's one thing to not attend services, it's a bit of another to work on the Sabbath."

"And what could make you think we've been working?"

"We went to call on my family," Will interjected.

"Indeed! Doesn't it seem curious that John Parke should be so interested in his servant's family?"

Parke's ire was rising. "Deacon Bridger, has your hide become so thick as to find no solace in a cup of tea from hand of a lady? Now, you will kindly return to those folk who may actually welcome your conversation and we shall return home without further molestation from you." He began walking and Will fell in step with him.

"I'd watch my mouth, Mr. Parke. You would not be the first in this parish to wear stripes for breaking the Sabbath," Bridger called after them.

"What bothers me most with pious fools is when they find their precious hereafter is a long dreamless sleep whilst moldering away in the ground they can't hear you say 'I told you so'."

William was momentarily taken aback by the baldness of the blasphemy then he laughed. "That's a curious observation."

* * *

He took well to mortar and bricks, but he lacked patience for stone cutting. Parke was indulgent. "Don't fret, Will, when you're made a master you will get some Negroes for the rude work."

"Why don't you have one?" Will asked.

"I have you."

In the winter of the second year of William's indenture Parke fell ill. He lay abed for three days while Will nursed him as best he could, but the wheezing became dense and there was hemorrhaging during the coughing spells. That night the pneumonia carried him away in his sleep. Will buried him on his land because he thought that he had no love for the churchyard. Still when the grave was filled he made a wooden cross for the head of it. "In spite of what you think," he said aloud to the grave, "I hope you can hear me say 'I told you so'."

He died intestate, left no inventory and had no heir in America. The Quarter Court showed a great amount of zeal in pronouncing that the land escheat to the Colony. Will had surreptitiously removed Parke's tools to Francis' house, but the Colony took all else for auction. An adjacent planter bought the land and set his slaves to making bricks and mortar in the kilns. He had no interest or skill in acquiring the remainder of Will's indenture, and the court, finding no way to profit from it, chose to pretend it no longer existed. He returned to live at Frank's house and resigned himself to yeomanry once again.

"I'm not a Master Mason, nobody will complete my apprenticeship, I'm not likely to find a commission and if I did, I've got no money for materials," he whined while he applied a hoe to a row of squash. Frank feigned not to hear.

* * *

On an afternoon of thundershowers while the heat made steam tendrils rise from the leaf mold, George arrived with his wife and son. Joy was manifold. Ann cooed and gushed and could barely force an intelligible phrase across her lips. John cut through the flood of emotion, "What did you name the boy?"

"George. Mary insisted."

"Of course she did."

"Although I had a struggle to call him George Skipper. Their custom is to take the mother's name. Bloody savages."

"And what was the mother's maiden name?" Ann

inquired.

"Turner."

"There's a savage's name, if I ever heard one."

John turned his attention to Mary and appraised her so thoroughly George thought he was going to inspect her teeth. "How lovely, my dear, and how do you come by such excellent English?"

Indian Ann grumbled, "Nansemond."

George was burdened with a haunch of venison from a buck that he had shot two days previous. The women used it as the center of a feast for the reunion, preparing it on a spit over the stone circle where they cooked their meals, and afterward George produced the ubiquitous jug. "How do my kinfolk fare in the heart of civilization?"

"Heart of civilization?" John sighed. "We get by, but not ahead. Thank you for the first meat we've had for some days."

"No game left?"

"Not much. We have to invest two or three days to find a deer, and there's never enough money for a hog. The chickens just can't breed fast enough to stay ahead of us. Fortunately there are still a few fish in the river."

In a reflective moment George asked his brother, "Why do ye not build Annie a fireplace so she can cook your meals in the house?"

"There's no money for it."

"Must get a bit brutal in the winter."

"Aye, it grieves me. Cousin says he would do it but for want of bricks."

"Go on," George said derisively.

"No, he put himself out to a mason, but the old man died after just two years. Still, he's got the knack for it, don't you, Will?"

"Sure I do. It's a mite more rewarding than pulling weeds."

"Just the same," George observed attempting to dislodge a bit of venison from a bicuspid with the nail of his little finger, "if you devoted yourselves to a cash crop, you might be able to afford a few bricks."

English Ann took to Mary from the start and was deeply enamored of infant George. "Be firm with him," she counseled the new mother. "He mustn't turn out like his father."

At George's suggestion William joined him to hunt for some meat. They had the great luck to shoot a large boar before the sun passed zenith. After gutting and hanging it on a pole between them, they started home. They had to carry it across the land that had been Parke's, and when they passed the kilns, William pointed toward them, "Those dusky fellows, there, are my replacements as brick maker."

"It doesn't look too difficult, Will," he replied. The Negroes eyed them suspiciously while they approached.

"You there," George called, "where would we find your master?"

The slave had deep pockmarks over his face and neck. He made no response until he had finished packing clay into the mold before him, then he pointed his muddy finger toward the house that had been the old mason's.

"Can you say how many bricks it takes to build a decent fireplace, cousin?"

"Sure. Why?"

"Let's see what the gentleman asks for his product."

The planter was an amiable sort, but Will could not see him in any light except the usurper of his aims. George proceeded to negotiate the price of the quantity of bricks that William said he required. "Fine, then," he told the planter, "I'll be back in a fortnight for them. See that you have them ready."

George left Mary and the baby with the families, and he and William left for Chounteroute. It was the farthest William had traveled into the interior. The summer days were oppressively hot and the nights were mild and magically transporting, if fraught with mosquitoes. When he approached the Indians' village he detected a certain fecundity on the breeze. When he saw it he was astounded. "These people's town is more orderly than ours," he gaped.

"It's orderly, but don't get any ideas they're civilized. There are about sixty warriors here who think it a fine time to keep themselves keen by skulking through the woods and ambushing anyone they come across. To make matters worse, half of them are Cheroenhaka and half Nansemond. If they can't find strangers, they ambush each other."

Bayley and Auteur Awwa were pleased to see William again, and the Turners greeted him warmly. Chounteroute had his younger wives prepare a feast. As usual Eteshe Ena boycotted the event. The men passed the moonlit evening drinking and smoking until the dew chilled them and all but Sam Turner retired to their houses. Turner was too drunk to rouse, so they covered him with a bear skin and left him where he lay.

William found the several days with the Indians liberating. His days among the Winyah had been anxious and uncomfortable, but in the hospitality of the Cheroenhaka he found release from care. He sensed the inkling of a future and determined to confront it. Chounteroute sent Youhanhu to William's bed which made a large contribution to his release.

* * *

George prepared his pack with the items he needed, and on a cloudy morning they began the walk toward the plantations. Before noon a thunderstorm drove them to the cover of a dense pine grove, but they were already wet before they found sanctuary on the dry needles. The sky cleared in the afternoon but the late summer sun baked the wet ground until the air was so thick with humidity the sweat stood in beads on their skin and their clothes refused to dry. They chafed to walk in them and decided to relent in their march and let their clothes dry on the gnarled limbs of an ancient oak. The flies pecked at their naked skin before the mosquitoes rose from the standing water. Even though it was much too warm, they built a smoky fire to discourage the plague which otherwise left a black and bloody paste on their limbs when they rubbed them.

"Cousin," William said with as much stoicism as he had in him, "every time I convince myself I'm getting used to life here, I have a day like this and have to reckon otherwise. How is it you adapted to life with the savages so easy?"

"Easy, you say. Well, I suppose it was easy since I wasn't getting on well with our tight arsed brethren in the parish, and the savage wenches did have a strong appeal for the likes of me. In truth I had very little trouble in getting used to their bear grease stench and watching out for the bucks who like to test your mettle by trying to peel off the top of your skull with their stone hatchets. Once they accept you, and you them, they make better neighbors than a pious hypocrite with a lacey ruff at his neck and a mind to denounce you to the constable every time you take a dram on the Sabbath."

William stood and placed himself downwind from the smoke until his eyes burned and he began to choke. Sitting again he said, "I know I couldn't live with the Indians, and I truly hate farming, the masons' trade was a hope, but I don't know how I'll ever finish the apprenticeship."

"Build John's chimney and let 'em see you can do it. Then make your own kiln. They don't look all that complicated." George was also shooing the pests, but not with the same urgency as his cousin.

"How many bricks do you think the parish needs?"

"I don't know. Maybe there's another part of the colony that's suffering a dearth of bricks."

George paid for the bricks, delivered William a motivational speech, collected Mary and the baby, bid the family adieu and departed for Chounteroute.

The success of the fireplace put enough confidence in William to build a kiln. There was grumbling in some circles about his not having finished his apprenticeship, but that did not prevent his bricks from selling. A master mason in Yorktown offered to take him as an apprentice, but insisted on a full five year indenture. "I've already completed half an apprenticeship," he protested, but the man would not relent.

"I'll teach myself as I go," William told him. "What I see of masonry really just takes a bit of common sense."

"You can teach yourself all the common sense you like, but without a right apprenticeship to your credit, you will never be accepted by the guild. You'll never be ought but a brick maker," the mason sneered.

"Then I'll be a brick maker."

CHAPTER FOUR

Richard Turner had killed one of the white settlers who had caused the Nansemond to cohabitate with the Cheroenhaka.

Mary confronted him as soon as she heard. "What did you do this for? Now we will have no peace."

"By this I have become a warrior. Warriors do not seek peace."

"You are going to be a hungry warrior when the white men drive us out and burn our houses and crops. Can you never think about anyone but yourself?" Mary railed at her brother in English, but he insisted on responding in Nansemond which kept George from knowing how to get involved.

"Speak English!" Mary shouted. "If you would speak English sometime you might learn to get along with white men."

"Speaking English doesn't help the white men."

She groaned. "You are the most lame excuse for a brother. You forget that part of you is white."

"I deny it. In our family the white blood all went to you."

Mary stomped from the house in a rage with young George hung upside down on her back. Senior George was left gawping, but snapped his jaw shut without speaking. The probability that anything he could say would have a settling effect on the young savage seemed remote, so he swaggered slowly in the path of his wife. At his door he heard Mary still fuming and decided to continue his swagger. At Chounteroute's house he found the *werrowance* smoking with Sam Turner. "Your son and daughter just had quite a row," he told him.

"I expected as much. Few women understand that a young man must become a warrior or his life will be worthless. It does seem a poor choice of target, though."

"So you can't think of a different rite of passage?"

Sam offered, "There is the *huskanawing* where we select boys to become shamans. It makes men of boys with no one being killed—except some of the boys."

"There," said George, "wouldn't it be better to put all the boys through that than have them starting wars?"

Chounteroute said, "Oh, no, George. Having too many shamans is like not being able to shit for five days." Then he waxed nostalgic, "They say our brethren beyond the sun's setting place consider it a great coup to touch an enemy with a stick. In my day we found it much more satisfying to kill him. Habits are hard to break."

"You do know that the settlers won't let it rest?"

"Yes, and that is why we must always have warriors."

"Bit of a vicious circle, don't you think?"

"It has always been this way," Chounteroute said solemnly as he drew on the pipe and held it.

George took the proffered pipe from him and thinking, "*What the hell*" did the same. When the narcotic effect had carried him to the same place as his companions he asked, "How long has it been since Richard killed the man?"

"Only a few days," Sam replied. "If they plan a serious retaliation, it will take them some time to bring soldiers. In the meantime, they will probably snipe at us from the woods."

"And what is our plan of defense?"

"The Nansemond and the Cheroenhaka combined have sixty warriors—sixty-one now. Their blood is up. I only hope they do not turn on each other."

"You fill a man with confidence."

When George thought that Mary had had enough time to compose herself, he wandered home to find her skinning a hare with a vehemence he assumed was directed toward her brother. It seemed meet to George to clean his musket. "We need to get some more guns in this village," he mused to himself.

Mary heard his remark and reminded him, "They'll hang you if they find you bringing guns here."

"Seems somebody wants to hang me no matter what I do. At least it would be better to put up a good fight. Counting Bayley's pistols we have a total of four firearms, and sixty, nay, sixty-one braves with bows who may or may not kill each other. I don't like the odds."

George attempted to organize a defense, but the warriors were not used to being told what to do. Auteur Awwa cooperated because neither of the rival groups accepted him. Bayley let him carry one of his pistols and gave him a powder horn and some lead, but knew that hitting a man at any considerable distance with an unfamiliar pistol would be nearly impossible.

When the retaliation came it was cowardly and wanton. An unseen group of settlers fired on a family tending their garden. The man was killed outright, and the ball that passed through the woman's chest also struck her baby that was strapped to a cradle board on her back. When the killings were discovered the baby was still alive but died later that night. The dead family happened to be Nansemond which inflamed Mary's brother even more. He rallied the Nansemond warriors to stage a retaliatory raid from which they returned with three scalps.

"Well, there's nothing for it now," George told

Chounteroute. "We will have to build a palisade around the town."

"You mean like the English forts?"

"That's right, and there can be no delay in doing it. You'd best call a council."

Chounteroute convinced the elders of both groups of the value of the idea, but it took a great deal of persuasion to make building a wall appear more desirable than fighting to the young warriors. George assumed the role of overseer and within a month the palisade stood ten feet high and one hundred feet square. It was canted slightly outward and contained loopholes every few feet. The gate hung on rope hinges and took six men to operate. During the time of construction there were no further attacks by the settlers. George was quite enamored of himself over the scale of the accomplishment, and his prestige in the village soared. Not every house was contained within the walls, and what little land under cultivation inside soon got converted to new residential space. A cooperative system was begun where sentries concealed themselves in the trees around the gardens so people could tend their crops with some security.

George and Bayley were finishing a small bottle of the brandy that Bayley had kept hidden. Mary and Deeshu were nursing the babies. They had the habit of leaving the men alone after a meal partly because the custom of sitting at a table still felt a bit foreign. The Indians generally ate as couples sat on the ground with the food between them. When George and Bayley insisted that they join in social groups around a table it proved a culture shock, especially to Deeshu but less so to Mary who knew of the custom from her grandfather.

"We've got to get these bucks some guns," George told Bayley.

"Risky business," he murmured.

"Indeed it is, but those walls will prove a colossal waste of effort against a group of militia without some firepower on the inside."

"Damned shame we have to defend ourselves from our own kind."

"I'm beginning to think they aren't our kind anymore."

"I daren't think we could waltz into the Middle Plantation, buy a wagon load of muskets and saunter away," Bayley said.

"No, that seems a bit too direct. What's better is finding a gentleman who is more interested in a profit than sticking strictly to wishes of the Burgesses. Then we send some harmless seeming Indian to him from time to time who wants to trade some furs for a hunting rifle."

"It'll take a while."

"Aye, and we had best start it sooner than later."

* * *

Cockarouse Will was related to Chounteroute and had the same ingratiating way about him. He understood the plan and was enthused by the idea of having a gun. George supplied him with a couple good furs from his cache of rum proceeds and directed him toward Isle of Wight County since it was removed from the Middle Plantation's hierarchy. It only took him a week to return with an old blunderbuss, some powder and a little bit of lead.

"Well, it's a start," George opined when he tested the gun.

Will was sent again in a different direction, and after a suitable period of time another seemingly innocuously older Indian was sent to the plantation where *Cockarouse* Will had been successful. Thus began the program to assemble an arsenal for Chounteroute.

* * *

John decided it meet to cultivate a cash crop and the only cash crop in Virginia was tobacco. Tobacco was so prolifically produced that there was not enough cash to pay for it and it became a currency in itself. In fact the only thing more plentiful in Virginia than tobacco was land which was a very good thing as the soil was depleted so quickly by tobacco that in the fourth consecutive year the crop would fail.

It was late summer and a thunder shower ended. John stood with Ann at the edge of the field where their failed crop languished yellow and stunted. "I ought to have seen this coming," he told her. "I guess my land's as barren as my wife."

Ann winced, "Do you plan to get a new wife as well as a new field?"

"Ah, I didn't mean that. I'm just upset and didn't think before I spoke. Besides, if we had another mouth to feed it would only make things worse."

She did not respond but walked silently by the muddy field and enjoyed the scent on the damp air. The fact of being childless was a gulf of unexpressed disappointment that hovered between them each time they encountered on the conjugal bed. For John's part he thought the problem might be solved by quantity. Ann rarely rejected his advances and truly enjoyed the closeness of his frantic attempts to procreate.

He caught her and fell into stride. "Ann, I feel a failure as your husband. I wanted to do better by you."

"You're not a failure as a husband and not even a failure as a farmer. Considering I married a young gentleman whose only experience at providing was collecting the rents, I'd say you've done quite a fair job. Now, stop feeling sorry for yourself and think of something else to plant. In the meantime I need to get back to the house. It's time to begin supper."

When supper was served John was still in his funk. The fact that Frank's Ann was expecting another child after two babies stillborn did nothing to ease his sense of inadequacy. Will brooded and Frank did the best he could to lighten the mood. "It's not like we've used all the land," he reasoned to his sulking brother. "We got more useable acreage we can clear, and we can swap your tobacco field with the truck garden."

"The garden is hardly big enough for a decent tobacco field."

"Why worry about tobacco?" Will grumbled. "You won't get a penny a pound for it."

"So what do you think we ought to plant, cousin?"

"His Excellency the Governour says we're all to plant mulberry trees."

"Yes, well, seeing as he is a Royalist, if I happen upon a mulberry, I'll be sure to put it in the ground."

"How about rice, then?"

"They say rice is not so simple."

"Got to flood the field, I hear. Well, most of the land is a bloody swamp. I don't see why that's a problem. I've got to plant or build on my plot," Will continued, "before the Council takes it back."

Frank said, "He's right, you know. It's been quite a few years, and Will's done precious little to improve it."

"I built a kiln," William defended himself, "and I girdled more than an acre of trees so they'd be fit to burn. We could put tobacco over there and rice on your old field."

Ann nudged John's shoulder. "There, you see, you've got a sound plan, and plenty of cooperation."

"The very thought of clearing more land discommodes me greatly."

Ann pulled a crooked smile at the quirky word, and said, "Well then, finish your supper and we'll see what can be done to get you properly commoded again."

Apparently being re-commoded was all that John's potency needed for the very next month Ann missed her period.

All the winter they cleared land, and Will used the wood to fuel his kilns. In February George arrived. He brought Mary and young George who were riding a horse. He gave John a sack of small round seed, and said, "Brother, if you'll cultivate this for me, I'll buy it back at twice the rate for tobacco."

"What is it?"

"Sorghum. When I plant it outside of our stockade your countrymen burn it, and there's not enough room inside."

"*My* countrymen? Aren't they yours anymore?"

"Not when the evil bastards shoot women and babies and burn my sorghum."

"Well, what do I do with it?"

"Plant it like you would corn, in fact it will look like corn. When it's ten or twelve feet tall, cut it, take the seed for the next crop, and stack the stalks for me. Put it in the ground as soon as there's little chance of frost. With luck you can get two crops in a season."

John put his hand into the sack and let the seeds run through his fingers. "And what will I do with it, brother of mine, if one of your neighbors splits your skull with a tomahawk, or one of my countrymen puts a musket ball through you?"

"Now, you see, in every venture must be a little risk."

"Well, I've got to talk to Ann about it. It's her future as much as mine."

"I'd have it no other way, and I know that Annie trusts me totally."

"George Skipper, when they find out you're giving whiskey to those Indians, they'll flay you alive," Ann reminded him.

"It's rum, Annie, and generally I sell it to them. What's more, if they come for me, they'll have fair number of warriors to contend with, but just for that reason, Johnny, I wonder if I could further prevail upon you purchase me a wagon and new musket? Be best not to show too much of my face in the plantations, you know."

Eventually the family agreed to put the sorghum where

the rice was intended, and George stayed long enough to help clear some more space for tobacco. William negotiated the purchase of the wagon and the gun. He traded the beaver pelts George brought for tobaccos and then used that to pay for powder and lead. During his trip to the Middle Plantation he discovered that the governor had decreed the forts would be rebuilt with bricks and that the Council was amenable to buying all that he could produce. Barges began arriving every second day or so to carry another load of William's bricks to the forts.

* * *

George returned late in July with the wagon loaded with furs which he was able to trade directly to a merchant on the river who was bound shortly for London. He then procured another gun and more powder and lead, and while harvesting sorghum, Frank's Ann gave birth to her second son. Frank named him George. "I mean it as a way to thank you for our new chance for prosperity," he told his brother.

George told him, "It's nothing to do with me. It's this golden land of opportunity."

The following month English Ann began a hard labor that put the fear of death in every one's mind. She did survive it though, and so did the son who they named William.

* * *

Auteur Awwa took over the task of driving the wagon back to the plantation until the entire crop was at Chounteroute. George and Bayley had modified a suitable flat rock by the side of the stream to use as a mill stone. Chounteroute cajoled several women to work at crushing the stalks to extract the juice which ran through fissures and was collected in clay jars.

One humid morning George was beaming over the still's increasing rate of production when Mary came to him. She wore the doeskin apron that she preferred during the hot weather which prompted to George to remark, "Woman, it suits me that your English blood hasn't civilized you altogether."

She had her shining black hair tied in a fountain and her brow was puckered, but she smiled mildly when she told him, "I think you will be a father again soon."

He took her by the upper arms and looked at her dark eyes, and all he could think to say was, "Sure."

The child was a girl and was given the name Ann.

George, Bayley and Auteur Awwa kept production at capacity while steadily amassing furs and hides which they traded generally for tobaccos, and that in turn was sold for hard currency when the market was favorable. John and Frank continued to produce sorghum while William sold bricks as fast as he could make them. The monarchy was restored, and all was well in the country. A mite more than a year after the birth of Ann, Mary had another daughter who George insisted be called Mary.

Then settlers killed another Nansemond woman while she tended her garden. George was outraged. He neither said nor did anything to prevent Richard Turner from staging a raid in retaliation, although he confided to Bayley, "This can't continue without ending in a bloody massacre."

"Aye, any fool can see that. It might be that we have to move ourselves out of here."

"We ought to get us a piece of land of our own."

"What? Amongst the plantations?"

"Nah! The king granted some new colonies to the south of us. Could be we'll find some living space down there."

"Could be. How do you suppose a body would find out about that?"

George was leaning on his musket which he kept in

hand since the woman was killed. He said "Well, I suppose a body has to find the new Governour and see how he wants to do business. I heard as they set up their settlement not far from where I went with that fool Greene a while back. Shouldn't take us more than a fortnight to find out and get back."

"Now, I can't leave Deeshu, George. She's not far from delivering Watt a new brother or sister."

George scowled and fixed Bayley with his cold blue eyes when he said, "She's a wild Indian, man. She can drop the little bugger without a break in weeding the corn."

Richard Turner's raiding party returned with five scalps, one was clearly a woman's. Mary was more upset than anyone else. "George," she cried, "they're going to come to burn the town and kill the children."

"You're right, woman, but your brother may have thinned the herd enough to keep 'em at bay for a while. Meanwhile, Joseph and I are going to go looking for a new place for us to live."

"And if you come back to find us burned out?"

"I gave you a gun and showed you how to use it. Make sure your savage of a brother keeps a lookout in the woods."

The party was George and Bayley with his slave, and Auteur Awwa. Gideon and Auteur Awwa had to walk while the Englishmen rode. All carried arms. It was the height of autumn with red sumac and yellow poplar burning through the deep green of the live oaks. They followed big chevrons of geese going the same way, and the bears were fat and glossy. One morning they found a camp that appeared more English than Indian and tracked the occupants. Later that morning they found a surveying party engaged in establishing the boundary between Virginia and the new colony.

"Ho, sir," Bayley hailed the surveyor. "How do we find the seat of government of the new colony?"

"A day's march south, then turn east," he advised, "else you'll find yourselves bedeviled by all manner of bays and inlets. And what might be your business there?"

"Why, we would like to buy a piece of his land."

"Harrumph! His Excellency has got plenty of that, but you might call it more mire than land. Still, the man aims to sell it, so good luck to you."

"Thank ye," said George, "and what does he call his new colony?"

"Carolana."

At the end of the day the party was skirting a vast obnoxious swamp the heart of which was an oval shaped bay. It forced them more west than south and was producing sufficient mosquitoes to assure a miserable night. Auteur Awwa saw movement ahead, and pulled back on George's horse's bridle. Going forward alone he found two brightly painted Indian boys trying to hide in the stickers. With the travelling language he established peaceful relations and brought the groups together. The strangers took them to a place where a peninsula of higher ground intruded into the swamp, and if it did nothing to dissuade the mosquitoes, it at least offered dry ground for sleeping. George and Bayley walked the dry salient in hope of finding something more toothsome for supper than the dried venison they carried as a fallback meal. Bayley shot a turkey which was scarcely enough for six men, but was nevertheless a welcome contribution.

"Joseph," George said walking to camp, "this place has a peculiar defensiveness about it."

Bayley considered that for a time and answered, "Indeed it does. That quagmire would dampen many an attack."

In the travelling language, George asked the young strangers what they called the place.

"Potecasi," was their answer.

* * *

When they found the seat of government for the new colony, such as it was, the soldiers were still cutting trees for the stockade. Lord Carteret's land agent slept on his ship and came ashore to do business at a writing table beneath an oak tree with arms spreading a canopy a hundred feet across. George paid a fee to apply for a patent on four-hundred acres on the south side of Potecasi Swamp, and was told to return at such time as there had been built suitable confines for the Council to consider his plea—such time being presently indeterminate.

Waiting seemed a non-productive endeavor so they began the trek home, pausing for a day to explore the tract of land that George expected would be their new home. When he found the swamp abounding with alligators, he liked it even more.

At Chounteroute Mary was in an uproar. Richard Turner had stolen a hog from the settlers and butchered it. "Don't fret, woman," George soothed her, "we'll be away from here soon enough. Just keep yourself and the babies inside the stockade."

"Why don't we just turn my bother over to the English?"

"Ow, now, that's an idea lacking in sisterly love. Besides, I think there is more than one culprit amongst us."

"That's true, but Richard's the worst."

"Is he sharing the hog?"

"You're as bad as the rest. Oh, and Deeshu had her baby."

"Boy or girl?"

"A girl."

"I must go congratulate Bayley, but first you need to give me a proper welcome home."

She grinned. "You can be certain Deeshu is giving Joseph his welcome."

After all the conjugal welcoming was completed,

George found Bayley and inquired as to the girl's name.

"It's only right," he answered, "that she be a Mary."

* * *

George began planning his relocation. The first thing he did was liquidate his furs and tobaccos. The market was down, but he accepted the poor price to raise hard currency and lighten his load. He advised his brothers of the pending move, and his expectation of growing his own sorghum in the future. John took it philosophically. Then he bought a quantity of bricks from William who was thriving in the industry. Promising to return regularly, he bid them adieu—not that he thought they believed him.

He was home a day and engaged in recruiting families to join in the relocation when the attack came. A band of settlers began firing on a few Indians who were tending their gardens. The men who had guns returned fire and all were gotten inside the stockade unhurt, but the firing continued. George, Bayley and Auteur Awwa took positions at loopholes and, as they had practiced, the two *cockarouse* and Mary's brother stood behind with guns ready to take their places while they reloaded. The exchange lasted until a settler was hit and his comrades carried him away from the battle, but before that had happened, Bayley was shot through the cheek and died before he hit the ground. George stood stunned in rage looking at the ruined face of his friend until he knew what he would do. Giving Bayley's musket to Richard Turner, he led the way from the stockade in hot pursuit of the band of Englishmen. Carrying a wounded man made them easy to overtake. They were unaware of being followed and the pursuers opened fired without warning. There were a total of five in the party. Three fell in the first salvo, and the *cockarouse* fired a barrage of arrows while George and Richard Turner reloaded. The last man standing took a ball in the knee and crumpled. They were all smartly dispatched with tomahawks. George made no effort to prevent the Indians from taking scalps, but he did dissuade them from going to their cabins to kill the women and children.

Inside the stockade George found Deeshu sat on the ground beside Bayley's body with her arms around her knees rocking silently. Saying nothing, he went to dig a grave by the river bank near the place where they crushed the sorghum. He buried the body and left no marker.

Immediately then, he began to load the wagon and advised the men who had decided to follow to bring their belongings. He told Bayley's slave, Gideon, that he was free, but he refused to leave. "No, suh," he said, "if it be all the same to you, I'd prefer to follow long." And he began to help load the wagon.

They left that evening just before dark and continued until the sky began to lighten in the east. Chounteroute would not leave the place that was named for him, and Deeshu stayed with her parents but indicated she might come later. Of the forty people who joined the exodus, the division of Cheroenhaka and Nansemond was roughly even. Aside from George's horse pulling the wagon, there were three others and in the party there were a total of five muskets and two pistols. Naturally, George took the still, but he left the bricks for a later trip so there would be more room for their effects.

It was early May 1668 when they arrived at the edge of the Potecasi Swamp and began the tasks of building shelter and clearing land, and naturally, reconstructing the still. "If the council doesn't grant my patent," he told Mary, "they are going to have to send soldiers to remove us."

The council did approve the patent at the first Quarter Court convened in the colony of Carolana. George paid eighty pounds hard currency and a shilling for the clerk's cost. He was handed a printed deed bearing Lord Carteret's seal and his particulars entered in the clerk's fine hand, later he paid the surveyor to establish the extent of the tract and record a plat. After that he acquired the habit of shooting at strangers if they happened to be white.

CHAPTER FIVE

"I've a mind to do some traveling," William told his cousins when he had returned from Henrico where he collected payment for a consignment of bricks. "They say there is a town building in the southern colony. A change of scenery might do me good."

"More power to you," Frank replied, "but I rather think what you need's a woman."

"You might have a point there, and surely such a commodity would be easier found in a more urban setting."

John was sharpening a knife on a whetstone. "The nature of a Virginian is staunchly agrarian," he observed.

"Isn't it! I swear Jamestown not to have changed since we first laid eyes on it—excepting the fort is brick, of course."

"When will you leave?"

"I've booked passage on a packet leaving in a few days—might be gone month or two."

The family was enjoying the late afternoon in the kitchen yard at John and Ann's house while the children played in the woods. Ann paused from plucking a hen to remark a bit sarcastically, "So the young gentleman has decided to pass the season touring the Continent."

"Well, why not. I think I've earned it," he said defensively.

"I say again, 'more power to you'. If I had made my fortune in bricks, I would probably do the same."

William blushed. "Hardly a fortune, but just the same, it seems prudent that I make a will."

"Oh, don't be gloomy," Ann told him.

"Just the same, I mean to leave everything to my two cousins. Mind you, that will change if I come back from Carolana with a wife."

"Seems to me you might have three cousins," Frank observed.

"Well, right, but frankly George doesn't seem to need it, and how would he be able to claim it without getting his neck stretched?"

John honed his knife in slightly rueful silence. He had taken to growing rice after the passing of his sorghum market, and though he could grow it, it did not thrive. The period of prosperity he had enjoyed through his brother's largess had deluded him to believe that he had achieved an upward momentum. The reversal was as galling. "Well, you must have supper with us so I can have a good look at you in case you decide to vanish like my fugitive brother, and your gesture is appreciated, however, leave the land to Frank. He does better with it than I do."

"I'll not pull a George on you, but the invitation is accepted, for your kindness, I shall bequeath you my personal property."

"Lovely. I get the bricks."

Three days later the packet hove to and sent a tender to fetch William. It was late September and as was usually the case, if there was no hurricane, the weather was fine. The short passage was free of problems and pirates, and in a few days the packet entered the River Ashley. The settlement was several miles upriver on a small island. A few houses were scattered on the shore and the harvest was visible in the fields. Clouds of midges blackened the sky, and the air was redolent with the fecundity of the salt marsh which struck him as vaguely erotic.

William took a room in the hotel which was not yet finished. He had a meal and a glass of beer then went to explore his surroundings. Indians loitered in the dusty streets with scarification on their cheeks and chests. Few if any buildings were fully constructed. Marines stood guard at the end of the footbridge to the mainland, and a man-o-war was anchored in the river. Small, raucous parrots hid in short bushy palm trees. The brutally intense afternoon sun drove people to pause to converse only in the shade of huge spreading magnolias and oaks. William found himself possessed by an odd sense of homecoming.

He rented horses from the stable to explore the country first downriver then upriver. The industry with which the newly arrived settlers had developed the land astounded him. The plantations unfinished appearances did nothing to diminish their apparent productivity. Everywhere black bodies sweated to bring in harvests of truck produce, indigo, and tobacco in a manner more businesslike than he was used to seeing in Virginia. The majority of the gentlemen with whom he conversed in the evenings had come from the Caribbean, principally Barbados. They had brought their slaves, their tools, and their households which gave them the means to settle their plantations seemingly overnight.

A gentleman of the name Middleton enjoyed conversation and good red wine in the common room of the hotel. He found William of interest and quizzed him on the state of things in Virginia. "The plantations follow the rivers," William told him, "and they rarely have a depth of a mile from the banks. Trading ships call on them individually, so there is little tendency to town building."

"Curious," Middleton pronounced. "Well, we mean to have a town here, but not on this speck of an island. The military governor got himself persuaded to sit here by an Indian. He wants our guns between him and his enemies farther inland. As soon as we pacify the place we'll start the real town building down at the natural harbor. How do you deal with the Indians in Virginia?"

"For the most part we try to avoid them. Having said that, two of my cousins have gone and married squaws."

"No."

"Quite. One, in fact, has gone off to live with them. He went so far as to kill some Englishmen who had the bad manners to open fire on their village. With that, he took to hiding deeper in the woods, and we haven't seen him for years."

"Remarkable. I myself would have a hard time fulfilling my marital duty what with the layers of bear grease, the paint and the tattoos." Middleton quivered and quaffed his wine.

"Well, Middleton, I'll tell you this, my cousin took me once to the Indian town, and not all of women are undesirable in the least. And the young ones have a disarming bawdiness to them that is powerfully hard to ignore."

"Well, sir, I say to each his own. Here, here, have another glass of this claret." He refilled William's glass. "Now, when do you plan on going back to Virginia?"

"On the next ship bound thither, I suppose, but I intend to be back. Something here makes me feel at peace."

"I believe you could do no better."

A man and woman with a little girl entered the common area and greeted Middleton. The child ran to sit on his knee. Middleton bounced her while he said, "Mr. and Mrs. Barker, meet Mr. William Skipper of Virginia. I should say lately of Virginia for he has just announced the intention of removing to our more virginal country."

"A pleasure, Mr. Skipper. May I present my wife, Sarah and our child Susan?" The man was tall, thin and fair, the woman comely, and the child toe headed and irrepressible.

"The pleasure is mine, sir. You have a most handsome family."

"Thank you for the compliment. What will be the nature of your business here?"

"I'm a brick maker and a mason."

"Certainly will be a need for those arts." Thomas Barker and his family bade them a polite goodbye and moved on to take their supper. Middleton fell back to his quizzing William on the fine points of life in Virginia until the second claret was gone and William's eyes were heavy.

A ship in from Jamaica called at Charleston. William learned it was further bound for Virginia, so he booked passage. Barring a change in weather, it planned to sail in seven days. In the tender returning him to shore was a young woman dressed like a man. Her *je ne sais quoi* impacted him such that the usually awkward William just gushed chitchat.

"Martha Whaley. You can call me Polly," she replied when asked for a name.

"Well, Polly, have you come from Jamaica?"

"I'm afraid so, at the insistence of my father who was fool enough to leave a perfectly excellent business in Kingston to begin planting in this God forsaken place."

"And he has uprooted you from a perfectly excellent life in town to languish on a plantation, I suppose."

"Couldn't have phrased it better myself."

"How far up river is his plantation?"

"Oh, I don't know. Here, he sent me instructions. I've got to find it all on my own." She handed Will a map.

"Do I detect some estrangement betwixt you and your father?"

"What kind of question is that to ask a lady you've just met?"

Will gulped.

She went on, "But to answer your question bluntly, yes."

"Well, perhaps you'll meet a gentleman to marry and be free of him soon." William couldn't believe that came from him.

"Well, perhaps I shall," her tone changed from confrontational to a fierce sort of purring.

William offered and she accepted his help to procure a drayman to carry her trunks to the plantation once they were brought ashore, then he suggested they dine together that evening. Her response was, "Nothing sadder than eatin' by yourself, is there?"

When he called at her room at the hour agreed she greeted him in the same clothes she had worn during the afternoon. "Bastards haven't brought my bag 'round. It's either this or nothing," she offered in explanation.

"Would my opinion change your decision?"

"It might have some influence on me, but probably would not mean much to polite society in the dining room."

They shared oysters with Chablis, and claret with steaks and collards, and of course, rice. William had not had such a lavish meal since leaving England. Polly seemed unabashed by the looks her costume drew. She relished the meal and when it was over said, "This place has promise." She slouched in her chair with the wine goblet to her lips, then went on, "Master Will, I have no intention of waiting for those clods on the riverbank with my baggage, nor do I relish the idea of riding to my misguided father's plantation alone, and, as I am unnaturally anxious to have the happy reunion, I wondered if you might be disposed to accompany a helpless maid across the savage wilderness."

Will could only open his eyelids halfway. "Miss Polly, I would not be a man if I were to let a helpless maid face the vicissitudes of this wilderness alone."

She looked him coolly in the bloodshot eyes and said, "No, you would not."

They left the dining room and were seen mounting the

stairs together. There was some harrumphing, some shrugging and a little winking, but all returned to their respective meals lest they should get cold. At the door to her room he kissed her hand and thanked her for her pleasant company, then stood vacantly. She tilted her head to the side as she reached behind to left the latch and took him by the lapel dragging him through the door. "Don't play silly buggers," she said.

William hadn't had a woman since his visit to Chounteroute, as such their first coupling did not last long. The second proved a bit more satisfactory.

* * *

Polly rode a horse like a man, and in the sweltering Carolina air, she sweated like one also. Removing her hat to dab her forehead, she asked, "Is it like this here always?"

"I couldn't say with certainty. Virginia tends to cool a little this time of year."

"At Kingston we had a lovely breeze from the sea. The only thing moving in this air are those damned horseflies."

"If your father's map is true, we should arrive soon."

"He probably lied about the distance."

"How did you two drift apart?"

"Drift? It's more of a rift, and it's his own bloody fault. After my mother died he had no earthly idea how to raise a proper little girl, so he raised me to be a Tomboy. When I came of a certain age he expected me to undo what's been done, but you see there's nothing for it."

"Well, I don't see anything about your ways that needs to be undone, save possibly a few buttons."

"Don't start that, Master William. In this heat I'm certain I'd suffocate."

"A little rest in the shade might do you good."

"Onward!" she pointed, "before one of these horseflies bites me."

Nathaniel Whaley's plantation was a flurry of activity. He had several score of slaves who were engaged in tending his fields, building his house, and planting magnolias along his carriage way. Craftsmen brought from Jamaica labored on the finer details of the mansion, and overseers swaggered with whips wherever the slaves toiled. Whaley greeted his daughter with affection. She responded coolly. He eyed William evilly, not offering his hand.

"And who is this character you've been out in the wood with?"

"This is Master William Skipper of Virginia. He was gracious enough to offer me the security of an escort, which is more than my own father did."

"As if I knew when you'd arrive. Well, he had best not have gotten smart with you."

"Master William is a perfect gentleman. I couldn't ask for a better suitor."

William felt his cheeks burn, but he was unaware that his jaw dropped.

Polly closed his mouth with her pretty finger. "Remember the horseflies," she told him.

Whaley became increasingly agitated. He was big man with huge hands and a day's growth on his face. He dressed for the work of the day not for idleness. For the first time he addressed William, "Suppose you explain your intentions."

He began to stammer and Polly watched him grinning. "Well, I—uh, would like your permission to call upon your daughter."

"Appears to me you've already called without my permission."

"Well, I couldn't very well let her ride out here alone, could I?"

"The courtesy of a message would have caused me to send a proper escort, would it not?"

"And deprive me of the sooner pleasure of being with

my adored father…" Polly interrupted.

"Save it, girl. What's done is done. If he comports himself with propriety, he may court you. God knows I couldn't prevent it if you had a mind to let him, but if he dishonors you in any way, there's nothing to keep me from putting the hounds on him, is there?"

"I'm sure he'll be on his best behavior. Won't you, William?"

"Yes, ma'am," he nodded lamely.

Only two rooms of the plantation house were habitable. William slept in a rude bunkhouse with the overseers. They roused him at daybreak as they went to tend their charges, so he strolled the grounds until breakfast was served. Polly bubbled while her father glowered and William struggled to seem charming to her and harmless to him. She put a hand on Will's and said, "After breakfast has settled, will you bring the horses and accompany me so that I may become familiar with my new confines?"

Whaley grumbled, "I'll send Leviticus with you so you don't get lost."

"I'm sure William can prevent me from getting lost. After all, he brought me here didn't he? And I'm sure you have important things for Leviticus to do."

"Nothing more important than keeping an eye on you."

"Nonsense! I'm fully capable of keeping an eye on myself."

Whaley's grimace soured.

The horses had a decent stable, and William found the two he'd rented. He saddled them and led them to the house. The bags arrived so Polly changed into riding clothes and waited on the finished half of the veranda. As they rode from the chaos of the house under construction Whaley was nowhere in sight. The day was the same as the previous with intense sun, and humidity to make one's breath seem to gurgle in the lungs. Vast tracts of sea grass forced them to make sweltering detours away from the river to ground that could be negotiated. Whaley was apparently trying to find his niche. They rode past fields of indigo, cotton, corn and tobacco. The crops were ready and slaves and their minders were ubiquitous, but following the road to the river and then up steam eventually took them beyond the limits of Whaley's holdings. The water looked brown from a distance, but from the bank its clarity was apparent.

"Why did you tell your father I was a suitor?" William found the courage to ask after an awkwardly long silence.

"Aren't you?"

"Well, I suppose I am, but it's like putting the cart before the horse."

"We've already put the cart and the horse in their proper places. So now you have to marry me," she tried hard not to smile.

"What? How can you be sure? Oh, I mean really, not that I wouldn't, but it must be too soon to be certain."

"Not that, simpleton, but you've had your way with me. Now no one else would have me."

"That I doubt, and if you'll pardon my effrontery, there seemed little virginal in your comportment—but there is the matter of your father."

Laughing now, she said "I think he should like nothing more than to unburden himself of me. Now, get off your horse, take me to that mossy bank and show me that you're worthy."

William thought he showed himself worthy, and Polly's response scared the parakeets from the palmettos. She lay panting with beads of sweat on her upper lip. Rising suddenly she pulled him to his feet. "Let's cool down. Can't catch me," she said and pranced into to water.

He started after her when the explosion froze him. Whaley stood by the bole of the tree with a pistol in each hand. The left was pointing upward and still smoked, the one in his right hand was aimed at William's genitals. "These buck a bit, so I might miss and put hole through your gut," Whaley snarled. "Now, get the hell out of here and don't ever let me see your stinking hide again, and Polly, you stay in the water so this filthy bastard can't lay his eyes on you again."

"No!" she cried and began wading to the shore.

"Git!" he gestured with the still loaded pistol. "Get on that horse and get out of my sight."

Polly ran to her father but he took her upper arm and threw her down. "Have you no shame, you little strumpet? Cover yourself." Then to William, "I'm counting to myself. You will have to guess what number I picked. Take both horses and go."

He bundled his clothes to his chest, untied the reins and began walking backward. "Get on the damned horse and leave!" Whaley bellowed. Polly sat on the ground, beat it with her fists and cried, but Whaley turned his back, took a few steps after William and shooed him with the gun. When William was mounted and moving away, he said to Polly, still turned away, "Get dressed and be quick."

Painful though it was, William galloped the horse until he was out of sight before stopping to dress. He continued on to Charleston agonizing over how he was going to renew contact with Polly. She was forced to ride behind her father in sullen silence, and at the plantation house went to her room and cried again.

When the day to embark arrived William had not thought of how to get past Whaley. He had been hoping vainly that she would come to him, so he concluded glumly that she really did not care and he boarded the ship. As the ship glided down the river the emptiness in him smothered the sense of belonging that the new colony had instilled.

She would have come to him, but her father posted a guard on her until she realized she was pregnant. Then they both went looking for William. On learning that he was gone, she assumed that *he* didn't care. Whaley stood for the bastardy bond, and when the baby was born he was given the surname, Whaley, and not Skipper.

CHAPTER SIX

Chounteroute, the *werrowance* of the Cheroenhaka, received the delegation of Pamunkey, Mattaponi and Chickahominy with his usual hospitality. He offered them his pipe, a feast and the girls of the village. Sam Turner was with him in the inner circle along with the several *cockarouse*. When business was finally broached the leader of the Pamunkey said, "King, we are being driven from our lands, and all the game is being taken by the English. We can no longer pretend that they will ever leave us in peace. They have even defiled *Uttamussack*. You, Chounteroute, have made the pilgrimage to *Uttamussack* and made offerings on the *pawcorance*. Do you mean to see it abandoned and the bodies of our ancestral kings defiled? This we cannot let happen, so we come to ask you to join us in driving the English out."

Chounteroute guessed the purpose of visit and had been considering his response. "I have known some English, and I found them to be much the same as Indians—some are good and some are bad."

"Look at how they force you to live here inside these walls. There is not enough space for all of your people."

145

"We have more land a short march from here. It is not disagreeable, but there are those among us who feel as you do."

"We are ready to kill the white men!" Richard Turner shouted from the outer circle. His father rose silently, walked to where he stood, and hit him hard on the bridge of his nose. He crumpled and refrained from interrupting again while he held his head back to staunch the blood. Sam reseated himself next to his king.

"That one and several others will join you if you can stand their insolence," Chounteroute assured the Pamunkey chief. "I am too old to fight and will stay here with the rest of the old men to protect the town from the reprisals that will follow. I will also make a large offering to the *quioccos* to give luck to your war."

The Pamunkey *werrowance* clearly was less than overwhelmed by the level of support, but he took what he could get, and made the best of Chounteroute's hospitality. The next day they left with a dozen Nansemond and Cheroenhaka warriors including Richard Turner of course. Chounteroute was an abnormally reliable Indian. He often kept his word. The next day he offered both rum and tobacco to the idol as he had promised, but it grieved him deeply.

* * *

Francis acquired another parcel of land. William baked his bricks in sullen resignation, and became the favorite uncle of the families' children especially him namesake. George, who remained in isolation, sent young George to live with his brothers for the sake of attending school, but when school was not in session, he insisted on leaving for the village of the Cheroenhaka where he was deeply fond of his grandfather, Sam and Chounteroute. The old men filled him with stories of the mysterious times before the English came. He loved to hear of spooky ceremonies around the fabulous crystal altar known as the *pawcorance* under the eyes of mummified kings, and vowed to go see it as soon as he determined where this shrine called *Uttamussack* might be.

Young William loved to play in the mud and was happier packing a brick mold than hunting or fishing. Elder William could not have more pleased. The children of Francis were more anglicized than George, Jr., but their mother made sure that they stayed in touch with their roots. This was especially difficult for them when the Indian attack finally came.

It was much more concerted than any previous attack. Squads of warriors fanned across the counties, lying in wait by the individual plantations until presented with propitious opportunities to ambush the families. John and Francis were walking back from the fields when two Indians appeared from the trees each carrying a turkey. The Indians were strangers and did not have much English, but they managed to convey that the fowl were gifts. John and Frank stared at each other in amazement. "Thank you," Frank said as he took the birds.

The Indians vainly attempted to communicate in sign language, and repeated, "Gift. Friend. Brother." Then they left as mysteriously as they appeared.

"What do you make of that?" Frank asked his brother.

"Being that nothing like that ever happened before, I'd say they were up to something."

"Think the turkeys are poisoned?"

"I think we should look them over pretty well."

They went to the house and found William talking to the women. "Look what some Indians gave me," he said and raised the ankle of a leg of venison.

"Indians you ever saw before?"

"Never."

Frank asked his wife, "Ann, could they be trying to poison us?"

She looked serious and shook her head. "Indians not

147

use poison. You keep guns near. This is bad sign."

The other Ann asked her, "What do you mean a bad sign, Annie?"

"Their tribe not live near here. They come to maybe attack and bring gifts so you think they're friends. We see it before."

John said, "Well, I'll get the guns. You pluck the turkeys. Where are the kids?"

The next day Frank and John carried their long guns loaded to the fields and stuck pistols into their belts. As they hoed down the rows they kept the guns at hand. The day was sultry and dead still with much buzzing of green flies. Just at noon four painted Indians broke from the trees whooping and flailing tomahawks over their heads. The sudden eruption made the two men jump and shout involuntarily. They raised their pistols and fired quickly, missing cleanly, but causing the Indians to hesitate. When they got the muskets one of the red and black devils was coming at them again. Frank aimed carefully and hit him square in the chest. John hit one of the other three but did not drop him. John raised his gun by the barrel as Frank frantically reloaded. The wounded Indian began to run for the cover of the trees. The other two followed outstripping him, and the one with a ball in his gut fell before leaving the clearing. His comrades didn't stop. Frank fired at their backs to no effect.

The first Indian shot was already dead. The second looked into their eyes grimly resigned. The wound wasn't bleeding much, at least not externally. "We best see where the women are. This one's not much of a threat anymore."

They took the time to reload before jogging to the house. Howerac insisted they all stay inside with the door barred and that is how the men found them, unmolested. John collapsed onto the stoop, put his head in his hands and vomited. When the heaving passed, he told Frank, "One of us should warn William."

"I'll go. Don't want anybody to see *me* puke."

Frank took the horse and galloped toward William's land while John went into the house and stood guard at the window. Ann caressed him but he just stared rigidly through the glass. She had the delicacy not to ask.

In something over an hour Frank suddenly appeared on foot in front of the window startling John. He motioned for his brother to come outside. There was blood on shirt and his face ashen.

"What is it?"

"The savages cleaved his head open with his own axe. They scalped him, John. I put his body in the shed so the kids and women wouldn't see it."

John made no outward reaction. He only sighed and said, "Well, it's going to be a long night, isn't it?"

* * *

The governor organized the militia. The two Skippers answered the call, but paradoxically, the two Anns took the children to Chounteroute. For English Ann it was the first time in an Indian town since they had stayed with the Winyah. She was decidedly uneasy.

"Aunt Ann," George asked on seeing her in the Cheroenhaka town, "will my uncles come here when they're done killing Indians?"

The issue of killing Indians and living with them perplexed her. "I don't know if they'll come here or just send a message," she told her nephew, then added, "and please put some clothes on."

"I should tell father about this. He may want you to stay with him."

"But you can't go out in the woods alone now. It isn't safe for an Indian."

"Don't worry, auntie, either side I meet, I claim to be one of them."

Ann was adamant that he not leave, but as soon as she

was occupied, he sneaked out of the stockade. George had a pony that he rode bareback. Riding by himself he could make the trip to Potecasi in less than half a day. The settlement in the swamp had grown. More than two dozen houses were scattered through the woods. George whooped and waved as he passed people he knew, though he did not know them all. Strangers had begun drifting into the swamp, people of indeterminate pedigree and strangely mixed features.

Mary hugged him and his sisters rolled their eyes. "Have you heard what is happening in Virginia?" he asked his father.

"What now, boy?"

"The governor called out the militia and Uncle John and Frank have gone to kill Indians. Aunt Ann and Aunt Howerac took the kids to Chounteroute so they'd be safer. Do you want me to bring them here?"

George rubbed the stubble on his chin pensively before he answered. "No, it'd be better I go there so they don't have to lie when the sheriff asks them if they know where to find me."

"Oh, I almost forgot. The Pamunkey killed Uncle William and took his scalp."

"What? You almost forgot?" George sat heavily on the stoop and stared at the ground.

"Father, isn't it a bad thing for Uncle John and Frank to go out killing Indians?"

George's heart was pounding and his eyes burned when he fixed his gaze on his son. "It's no worse than Indians killing them."

In the morning George put Mary and the children into the wagon, his oldest rode his pony, and they began the trip north. Through the years he had kept in close contact with the town of Chounteroute which was his largest market for rum. Rarely was anyone encountered en route, and never anyone who was looking for a renegade Englishman who was rumored to have participated in the killing of some settlers.

"Annie, you look as fresh and sweet as the last time I laid eyes on you," George exclaimed when he found her at Chounteroute.

"And I'm quite relieved to find you fairly dressed."

"Well, of course. I've been bringing the trappings of civilization to our new settlement."

"So you say."

"Yes, but tell me what happened, and how did poor Will meet his maker?"

"It was bloody awful, George. The savages attacked from ambush. They say they attacked plantations all over the colony at the same time. John and Frank saw them coming, thank God, but Will was all alone and they overpowered him and mutilated his dead body. I tell you, it's a queer feeling being here after that."

"You're among friends, Annie. There's Indians and then there's Indians."

"Indian Ann tells me some warriors from right here went off the join the massacre."

"Mary's brother I suspect among them. Like I said, there's Indians and there's Indians, but Chounteroute won't let anything happen to you while you're here, and neither will I. Does John know you're here?"

"Yes, Ann convinced us all this was the safest place to wait for them to come back."

"Well, I'll stay until they do. It'll be good to see my brethren after so many years. Here, now, you must meet the rest of my brood."

George went to see Chounteroute to see if he would organize a feast. It wasn't particularly difficult to convince him. "Yes, it will be good to have a celebration. I doubt if we will have the Green Corn Dance as long as your brothers are on the warpath. The Corn God will be angry with us but we might as well enjoy ourselves."

"He'll get over it. Besides, my brothers couldn't hit the side of a barn."

"Your brother's woman tells me he killed a Pamunkey warrior, but he did not collect a scalp."

"He always was a bit squeamish."

"Such a waste. Tell the women to prepare the feast for two nights hence. The moon will be full then."

By the gentle nudging of Mary and Howerac, English Ann was induced to participate in the dance at the feast, although her participation was limited to the tentative shaking of a rattle. In addition to the requisite venison, the hunters had killed a huge boar. It's liver was much relished by the chief men and George had naturally transported a cask. While the adults feasted and danced Ann remarked to her brother-in-law, "All the children are playing like little savages." When her William appeared in the moonlight having been painted by his cousins, she even managed to laugh.

* * *

The campaign against the Indians lasted a bit more than a month. Precious few were tracked and engaged in running battles, the survivors of which were captured and hung. This was infuriating to the warriors who considered hanging to be a disgraceful way to die. Most of the violence took the form of storming Indian towns and wantonly killing as many inhabitants possible.

At last in frustration the Indians went home, if they had one, to pack their belongings for the inevitable relocation to lands farther west that were graciously granted by the invaders, at least for the time being. John and Frank found their way to Chounteroute to reclaim their families and were astounded to be greeted by their brother.

"We never thought we'd see hide nor hair of you again," John told him.

"You'll not be rid of me that easily."

"Just the same, you shouldn't be here. When we got to the Middle Plantation the sheriff asked us again if we knew where you were. I wouldn't put it past him to follow us here."

George thought for a time then said, "I wouldn't either, but I'm not going to run away the minute I see my brothers after so much time. Let's see if the king will throw another feast."

Well, of course he would.

Richard Turner and the survivors of the warriors who had joined the war returned and were surprised to find two white men from the militia. Mary confronted him finding that he had shaved the right half of his head, gathered the hair on the left side into a shoulder length lock, and still had half his face painted red and the other black. "Richard, no one wears their hair like that anymore."

"Warriors do. What are these English doing here? We have collected many English scalps, but maybe there will be more."

"These are George's brothers. They are guests here for a few days, and you will not bother them."

"Girl, you must be crazy. A few days ago they were killing our people."

"And you were killing theirs. While we're all here we're going to live in peace."

"It is madness!"

"The whole business is madness, but if you or any of your friends harms anyone here, I will cut your throat while you're asleep and collect your scalp for my pantry door." The tone of her threat had a profound effect on her brother. He backed from her with wide eyes and decided to go hunting for a few days.

Eteshe Ena was very critical of Chounteroute when he ordered another feast since it appeared the Green Corn Dance might proceed as planned, but he was adamant that the brothers of *cockarouse* George had to be feted.

The dancing began in the early evening and had not progressed very long when then whooping of the women sentries brought it to a halt. The warriors who had been dancing in their full regalia dropped their rattles and seized their weapons. The guests looked to George for explanation. "Strangers are coming," he told them. "Don't be alarmed yet. A runner will get here shortly to tell us what it's about."

A girl ran toward the stockade and was admitted through the sally port. She reported to the war chief, Doctor Tom, who waited with his men inside the gate, "It is a party of English soldiers. They come with a white flag."

Doctor Tom went to Chounteroute who had not wanted to interrupt the celebration unless it was absolutely necessary. He directed Sam Turner to meet the delegation. "See if they can be convinced to come back tomorrow. I don't want George to miss the feast."

Sam Turner took a few warriors with him. He approached the Englishmen alone and unarmed. One of the soldiers in an officer's coat stepped forward also unarmed. He spoke first, "I have come to speak to King Chounteroute about the renegade George Skipper."

"Chounteroute is busy right now. Would it be possible for you to come back tomorrow?"

The militia officer looked like he had been slapped. "No, I can't come back tomorrow. I insist on seeing Chounteroute, now."

Sam sighed. He motioned for one of the warriors to come forward, took his gun and arranged an exchange of hostages then he escorted the officer into the stockade. He took him to the longhouse where he left him under guard, and went for his king. Chounteroute shook his head and slowly got to his feet. He had Sam tell John and Frank to come too. "It will save time." Then to George he said, "Look not so white."

That made George laugh. "Sorry, Annie," he said as he removed his breeches and shirt and tied a breechclout across his loins. Mary took some red paint from her bag and applied it to his upper face.

Chounteroute entered the longhouse and greeted the officer through Sam Turner. "Greetings, King Chounteroute, I'm Captain Sommers of the Virginia militia. These gentlemen already know me. We've come for their brother. I know he's here, so don't bother to deny it."

The chief stepped toward Sommers in a way that told the brothers he would handle it. He locked eyes with the officer for several silent seconds as he sucked his teeth, then said, "The Englishmen are not here because their brother is here, they are here because their wives are here. Frank's wife was born here. She is one of my children. She came here and brought her sister-in-law so we could protect them while their men were with you. As for the other, he is a good man, and if I knew where he was I would not give him up to you. Now, we have interrupted the feast for too long. You will take some food with us before you rejoin your men." He left the longhouse abruptly and John and Frank gestured that Sommers could precede them.

George danced when the men danced so not to call attention to himself. The rest of the time he sat with the men keeping his back to Sommers who remained close to the other two Skippers. A glazed ceramic jug of rum was passed and Sommers was quick to ask, "How did this get here? As if I didn't know."

John took a swig and replied, "You'll have to ask the chief." He gave the jug back to the Captain who condescended to try some.

"Look at that," Sommers pointed at George in the line of warriors. "That Indian can't dance!"

John moaned, "Probably too drunk."

It was then that Frank's boy shouted, "No, George," and ran through their midst. The name jolted Sommers who stood as a tall slender youth came in pursuit. He grabbed the boy by the upper arm and examined him critically.

"I know that nose. You're his half-breed son. Where's yer old man?" he growled.

Young George sank his fist beneath the man's rib cage. He lurched forward from the waist but kept his feet and did not lose his grip on George's arm.

John caught his nephew's second blow before it impacted. "Let go of his arm, Captain,"

"I'll not. I intend to keep a hold on this boy until his father surrenders himself."

"Captain, look around. Exactly how do you intend to accomplish that?"

Sommers turned his head toward several score of baneful black eyes and he released George's arm who stared at him scowling for a few seconds then left calmly. Before he could resume his seat, Chounteroute arrived and said, "Captain, the feast is nearly over and you are anxious to return to your men. Sam will take you and the hostage back. Sorry you couldn't find the one you wanted."

Sam Turner and a couple armed warriors pushed Sommers and the English hostage through the sally port and when they had recovered the Indian hostage, they dismissively returned to the stockade where the feast was just getting started. By sunrise most of the revelers had drifted to their beds, but young George had just arisen from the bed of one Suntetung, a tall fiery girl who was the daughter of a Cheroenhaka shaman and George's favorite when he was at Chounteroute. Suntetung plaited his hair and tied it then she painted his face red and black.

"I've done all I can do to make a warrior of you," she told him. "Now it's up to you."

He smiled at her chiding and said, "Don't worry about that. I'll bring you his scalp before this time tomorrow." Then he stole from the stockade without being seen and ran into the woods where the soldiers had last been. Their spoor covered the entire width of the trail. He was able to follow at a trot and by mid-afternoon was stalking them from cover. They made an early camp and George found a tree in which he could secure himself sufficiently to get a small nap. When it was almost dark he was watching the movement in the English soldiers' camp. They were preparing for the night and the captain clearly in need of some privacy wandered into the trees followed discreetly by a lookout. When the costive captain found a comfortable spot, George was gratified to note the sentry kept his eyes averted and remained screened by foliage. He slipped soundlessly from the tree and crept to within reach of the preoccupied officer. George slapped his palm over the man's mouth and slit his throat nearly cutting to the spine. Sudden death completed the release of his bowels nearly causing George to gag, but he managed to pull the body away from the mess as, quite deftly for his first time, proceeded to collect the scalp. He was gone long before the lookout felt compelled to investigate.

George presented the scalp to Suntetung who promised to display it proudly; however, he neglected to mention what he had done to his parents who were preparing to return to Potecasi. Nevertheless the news got to Mary quickly and she confronted her son while he was helping load the family's wagon. "Have you lost your mind?" she demanded with venom. "Now you have to live like your father. You can't be seen amidst the plantations. You'll never see your cousins and you can't even spend time here like you always want to. You won't see Suntetung and when you don't come as often as she wants, she will let another boy into her bed."

George had expected this from his mother and he coolly gave her the speech he had rehearsed. "The man was determined to capture my father, he insulted me and it is past time I became a warrior."

"It's past time that we put that custom behind us. You are more than half English, and an Englishman does not have to murder someone to become a warrior."

"What's done is done, mother. I've been raised Cheroenhaka more than English. That's the world I live in."

She was too stoical to cry and returned to her packing. His father's reaction stung. "That was a mighty cowardly way to become a warrior."

"He had a sentry. If I had confronted him he would have shouted and the sentry would have shot me." Young George stiffened his spine and left indignantly.

When he was out of earshot his father muttered, "I didn't say it was stupid."

* * *

George found his brothers to bid them goodbye. "I reckon it will be awhile before I see you again. You heard what the boy did?"

John frowned, "Yes, like father, like son I suppose."

"Here now, was that called for?"

"Sorry, but you may be right about not seeing me. I've got a mind to leave this country."

"What? Not going back to England?"

"No, no, not that. Our poor departed cousin put a bug in my ear about Charleston. He says the land there is most conducive to the cultivation of rice which I think superior to tobacco as a cash crop."

"What kind of spirituous liquor is made from rice?" George asked with sarcasm.

Ann groaned, "You're a hopeless case."

"Well, then perhaps we will see each other. As far as I can tell I'm not a wanted man in Carolana."

John slapped his back. "There you go! I'll send a letter when we get settled."

George looked at Frank and asked, "So, are you going too?"

"Not likely," he replied, "I've agreed to buy John's plantation, and seeing that I'm only possessed of two good arms, I suppose I'll be in the market for a Negro."

"'My brother, gentleman planter.' It has a certain ring

to it."

"Not so much as 'my brother, Indian chief'" Frank retorted.

"All right, then. You've got me there. Well, best of luck to both of you. It's back to the swamp now. Don't forget to send that letter, Johnny. Annie, keep him out of trouble in Carolana, and Frankie, don't be too surprised to find one of my urchins on your doorstep looking for an education. That is if I have one without a price on his head."

Most of the route to Potecasi followed well maintained Indian trails, but the in area immediately surrounding the swamp the underbrush was not cleared. George did all he could to keep it that way. Each time he passed he forced his way across a different patch of saplings and vines so no clear trail developed, and he harped at his neighbors to do the same.

There was a new arrival in the community. A man with a strangely yellow complexion, nappy, if somewhat fine hair and hazel eyes had built a rude half shelter. George went to meet him after unpacking. He spoke the kind of English normally heard from the black people and introduced himself as Silas Oxendine. "Is youse da chief?" he asked.

George studied him at length before he pulled his chin and replied, "I'm more of a landlord. For a pound a year you can use enough land for a cabin and truck garden. When you come and go, don't make a trail through the underbrush. Rum's one tobacco a jug, or equal in skins or hard money."

"Yessir, I's right glad to make yer acquaintance."

Not very much later a Nansemond woman moved into his partially completed cabin. Curiously when their children were born they could pass for white.

* * *

Young George resigned himself to the domesticity of Potecasi for a time, albeit a short time. Mary had warmed to the un-Indian-like habit of dining with the whole family so George fashioned a respectable table and set of chairs although each varied in height they were suitable to accommodate the various sized children. Since establishing themselves in Carolana two more sons, John and James, had been born. John was tied to the tallest chair while James was slung across his mother's back waiting to be slung across her front where his dinner waited. In the autumn afternoon with the sun sparkling on the red leaves of the maples and the still green oaks, the Skippers enjoyed steaks from a black bear that made the mistake of raiding the midden heap behind the house. George, Jr. dispatched him with a single shot and was feeling somewhat full of himself.

"I'm going to Chounteroute when Auteur Awwa takes the rum tomorrow," he announced.

"It's not safe yet," Mary told him knowing it was futile.

His father was more circumspect. "Why don't you bring the girl back here?"

Caught off guard the boy hesitated before he said, "Suntetung's not the only reason I want to go. I like to see grandpa and Uncle Chounteroute too."

"Well, just don't be a fool and go near the plantations," George warned. "As soon as he sees that nose, the constable will know who are."

"Why? I look like an Indian."

"No, you don't. You look like a Skipper, and don't think anybody up there is going to forget about us."

"I can't spend my whole life stuck in this swamp."

"Being stuck in a swamp is better than dancing at the end of a rope."

"Nothing will happen to me. Auteur Awwa and I can take care of ourselves."

George picked a piece of meat from his teeth while he thought of how to answer that. "Nothing short of tying you to the gum tree is going to prevent your leaving, but don't be gone so long your mother gets worried about you."

The prestige of being in business with George Skipper gave Auteur Awwa the status to acquire two wives, who gave him five children, but the women could not get along, so he kept one wife in Chounteroute and the other at Potecasi. Each time he left Potecasi the wife there became sullen and angry, and the same thing happened when he left Chounteroute. As he and George proceeded toward the barrier of blackberries and poison ivy that shielded the settlement from interlopers, she followed berating him for running to "that reptile", and she launched an oily black walnut that caught him on the back of the head and raised a fair knot.

"I married two she devils, George. Try to let it be a lesson to you."

George was riding his pony along side of the wagonload of rum. Midges buzzed in his nose and ears. The annoyance reminded him of the woman's shrilling. "Why do you let her show you so much disrespect? I will never let a woman do that to me."

Auteur Awwa looked at his young friend and smiled the smile of experience. "Years ago I learned that it served me better to pretend I didn't hear than to try to put a stop to the noise, but it is necessary to have two women so when one is angry with you the other will not be just to get the better of her rival. When you marry Suntetung take her sister too."

"What makes you think I'm going to marry Suntetung?"

"What you want doesn't matter. She will decide the matter for you, but if you insist that she bring her sister to your bed you will at least have a little bit of control."

"I'll give it some thought, but Aheeta doesn't even have women's breasts yet."

"That's good. When Suntetung's become long and

unappealing, Aheeta's may still be firm."

"I hadn't thought of that."

"One has to keep these things in mind when choosing wives. You should also look closely at her mother, for the girl will surely become like her mother with time. Pay close attention to how her mother treats her husband. Does she shrill at him with prideful meanness? And be certain to examine her thighs."

George gave this much consideration and found a flaw in the logic. "If you are so wise about women," he asked after a time, "why did you marry two she devils?"

"It's because I did not have someone like me to offer good advice."

By the time they arrived at Chounteroute George had determined to never marry, but that did not prevent him from running straight to Suntetung who received him with anxious enthusiasm, and then again. Later he found his grandfather, Sam Turner, and the old king who he called uncle though they were unrelated, seated on the mat at the door of Chounteroute's house.

Sam beamed at the sight of him. "George, how good to see you here so soon. We have been concerned for you. Did you come alone?"

"I came with Auteur Awwa."

"Excellent," Chounteroute said with a broad smile knowing what the Winyah would have brought. "How is your family?"

"Everyone is well, Uncle. The harvest is good this year and there is plenty of game. How are things here?"

"There is still much trouble with the English. Some men attempted to burn the corn which was just full on the ear, but your Uncle Richard shot one of them, and ran them off before the fire could spread. They have the same trouble at Tamahiton."

"Why doesn't everybody move to Carolana? We never see Englishmen at Potecasi."

"That's fortunate, but we are too old to move, George,

besides, the fork in the river is the place of our ancestors. It is important that places like this do not fall into the hands of the English."

"And places like *Uttamussack*?"

"*Uttamussack* especially," Sam said as he began to fill his pipe. "What do you know of *Uttamussack*?"

"Only that it contains the *pawcorance*. Why is *Uttamussack* more important than Chounteroute?" George asked taking the proffered pipe.

His grandfather was holding his lungs full of smoke, so Chounteroute replied, "*Uttamussack* is the resting place of great kings, so it is very sacred."

"Will you go to *Uttamussack* when you die?"

"Probably not, George. The families of *Tsenacomoco* consider me to be a very ordinary king."

"What do you have to do before they consider a king great?"

"Oh, kill many enemies or have useful visions."

Sam laughed which made him choke on the smoke. "Then you will surely be preserved at *Uttamussack*, Chounteroute. You have visions every night after the pipe gets passed."

The king ignored the jibe and reached for the pipe.

"Tell me about the *pawcorance*," George urged with a sort of childlike guilelessness that belied his usual bravado.

Being in his element, Chounteroute assumed the posture of the all knowing. "It is a wonderful thing to see, George. It is as big as the stone by the longhouse where the women grind the acorns and it is clear as the glass in the Englishmen's windows. It is warm to the touch and when the *quioccos* is pleased with the offering, the *pawcorance* buzzes like a bee."

"Have you seen it, grandfather?"

Sam was as rapt as his grandson. "No, son, I never have. Why don't you go to see it before you become occupied with the burdens of being a man? A vision quest is part of becoming a man."

"Mother would scalp me for going near the plantations."

"Did you mother approve of you coming here?"

"No."

"So, now you have become the obedient son?"

That was all the license he needed. "How will I find *Uttamussack*?"

Chounteroute answered him. "It's on the north side of Powhaten's river just above the falls. The town of the Chickahominy is two and a half days' walk north of there. The English militia might be watching that place. You will have to be very careful."

Sam Turner took his grandson home for supper. Richard Turner, who built his house next to his father's, had taken Deeshu as his second wife. He beat her and treated her children by Joseph Bayley dismissively.

Deeshu's son, Watt, was George's closest friend. "Watt, I'm going on a vision quest to *Uttamussack*," he told him. "Want to come, too?"

"What vision did you have?" Watt asked a little mockingly.

"I haven't had one yet. It will probably happen when I see the *pawcorance*."

"I'll go just to get away from your uncle."

"I can't believe you still let him treat you like he did when you were a boy."

"He no longer tries to hit me, but if I stand up to him, he is cruel to my mother."

"Why don't you kill him, and take care of your mother yourself?"

Watt did not remember his father, but he had the same sense of fun. "I'd rather go on your vision quest," he said.

George passed a couple of days joined to Suntetung in the hope of sufficiently draining his carnal needs until he returned. The morning the two half breed pilgrims left was fresh and clear. George stepped from the sally port with his gun in one hand, a travelling bag over his shoulder and a sense that this was the moment that defined him as an individual. The pair walked because Watt did not have a horse, but he did have his father's quite excellent rifle. There was no game, however, and the jerked venison and parched corn that they brought was exhausted by the third day. They had found the falls but *Uttamussack* eluded them.

"We need to find the Chickahominy town," George told Watt on the evening of the fourth day of their journey.

"Chounteroute said it was north of the falls," Watt recalled. "If we walk north, we should find a trail that will lead us there."

"Which way do we turn when we find this trail?"

"That will be the time for your vision, George."

They were attempting to kindle a fire when the smell of wood smoke from someone apparently more successful froze them. "We'd best see whose fire that is," George advised. "It might be some Chickahominy."

"Or it might be militia."

They stole soundlessly into the direction of the wind and found the camp without difficulty. Three white men sat next to a fire watching a large catfish roast.

"We've got to get that fish," Watt whispered.

"Well, we can only shoot two of them," George mused. "We'll shoot the two facing us then you rush the other and tomahawk him while I reload in case there are more of them."

"Why don't you tomahawk him while I reload?"

"Just don't miss. If we miss one, we'll both have to rush them."

"If we miss two we'd better run the opposite way."

"I'll take the one on the right. You take the one on the left. Fire as soon as you hear my shot."

They crept closer and indicated to each other that they had their targets. George fired and heard Watt's shot. Both men were struck in the chest and collapsed. George leaped forward with his tomahawk raised expecting the third man to reach for his gun, but instead he covered his head with his arms waiting for the blow. He hesitated to strike him, and the man said, "I give up!"

George hesitated with the hatchet held aloft but did not strike. Watt ran into the camp still pouring powder into the pan. "Hit him," he said.

"I can't. He gave up."

"If we don't kill him, what are we going to do with him?"

"I don't know."

"So hit him."

"No, we'll take him prisoner."

"Then what?"

"We'll take him to Chickahominy."

"We don't know where Chickahominy is."

They were talking in English which was their habit, and the man followed their conversation with wide eyes.

"Maybe he knows where it is," George gestured toward him with the tomahawk. "Do you know where the Chickahominy town is?"

"If I did, wouldn't I be a fool to tell you?"

"If you don't we will kill you now."

"And if I do you will take me there and they will kill me."

"Maybe not. You'll run a gauntlet probably, but you might survive that. We can ask them to spare you."

"You just killed my friends. Why should I trust you?"

"Well, you can think about it while we eat your fish."

"Now, that's enough fish for all of us. You don't mean to eat it all do you?"

Watt considered the drift of the conversation and added, "You think about telling us where Chickahominy is, and we'll think about giving you some fish. Now, we have to tie you to that tree while we scalp your friends."

The man went even more pale than he had been. "You're not going to do it right here are you?"

"What kind of savages do you take us for?"

They tied his arms around a sizeable beech and dragged the bodies out of sight to collect the scalps. Watt had never done it and made a mess of his. "I don't think I want to do this again," he complained.

"You might not have to, but be sure to show that to Uncle Richard. It might win him over to you."

They shook the blood from the scalps and rinsed their hands with the men's water before carving the catfish. It was a good ten pound fish and they tucked into it with relish. George held a chunk of it aloft for the Englishman to see and said, "This is excellent fish. Did you catch it on a line or gig it?"

"Line."

"There is plenty of it left. Did you decide to take us to Chickahominy?"

"I never said I knew where it was."

"You do though, don't you? Come on, now, just agree to take us there and we'll untie you and you can have some fish."

"If I tell you where it is will you let me go?"

"Then how would we know you were telling the truth. No, I'm afraid you have to take us there."

The man thought for a while. "How is it you speak English so well?" he asked.

"We're half English," Watt told him.

"You're renegades."

"No, that's our fathers. We're half breeds," George corrected. "So what's your name?"

"Eli."

"Well, Eli, you really should get some of your own fish, so just agree to take us to the Chickahominy town and we will untie you, and we can all be friends."

"Fine. I'll take you."

"There, that's better," he untied the man's arms and let him sit across the fire although he kept his gun trained on him. He pulled a piece of white meat from the catfish and swallowed it eagerly.

With their captive securely trussed George and Watt retired. At dawn Eli told them where to look for the hobbled horses. The Chickahominy town proved to be a short ride from their camp. It was nearly deserted. An old woman greeted them. "After the soldiers attacked us, the warriors took their families over the mountains," she told them. "Only a few who are too old to go remain here to die." She showed them a house to use, and gratefully accepted the captive. "There aren't enough of us to form a decent gauntlet, but we'll find something to do with him," she said fiendishly.

George said, "He's been a good prisoner. We'd like it if you don't kill him."

"You wouldn't say that if you had seen the bodies of the women and children after the English attacked us."

"Maybe not, but the real reason we came here was to go to *Uttamussack* to see the *pawcorance*. Will you tell us how to find it?"

The crone looked queerly at him, spat, then said, "No, I can't. *Uttamussack* is no more."

"What?"

"Before the people left we had to prevent the sacred things from being defiled by the enemy, so we buried the bodies of the kings and the *pawcorance*. Then we tore down the house and scattered the pieces."

"Damn," Watt said in English, "you're never going to have a vision."

The woman gave them some food and left them alone. She put Eli, firmly bound, into an empty house. Later there was drumming and the two found a few old men by a fire chanting softly. Eli was stripped naked and tied to a post before them. George didn't want to make eye contact and stepped into the shadows. The old woman appeared in the circle of firelight. She was naked and had painted her sagging folds of flesh red. In each of her hands was a mussel shell with sharpened edges. Starting at his face she patiently and expertly used them to skin him while the men drummed and chanted.

Watt turned and vomited. George wished he had tomahawked him the day before. He never would get the sound of his scream out of his head. They left the next morning before anyone stirred taking two of the horses and leaving the third. They both avoided looking in the direction of the pole where Eli was bound, and neither of them said anything until they made camp for the night.

Chounteroute took the news of *Uttamussack's* demise badly. Richard Turner grudgingly acknowledged Watt's warrior status. The story of Eli's skinning was not mentioned. George offered the scalp he had collected to Suntetung and asked her to be his wife. He raised the issue of taking her sister as well. She told him he was crazy and firmly killed the notion but agreed to marry him.

After visiting Potecasi they returned to Chounteroute intending to live there, but the constable came with three men under a flag of truce. They were armed but left their weapons outside the stockade. Carrying gifts they asked to speak with the *werrowance* who sent for Sam Turner to translate.

After the gifts were distributed the constable said, "Brothers, we have come for the half breed who killed the captain of the militia. He must stand trial in an English court."

Chounteroute fingered the beads the men had given him. "The *wampum* is very good and the looking glass is nice, but steel knives and tomahawks are more useful."

The constable began to look irritated as he said, "Brother, give us the half breed and we will bring you a good tomahawk."

"Well, I am too old to make good use of a tomahawk, and the boy you want to hang went with the Chickahominy who you drove over the mountains."

"The Chickahominy fled before he killed the captain," the constable glowered.

"See how feeble I've become? I get confused about many things." Sam could not suppress his smile when he translated, neither could the other Englishmen.

"I think you are hiding the boy. Perhaps we will search the village and if we find him, perhaps we will burn it."

"Brothers, you call me a liar and you threaten me, but you left your guns at the gate. Perhaps it is I who will start a fire in a circle around you while you are tied to a post."

The white men jumped to their feet, but Richard Turner with his warrior clique materialized with the muskets they stole from where the Englishmen left them. Sam did not wait for Chounteroute to speak. "The boy followed the Chickahominy over the mountains." He reached for the white flag which his son was carrying and handed it to the constable. "Here," he said, "you will need this to pass to the plantations unarmed."

When the warriors prodded the four through the gate, Chounteroute told Sam, "Four more guns is a better gift than a tomahawk."

That night the newlyweds decamped to the swamp and Chounteroute died in his sleep.

The following autumn Suntetung delivered a son who was duly named George, and the following year she gave birth to a daughter, Jean.

* * *

In Williamsburg the recent sneak attack moved the Governour, His Excellency, Herbert Jefferies, to have a treaty drafted and he sent messengers, bearing gifts, to all the remaining Indian nations. Chounteroute's son, Serrahoque, and the chief men received the delegation at Chounteroute on a blustery day in the late winter. "Brothers," began the English interpreter, "the Governour has decided that it is time we put all enmity behind us and live together in peace. He has sent me to invite you to his great capital where he will celebrate with you and all the

Indian nations a treaty of mutual protection."

Serrahoque was a young man and had not much experience being king so he turned to Sam Turner to confer. "What do you think of this idea?" he asked the old man whose father had been English.

"The treaty is not worth the parchment it's written on," he replied, "but it won't cost us anything to sign it and there may be more presents for us."

Serrahoque saw wisdom in this and had always wanted to see Williamsburg. "Brothers," he said in his most kinglike tone, "we will come."

It was late May to the English point of view but to the Cheroenhaka it was *shautaroswache* when the chief men of the various tribes converged on Williamsburg. Each of the five nations sent delegations of five to ten men. The influx of surly looking savages put the town on edge in spite of the increased number of militia who stood guard at the Council chambers. On the morning of May 29, the speaker rose in chambers and read aloud the treaty wherein was stated that in exchange for the goodwill and protection of His Majesty's troops each tribe would be required to pay annual tribute in the amount of three arrows and twenty beaver pelts of good quality.

Sam Turner was too old to travel but if he had been present Serrahoque would have cuffed him. Nevertheless, he signed the treaty making the mark of the three rivers that represented the Cheroenhaka patrimony and he was presented with a crown and a purple robe which he donned with pride.

CHAPTER SEVEN

In Norfolk County Francis and Ann were bereft over the loss of their children to smallpox. Their plantation prospered with the aid of two slaves who had been born in the West Indies, and an indentured servant named Sarah. The family had moved into John's house since it was larger and better appointed. The servants lodged themselves in Frank's house quite comfortably.

Auteur Awwa delivered the six year old grandson of his friend and partner, George Skipper, Sr., to his brother Francis for the purpose of attending school. Ann took to him instantly and was delighted to have another Cheroenhaka speaker in the house. The couple found the boy a welcome diversion, although when school commenced after the harvest time, they saw little of him. A Presbyterian bishop from Sterling ran the closest school to the Skippers' plantation. His fire and brimstone terrified the boy, in fact all the boys, but it failed to put the fear of God into him. At Christmas he asked Ann why the teacher claimed God made everything when everyone knew the creator was called Quakerhunte. Ann thought before answering. Since being with Frank she had had little exposure to Christian religion, but she was aware that her sister-in-law was rather proud of having been baptized, although she was fairly certain that was the last time she had seen the inside of a church.

"The white people have different names for everything," she finally said hoping to avoid the rest of the conversation.

"But it's not the same story," George explained. "The teacher doesn't know that Otkum kept everyone in a bag until Quakerhunte released them."

"Maybe the creator tried something different when he made England."

"Mr. Marvin is from Scotland. We get our knuckles rapped if we call him English, and I got switched for telling the story of Quakerhunte."

"Then that explains it. If the people in Scotland had been freed from Otkum's bag, they would not be so mean spirited like Mr. Marvin." This seemed to satisfy the boy.

Late in winter when it seemed that the gloom of February would last forever, Frank was felled by a high fever. In a week he expired. Ann sat by Frank's rigid body moaning softly in the rhythm of an Indian chant until Sarah found her and tried to comfort her. Ben and Urias, the slaves, made a coffin and when the afternoon sun thawed the ground, dug a grave next to William.

A sense of isolation descended on Ann. Without even young George to cling to her, she felt as if she were the only person on Earth. The Negros and servant girl may as well have been members of another species, and the fact that they did not run was inexplicable. She lay on her bed staring at the ceiling rarely noticing the meals Sarah left until the sheriff came for the quit rent. When told that the master of the house had passed away and the mistress was in mourning, he barged into her room stood over the bed and said, "It may be a pity that Mr. Skipper is defunct, Indian, but the Governour will have his rent."

Ann looked the man in the eye, her face impassive.

She rose and crossed the room without speaking and pulled open the top drawer of the bureau from which she removed a stack of coins and a pistol. She cocked it and said, "There is your money, white man, take it and leave me in peace before I take comfort in putting this ball through the center of your chest."

"You'll not hear the end of this, squaw." He swept the rent from the top of the bureau and backed from the room. Her outrage with the white-devil was the tonic Ann needed. She left her room, took charge of the plantation and, working beside Ben and Urias, put the crops in the ground. Eventually the sheriff came and demanded a copy of Frank's will. "And I'll thank you not to point any guns at me," he added grinning.

Ann had a vague idea what a will was from the time of William's death. "My husband never showed me such a thing."

"Madam, I am afraid in that case that the court will have to decide the disposition of the land. It would not be a bad idea for you to engage the services of a lawyer." The sheriff's manner did not have the polarizing effect on her that it had before, but he wasted no time in retreating just to be safe. She was confused by what he said, and only had a hazy notion of what a lawyer was.

"Miss Ann, they mean to put you off the land," Sarah counseled. "You need a lawyer to try to stop them."

Ann thought she needed a gun more than a lawyer, but she consented to retain one. Sarah was the only person on the plantation who could write and her proficiency was seriously lacking, but she scrawled a childishly crude note requesting legal help. Ben was dispatched to Williamsburg with it. He had never been to Williamsburg and was scared out of his wits at the thought of attempting the journey. On the second day he met a planter.

"Boy, you wouldn't be running away, would you?"

"Oh, no suh. I's delivering dis here message for da Missus." He held the note aloft offering it to the man.

It took him a fair amount of effort to decipher the thing. "Who are you delivering this to, boy?"

"I doan rightly know, suh. I's 'posed to find my way to Willumsburg and deliver it to da first loyer I find."

"God help you. You be sure that when you deliver that note that you turn right around and get back to where you belong, and be sure you ask the lawyer to write you a safe conduct pass, otherwise somebody is going to take you for a runaway."

"Yessuh, I do it. Oh, an' there any chance you know which way is Willumsburg?" Ben's lack of guile got him past all the white men that he met on his journey, and against all odds, he eventually found his way to Williamsburg where it was not hard to find a lawyer. Thomas Jones, Esq. agreed to handle the matter. He hired a boat and took Ben along to identify the plantation of the late Francis Skipper. The trip that, with much wandering about, had taken Ben five days, they managed in a day by water. Ben led the man to the house and was relieved to have his task successfully behind him.

Thomas Jones was surprised to discover that his client was an Indian. "Mrs. Skipper," he began, "did your husband have any male relatives in the country?"

Ann appraised the lawyer and pronounced him adequate to herself before she replied, "He has two brothers. One has killed Englishmen and cannot leave his swamp. The other left several seasons ago."

"Do you know where the brother who is not hiding in the swamp left for?"

"To Carolana to the town named for the King."

"Ah, Charleston. Well, we must try to get a letter to him. I will dispatch it at once, and file the necessary pleas with the court. In the meantime, madam, you may reside here in peace. I shall be in touch." With that extremely brief meeting, the lawyer retired to the boat where he and the boatmen passed the night and departed for Williamsburg at daybreak. The letter addressed to John

Skipper of Charleston failed to find him. A year later, in late April, the clerk read the decision of the court.

"Two-hundred acres according to the most ancient and lawful bounds thereof, which Francis Skipper died seized of intestate and was found to escheat. Location Lower Norfolk County."

Thomas Jones was disappointed but he dutifully composed a letter to his client and put it into the post. It was faithfully delivered into the hands of the addressee, Ann Skipper, but nobody was there who could read it. When young George returned from school he read it to his aunt, but there was nobody there who could understand it. Eventually George returned to school carrying the letter which he showed to Mr. Marvin. The cranky old Scot read it and explained to the boy that the land whereon his aunt resided would revert to the crown and she would have to leave, however, since the session had just begun George could not relay the information for some months. By the time he returned to the plantation at Christmas time, he forgot. Ann forgot too, and was oblivious to the machinations happening beyond her comprehension until the man who had patented the land sight unseen arrived on horseback to inspect it.

"I didn't know the plantation came with a workforce and an overseer," he muttered. Then to Ann he said, "I take it you are the widow Skipper."

She admitted as much. "So what's to be done with you?" he mused. "Permit me to introduce myself. John Ivey, planter, and your husband's plantation is now mine."

The entire concept of land ownership was something that Ann had never fully assimilated. She considered shooting this man who said he was taking her late husband's land, and she considered marrying him. Finally she said simply, "I can't leave."

Ivey was as perplexed as her. "Why is that."

"My nephew needs a place to live while he goes to school."

Ivey chuckled saying, "Well, ma'am, maybe we can work out an accommodation."

He moved his wife and four children into the big house and, in lieu of paying rent for Frank's house, Ann provided the labor of Ben and Urias to the plantation. She retained Sarah as her personal servant although Sarah had gotten pregnant by Urias and for a time Ann attended her instead of how the indenture said it should be.

George went to school until he was fifteen and spent most of the free time with Ann who he insisted on calling Aunt Howerac. At the end of the term he walked alone to the plantation and found his aunt shelling beans in the shade of a grand old oak behind the house. "I've finished my studies and want to go home," he told her.

She handed him some beans to snap and looked him in his eyes. She had always thought he had doe eyes, but there seemed to have been some change. Shiftiness sparkled in them and his boyish grin had hardened into a manly smile. "Where is home, boy?"

"I'm not so sure, but it's not here anymore."

"That is good," she said nodding and the nodding became rocking. "It is time for me to go home too. There is something growing inside me that is a burden. I need the comfort of the people to bear me through this."

"Are you in pain, Aunt Howerac?"

"Sometimes. It comes and goes."

"Maybe you should go to Williamsburg to see a doctor."

"No, I should go to Chounteroute to see a shaman."

The boy stood to press his cheek to hers and pat her shoulder. "Of course you're right. Let's go tomorrow."

"We will go soon. No need to rush."

Ivey was put out at losing his tenant but took it with good grace. "So, where will you go?" he asked George who brought him the news.

"We're going home to our Indian town."

"Wouldn't it be more fitting for an educated young

man to find his way among the plantations?"

George was amused by that. "No, sir" he said, "I'm an Indian. I need to find my way with my own kind."

Sarah's indenture had expired after seven years but she continued to work on the plantation to be with Urias. However, she could not bring herself to move to the Indian town. "Sell Urias to Mr. Ivey," she pleaded to her mistress.

"Where I'm going, I'll need Urias more than I'll need money," she argued.

"But you're breaking up our family."

"You can come with us."

Sarah looked terrified and said with venom, "I won't have my children growing up like Indians."

"What's wrong with that?" Howerac sounded more puzzled than angry.

Sarah realized her faux pas and dissembled, "Well, it would be all right for you, but I'm white."

"That's right and your children are half black, but my people will accept you anyway."

Howerac was adamant. Urias went and Sarah and the children stayed. She had her personal effects and those of her entourage loaded onto a hay wagon, and began the trip west. She drove the wagon while George and the two slaves walked.

Eteshe Ena was running the town that still bore her husband's name in spite of the fact that her son, Serrahoque, was titular king. The queen had gotten more frugal, if that was possible, since the death of her extravagant spouse. She hoarded food and refused to permit feasts for frivolous reasons. The prospect of new mouths to feed did not sit well. When she was told Howerac intended to stay she asked her, "How will we feed all these people?"

"You silly old woman," she snapped, "I have two slaves to grow food for me."

"It's is months until harvest time. I do not have

enough food for you until you can grow your own."

"This is my town," she argued. "Where is my brother?"

"You have been gone too long. Chounteroute is no longer your town, and your brother does not live here. He moved to Assamoosick when the people from Tamahiton went there." Eteshe Ena folded her arms and looked away.

* * *

George loved the river and went to have a look at it while Howerac and Eteshe Ena argued. Two young girls playing in the water were startled by his sudden appearance. They froze at the sight of person wearing English clothes and waded toward the opposite shore. "Don't leave," he shouted in Cheroenhaka and they stopped. "Can I join you?"

"It's cold," one said.

"I don't care."

"Take off your clothes."

He undressed slowly staring at her stunning breasts and the fiery color of her hair. It was cold and when the depth was near his crotch he hesitated. The girls came to him taking his arms one pulling one pushing. Their touch gave him an erection which made them giggle and embarrassed him enough to wade deeper to let the chill dampen his arousal. That was when Howerac arrived on the bank.

"George," she called, "we're leaving. We won't stay here as long as that she-wolf runs Chounteroute."

"Do we have to go now?"

Smiling broadly she said, "No, we can leave tomorrow. I just wanted to let you know." She returned to the longhouse.

George returned his attention to the girls. "What are your names?" he asked while splashing water at them.

Giggling, the taller redhead answered, "This is Dekanee

Queru and I'm Mary Bailey."

"Are you related to my father's friend, Watt Bailey?"

"Sure. He's my father and I've got a brother called that too. Now you tell us your name."

"George Skipper."

"I've met your father. You have the same name."

"Yeah, there's a lot of Georges in my family."

"Who is the woman who wanted you to leave?"

"That's my aunt. Her name is Howerac, but English people call her Ann."

"If my name was hairy, I'd change it too," said the other girl.

"Her full name is Howerac Unke."

Dekanee Queru asked, "Why is she called that?"

"Why do you think?" George retorted.

"Do you think she was born hairy?"

"I don't know. Maybe she changed her name when she grew up."

"Are you going to leave?" Mary asked.

"I suppose so. I haven't seen my parents in a long time."

"Maybe you can come back sometime."

"I will as soon as I can."

It got too cold to play in the water so they went into the stockade to stand by the fire. When they were dry they redressed, and George went to find his aunt. "I see you take after your father and his father before him," she said when he found her in the longhouse.

"Is that bad? Mr. Marvin said we ought to keep our carnal urges in check."

"Why did he tell you to do that?"

"He said we'd go to Hell if we give into them."

"Your Uncle Frank used to say I'd go to Hell if I didn't control my need to take him between my legs, but he never refused to go there."

George looked at her curiously and felt the yoke of Marvin's civilizing influence slip from around his neck.

"The English have some strange ideas," he concluded.

"They have the same ideas that we do, but they say they don't."

"Hell must be a very crowded place, then."

"I often thought that."

"Where are we going?" the boy asked.

"Assamoosick," she said. "When the English started raising plantations near Tamahiton, the people went to Assamoosick. The viper that calls herself queen said my brother went there, probably to get away from her after Chounteroute died. I don't know how he could live with her without cleaving her skull open with a tomahawk."

George grinned at the thought.

Assamoosick was nearly as far northwest from Chounteroute as Norfolk County was northeast. The party arrived there on the second day. It was a raw looking settlement, not having been established for long. There was no stockade and the houses seemed a fusion of Indian and English style, posts set into the ground with logs lashed to them, mud in the chinks, and either hide or bark roofs. Howerac settled into her brother's house and put Ben and Urias to the task of building her one of her own. George wandered about the town and explored the swamp. It was loud with frogs and egrets that hunted them. The water was black and still and the air buzzed with mosquitoes. He sat on a log and daydreamed about Mary Bailey, but the mosquitoes were very distracting—to the extent that he could not keep the image of her body in his mind. The red hair fascinated him and he wanted to explore it with his fingers.

After a few days he was bored and told his aunt he was going to Potecasi. "You should," she told him. "It's been too long since you saw your family."

"You're my family, too."

"I know. Tell them I'm well and where I am."

"Sure."

She gave him a bag of food and Frank's musket. He

left alone and on foot only to stop before midday to take shelter from a storm beneath an ancient beech tree. Later the heat rose and the air was damp. He had to take a long detour around a branch of the swamp and before the end of the first day he knew he was lost. Other times travelling to Potecasi he had started from Chounteroute and the route was second nature to him. The route was to the south but the swamp pushed him west. Though he felt himself capable enough, anxiety would not stop rising and he agonized over returning to Assamoosick where he could find someone who knew the way. That night he made a cold camp and completely wrapped himself in his blanket to get some relief from the mosquitoes even though the air was sweltering. Sleep would not come and his fretting would not go. It was not enough to worry over being lost, he dredged every incident of shame and regret from the back his mind and relived it. He rehashed the isolation of first being left with his aunt and uncle, emptiness of the time after Frank died, the impotent rage of the time some older boys beat him and kicked him after school, and the uncertainty when he thought Ann would be put out of her house and fear when she told him she was sick. So in discomfort and distress the starless night crawled past interminably until he finally did fall asleep.

It was still dark when he was jolted awake by a tongue in his ear. Flinching, he squawked and tried to see what it was in the nearly total darkness, and he would not have been able to tell if it hadn't barked. He held his hand forward and the dog tentatively sniffed and licked it then it crouched with its nose between its paws and began to play. George patted the ground before it, and it jumped back then lunged forward growling and pawing the ground. The two played for a time in the pitch black until the dog simply lay down next to him and went to sleep. Thoroughly awake, he sat with his back to a tree and returned to his worrying while time simply stood still. He was almost in a panic when he thought he saw a brightening if the eastern sky. Dawn came ever so slowly. Finally he was able to see the dog. It was bigger than a hound but smaller than a mastiff with a great mass of gray fur that was enormously matted with burrs and stickers.

The dog woke, sat and made eye contact, even though the eyes were hidden by fur, with its tongue hanging out of the side its mouth. The sun finally rose and everything was fine, so the pair stood and went to find the way to Potecasi.

"You look like a dog in a picture Mr. Marvin had. He said it was Scotland and there was a black and white dog herding sheep with black faces." The dog reacted to his voice with its head cocked and one ear forward. "What am I going to call you? Maybe Marvin. No, that's a lousy name and I don't want to think of the miserable bastard every time I call you. *Cheer* means dog in Cheroenhaka, but it means something in English too, so that would be a stupid name. What do you think?"

The dog woofed.

The sun was still below the treetops when a village came to view. It was tiny and desolate, not having more than a dozen houses. George was reluctant to approach not knowing who lived there but the dog went ahead so he followed. A man sat on the ground with his back against his house apparently asleep. The dog stopped and growled which made the man look.

"Does he bite?" George was surprised to hear him ask in Cheroenhaka.

"No, he's friendly," he replied though he really knew nothing about the animal's nature.

"Are you hungry," the man asked without showing any sign of rising.

He nodded.

The man turned his head toward the door of his house and called, "Woman, bring this boy some food." Then to George he asked, "Where are you going?"

George sat in front of him and replied "Potecasi."

"Where's that?"

"Somewhere south of here. I got a little lost yesterday."

"What's there?"

"It's where my family lives."

The man grunted and his wife came from the dark doorway with a bowl of corn and beans. She gave it to George and returned to the house without a word. He ate in silence for a time until the silence felt awkward. "I never knew this village was here," he said by way of making conversation.

"We watch the *quiocosine*."

Watching the cemetery struck George as being a thoroughly tedious occupation. He'd seen a burial ground on an English plantation with its wooden crosses but he had never seen one of his own people's. "Where is it?"

The man looked closely at him as if he wasn't sure he could be trusted with the information. Finally he raised an arm and pointed. "Follow the path."

"Thank you for the corn," he said standing and feeling uncomfortable with the taciturn individual. He whistled at the dog and turned to the path.

A short way from the decrepit village the ground was cleared of trees and short mounds were piled haphazardly. He walked among them noting much variation in height though none were much taller than him. It was eerily still and oppressive. Even the cicadas were silent. The dog stayed close and kept looking at him until, as if to say he'd had enough of the place, he lifted his leg and pissed on a mound.

"Oh, that wasn't nice. Let's get out of here."

* * *

Potecasi changed each time he returned. Indians and half breeds from sundry tribes came to escape the English intrusion, and runaway blacks from the plantations arrived and mingled. When young George went to his parents' house he also found his grandfather who greeted him warmly and sent an order to have a hog butchered and spitted. The feast that followed caused the boy to reflect on how it differed from those he knew at Chounteroute. The people sat at tables, a fiddle was added to the drums and rattles, the dancing was more spirited and involved men and women together, and most of the revelers were attired.

"So, now that you have a proper English education, will you be staying with your family or be going back to civilization?" his grandfather asked.

"I've come home and I don't want to leave again."

"That's my boy."

"I was always an outsider to the plantation boys," he confided pensively. Then he added, "Aunt Howerac is sick."

"What's the matter with her?"

"She doesn't know. She gets pains in her belly and it hurts to touch."

"She hasn't gotten herself with child has she?"

The boy laughed. "I don't think so, Grandpa. She took all her stuff to Chounteroute, but Eteshe Ena wouldn't let her stay so she went to Assamoosick."

George sounded nostalgic when he said, "Things haven't been the same since the old king died. We'll have to get up there to see her soon. Meantime, let's not have anymore sad talk tonight. This is your homecoming party."

"Thanks, Grandpa. Did you see my dog?"

"Fine animal. Could use some soap and water, though."

The boy's father came and urged him to join the dance which he did, but he had inherited his grandfather's sense of rhythm and shortly retired. Suntetung hugged him laughing. "Now that you're back with you own people, you'll soon get better," she told him.

"I hope so. That was embarrassing."

An older boy who was full blooded and came to the feast in breechclout and paint laughed at him and said, "It's time to stop being a white boy and time to become a warrior."

George felt his balls shrivel. "Not all the white customs are bad," he said lamely.

"I guess you were among the English too long and lost the spleen to become a warrior."

"We don't need any warriors at Potecasi," the most senior George interrupted. "We have the swamp."

"You may be right about Potecasi," George, Jr. challenged his father, "but what about the other towns?"

"That is a different story," he conceded, and the youngest George absorbed this with apprehension.

* * *

The next morning his grandmother, Mary, gave him a bar of soap and the use of a wooden wash tub. He spent the whole day trying to make an inroad into the dog's coat. Many of the mats were hopeless and had to be cut, but at the end of the day it was a white dog that jumped to lick his face.

"Owheryakun! That's what I'll call you," he announced.

Mary winced, "That's a little long. Why don't you just call him Whitey?"

"But he's and Indian dog."

"I really doubt that, dear," she smiled the grandmothers' smile.

"Maybe you're right. Whitey it is."

CHAPTER EIGHT

John, Ann and their son, William arrived at the mouth of the Ashley River to find that a town of sorts now stood there. A few tall, narrow frame houses with verandas on their shady sides fronted the tabby sidewalk. There was an inn and a Government House as well as a few taverns. The family found residence at the inn and John immediately began inquiring as to the availability of a plantation.

"There is a gentleman by name of Taylor who is here in the inn," the innkeeper told him. "I have heard him say that he intends to sell his holdings and remove himself to England for reasons of health."

"When you see him would you kindly ask that he call at our room?"

"Surely. I believe he is out making inquiries as to his passage."

The innkeeper introduced John to Mr. Walter Taylor that evening in the common room. "Would that we had met a fortnight ago," he said, "the plantation was sold at a discount to a certain John Meader, and it's sweet piece of land, too. On the river, not altogether marshy, and some decent buildings all ready in place. It'll pay you to talk to this Meader for I believe him to be a speculator, but don't offer more than fifteen pounds and don't settle for more than twenty."

"How big a parcel is it?"

"Just not twenty acres and all of it usable."

"Where can I find this John Meader?"

"Oh, he was my neighbor. Has a plantation just to the north of mine. If you've a mind to on the morrow, what say we go have a look and see how amenable Meader is to parting with it? There's nothing for me to do until there's a ship bound for England. Got to get treatment. Dearth of doctors here is a bit of an inconvenience."

John readily agreed and then he and Ann had to endure a lengthy description of Taylor's unfortunate condition. In the morning to spare Ann the discomfort of a horseback trip, John hired a boat to take the four of them up the river. They arrived by midday at the mouth of Noisette Creek where Taylor directed the boatman to go ashore. The house was set on a rise away from the river. It was rough sawn planks with a puncheon floor, three rooms and kitchen lean-to. Fruit trees had been planted to the rear and a barn of sorts stood beyond that. The fields were gone to weeds as Taylor's health prevented him from attempting a crop in the previous season.

"Looks like a great store of work," William grumbled.

"No worse than starting out in Virginia," John advised him.

"Yeah, well I wasn't born then so it didn't bother me so much."

Taylor pointed beyond the barn. "Meader's house is that way about a twenty minute walk. You can't miss it. I believe I'll wait for you in the shade."

A grove of oaks stood between the parcel that had been Taylor's and the home of John Meader and the path through it was well choked with poison ivy. "I'll be scratching for a month," Ann predicted.

John kept his peace.

Mr. Meader was being paid a visit by the Barker family, Thomas, Sarah, Susan and Anne. He was somewhat surprised to find the Skippers emerging from the woods. "How is Taylor doing?" he asked after explanations and introductions.

"He's resting in the shade at his former homestead apparently drained by his consumption," John replied.

"He's a man of many problems. Perhaps Mr. Barker will excuse us for talking business during his social call?" Meader said to the group.

"By all means, Meader," Thomas Barker said. "Take as long as you need. We'll relax and partake of your punch."

The Barker girls took William aside to converse on youthful topics. Ann chatted with Thomas and Sarah while John and Meader walked out of earshot. "You've seen the place. It's a fine piece of land, so how much are you prepared to give for it?"

"Fifteen pounds cash in hand," John offered.

"Well, now, it's worth at least twenty-five."

"Twenty then."

"Done," Meader said, and extended his hand. John shook it and Meader continued, "I'll have a deed drawn within the week and find you at the inn." They returned to the others and the newcomers became acquainted with their neighbors.

In time John stood saying, "Perhaps we ought to relieve old Taylor. We'll need to get back to Charleston before dark."

"Oh, yes," Meader concurred, "else he'll bend your ear with his ailments. Probably will anyway."

"William," John shouted, "we're leaving."

"Oh, when you're settled, will you call on us?" Anne asked as he was rising.

"I surely will. It's been a pleasure making your acquaintances. Good day, now." Suddenly William had a better opinion of his new home.

John admitted Meader and his lawyer to their room late in the afternoon when sunlight was softening and the heat abating. The lawyer carried a folio of ledger pages with the deed inscribed in a flowery hand. It began: "To all people to whom these presents shall come I John Meader of the province of Carolana send greeting."

"Here, Skipper, we had to leave a blank space after your name as we didn't know where you hark from," Meader pointed to the fifth line of the document.

"As I said, we have recently removed from Virginia."

"Oh, no, we need your province of origin."

"Ah, well, my home in England was called Thiobridge Brassior," he replied and was struck in the gut by a pang of nostalgia at the loss of his patrimony and the cozy rents he never received. Ann saw the look on his face and felt it too.

"See here," the lawyer said, "that will never fit. Is the place most commonly known as Thiobridge or Brassoir?"

John smiled recovering from his sense of loss. "Brassoir is the common name."

"Very good," the man conceded, "that fits without crowding. Shouldn't want to have to do it all again." The deeds were signed, witnessed and sealed. Each man kept a copy of two pages describing the land, the appurtenances, the adjoining estates and their owners.

"Who's this Ohoch Midwinter character?" John inquired. "Sounds like an Indian name."

"Indeed. Full blooded. Don't know how he came by the place, but it's a fine plantation some five-hundred acres in indigo and cotton, plenty of slaves. Keeps to himself mostly. Never met his wife. Decent sort, though. Gone over to the King's religion, or says he has. I've got no truck with him."

"Curious race, Indians," John said meditatively.

* * *

He and William set themselves to building berms, ditches and weirs to flood the field for his rice crop. It flourished and John had the satisfaction of achieving his goal and showing a profit, for the commodity was much prized in the marketplace. William, meanwhile, was calling frequently at the Barker plantation. At first he was ambivalent as to which daughter he preferred, but his interest quickly gravitated to Anne who was the younger of the two. Each time he made his way to Oak Grove, which was the name of Barker's sprawling estate, he skirted the land of Ohoch Midwinter, in truth he trespassed, though no one ever challenged him. On a perfect evening in December he passed the indigo processing tanks and was hailed by a man who was stirring air into the mash.

William responded, "Greetings, neighbor, working late, aren't you?"

"You work late everyday on this plantation," the man replied with animosity in his tone.

"How's that?" William asked.

"My master is a beast. I'll be stirring this slop past dark for a dollop of pemmican and water, and it's the rod across my back if I object."

"Oh, so you've been put out."

"Put out and put upon these three years with seven more to go. Then do I have a trade? Hah! There ain't no trades on this plantation, just work like stirring this shit."

"Well, I'm William Skipper," he said stepping forward with outstretched hand, and while he shook hands with the man, he saw his face clearly for the first time. A compulsion to examine that face made him stare so intently he forgot to release his hand. On recovering he said, "Sorry, I just thought you seemed very familiar."

"I might say the same about you. Name's Patrick Whaley. You from hereabouts?"

"My old man just bought the Taylor plantation from John Meader."

"Did he, now? Don't suppose he'd like to buy out an

indenture?"

"Probably not. He seems to think of me as his servant. So how did you come to get put out?"

"I ain't got no father, ya see, and my mother married a right bastard who didn't want me 'round. I didn't want him 'round neither, but my mother went along with it to make him happy. Getting put out might not be so bad if it was to a human being. My master is a bloody savage, and I do mean that literally."

"Have you tried to make a complaint to the Quarter Court?"

"And how would I do that? I haven't set foot off this plantation in three years."

"Perhaps I could do it on your behalf."

"When he found out I complained it would be worse for me. There's more. He's a sodomite. So far I've been spared the pleasure, but I've seen a runaway slave brought back in chains get bent over a rail an' given a lesson he won't soon forget. I mean to run, but I've got to *know* I won't get caught."

"Sorry to hear all that, but I am glad to make your acquaintance just the same, and if there's anything I can do to help, I will."

When William told his parents about Patrick Whaley he said, "I thought I might be looking in a mirror."

"He carries the curse of the Skippers, does he?" John laughed.

Ann asked, "How old is he?"

"Just about my age."

She looked troubled. "Oh, dear, you don't suppose?"

John's laughter kept coming. "Do you recall the peculiar state Will was in when he came home from Charleston? Maybe his return to Virginia was more of a fugitive nature."

"How could we find out?"

"Why would we want to find out?"

"Well, he might be your flesh and blood, and he's in a

distressful place."

"It's not our business. We can't meddle with a lawful indenture."

"You can't let your own nephew be used that way."

"We don't know he's Will's, but just the same, I'd like to have a look at him. I'll ask Midwinter if I can hire him for a couple days. He could help shore up the berms."

* * *

It was a rainy, cold morning not good for much else when John and William went to see the Indian planter.

"Morning, Mr. Midwinter, we're your neighbors to the north," he said when the house nigger showed them to his master.

"Is that why you are interrupting me?"

"No, it's because introducing yourself to your neighbors is a neighborly thing to do."

"I don't have time to be neighborly."

The man's rudeness amused John a little more than it irritated him. "Suit yourself. I was going to make a business proposition, but perhaps you're too busy to hear it."

"I know who you are. Your son uses my plantation for a bridal path."

"He's just helping keep the weeds down," he baited.

"So what's your business?"

"Well, we could use some extra help and I've heard you have a man with a strong back. I'd like to hire him from you for a couple of days."

"I don't hire my servants out." He turned his eyes back to his accounts.

"Glad to hear you're doing so well as not to need extra income, so we'll not bother you much more, but tell me, how did an Indian come into such a prosperous plantation?"

Midwinter raised his gaze and looked the two men in

the eyes one after the other. His scowl hadn't waxed or waned since their arrival. "I kidnapped the planter's wife and fucked her better than he ever did so she came over to me and I killed him then married her and the place is now mine under your English law."

"I hear some revisions in the right of inheritance are being worked on in Parliament," John muttered and took William by the arm, turning and leaving he made a dismissive flap of his fingers behind his back.

Outside William said, "Right proper piece of shit, isn't he? Just like Patrick said."

"Still want to have a look at Patrick."

"So let's go over by the indigo tanks. That's where I met him."

He was there draining liquid from one tank to the next in the stair step series.

"Ho! Patrick, we just came from meeting your master. You didn't do him justice. He's a perfect arsehole," William called to him as they approached.

"Only kind of perfection he achieves," Patrick wiped the rain and indigo slop from his hand before he offered it.

John took the extended hand and like William had he gripped it overly long while he looked at that face. "Son, William tells me you never knew your father. Did you ever hear his name?"

"No, mother refused to talk about him. When I was old enough to understand under what circumstances I came about, I could see she was pained at the thought of him and she would brook no questions."

John took his chin and turning his face to profile said, "Mr. Whaley, I think properly you ought to be called Skipper."

Patrick looked from John to William and said, "Truth! There is a strong resemblance amongst us."

John smiled wryly. "There's one resemblance and it's hard to deny that there's little difference between one Skipper male and the next. Thank God it rarely afflicts the females. Well, Patrick, we tried to get your master to hire you out for a time, but he was intractable. Nevertheless, we'll see what we can to do to improve your situation."

Patrick dropped his head and shook it slowly from side to side. "I appreciate your concern, but there isn't a way out of my predicament short of flight or the grave."

"Choose the former over the latter, please," William interjected.

With that, they parted.

* * *

Polly Joyner, nee Whaley, was in Charleston shopping for a bolt of good linen, not that she was inclined to sew but her maidservant was especially handy. It had come to her attention that a certain William Skipper of Virginia had arrived in the area and it made her very nervous. The news had come to her through a circuitous route and she had not had the opportunity to interview anyone who had actually met the man. Her informant had said that a father and son of that surname had purchased land a little way up the Ashley which was sufficiently removed from her home several miles to the west that she had little fear of encountering them, but a two minded demon within her craved to know who this William Skipper was.

John and William went to Charleston specifically to call upon the attorney who had drafted the deed for Meader. It was a waste of time. The lawyer dismissed the matter as hopeless. Without being able to see a copy of the indenture, or having an eyewitness account of the misuse of Patrick Whaley, he could see no way to intervene. For this insight he charged three shillings.

"He needs to runaway to Uncle George's swamp," William opined when they were again on the street.

"It's a serious business to aid a runaway," John warned.

"I wouldn't really aid him. I'd just tell him where he could find a place to hide."

"And how would you do that? Neither of us has ever been there."

"But you know where it is, don't you?"

"Only generally, and my reckoning of where it is would be based on starting in Norfolk County."

Polly Joyner and her maidservant exited the yard goods shop and turned toward the advancing Skippers. She dropped the bolt of fabric that she was admiring and was unable to stifle a gasp.

"Laws, missy!" the black girl cried retrieving the fabric and making a fuss over brushing the dirt from it, "yous look like yous seen a haint."

John stopped short, puzzled by the peculiar response of the woman. "Begging your pardon, ma'am, did we do something to startle you?"

"Oh, I just," she stammered awkwardly, "it's just that for a moment I thought perhaps we had met."

"I don't believe I've had the pleasure. John Skipper at your service, and this is my son, William."

"William? William Skipper?"

"Generally a son takes the same name as his father, doesn't he?" he chided good naturedly.

"Yes, of course, it's just that I once, uh, knew a gentleman of that same name."

John had the sense that this woman had a backbone and could hold her own in a verbal sparring match, so he went for the opening. "By any chance did this encounter take place here nigh twenty years ago?"

"Why, yes, it was twenty years ago. You're related to him, aren't you? And what exactly do you mean by encounter?"

"Only a figure of speech, but unless there are more Skippers in this country than I know, that man was my cousin."

"Was?"

"He was killed by Indians soon after he returned from Carolana."

The bottom dropped out of Polly's stomach and she wasn't sure why. "I'm so sorry. We met only briefly, and it was so long ago."

"Yes, it was but I still miss him sorely," John's expression did not match the lugubrious note of the phrase. Smiling slyly he continued, "It's possible we have another acquaintance in common."

"Is it?"

"We have recently come to know an unfortunate individual by the name of Patrick Whaley."

"Oh, good Lord!" Her eyes widened and mouth gaped. Recovering she said, "What did your cousin say about me?"

"Be assured, madam, he did not mention you. Any assumption we have made about Master Whaley is based on family traits."

Polly sighed saying, "Yes, my memory of your cousin would surely have faded if I hadn't had his spitting image in front of me everyday. I guess you can never escape the past, but tell me, are you trying to spare me embarrassment when you say that he didn't mention me?"

"No, ma'am, I can tell you he was in a rare state when he returned, but he kept his silence."

"I suppose I appreciate that he protected my reputation, but it would unburden my heart to know the truth of why he left. He left without knowing about the child. Was he simply a rake?"

"Well, he was a man, and a Skipper man at that—one or two might have been known to womanize—but he was also an honorable man and would never have left you had he known."

"I believe you, sir. How different my life would have been," she mused. "How is my son?"

"Well, he is in rather difficult straits. I'm afraid that Mr. Midwinter misuses him." Then taking her arm and drawing her out of earshot of the young Negress he whispered near her ear, "I'm afraid he may flee his indenture."

She drew a sharp breath and said, "I hope he does."

John took his hand away and asked, "May I ask as to your name."

"Oh, I'm so sorry. Polly Joyner." She extended her hand to be shaken. "It's been a pleasure to know you, if somewhat saddening. I fear that we will not have the pleasure of social familiarity, however, there is no chance that my husband would miss the resemblance between you and his stepson, and that would be rather awkward."

"Of course. I understand."

"If you have occasion to see him again, please tell my son that I love him."

"Of course."

Polly said to her slave whose eyes were open so wide as to show white all around, "Come along, Lizzie, we have to get back to the inn. Mr. Joyner will be worried."

* * *

William's infatuation with Anne Barker took him across Midwinter's plantation with regularity so it was not long before he encountered Patrick Whaley at the indigo plant. "My father consulted an attorney who said there was nothing to be done for you, and by chance we met your mother. She sends her love."

"My mother? How did you know it was my mother?"

"She recognized a certain resemblance between us."

"How is she?"

"Quite fine, and she says she hopes you'll run away."

"I'd go today if I knew where to go that I wouldn't be found."

William hesitated before saying, "I know a place. My uncle is a fugitive. He has some land so far back in a swamp that no one can find him. He lives there with some friendly Indians and other runaways."

"Why would he take me in?"

"Because he likes the look of you. Of course he will take you in. Just tell him who you are."

"And who am I to him?"

"You're his nephew."

"I'm what?"

"You're my cousin."

He stood there with his mouth opening and closing and nothing coming from it. William continued, "Your mother confirmed it. Your father was my namesake, Uncle William."

Patrick got his wits back in order sufficiently to ask, "Is my father in this swamp?"

"No, sorry, he was killed by Indians when I was a boy."

"My God. I don't know what to make of this."

"I don't either, but I think you ought to get out of here soon. I'd hate to hear of my cousin getting skewered by that bastard Indian."

"You and me both, but how am I supposed to find your uncle's swamp?"

"He's your uncle too, remember. It's not going to be easy as none of us has ever been there, but it called Potecasi and it just a little bit below the border with Virginia, not too far from the coast. If you don't find it before you get into Virginia, ask directions to either of two Indian towns that are called Chounteroute or Assamoosick. In either place someone can guide you to Potecasi."

"I'll never remember the damned Indian names."

"Here, I wrote 'em down for you. You can read can't you?"

"Sure, I can read, but I'm a bit uneasy about Indians."

"Your new uncle is an Indian chief. They will take you in with open arms."

"Sweet Jesus! Who am I, and where am I going?"

"You're a Skipper, and you best get used to the idea."

William shook his cousin's hand and slapped his back, wished him luck and sent his regards along to his uncle

George, then he continued his quest for the hand, and presumably the body, of Anne Barker. She was a proper girl who kept her suitor's hands in check, in fact rarely allowed herself to be alone with him.

John invested the proceeds of the sale of his crop in slaves which offered sufficient free time for William to indulge a whim he inherited from his namesake. He developed a brick works on the plantation, and found an ample market in Charleston for his product and skill as a bricklayer. He was to the point of relocating to the city when his father was felled by the ague. The administration of Peruvian bark rallied him only a little. William was forced to assume the management of the plantation. John hastily made a will in which he left the estate to his son with the proviso that Ann was let to reside there all her natural days.

On a night when the air was heavy with a gathering storm, and an owl dolorously called for her mate, John expired. William's grief was silent and inward, Ann sobbed stoically.

CHAPTER NINE

Patrick Whaley's indenture specified a new suit of clothes annually, but he never got it; therefore, he had nothing to pack except what little food he stole from the kitchen while the cook was asleep. A half moon lit the trail and cast deceptive shadows until the sky began to lighten. All night he debated whether to travel by day. Reasoning that he only had a six hour start on the hounds, he decided he had no choice but to keep walking and in fact before the sun reached zenith he heard baying. At a dead run he made for the river and splashed into the shallows. When waist deep he dived and swam as far as he could underwater. The Ashley River was a half mile wide and still tidal at the place he was crossing. Flood tide made the current nearly stagnate which may have been the only reason he didn't drown. When he hauled himself onto the opposite bank his heart was pounding against his ribs so hard that he felt it throbbing in his ears. He craved to lie where he fell but he knew the Indian would drive the dogs into the river and swim his horse. His lungs ached, his throat constricted and his mouth was dry, but he kept running, and even though it was slower, he slogged through water whenever it was possible. It did no good. The dogs followed his scent through the air. Still, he stayed ahead of them, and by sunset Midwinter abandoned the chase and made camp for the night.

At dawn the Indian made his way directly to the Joyner plantation and confronted Abel Joyner about the runaway. "Your boy ran," he told Joyner. "You pay me what I gave you for him."

"Offer a reward. You'll get him back sure," Joyner argued, and Polly heard the heated voices through the open window.

"Patrick ran?" she asked.

Midwinter looked at her. "Yes, he ran and I'm glad to rid of him, but I want the money I paid."

"You'll let him go if you get the money back?"

"It's not my problem that he ran," Abel Joyner said before the Indian could answer Polly.

She turned on her husband: "He won't come here. You're rid of him either way. Now give the damned savage his money and be done with it."

Midwinter said, "I don't want him back. He's worthless, but you give me the money."

"You'll give him the money, Abel, or there'll be Hell to pay, I promise you that," Polly warned him with clenched teeth, and he went into the house to get the money.

The money placated Midwinter and Joyner said to him, "Those are fine looking hounds. Let me know if you want to sell any."

"Dog's worth more than your boy."

"Well, he's not really my boy. He's my wife's bastard. You know that."

Midwinter gave Polly a hard look. She returned his gaze but a tear welled in her eye. He took the money, of course, but he also used some of it to advertise a reward.

* * *

On the third day Patrick was far from settled territory where anyone who saw him would assume that he was a runaway because he was unarmed, unprepared and utterly lost, so he traveled only by night. The moon was nearly full and even in the forest he picked his way with relative ease so he saw the man even before he heard him splashing through the cypress knees. That he was a black man was unmistakable and, therefore, also a runaway. Patrick sat on a log and waited for the escaped slave to get out of sight before he continued. When the light was rising he found fairly dry ground and a good bed of pine needles and promptly fell asleep. The jab of a fly bite woke him, he slapped the stinging spot and that startled the Negro who was sleeping next to him.

"What are you doing here?" Patrick demanded. The slave just looked at him. He had scarification on his cheeks and his bare chest. "I said what do you think you're doing. Go away."

"I knows yous runnin'," his voice was low and deep.

"Yeah, and I intend to keep running, alone."

"I's got nuthin' t'eat."

"Neither do I, now git!"

"I go witch you."

"No, you don't. I'm going alone."

"I doan knows da the way."

"Neither do I."

"We finds it."

"I'll find it by myself, and you find it by yourself."

"Wheres you goin'?"

"I'm going to Potecasi Swamp, alone." He stood, reckoned which way was north, and started walking with the Negro right behind. "Do not follow me," he insisted and gave the man a shove that put him to the ground. When he resumed his march the African waited twenty paces before following which excited Patrick to run and also his shadow. He slowed and grumbled to himself, "I'll lose him in the dark."

It didn't work. When the sun rose, there he was, fifty feet back grinning foolishly. Patrick groaned and so did his stomach which had not taken nourishment for a day and a half. The black man may have heard that rumble for he produced a turtle from the pocket of his baggy trousers and held it toward Patrick whose eyes got wide.

"Truce," he said and approached his pursuer.

"Cook," the slave said.

"Cook, indeed."

Neither of them had a knife, but Patrick had flint and steel with which he got a fire going in short order. The turtle objected to being roasted and did his best to crawl out of the flames. They held him with a stick until he succumbed and thereafter baked peacefully within his shell. Getting at the meat proved quite a chore until the Negro bashed the shell apart with a rock and teased the flesh away from the carapace with a stick. It was a meager meal but appreciated and bonded the two together.

"What's your name?" Patrick asked when the last scrap of meat had been picked from the turtle's shell.

"Cavauso. You's?"

"Patrick. I take it you were born in Africa."

"Doan knows. Ngomo," he said pointing to his chest.

"Did you come in a boat?"

"Long times boat."

"Well, I see we will have plenty to talk about on the trail, so let's get some sleep."

They resumed their trek before it was dark and Cavauso quickly discovered grapes that were sour and made them grimace but they ate them gladly and carried as many and they could. Some days later they stumbled upon some Indians who seemed mostly indifferent to them but offered dried meat and pemmican. The Indians were completely unintelligible which meant they offered no clues as to the whereabouts of Potecasi, Chounteroute, nor Assamoosick. Eventually they found an Indian who pricked his ears at the sound of Assamoosick. He was unable to communicate in either English or Ngomo, but he laboriously drew a map on the ground and pointed a great deal. The pointing was more informative. As it happened, once they got near Assamoosick the terrain, or more accurately the lack of it, directed them to the dry ground where the town sat. Patrick's countenance was the key to the city. He was dumbfounded.

"I never thought of this nose as anything but a curse," he confided in Cavauso who grunted uncomprehendingly.

The chief man at Assamoosick took them to Howerac who was prostrate on her deathbed. "I'm seeing a ghost. Who are you, boy?" she croaked.

"Lately I'm told my father was named William Skipper."

"He was cousin to my husband. I miss them both."

"You knew him then?"

"Oh, yes," she began to cough but was able to continue. "He was a good man though he seemed frustrated much of the time. I would have given him release but my husband wouldn't allow it. I never understood English customs. I knew it was bad to do it with brothers, but I thought cousins were all right."

Patrick brushed that aside. "I was told that I should go to Potecasi Swamp, but I don't know how to find it."

"Just wait here. Someone will come from there to bring whiskey, then you can go back with him."

"Whiskey?"

"Maybe rum."

Someone did come the very next day. It was George Skipper, Sr., and though he was carrying some rum, the purpose of the visit was to see Howerac.

"I heard you were under the weather," he told her.

"No, I'm dying, George. Dr. Tom has given up. It's all right. I haven't cared much for living since Frank died."

"You're too tough to die. I expect you'll be on your feet in no time."

"Not this time. There is something growing inside me.

When it gets as big as a head that will be the time for me. I wish it would hurry. Did you see the boy?"

"What boy?"

"He says he is William's son."

"John's William?"

"No, the dead William."

"You don't say. So William spread some wild oats."

"It was probably his man juice. Oats won't do the job."

"Yes, well, then where did he come from."

"The other William found him and told him to come find you. He ran away from his master."

"Oh, he got put out did he? I'll go find him. Don't die in the meantime."

"Don't be a long time then."

He found Patrick and Cavauso huddled in the longhouse and he was thunderstruck. "There's no mistaking who you are," he told him. "Did your father know about you?"

"No. I was raised with the name of Whaley. Ma never told me nothin' about him. In fact she said she found me under a rock."

"Now, that was right unkind." George looked at the black man. "I take it you're both runaways."

Patrick nodded. "William said you got a place I'd be safe. I found Cavauso here in the woods."

"I think we've got room for you. We'll go after Howerac dies or gets better. Who's taking care of you here?"

"The sick woman's got some slaves. They bring us food. We mostly stay in here 'cause we're kinda nervous around the Indians."

"You best get over that. You're going to *be* Indians from now on."

Howerac didn't make them wait long. She died in her sleep. After they buried her George told the slaves they were free and offered to take them to Potecasi. Ben accepted, but Urias chose to go back to Sarah. "Do as you like. I'd do the same myself, but you be mighty careful getting there. According to the powers that be in Virginia you're still a slave, and I am in no position to free you according to the law," George warned him.

* * *

Watt Bailey had married a white girl who was orphaned when some of Richard Turner's band massacred her family. She was fair and Mary Bailey was born with red hair and hazel eyes. This, among other attractions, drew young George to her side with regularity. The pair would steal to secluded places and excite each other in corporeal play. Mary's mother became suspicious and gave her daughter a sermon that harked to the time of her Presbyterianism. Mary took it to heart. The next time she and George were alone she told him, "We can still touch each other but I can't let you put that in me anymore."

"Why?"

"Because it's a sin."

"It's a sin to get me all excited and not finish it," he insisted.

"I'll finish it. You just can't get any of that stuff in me."

George decided to take what he could get and continued to spend all his free time with her, but eventually he felt compelled to return home, at least for a visit. The Oxendines had a daughter who was a little older than George. She noted his return to Potecasi and sought him to say, "George, if you get us some of your grandfather's rum I'll let you do it to me."

"Really?"

She gave him a wry look. "Well, don't wait until I change my mind."

"Where will I find you?"

"Old Jack Quinto's barn. He's deaf and won't catch

209

us."

"I'll be there as soon as I can get it."

He sneaked into the room where his grandfather stored his finished product and filled a small jug from a keg that had been tapped for daily usage. He resisted, with straining effort, the urge to run with it to Quinto's barn. Inside was dark and hot with the heady smell of the fodder stored there. Laura Oxendine was hiding in the shadows and jumped on his back. Together they fell on the haystack.

"Hey, you're gonna make me spill it."

"How much did you get?"

"A whole jug."

"Well, let's have some." He gave her the jug and she took a mouthful. She choked and lost most of it down the front of her dress.

"Don't take so much. It's really strong."

She tried again and passed it to George who drank a moderate swallow that made him gasp. When they had gotten a few mouthfuls down their burning throats, he set it aside saying sagely, "It will take effect pretty soon. You don't drink too much at once or you get sick." He sat back and looked at her not knowing how to start claiming his reward.

"Have you gotten really drunk before?" she asked.

"Sure," he lied.

"We drink beer all the time at my house, but it hardly does anything. Let's have a little more."

He gave her the jug and her hand touched his. "Here you have some more, too," she offered it back to him. He drank and then put his hand on hers. She laughed nervously and he stroked her arm but got no reaction. Moving closer he was searching for some sign as to how to begin but she remained impassive. His cheeks felt either flush from the rum or embarrassment and he became afraid she was changing her mind so he took her by the shoulders and laid her down on the hay. She complied smiling which emboldened him to proceed. By comparison to the tentative groping with Mary Bailey making love to Laura Oxendine was life threatening. She bucked and moaned and scratched and clawed panting to climax. The two lay spent sweating, she on her side with her head on his arm. "You're grand," she told him stroking his chest.

George felt mature, independent, and unencumbered, he began spending all his time with her to the consternation of his father who said, "I don't know what you see in that girl. She's nothing to look at."

"She knows how to make me happy," he defended.

"Oh, that," his father smirked.

Suntetung took it in stride though she didn't like the girl, George, Sr. and Mary shook their heads. They were preoccupied by their second youngest, John, who had turned eighteen with no observable compass. He had not attended school but had learned to read and write not that he ever applied either skill.

"Boy, you're useless as tits on a boar. It's time you find an occupation that suits you," his father warned.

From nowhere he answered, "I've a mind to be a joiner."

"A joiner? I didn't think you knew the term?"

"I've always wanted to do it and I know how I'm going to go about it."

"Oh? How's that?"

"I'm going to Virginia to put myself out."

George considered it. "Well, I've heard worse plans. You'll be on your own, though, I have few friendly connections in that country."

John left Potecasi nearly unnoticed since the buzz over young George and Laura Oxendine predominated. He found a certain James Alexander, carpenter, of Nansemond County who needed an apprentice and took his indenture for seven years.

The newly individuated George III, built a house with

the help of his father and grandfather, and took his paramour to live there. The Oxendines helped her move. "Aren't you going to marry her?" the eldest George asked.

"Maybe," was all the answer he had.

George's younger sister, Jean, was receiving calls from a certain David Herrin who was newly arrived at the Potecasi settlement. He was a farmer's son with respectable presence and Jean was smitten by him, but her father played relentless chaperone whenever Herrin called.

Suntetung did not acquire much English and she wanted to be precise in meaning, so she addressed her husband in Cheroenhaka when she said with considerable excitement, "You look away while your son ruts with that sow but you sit between your daughter and a good man! I think I'll start acting toward you the way you make Jean act toward him."

"But we're married," he whined.

"Never mind that," she growled.

George softened.

* * *

The next year John Skipper came back to Potecasi. "I can't do it," he said, "the man was a real arsehole and I'm not cutout for it."

His father doubted he was cut out for anything, but he asked, "Does your master know where you are?"

"I might have mentioned the name of the place, but I didn't exactly announce my destination when I sneaked out in the middle of the night."

George felt the inevitability of confrontation looming. "Boy, you vex me," was all he could say.

Under steady pressure, mostly from his grandparents, young George asked Laura to marry him and she said, "I've been ready to marry you from the first day in the old Quinto's barn." He immediately regretted it. He saw the ginger hued nether regions of Mary Bailey in his mind and his innards felt heavy. There was no clergy at Potecasi so the matriarch, Mary, administered the Cheroenhaka nuptial ceremony. Afterward, the couple retired to their house and did what they always did, but this time the elders were less disapproving.

George ached with guilt for not saying goodbye to Mary Bailey. It gnawed at him while he was making love to his wife and it rode heavily on him when he wasn't. "I'm going hunting," announced one evening.

Laura said, "You never go hunting."

"It's time I start. I need to do it and we need meat. I'll only be gone a few days."

"I can go with you. I'm not afraid to sleep on the ground."

"You'll be in the way."

"What's that supposed to mean?"

"Well, uh, I have to find the game and stalk it, move fast, and not have to worry about you making noise."

"And at night you'll be playing with yourself."

"Dammit! It's just a couple days and I'm going and you're not."

She threw a trencher at his head and ran into the bedroom. He slept on the floor in front of the fire, and before dawn he took his gun, mounted and rode the horse hard to Chounteroute.

"Why did you stay away so long," Mary asked obviously offended.

He lost his courage and groveled, "I had to help on the farm."

"Are you going to stay here now?" she was still defiant.

"Can't. I promised I would come right back."

"Well, why did you come at all," she kept hammering.

"Because I missed you."

"You really missed me?"

"Of course I missed you, I love you."

Her anger relented and she took his hand. "You want to take a walk?"

Now he was flummoxed. "I don't know."

"You don't know! You've been away a long time and I missed you too."

"Yeah, I want to take a walk, too."

He took her hand then asked, "How are things here?"

"There's been a lot of hunger. The English burn our fields to get us to leave. There has been some fighting and we steal their cows."

"There needs to be a permanent solution," his voice drifted away from the half formed thought.

When they got to the favored bed of pine needles Mary was voracious in taking control of their frantic coupling, so much so that George felt somewhat cowed although he got through it. "What about sin?" he asked sheepishly.

"Dammit, George Skipper, did you want me or not?"

"Yeah, of course I wanted you," he waited then he blurted, "I came to tell you I got married, though."

"You what?" She began pounding him with the sides of her fists. "You just said you loved me. What is wrong with you?" still pounding.

He rolled away from her onslaught and sat saying, "I don't know what I was thinking. It was a big mistake. I wanted you but you were too worried about going to Hell."

"Go away, you big nosed goon!" She tried to hit him again then she snatched her dress from the ground and began pulling it over her head, when she was mostly attired, she stomped from his sight.

"Wait," he called after her but she refused to turn. He stole back to where he left his horse and rode hard for Potecasi.

Laura received him stiffly, "So what did you shoot?"

"Nothing."

"Nothing?"

"I hurried back because I didn't want you to be mad at me."

"You were only gone a day. You didn't have time to

shoot anything!"

"I wanted to see you."

"Then you should have taken me with you."

"I know. I'm sorry. Let's don't quarrel."

"We'll see," she said and went to the bedroom again with a little less venom in her demeanor.

Later that night he tiptoed into the bedroom and slid along side of her. He caressed her and she submitted rigidly and without comment.

CHAPTER TEN

In Nansemond County, Virginia, James Alexander filed a lawsuit against John Skipper for fleeing indenture. The matter was moved to the Chowan Precinct in North Carolina and it took two years for the court to decide to send someone looking for him. One David Blake, an ambitious young magistrate, was given the task. After recruiting two cousins to watch his back, he headed in search of a place called Potecasi.

It was not hard to find the general area but the three met an Indian travelling from Potecasi to Chounteroute and asked directions. He was quick to point them in the wrong direction and then hurry back to warn George. The Skipper men and Patrick Whaley took arms and began watching the narrow and overgrown entrance to their refuge. When Blake and his team finally arrived, the youngest George, who was the only George not actually wanted, met them to see what was their business.

"We're here to arrest the body of one John Skipper for fleeing indenture," Blake told him.

"Wait here. I'll tell him the nature of your call."

"And have him run into that infernal swamp? Not

likely. We'll accompany you directly to Mr. John Skipper if you please."

George shook his head while saying, "My family is a little sensitive about who comes to visit. It would be in your own best interest to let me be the intermediary."

Blake made a move to seize George by the arm but one of the fugitive Skippers fired a shot into the bole of a tree directly beside him making a sharp splat and freezing the man where he stood.

"There are several more of us than there are of you," George said firmly. "Now, I will deliver your message to my cousin and we'll see if he decides to cooperate." With that he turned and left the three men stood there in a state of consternation.

"If I don't turn myself in they'll just come back with more men," John said in response to his cousin's report.

"And once they find us they are likely to remember a militia captain with his throat cut and a couple of dead settlers," the elder George opined.

John told his father, "Pa, I didn't mean to bring trouble down on you. I'll just go peacefully."

"Do what you have to, boy, but I'll send for a lawyer to represent you. There won't be much to come of this."

John got his horse and surrendered without incident. George traveled to Williamsburg with his grandfather's money and paid Thomas Jones, of Howerac's failed effort to keep Frank's land, to travel to Edenton to arrange bond. In the course of conversing with the attorney he asked, "How could Indians go about getting the King's protection from settlers?"

Jones looked astonished. "That's a pretty tall order. It would take a petition to the Council and need the blessing of his Highness, the Governor, but there already is a treaty that is intended to do just that."

"The only thing the treaty does is cost us twenty beaver pelts and a few arrows—why do they want arrows? We need a better solution."

Jones pondered the matter and considered his fee. "Well," he said, "if you had title to your lands you could demand the same protection as any land owner."

"So how would I get it started?"

"I'd need a fairly substantial retainer, say twelve pounds."

"I'll see what I can do about that," George assured him.

John was ordered to appear at the next court session, but of course, he never did. The bond money was forfeited and the sense of the court was to the effect that having the money was preferable to having John Skipper, so they were satisfied. James Alexander was less so.

George spoke with his grandfather on the subject of petitioning the Council for protection from the depredation of white settlers. He said he would give it thought.

CHAPTER ELEVEN

At Chounteroute Serrahoque died of smallpox. The chief men from the Cheroenhaka towns met in council to decide how to deal with the vacuum of power. The men smoked and each spoke his peace at length, then they smoked again without the threat that a consensus would ever be reached.

Watt Bailey rose waveringly to his feet, steadied himself, and said, "We need the opinion of George Skipper."

Cockarouse Will agreed, "He has a way to bring us to one mind."

"He does it with rum," Robin Scholar reminded him.

"Nevertheless," William Edmonds replied, "he is a unifying influence. We must send for him. Until then nothing will be decided."

Robin Scholar again reminded, "The Green Corn Dance will come before we will be able to meet again in council."

"We will convene the council the day after the dance. Our minds will be clearer then."

So a delegation of Watt Bailey, Robin Scholar, Wainoak

Robin, *Cockarouse* Will and *Cockarouse* Sam rode to Potecasi. They were familiar with the route and the protocol of not tramping the underbrush at the dry entrance so they left the road and waded their horses through the swamp arriving from different directions so not to make trails. The dog, Whitey, couldn't decide which of them merited barking. George, Sr. greeted the son of his long departed friend warmly and remarked to the others, "Seeing you come at us from four corners, I thought for a minute we were surrounded by hostile Indians."

"You were, George," Wainoak Robin told him, "we're mighty hostile toward your countrymen, and since we lost Serrahoque, we decided to select a *teerheer* who can lead us to an end to the English problem."

"You're not thinking of me are you?"

"Maybe, maybe not. We've come to ask you to join us in council. You have a way of solving problems."

George ran his tongue around his teeth while he thought. "Come inside," he said. "Mary will give us some dinner and I'll get us some rum."

"See what I told you," Robin Scholar grinned.

"Mind the shit. Place hasn't been safe to walk since the boy found that dog and Mary'll skin us if we track it inside."

Mary was surprised and happy to see the company and, after greeting them all, began to serve the hog she prepared. George returned from the storeroom with a jug and said to Patrick Whaley, "Go get George two and three, will you. They ought to hear this."

Mary told the children to take their dinner in the kitchen so there would room for the guests but she sat with the men from Chounteroute and asked after her kin.

Watt Bailey answered, "We miss your father and mother sorely, and the more trouble we have with the white bastards, the better opinion we have of your brother."

"Watt, if I recall, you're a full half white," Mary chided.

"I didn't have nothin' to say about that. I wish I wasn't."

George grunted, "He was a good man, Watt. He died trying to protect the town from English."

"I wish'd I'd known him. Mother still tells stories about him. Did you really tie her to the bed to keep her from goin' home with him?"

"That was your grandfather, but I supported the idea. Now, back to this council, when is it?"

"The day after the Green Corn Dance at the ceremonial camp."

"Oh, George, let's go to the dance. We haven't gone since we came to Potecasi," Mary laid a hand on his forearm and gave him the look that would not be refused.

"You want to get me hung, don't you, woman?"

"You're too o'nry to hang, George Skipper. Besides, the white-devils are scared to come near once the music starts."

George chuckled. "White-devils be damned! We'll go." Then again to the delegation, "You still haven't said when."

"Seven lowerings of the sun," replied Robin Scholar. "Is there anymore of that rum?"

George refilled the jug and produced his company pipe. "The tobacco that grows down here is a wee bit weak, so we add a little hemp to give it some chine."

* * *

George III returned to his house a little addled. He leered foolishly at Laura and pawed her breast. "We're going to the Green Corn Dance," he said.

"I've never gone," she confessed.

"Me either. That's where Grandpa met Grandma. They say it's important that we go at least once." He continued his fondling.

"What did you have over there?" She squirmed but didn't quite object.

"Just rum and a pipe."

"Well, you best start bringing some of that home with you if you plan on getting what you want from me."

"I'll see if I can and be right back. You wait for me in there."

Watt Bailey found George, Jr. on the path between the houses of the two elder Georges. "My Mary is pretty broken up since your boy married that Oxendine girl," he told his boyhood friend.

"Sorry about that, Watt. I'd much rather have your girl for a daughter than the other one."

"I ain't even sure what that Oxendine fella is."

"Some say he's a Portuguee."

"Whatever that is."

"It's like a Spaniard but worse. I've never seen either one, so I don't have an opinion."

"I can't figure how he managed to keep Mary from gettin' knocked up. I thought she'd show up pregnant and we'd make him marry her."

"Well, I imagine he'd be willing to service 'em both."

"Naw, her mother'd never go for that. She still thinks she's a Christian."

"That's just women. Mine's full blood Indian and she won't let me have another one either. I even offered for it to be her sister so they would already be used to each other."

The youngest George came along the path on his way to try to steal his grandfather's rum. Seeing Watt Bailey gave him a twinge of conscience even though he had been civil toward him at dinner.

Watt caught his wary look. "Don't look scared, boy. I ain't gonna hold it against ya."

"Could you tell Mary I still care about her?" he said foolishly while staring at the ground.

"I don't know how that would go over."

"Well, just 'hello' then?"

"I'll do that."

He kept walking and staged his raid successfully.

* * *

When it was time to leave for the corn dance the caravan had swollen to a few dozen. The five from Chounteroute took the lead to provide ample warning to those not welcome in Virginia should any threat appear. None did. The crowd at the ceremonial center was diminished from the year that George and Mary met and, without the guidance of old Chounteroute, the attendees from the town named for him played a lesser roll.

The men and women were separated when the shamans passed their black concoction to the waiting dancers. George had been taught what to do by his late aunt and he had instructed Laura before they were segregated. When the women danced he noticed that Mary Bailey was among them. She and Laura had never seen each other and George was certainly happy about that. Later as the hallucinogen's effect began the slow decline from its peak, he wandered to the place where the people from Chounteroute were camped and he found Mary alone singing to herself ecstatically.

"George—hi," her fair face scintillated in the silvery moonlight.

"Hi, Mary, enjoying yourself?"

"Yeah, are you?"

"Sure. It's good to see you. Mind if I sit down?"

"Sit down. It's good to see you too. This is your first time, isn't it?"

"Yeah, I was always away at school."

"What do you think of the shamans' medicine?"

"It's good. I never felt this way before. You're not mad at me?"

"The corn dance is a time of forgiveness."

"That's good. Do you feel like walking?"

"Yeah, I do. I feel like I can't sit still."

He took her hand and they walked in the woods for a long time laughing at the peculiar visions until their guts ached. They found a vantage to watch the moon set and were quiet for a time. At the first trace of light behind them, George touched her cheek and then her breast. She was smiling serenely. Without a word he pealed her dress over her head and turned her face down on the grass then he raised her hips until she was on knees and elbows. He paused a moment to admire the wisp of silky orange fluff that flowed from between her thighs then he parted it and penetrated her controlling the thrusts by pushing and pulling her hips. She looked over her shoulder and said, "Is it beautiful, George?"

"Oh, it's very beautiful."

The narcotic effect of the drug deadened his sensation sufficiently to let him bring her to climax more than once before his erupted with a preternatural intensity. He collapsed onto her back and when their hearts slowed, they dreamt. He woke first and disturbed her. She opened her eyes slowly against the rising light still smiling beatifically.

"I have to go," he told her.

"I know."

"I'll come see you."

She still smiled as he left her.

As the disorientation subsided some slept, some couldn't, and when the effects of the drug were gone, everyone was ravenous. Women prepared meals, men smoked and all felt uplifted by a sense of rebirth. Laura was asleep when George found her and he tried not to awaken her.

George, Sr. was talking with Doctor Sam and gnawing on a piece of jerked venison. "What do put in that black stuff?" he asked.

"That's a secret only shamans can know," Sam replied.

"Well, couldn't you mix it with something so it doesn't

taste like dirt?"

Sam shook his head and said, "You make your poison your way, I'll make mine."

"I have an idea," piped the young George, "mix it with rum. It'll taste better and it won't take so long to take effect."

Sam groaned, "That way is madness."

* * *

The council began late morning on the following day. William Edmonds spoke first. He began as Indians are wont, "Brothers, we have lived and hunted on these lands for more generations than can be remembered. We have had wars with those who would take our lands from us, and we have driven them off, but we cannot drive the English away. They are too many and it is foolish to believe otherwise. Why can we not then live in peace with the English? People are people. There is a way for us live beside the white men and be their brothers, but none of us know how to do it. We don't know their ways, but George Skipper is English and is our brother and he knows their ways. We must listen to his advice for he has found peace at Potecasi with all manner of people."

"Oh, God," George muttered under his breath and there was murmuring of assent all around as he was lifted to his feet. He stroked his whiskers for a time and looked into the expectant black eyes that fixed on him. Clearing his throat he spat and began de rigueur, "Brothers—the only difference between your land and my land is a deed. Englishmen put great stock in a legal document, and if we had deeds to all our lands, the power of the English King would protect them."

There was much hemming and hawing as the chief men seated all around conferred with each other in puzzlement. "Brothers!" he continued, "There are two ways for us to get deeds to our lands. We can buy them with money or we can petition the Council for grants. My little plot of swamp cost me eighty pounds. All the furs and tobaccos and hides we have will not be enough to buy the hunting grounds of the Cheroenhaka, so we must petition the Council. It will still cost some money because we need an attorney, but that will cost much less than the cost of the land."

Robin Scholar spoke still seated, "Can you do this for us, George?"

"Now, it would be difficult for me to waltz into Williamsburg, state my name and my business. They have a long memory over there, but I have a grandson who knows his way around that part of the country and hasn't yet done anything there that would be frowned upon— yet."

People began to look for the youth who tried to make himself invisible.

Edmonds rose again saying to George, Sr., "Can the boy really do this?"

The grandfather was amused by the question and answered with a laugh, "The boy can't find his arse with both hands, but he's got enough head on his shoulders to hire the attorney if we can furnish him with the money. Now, mind you, this won't happen overnight. The wheels of justice move like one of those terrapins down at the swamp."

Edmonds still standing addressed the council, "Brothers, we must make George Skipper our king so he can guide us to this end."

There were shouts of agreement but none as loud as the shout from George. "Ow! None of that. You expect me to be your king while hiding in the swamp? If we are going to live beside the English as brothers, we are going start by adopting some of their better habits—"

"Making rum?" from Robin Scholar.

"Eh, no, we'll start with free elections."

Edmonds was still on his feet and asked, "How is this

done?"

George thought for a minute before replying, "Well, first someone nominates a candidate, and somebody else seconds it. Then we get a jar and a bowlful of white and black stones. All the men take a black stone and white stone and if they like the candidate, they put a white stone in the jar, if they don't like him, they put a black stone."

Edmonds eyes were wide. "Is this how you choose your king?" he was incredulous.

"Well, no, but it's how we choose the men who represent us to the King. Anyway, I nominate William Edmonds," he said above the crowd noise.

The council fell silent until George III shouted, "I second."

His grandfather beamed, "Good lad. Now all we need are some stones. Let's have a drink while we send a couple of girls to the stream to fetch 'em. Remember, brothers, the way to live in peace with the English is to become them." As soon as he said it he remembered the head of a king vainly trying to speak its last word but thought better of mentioning it.

The election was a landslide largely due to George's endorsement, and King Edmonds asked young George if he couldn't bring him a red coat from Williamsburg, the sort he'd seen officers wearing. George promised to try.

The council adjourned and all the chief men returned to their homes to pool their resources for the attorney's fee. George told his grandson, "I fear you're going to collect a divers heap of merchandise to negotiate before you can count out the sterling to the lawyer. You'd best take the wagon, and mind, the traders'll hold their money dear. Bargain hard for the furs and don't take less than a pound for a good hide. Tobaccos have a set value but it changes every day. Make sure you know where it's at before you take their coppers. Trade goods for the king's scarlet coat. That won't do a harm, but hoard the hard money for the lawyer and the court. Take these pistols with your musket and be sure that girl of yours can load them for you. This cask is my contribution. Get two shillings per jug and not a farthing less."

George did receive a 'divers heap' when he visited Chounteroute and Assamoosick to collect the towns contributions for the attorney's fees. The only commodities he did not note in his inventory were weapons and liquor being too dear to give to the cause. The fanfare of his arrival at Chounteroute flushed Mary Bailey into the street to greet him but her childlike glee was crushed by the sight of the woman beside him in the wagon. She dropped her gaze and ran from sight. George pretended not to notice. King Edmonds posted a guard on the wagonload of trade goods through the night and sent three warriors to accompany George and Laura until they reached the plantations. They were *Cockarouse* Tom, *Cockarouse* Will and Robin Scholar. Richard Turner wanted to go but the king considered his presence would be at odds with the new spirit of brotherliness.

On the first night the horses were scarcely hobbled and the fire had not yet kindled when strangers painted for war raced whooping into the camp with tomahawks raised. Laura screamed and lost bladder control. George threw an arm across her midsection, knocking the wind from her and tumbled with her under the wagon banging her head in the process. He rolled free of her and drew a pistol from his belt hoping it was still primed. Tom and Will fended tomahawks with their muskets and Robin Scholar sidestepped his attacker tripping him going past then swung his gun by the barrel smashing the back of the fallen Indian's skull. George fired the pistol dropping Tom's threat with a gut shot. The third man fled but Will leveled his gun and hit him square in the back. Tom took the wounded Indian by the scalp lock and holding his knife to his throat demanded to know his tribe.

"We are Meherrin, Nottaway!" he spat.

"You *were* Meherrin," he sneered coolly cutting a circle

around his hairline. "Anybody else would have known not to rob Cheroenhaka warriors." He yanked the scalp off his white skull. Laura gasped then fainted. While she was oblivious to what they did, the men scalped the dead and took the wounded man out of earshot and tied him to a sycamore where he could bleed to death without disturbing their sleep. They left the bodies with him for company.

"They may draw wolves," George observed.

"Better them than us," Tom reminded him.

"Good point."

Laura recovered and was cleaning herself when the men returned from their tasks. "How about a little privacy?" she scolded.

"People from Potecasi turned modest?" Tom asked George.

"'Pears so."

Laura scowled at him saying, "George, you put a tap in that cask and get us all a gill right now and don't even think of arguing. I got to find somethin' dry to put on, now hurry, my head hurts."

George scratched the back of his head pondering her tone. "Under the circumstances I think my grandfather would not object."

Robin Scholar said, "I'm sure he wouldn't."

Laura was still shaking when she took the cup from his hands. She drained half of it in a swallow and winced at its fire. "I hope that doesn't happen every night," she said breathing hard.

"If only Meherrin attack us you don't need to worry," Tom reassured her sipping his rum a little more judiciously.

They finished the meat that was fresh from the day before and Laura, enervated by rum and adrenalin, chattered nervously. "Why do you have to take scalps?" she asked Tom.

"The women like it," he teased.

"If you had a hundred scalps it doesn't make your prick any bigger," she shot back and the others laughed.

"Is that all women at Potecasi care about?"

"It's all any woman cares about. They just tell you they like your scalps so you feel important. George doesn't need any of your nasty scalps to get what he wants." Then she stroked George's thigh purring, "George, could I have a little more rum?"

Tom looked at her grinning in amazement. "I got second watch and need some sleep before then. Try not to let her cry out while you're giving her what *she* wants."

She threw a bone that hit him in the chest and he said while he reached for his blanket, "George, you're braver than a man with a hundred scalps on his saddle."

Each took to their blankets except Will with the first watch who moved into the shadows to investigate a noise. Laura immediately unbuckled George's belt and set to fondling him with both hands. "I love you, woman," he whispered. "Just don't make any noise."

Will found one of the dead Meherrin's horses and hobbled it, then he returned to the fire and kept himself awake by studying the silent commotion of the couple's blankets. He observed a convulsive shaking followed by stillness and turned his attention to the darkness where the danger might come until a renew rhythm caught his eye. He stared raptly again until there was a second convulsive shaking followed eventually by the appearance of heads then he woke Tom for his watch.

The group reached the plantations and the three warriors became more of a provocation than an aid, so they parted with the idea to return by way of the Meherrin town to see if they could collect another scalp or two. Laura called to them as they were departing, "Next time I see you I want to measure your pricks to see if all these scalps are makin' them any bigger."

The warriors laughed till it hurt and George shook his head.

* * *

The first few days in Williamsburg George devoted to converting merchandise into cash. Furs and hides were eagerly accepted by traders preparing to embark for England. It was more difficult to find buyers for baskets and pottery but they did sell if rather cheaply. Bushels of corn were a welcome commodity but he had to accept tobaccos in exchange for them. He had to defy his grandfather's admonition as to the value of the rum because he had no license to sell spirituous liquors and would end in the pillory if he had been caught. Nevertheless, it moved quickly at a small discount. The inn was willing to accept tobaccos for room and board so he was able to gain lodging without using hard currency. The couple passed the evenings playing cribbage in the common room. Their appearance struck the other patrons as a little rustic. When Laura, into her third rum, caught a woman appraising George with derision she gestured dismissively and said loud enough for the room to hear, "Hey, hussy, keep your eyes to yourself." The next day George suggested they buy some new clothes.

George located Mr. Thomas Jones, Esq. who was surprised to see him again. "Don't tell me you have another cousin in trouble," he said.

"No, sir, I'm here representing the Cheroenhaka nation." Jones' eyes widened but he continued, "We think it meet to take legal title to our lands and we'd like you to petition the council on our behalf."

"What has brought you to this conclusion?"

He had been rehearsing his speech for several days. "We are constantly encroached upon by white settlers who poach our game, burn our crops, and squat on our ancestral lands. We hope that if we have legal title to those lands that we can seek redress in the courts."

"I don't know of any precedent but the idea may have

merit. How shall we indentify exactly what comprises your people's ancestral lands? Are you suggesting that each of your people patent his own estate?"

"No, nothing like that. We don't conceive of land ownership the way the Europeans do. What we would like is two parcels at the locations of our principle towns to be held in common by all the inhabitants."

"Fascinating. And just how much land are we talking about?"

"Well, I reckon that the larger town has about three-hundred inhabitants now and the smaller about a hundred and fifty. Each person requires one-hundred acres to allow space for agriculture, game and residences."

"My boy, this is a unique concept. I accept your case. My initial retainer shall be twenty pounds."

"Two years ago it was twelve pounds."

"We live in inflationary times."

George counted the money onto the desk saying, "We are hoping to put the petition before the Council during the January session."

"Boy, where did you study law?"

"Oh, I didn't, but I did read a law book that belonged to my headmaster, a certain Mr. Marvin."

"Marvin? I know him. I'll have to compliment him on his success with you."

There was nothing more to be done until it was time for Jones to argue their petition before the Council except to take advantage of the relatively cosmopolitan life in Williamsburg. Laura took to it decadently and knowing little of the mores of the plantation folk, George had to remain on guard to prevent her from making some faux pas that would land them in the stocks.

"Laura, my love," he warned, "it is not fitting for a lady to be drunk on the Sabbath. Leastwise not in public."

"Go on, now, Sunday's the day you need it the most."

"Yes, I know, but we'll have to be clandestine about it."

For Christmas George gave her a brooch for which he

was rewarded until it hurt. For appearances, and to see what it was like, they attended services that day. He had to restrain her from leaving in the middle and as soon as they were in the street she demanded too loudly, "It ain't Sunday! Can we get a drink today?"

Between Christmas and the New Year it was cold and rainy. George had left the inn to look for an umbrella. When he returned the innkeeper hailed him from the bar. "Mr. George Skipper, a piece of mail has found you."

"Mail? Whoever from?"

"Well, I'm sure I don't know. You'll have to break the seal and find out."

It was the first letter he had ever received and he stood in front of the innkeeper turning it over examining every detail of it. The seal bore an impression of oak leaves and the address said simply "Mr. George Skipper, Virginia". His complete unfamiliarity with what a letter might contain convinced him to take it to his room and sit down before opening it.

Laura eyed him suspiciously. "What's that?"

"A letter."

"Who from?"

"Don't know"

"Well, open it."

His hands actually trembled as he cautiously broke the seal. He read: 'My dear uncle,' and knew that he had opened his grandfather's mail in error.

"Oh," he said, "it isn't for me. It's meant for my grandfather."

"Well, it's already open so you may's well read it."

He shrugged and read aloud:

> My dear uncle,
>
> 1 August 1702
>
> My mother—rest her soul—passed from this life on the second day of July in the year of our Lord one-thousand-seven-hundred and two. As I have no

confidence that her last ever reached you I will repeat its contents as far as appraising you that your brother and my father died in the year of our Lord 1687/8. He succumbed to the ague of which there is much in this country owing to the pestilential airs. It had been my good fortune to find gainful employment in the manufacture and laying of bricks to which I owe much gratitude to my late uncle and namesake. In the past year—viz. 1701—I have become married to the former Miss Anne Barker whose family has a large and prosperous plantation known hereabouts as Oak Grove. As yet we have not been blessed with increase. If you would favor this with a brief response I would look upon it as a great kindness as I feel myself sorely isolated from family. It is my fervent hope that this finds you and yours in good health.

I remain, sir, your loving nephew,
William Skipper
Berkeley County
South Carolina

"Your cousin writes a pretty letter, don't he?"

"Indeed, pity he doesn't have some prettier news."

Later in the week the innkeeper handed him another letter this time addressed to 'George Skipper III c/o the Bull & Bear Inn, Williamsburg, Virginia'. George now felt sufficiently adept at receiving letters and opened it immediately. It was from the attorney advising him to appear at the meeting of the Council on January 15. The sensation of falling gripped his viscera.

The morning of the Council meeting he donned his new suit of clothes, covered it with the square tailed frock coat and topped it with his cocked hat. Laura whistled at him. The Council chambers were cold and dominated by an air of arrogance. Jones met him at the rear of the chambers and ushered his provincial client to a pew behind the attorneys'. When the clerk finished reading the petition the Speaker studied a ledger before him. "Mr.

Jones, I don't find reference to Cheroenhaka Indians in my registry of native tribes."

Jones replied, "Perhaps the Council is more familiar with them as Nottoways."

The Speaker returned to his registry then lifted his eyes saying, "Yes, here they are, principle settlement on the Nottoway River. You will please revise your petition to that effect and return it to us in the Spring Quarter. The matter is continued."

Jones turned briskly, noticed George's open mouth and discreetly wagged his finger. Outside George protested the delay and added, "We're not fond of being called Nottoway. It means 'snake'."

Jones gave him the timeless look of the attorney and told him flatly, "If it gains approbation for your petition, you will be snakes."

At the inn George scowled silently for a time before he began to rant, "The evil bastard could have given us one minute to make the change he wanted, but no. Now we have to wait till fucking April. I suppose there's nothing to do but go home and tell everyone what's gone on."

"Well, ain't that fine fucking language?" she said striking an indignant pose. "Do we have to go? I'm getting to like the life of high society."

"We can't stay here for three months. We're almost out of money now."

"Can we stay a little while longer?" she stepped close putting her left hand on his shoulder and interposed her left leg between his while she stroked his chest with her right.

He pulled her tighter and said, "Oh, I suppose we could wait a few days to see if the weather improves."

* * *

They first went to Chounteroute where King Edmonds called the chief men together to hear the news. When

George finished his report an angry Richard Turner stood and declared, "We were fools to think the English dogs would give us our own land and leave us in peace and now the money is gone and we have nothing."

The king rose slowly all the time glaring at Turner who remained defiant. He locked eyes with the older man and did not speak for many seconds. Finally he said, "For your whole life you have made war on the English and it has brought us only unhappiness and hunger. It is madness to think that by doing the same thing over and over again you will ever have a different result. The money is gone and it will not be brought back by withdrawing our petition. We will wait until the next Council and we will go to Williamsburg to hear what they say. I have been chosen your king in the manner of the English, but I am still a warrior at heart, and I tell you this, Richard Turner, if you interfere with our plans I will give you to the English and tell them everything you have done. That is if I don't decide to bury my tomahawk in the back of your skull first. This council is over."

Laura was waiting in the longhouse but George walked with Watt Bailey and his son, Watt, toward his house. "Do you think Richard Turner will accept the king's will?" he asked.

"Richard Turner has been driven mad by his hatred. He will make more trouble," Watt replied.

"If my grandmother were here she would put the fear of God in him."

Watt gave a laugh at that. "Yes, indeed she would," he agreed.

George felt he had waited long enough to ask, "How is Mary?"

A cloud of pain crossed his face while he answered shortly, "Mary put herself out."

"What? Why?"

"Well, we haven't had enough to eat this whole year was one reason," he hesitated then continued. "No, it was because of you, George."

"Where is she?"

"She's gone a long way away and I won't tell you where because you will interfere and cause her trouble."

Crestfallen and shamed he dropped his head saying, "I'm sorry, Mr. Bailey," and he walked the other way.

George went to Assamoosick to deliver the news. On the way Laura was chipper and George was sullen. "All right, don't tell me what's wrong," she said shoving him.

"I'm worried about the problems Richard Turner will cause."

"I don't believe you."

"Fine then, believe what you like."

She crossed her arms fell silent.

That night under the bear skin that kept them from the frosty air he stroked her breast and she turned abruptly away from him. "Don't."

At Assamoosick George's father and mother were visiting the part of Suntetung's family that relocated during the unpleasant reign of Eteshe Ena. Suntetung gushed over her son to his embarrassment. "I am proud that my flesh will bring peace between us and the white dogs but I wish you had better sense about women," she finished her greeting.

"She's a stopgap, mother."

Not knowing the word Suntetung thought it probably meant she-devil and said, "I will get the shaman to remove your curse."

George patted her hand and smiled woefully, "Thanks, I could use that."

Howerac's brother, Hahenu, had become teerheer of Assamoosick. He was enduringly fond of George's rum and welcomed his son and grandson enthusiastically with a feast although the fare was lean and the rum George, Jr. carried from Potecasi was the only libation. Nonetheless, a pipe was passed and the drumming began.

Suntetung said to her son, "George, you must dance

with the men."

"But I'm not very good at it."

"Neither is your father or grandfather, but they still do it. Now go get painted."

Laura interjected, "Maybe it will help your attitude."

With a sigh and shrug he stood and went to where the other men who would dance were being painted. A girl who had finished making a warrior's face red and blue noticed his aimless milling. "I can do you," she called.

He sat cross legged in front of her and looked at her face while she studied his. "Think you should be all red," she said.

"Really, why?"

"You have the face of a devil and devils are all red," she locked eyes with him and smiled wickedly.

"So you think I'm a devil?"

"I'm certain of it."

He contemplated this feeling awkward then asked, "What's your name?"

"Youhanhu—and you're one of the Georges."

"How do know my name?"

"Everyone at Assamoosick knows that you are making our land secure from the white-devils." She began smearing the thick paint on his cheeks.

George wanted to keep the conversation rolling so he asked, "Will you dance with the women?"

"Sure."

"It's cold tonight. Are we going to dance with our clothes on?"

She laughed, "Yes, we'll dance in our winter robes, silly."

"Pity."

"See, I knew you were a devil. Now close your mouth so I can make your lips red. What's it like in Williamsburg?"

He waited until she moved her spreading to his neck then replied, "The houses are bigger and many are made of bricks, and there is a lot of good things to eat all the time if you have money. But they don't have feasts or dances and you can get put in the stocks for almost anything."

"There, now you look like a devil should. What's the stocks?" Having finished, she sat back to admire her work.

"It's like the gauntlet except instead of running they trap your feet and hands in a block of wood and people pass by and throw things at you."

"Why? Can't white people hit a moving target?"

"It's just how they do it. Do you want me to paint you now?"

"Sure. Make me blue with red suns on my cheeks. Is that woman you're with your wife?"

"Uh, no," he was taken aback and wished she hadn't asked. "She's a concubine." He was immediately angry with himself for lacking the courage to be honest. Why couldn't he say that she was a wife and he might be looking for another? Too much English influence he supposed.

"She's pretty."

"You're prettier."

"Do you think so?"

"Very much."

"Devil!"

"Don't laugh now or your suns will be crooked."

"I wish I could see an English town," she said trying to keep her face still. "It sounds exciting."

"Someday you might get a chance. There, your suns are straight and the same size."

"Come on, boy," his father said passing behind him and pulling him by his hair, "it's time to dance."

"Thanks, Youhanhu," he called to her, "maybe I'll see you later."

"Now, that's a nice one," his father said without looking at him.

* * *

In a few days the Skipper family found their way back to Potecasi. When George saw his grandson he said, "Good to have you back. Now you can clean up after your dog. The beast has laid a gauntlet of shit all around the house."

Looking around he said, "That's what he does best and it looks like he needs a bath again."

Slapping him on the back his grandfather said, "Good to see that education money wasn't wasted, but I guess it can wait a little longer. Come on inside and tell me how you're getting along with the powers that be, but watch where you walk."

"Here," he said holding the folded paper, "I've got a letter for you. I opened it by mistake."

"My stars! Who's it from?"

"Cousin William."

He began reading while they walked. At the stoop he remembered to check his boots. "Dammit! I knew better than to read while I was walking." He had installed a scraper on the step and a bootjack just inside the door. He told his grandson, "You can keep your shoes on if they pass inspection."

When he finished the letter the elder George said, "You remember your aunt and uncle, don't you?"

"Not really, it's too bad about them."

"It is but it's going to get us all sooner or later. Have a seat. I've got to tell your grandmother about this."

Mary came into the room and hugged him until he couldn't breathe. She had a unique scent about her that would have let young George identify her in total darkness. "Have you been taking proper meals since you've been away?" she asked when he finally broke free of her embrace.

"We ate great at Williamsburg, but nobody has enough to eat at Chounteroute and Assamoosick."

"Well, we'll get you something right now. I'll warm it

up while you fill your grandfather in."

After the information was imparted and the obligatory mid afternoon meal was laid George said, "Boy, that letter is making me feel a mite pensive. I've a mind to go down and have a look at William. Why don't you come with me?"

"As long as I can make it back for the Council session."

"Shouldn't be any sort of a problem there. Woman, you don't mind if the boy and I go for ride in the country, do you?"

"I would do me good to get you out of my hair."

"Now, I always speak well of you." Then to himself he said, "We'll see if Auteur Awwa will join us. We can visit his town on the way."

George told Laura about his intended excursion with his grandfather and she said, "Is this going to be like your hunting trip?"

He just scowled and didn't respond.

* * *

The territory between Potecasi and Berkeley County was unblemished by white settlers. The various Indian tribes, as usual kept the undergrowth in check with periodic burning and the forest had a light open aspect from the bareness of the deciduous trees while the live oaks and evergreens imparted a sense of shelter. "Idyllic, that's the word for it," the elder George proclaimed one morning as he beheld the freshness in the air. The other wasn't quite awake and made no reply. "You know, boy, I've been thinking. I want you to make me a promise."

"What's that?" he asked nervously.

"I figure you will be procreating fairly soon—it's a wonder the girl hasn't turned up pregnant long ago— anyways, I want you promise me that there will be no more Georges in the next generation."

"I promise," he answered laughing.

"So how is it she's not conceived already? We're not spilling our seed on the ground, are we?"

"Not that. Just been unlucky I guess."

"Good. I don't want you adding to your list of mortal sins."

"Grandpa, I never knew you to be so pious."

"I never object to doing the Lord's work if it doesn't interfere with having a good time. Now, don't go repeating that to your grandmother."

* * *

Perhaps it was his long association with Englishmen or maybe it was the prodigious amount of rum he had quaffed, but Auteur Awwa had lost his woodcraft. "My friend, there is no way we are going to be able to find your peoples' place," George admonished him, "unless we find the coast and follow it south."

"We can't even find the coast," he complained.

"I don't think it's been moved, we just aren't following the path of the sun contrary-wise for some reason that escapes my explanation at the moment."

"According to headmaster Marvin's cartographic lessons, we should be tending as much south as east, and though it grieves me deeply, I suggest we not pass the jug until well past zenith so we remember which way east was," young George offered.

They found the coast but never did succeed in finding the Winyah town but it found them. A family collecting mussels guided them to it and Auteur Awwa was saddened to learn of his father's long since passing. However, his fame earned the trio a feast in their honor with traditional accoutrements. After the food, dancing, smoking and the end of their travelling supply of rum, the maidens were offered. Auteur Awwa made his selection quickly based on the amplitude of her mammary glands and quietly retired to the dark side of the longhouse. Young George, in uncertain discomfort, pretended that he didn't understand the question while his aged namesake inspected a comely slip of a girl as if she were horseflesh.

"Grandfather, is this seemly for a man of your age and situation?" he asked with cockiness of intoxication which earned him a cuff behind the ear.

"Boy, it may come as a shock but you did not invent fornication. The only difference between a young man and an old man is that a young man tries hard not to come too soon and an old man just tries hard to come."

"Well, that clears that up. I guess I'll take the little one with the impish grin."

"Good choice, but I like to make sure the sacred forest has plenty of foliage." He lifted the girl's apron and whistled, "This will do nicely."

They did not tarry with the Winyah, after thanking the *werrowance* for his hospitality, they resumed their journey but in a meandering way. "I do admire this country," George said to Auteur Awwa, "the last time we were here I must have been too preoccupied to notice."

* * *

Oak Grove Plantation had a mature aspect. The magnolias along the carriageway had grown stately for twenty some years. The liveried servant that met the trail worn trio only partly hid his distain when asked, "Who might I tell Massa William is callin', suh?"

"You may tell him it's his uncle George then you can see to our horses getting stabled."

That curbed his uppity ways. "Yassuh, please falla me."

William saw them from across the parlor and might have been less shocked to see his own father resurrected. "Good God, what a surprise!" he said and threw his arms around his uncle.

"William! Your language," this came from an elegant young woman knitting in the light by the window.

"Uncle George, this is my wife, Anne. She's a stickler for proper language."

George noted she might drop her whelp at any moment. "Please to make your acquaintance, ma'am, we'll try to curb our heathen ways while we're here."

She studied Auteur Awwa curiously and turned eyes back to George saying, "I take it you must be the uncle who lives with the Indians."

"Yes, but you mustn't believe the half of what William has told you." Then to William, "I was most sad to hear about your parents."

"It was a blow but Anne's family treat me like one of their own, and as you can see, we're about to have a family of our own."

"Promise me you won't name the boys George."

"My God—"

"William!"

"—it's been more than twenty years," William said to the room and then to his cousin, "and you were no bigger than that." He held his palm at an improbable height.

Anne cleared her throat, "Dear, have you forgotten your manners? Our guests must be allowed time to refresh themselves from their travels."

"Oh, quite right. I don't know how a woman of Anne's breeding could have married a Philistine like me." He rang a bell and dispatched the servant for their luggage then showed them to the guest rooms. "So how is our secret cousin, Patrick?"

"He's doing quite well as a Skipper, though he still calls himself Whaley, says he's used to it. I've got a message from him to his mother if she's still in the realm of the living and you can arrange to get it to her."

"She is well and we'll have a boy fetch it to her today. God, it's good to see you all—I can say that now that we're out of earshot."

True to William's word the Barkers treated them like family and Thomas Barker was keen to hear Indian tales when Sarah and Anne weren't there to be scandalized. "Remarkable stuff," Barker commented, "noble savages, indeed."

George replied to that while enjoying his host's brandy, "Well, savages anyway. I suppose a few of us are noble."

Polly Joyner came to visit after she got Patrick's missive and was nearly overcome with nostalgia by the presence of those who were so like her lost love. Studying George III she said to his grandfather, "Promise me that while you're here you will keep that one away from my granddaughters."

To which he replied, "Oh, he's married and she neutered him." Anne nearly succumbed to the vapors.

The days passed in familial bliss until Anne's labor began. The doctor was summoned and, after a cursory examination of his patient, felt it meet to administer a draught of laudanum to the expectant father. The contractions lasted well past midnight. Anne's sobbing and wailing took a terrible toll on all who waited in the antechamber but when the bawling suddenly stopped it was worse. It roused William from his stupor. "What does it mean?" he demanded.

George, who was keeping Thomas Barker calm with his own whiskey, assumed his most sage demeanor and replied, "Generally it means the baby's been born."

All fell silent and strained to hear what was happening beyond the closed door. At last they were relieved to hear a scream that wasn't Anne's then a minute or so later they heard it again. A few minutes later the door opened and the nanny appeared with a bundle on each arm. "Bofe um dun be boys," she said. They were duly christened William and John.

* * *

While March was still waxing George grew increasingly antsy to start for Williamsburg. "It's a mite soon," his grandfather declared.

"What if something happens and I don't get there in time?"

"Then there would be further delay."

"That's what I want to avoid. The people are going hungry. They need their land."

"Hmm," he made a wry face, "I think there's more of the story of the Grasshopper and the Ants behind the people going hungry, but your heart's in the right place. Still I promised to stay until the babes' formal christening."

"You and Auteur Awwa don't need to leave. I'm fine travelling alone."

"Well, maybe, but your mother will scalp me if something untoward were to happen to you."

"Not to worry, granddad. I will be fine. I will need some money to live on in Williamsburg, though."

"Get some from your grandmother."

Young George dropped his eyes and shuffled his feet then he said, "I thought it would be faster to go straight to Williamsburg."

"This excitement to get to Williamsburg smells a bit fishy."

"I'm just trying to help our people."

"Sure you are. There wouldn't happen to be something female at the bottom of this? And not the one you're married to."

He could feel his cheeks redden. "Didn't you just remind me that I did not invent fornication while you examined a girl's *oranakewn*?"

"It would have been rude and even dangerous to spurn the Winyah king's hospitality, however, at Potecasi we attempt to hold ourselves to a higher standard," he lectured the boy.

Auteur Awwa had followed this with growing interest. "That's why I keep my number two wife at

Chounteroute," he interjected.

George, Sr. felt his teeth with his tongue and rolled his eyes. "I give up," he said. "Here's your money and do the best you can not to get caught. I think that Oxendine girl might stick something between your ribs if she finds out. Your mother should have pinched your head off while she had the chance."

* * *

Whereas on the southbound trip the travelers had hugged the coast to insure their encounter with the Winyah, George intended to follow a route nearly due north until he was certain that he was beyond Potecasi then he would turn east and look for Assamoosick. The first night it rained and he was exceedingly miserable. The second night the air was cool and damp so he made a large fire and banked it with plenty of logs to last the night. The hobbled horse was grazing on fresh new grass and George leaned his back against a lofty beech to chew on jerked beef that the Barkers had sent with him. A twig snapped in the direction the horse had wandered and the horse nickered, and then again. He checked the prime in his gun but continued relaxing and chewing. There was another horse sound which made him try peering into the darkness but the contrast of the firelight made the surrounding blackness impenetrable. Finally there was the sound of a hoof on hard ground that could only be made by an un-hobbled horse. With the gun cocked he stepped silently in the direction of the sound. When his eyes adjusted to darkness he saw a shape attempting to slip a noose over his horse's head. If he missed or the ball went clear through the man, it would hit the horse. Still advancing, and with his heart pounding against his ribs, he pulled the tomahawk from his belt and raised it over his head. A noise turned the man suddenly. He had a knife in his left hand which he quickly switched to his right. George started to sprint and scream which startled the horse bumping the thief with his flank. The tomahawk landed on the bridge of the man's nose, he slumped to his knees then fell on his face and lay convulsing.

Frozen by the sight George's heart still raced and his legs were quivery. As if one thing were responsible for the other, the dead man's twitching slowed and so did George's heart. He turned the body onto its back and realized he had killed an Indian. Without any sense of freewill he took the knife from the dead hand and collected the scalp then hobbled the horse again.

* * *

Hahenu received him warmly and was interested in hearing news of the plan to enlist the aid of the English great father to prevent the depredations of his subjects, although he was skeptical. After his courtesy call to the *werrowance* George found Youhanhu scraping a hide.

"It's the devil!" she cried and hugged him with her greasy hands.

"So," he said holding her by the arms, "do you still want to see Williamsburg?"

"What?"

"I'm going back to Williamsburg and you said you wanted to see it, so I'm going to take you."

"Oh, I can't."

"Why?"

"I don't have an English dress. I can't speak English and I won't know what to do."

"I'll get you a dress and make sure you know what to do."

"What about your woman?"

"She's not going."

"Well, in that case—"

"Good. And can I leave this here? It wouldn't do to ride into Williamsburg with it on my bridle," he said holding the scalp.

She wiped the scraps of venison from her hands and cupped his balls. "See? I knew you were a devil."

CHAPTER TWELVE

The date of the Council's session was approaching and George, Jr. was concerned by his son's absence. He told his mother, "Somebody has to go to Williamsburg to make sure that lawyer knows we are not abandoning the matter."

Mary thought through the issue before responding. "James could go. Nobody wants to hang him yet, so could Patrick, he's only wanted in South Carolina, and the Oxendine girl knows how to find the lawyer."

"Do you think we can trust those two with George's wife?"

"More than we can trust her."

"Who could we send along to keep them honest?"

"How about her father?" Mary offered.

"Not a bad idea. I'll go see him."

Silas Oxendine never did much more than to rock himself to sleep on the porch of the ramshackle house he built. That was where George found him. "Mr. Oxendine, good afternoon to you."

"How do, Mr. Skipper?" he said through the tobacco stains on his gray beard.

"I do just fine, but I come here on account of a

problem that you can help with."

"Pralum. What sort o' pralum?"

"You are aware that your son-in-law has been in Williamsburg trying to get the Council to make land grants to our people?"

"Oh, I hear tell from the girl she's been in Williamsburg but I doan rightly know what fur."

"Mr. Oxendine, we have been trying to find a way to prevent the white settlers from running us off our land."

"Ain't been nobody tryin' run us off our land."

"No, I mean at the other towns."

"What towns?"

"Chounteroute and Assamoosick."

"Ne'er bin der."

George took a breath and studied his tack. Minutes passed in silence that was awkward to him but Oxendine seemed unaware. Finally he found a new route to an end, "Mr. Oxendine, would you think it proper if your daughter were to be travelling alone in the company of two unmarried men?"

Oxendine rolled his bleary eye toward George, hacked and spit, then said, "I reckon not but I wouldn't put it pas' her."

"Would you be willing then to go with her to Williamsburg to protect her honor?"

He contemplated that for some time then sighed, "I doan thin I'se much good fur dat."

George stared at the man and wondered how long it would take his mother to forgive him if he throttled the cretin with his bare hands. If he were able to see the future Oxendine would have died right then. He left the porch without saying anymore and the miscreant didn't notice. He went next to Laura to tell her she was required to go to Williamsburg to introduce her cousins-in-law to the lawyer. "Your father and I would like your promise that you will behave yourself," he prevaricated.

"What's that supposed to mean."

"That means you need to keep the two boys who are going with you in line."

"Who's going with me?"

"James and Patrick."

All she said was, "Hmmm."

* * *

George was enjoying the time alone with Youhanhu. She was a generous lover whose long silky pubic hair clung to his member, tantalizingly, on the withdrawal stroke. His grandfather's fetish began to make sense. They had nothing to do but eat, sleep and make love and they did them in roughly equal proportions. It was during the afternoon interlude a few days before the Council session that they heard a commotion in the street. Being seized by an odd sense of doom, he left the bed to look from the window. What he saw put more terror into him than killing the Indian—his wife was arguing with the innkeeper. She disappeared into the building and he could hear her on the stairs. He checked the lock and hoped the door was stout.

The latch rattled and Laura began pounding with the side of her fist. "Open the door, George. I want to know who's in there."

"Nobody."

"Then open the door."

"No, I want you to go away."

"I won't go away until I see who you've got in there."

"What difference does it make?"

She was quiet for some seconds then began pounding on the door again.

"Quit making so much noise," he ordered.

"I'll wake the dead if I have to. Open up!"

There was some scuffling in the hall and Laura fell silent. A key turned in the lock and George felt the terror again. He frantically tried to get a leg into his breeches but was still hopping on one foot when the door swung open on squealing hinges and the innkeeper stepped aside to allow two constables to enter the room. They were followed by the innkeeper and Laura.

"Mr. Skipper, you will kindly make yourself decent and come with us," one of the constables told him.

Laura didn't look at her husband. Her eyes went to Youhanhu who was sitting on the bed looking stunned. "Man stealing savage," she screamed and sprang on her. The two men ran to separate them. Youhanhu, who couldn't understand what she said, leaped to her feet in self defense.

When the small melee was halted the man said to the Indian, "Cover yourself, savage." But again she had no idea what he said and simply remained standing naked.

George got his trousers and shirt fastened and started to protest. "What do you mean breaking into a man's room and letting her in?"

"We do not countenance adultery in this establishment," the innkeeper preached.

"We're Indians. Plenty of us have more than one wife."

"I'm no Indian! And when did you marry *her*?" Laura injected.

The constable who was doing all the talking said, "I'm sure that's lovely in your heathen towns but when you're in Williamsburg you will refrain from such practices. Now, will you please tell your squaw to put her clothes on?"

George ignored Laura and suggested Youhanhu get dressed. He began to protest again but the constables interrupted, jerking him by the upper arms and forcing him from the room. "What in hell are you doing?" he demanded.

"Arresting you," the man answered.

"What for?"

"Well, it's either fornication, adultery or bigamy. We'll have to let the magistrate sort it out." He attempted to break their grips but they held fast and one drew his sword. "I advise you to come along peacefully." They put him in the pillory without comment and left.

"Oh, it's going to take a very long time to forget this one," he said aloud to himself.

The first person to arrive to view the spectacle was Laura. "You pig!" she shouted and threw a stone. It took several more stones before she scored a hit and she accompanied each with, "Pig, pig, pig." The stone struck him on the side of the nose and it began to bleed.

"When I get out of here I'll take care of you, woman," he shouted.

"You won't be in any condition when I get done with you." She threw several more stones doing little more damage. In her impatience she strode to the pillory and punched him squarely in the right orbit then she left.

Lawyer Jones was the next visitor. "Isn't this a fine state of affairs?" he said. "Three days before the session begins and my client has himself arrested."

"It wasn't my idea. Can you get me out of this?"

"I don't know. We'll have to see."

* * *

Youhanhu walked out of the inn after the room emptied and went to the stable where she attempted to retrieve her horse. The stable keep stopped her and demanded payment but, of course, she had no idea what he was saying. She told him George would take care of it when he came for the other horse and the stableman had no idea what she was saying. In the end she kneed him in the groin, jumped on the horse's back and fled. She rode straight through the night to Assamoosick and told her story to Hahenu who summoned a council of the chief men who were present. With little of the customary oratory, they decided to leave immediately for Williamsburg and dispatch an express to Chounteroute.

The result was that when the Council session convened King Edmonds, Watt Bailey, Harrison, Peter, Wainoak Robin, William Hines, Frank, Wainoak Robin, Jr., Ned, Robin Scholar, Sam, *Cockarouse* Tom and *Cockarouse* Will, being all of the chief men less George Skipper, Sr., were present in the Council chambers. The Speaker eyed them warily.

Jones read his revised petition to the chamber which now included a more specific description of the tracts that he proposed the Council grant the two Cheroenhaka towns. He read: "Viz., the lesser town shall be granted a tract of land in the form of a square with its center being a stake to be placed in the center of the smaller town and each side of the aforesaid square shall be a measure of six miles; and the greater settlement shall be granted a circular tract of land with the center of said circle in the center of the aforesaid greater settlement, and said circle having a diameter of six miles."

The matter was continued until the following morning when, with as little oratory as the chief men's council at Assamoosick, the Speaker announced, "The petition of the chief men of the Nottoway Indians is approved by this Council pending approval by the Governor. The Clerk shall prepare the patent. Furthermore, to promote the general welfare of our Indian brethren, this body directs the creation of three posts decreed to be agents for the aforesaid Nottoway Indians. Candidates for the aforesaid posts may apply with the clerk."

Watt Bailey spoke the best English and so became the interpreter for the event. Jones had him tell the assembled chiefs that they would have to make themselves available to affix their marks to the document when it was ready. "What can we do about young George?" Bailey asked the lawyer when the business of the Council session was over.

"Someone will have to stand for him," Jones replied.

"I'll stand for him so long as he has the bond money," Watt volunteered.

"Well, that's a bit irregular. Generally the bondsman is a citizen of the colony."

Watt Bailey contemplated this for a moment then said, "So? Aren't I a landed citizen of the colony?"

This flustered the lawyer who was only marginally comfortable with his Indian clients. "Highly irregular, highly," he muttered, "but your point is well taken. I shall put it before the court."

As it happened that wasn't necessary. The sheriff confided to him, "The innkeep is disinclined to press the matter out of fear of retaliation. The wife got her pound of flesh and the other has vanished. Frankly, I'd like to not see the savage again."

He was released from the pillory and asked to leave town. Since the business of the petition was proceeding without him he was disappointedly willing to comply. It was just as well for Bailey that he did not have to stand for the bond as George—true to family tradition—had no intention of appearing for trial had he been ordered to do so. Jones informed him where to find his wife and cousins, and for want of a better idea, he found them. Laura examined his black eye trying to decide if it was adequate.

James said, "Now it's unanimous. All the George Skippers are fugitives."

George went innocently to collect his horse only to be blindsided by the stableman's moral outrage. "Sorry," he told the man, "she's a devil." He settled the bill and left a generous gratuity for his discomfort.

It was a bitter trip back to Potecasi for George. He was overwhelmed by a sense of failure for not being part of the closure of the land grant. The loss of Youhanhu hurt but was overshadowed by the disgrace of having been caught and that sting was certain to live a very long life. His three traveling companions, even Laura, were light and happy in each other's company and the sweetness of spring. Their buoyancy grated on his despair and as he looked on the verdant country his sadness put a harsh edge on the light, made the world feel empty and the keening breeze in the pines sound lonesome.

On their approach to Potecasi the lighthearted three gave no thought to their patriarch's standing order to not trample the brush and George was too sullen to care. He and Laura went home where he sat staring fixedly until the frosty silence was screaming in his head. For relief he stood and announced that he was going to report to his father and see if his grandfather had returned from South Carolina.

Laura said, "That's fine with me."

He stopped half way to his father's house to sit on a stump. How to tell the story and retain any shred of self respect escaped him. Finally he decided there was no way to make it pretty so he got to his feet and went into the house. His mother hugged him and chattered about how happy she was that he was back. He smiled wanly and muttered his appreciation while his father looked baffled. "You missed the Council date," he accused.

"No, I didn't. I was there early," he replied sounding wounded.

"Why didn't you tell anyone you were back?"

"I told Hahenu."

"You went to Assamoosick but didn't stop here?"

"It was out of the way."

"But you were early! Did the girl find you?"

"Yeah, we all came back together."

His father stared right into his head for what felt like a lifetime then he said, "You got caught cheating, didn't you?"

"Yeah," he replied barely audibly.

"Boy, you're as useless as teats on a boar. Nobody got killed, did they? "

"No, but I got put in the pillory."

"What the hell for?"

"They said I was being immoral."

"Damn fool English."

Suntetung said mildly, "If you don't love her your grandmother can undo the marriage. Everyone would be happy about that."

A series of emotions coursed through him that left his head swimming. "No, I want her," he said, "I just got tempted by somebody else."

"Somebody in South Carolina," his mother asked.

"No, Assamoosick."

"A Cheroenhaka girl?"

"Yeah."

"Why don't you let the matriarch divorce you?" Suntetung urged, "You'd be so much happier with an Indian wife."

"I want Laura."

"Does she still want you?" his father interjected.

"I guess so. She came home with me. We'll work it out."

"Suit yourself. You made your bed. Now you have to lie in it. But what about the petition?"

"It's been granted. King Edmonds is there with the other chiefs to sign the patent. Chounteroute gets a six mile circle around it and Assamoosick gets a six mile square."

"A circle and a square—huh."

"And there will be three agents assigned to look out for our interests, a Thomas Cocke, John Simmons and Benjamin Edwards."

"Hmm, I wonder who's going to watch them?"

"Did granddad come back yet?"

"Oh, he's back but he's pretty sick."

"What's the matter?"

"Might be pneumonia. You best go see him. And round up that dog when you're done. We can't get him to shit in his own yard."

* * *

Feeling a little better, George kissed his mother and went to his grandparents' house. The old man looked like he had aged twenty years since he had last seen him. He was propped in the bed and Mary was forcing sips of some herbal brew into him. More herbs were burning in a clay censor. His grandfather took one look and said, "You got caught, didn't you?"

"Yes."

"Just like tits on a boar hog."

"I've been hearing that a lot today."

"You're lucky she didn't cleave your skull open." His voice was raspy and weak.

Mary just tut-tutted softly.

"Well, it's good you're back. I didn't want to depart this world without saying goodbye."

"Granddad, you're not goin' anywhere."

"No, I'm afraid 'the old man's friend' is going to be carrying me away this time."

"Grandma, you've got make him stop talking like that."

"You know how stubborn he is, dear," she said. "Once he makes his mind, there's no changing it."

CHAPTER THIRTEEN

George, Sr. was true to his word. He died in his bed and the titles junior and senior were adjusted by a generation. He was interred in a plot that had been consecrated as a burying ground when twin infant girls were stillborn to one of the Indian families

George, Jr. and Laura wordlessly came to a truce of sorts. They spoke civilly but Laura's attitude in bed was a completely different thing. She would get into bed and lie on her back with her arms folded across her chest. George had to take the initiative but at some point Laura would become aroused, brusquely reverse their positions and pump her pelvis vigorously until she stiffened, shuddered and collapsed. If George hadn't yet relieved his tension he was made to do so in her inert body.

Finally he could no longer stand it and asked, "Why don't you act like you used to?"

"You know why."

"Aren't you ever going to get over it?"

"No."

"This can't go on."

"There's nothing I can do about it. It's just how I

feel."

His depression mounted with passing years but each night he put himself through the ordeal hoping her anger would relent.

The late George had made a will in accordance to the custom of primogeniture which upset Cheroenhaka convention, but Mary considered herself progressive and did not object. The eldest son took possession of the major assets with the proviso that Mary be allowed the use of the house as long as she lived. The other children were given a head of livestock and few tools. The current George, Sr. was also given the responsibility of keeping the stills running. Auteur Awwa was naturally a willing help. So it came to be that a new delivery man was needed to be found and George delegated the task to his son. Auteur Awwa still went along on most trips to spend some time with his wife in Chounteroute. It also happened that a stranger appeared in Potecasi with a piece of mail addressed to Watt Bailey. Mail was a rare event but the simple logic of forwarding it Chounteroute via the rum delivery was clear and it was entrusted to George, Jr. He took the letter and idly glanced at the address. It was dainty, if unskillful, handwriting and with a jolt he knew who had written it. The last time he had violated the seal of a letter that was not for him the result had not been disastrous, so when he was sure nobody was looking, he broke it and read the contents. The body of the letter was of little interest, she missed her family and wished the term of her indenture was shorter, but what really piqued his interest was the return address: 'Allen Plantation, Chowan County'. He memorized it and attempted to reseal the wax with the heated blade of his knife.

When Laura discovered that he was taking rum to Assamoosick she said, "I know you're going to go lay with that Indian whore."

He'd thought about it but he said, "What do you care?"

"What do you mean? I am still your wife."

"You don't act like it."

She began to cry for the first time since the incident in Williamsburg. "If you go there I'll never let you touch me again," she said between sobs.

He had a heavy feeling in his chest and hated her tears, but he said, "I don't feel like I've got much to lose."

Youhanhu said to George when she saw him at Assamoosick, "You're woman acts crazy. Why do you keep her?"

He replied, "I'm not keeping her any longer. I should have come back for you."

"Yes, but now it's too late."

Going to Chounteroute his demons tormented so that even Auteur Awwa's *joie de vivre* could not penetrate his gloom. The aged Winyah was relieved when George decided to return home alone rather than wait for him to fulfill his conjugal obligations with the women he kept there. "I once told your father he should follow my example and keep two or three wives in different places. He wouldn't take my advice, but I offer again," he told George as he departed.

"I'll work on that," was his response. And work on it he did. He headed straight for Chowan County where he began making inquiries as to the whereabouts of the Allen plantation.

The Allen homestead had a modestly prosperous look. George tied his horse to the hitching post and banged the knocker. Mary herself answered and felt her heart start pounding when she saw her lost love standing in his linen shirt and buckskin riding pants.

"You shouldn't be here," she whispered.

"Why not?"

"Father promised he'd never tell you where I was."

"He didn't."

"Then how?"

"That doesn't matter. I have to talk to you."

"I have work to do. Mr. Allen is very jealous of my

time."

"Meet me when your work is done. I'll make a camp by the river near the ford."

She vacillated and covered her mouth with her hand while weighing her fears and finally said, "I'll come after supper but I can't stay long."

* * *

An owl was hooting for a mate. He could see her raise and fold her tail with each hoot. Eventually a male answered first from a long way but each response was nearer. George reflected on the straightforwardness of the owl's courtship and the great size of the dame and it put him in mind of Laura whose stature had caused him, during coitus, to fanaticize floating on a sea of carnal joy. He grew apprehensive that Mary had would not show. The male owl finally landed on a limb in the same tree where the big female perched. They began bobbing and posturing and rather purring. The sight was making George feel libidinous and he thought he was going to get to see them mate, but on some invisible signal they both took wing and vanished to do the deed in privacy. An orange moon was rising. He could see it partly obscured by the trees. So was she coming or not? The longer time dragged and the higher the moon rose the more hopeless he felt. The moon was completely above the trees and illuminating the road when he saw her. He jumped and went to her and led her by the hand to the fireside. Before releasing her hand he leaned to kiss her softly on the lips. She made no response but she did not pull away.

"I was afraid you weren't going to come," he told her as they sat on the ground.

"I almost didn't."

"I'm glad you came."

"So, why are you here?"

"I came to tell you I made a big mistake but it's over

now and I want you to marry me."

"You're already married."

"Not anymore. I want to marry you in the church."

"What makes you think I want to marry you after what you did?"

"Well, do you?"

"I don't know."

"We had good times together."

"But you had to ruin it. Besides, I'm bound for five more years. I can't marry you even if I want to."

George studied her minutely trying to guess if touching her would get a positive reaction. He decided to err on the side of caution. "You can run away. We can build a house where he won't ever find you," he said and he touched her arm in spite of his resolution.

"Do you expect me to live in your swamp next door to *her*?"

Since she was discussing the matter instead of rejecting it outright he thought he could have a chance if he had enough to offer. The issue of where to live was a bit tricky. Allen must know that she came from Chounteroute, Youhanhu made Assamoosick seem a little uncomfortable, and he could think of no way to rout Laura from Potecasi that didn't involve killing her. "We can buy some land of our own and build a plantation. Your name will be Skipper and Allen won't have a clue how to find you. You can have a servant," he offered while cudgeling his brain to think of anything else that might sweeten the pot. "You can get a cat," he added though he thought it a lame thing to say but it made her laugh.

"A cat? I can have a servant, you and a cat? You certainly do know how to sweep a girl off her feet."

"And when I go to Chounteroute to deliver rum, you can go along to visit your family." He felt like he had won and reached to embrace her but she stiffened in his arms and held her face away from his.

"I'm not ready for that," she told him.

"I'm sorry. I thought you were over being mad at me."

"Not quite. I need time to decide. How long will you be staying here?"

"As long as takes to convince you that I've changed."

"You might be here a very long time."

That let the wind from his sails.

"I have to go now."

"When will you come back?"

"When I've made up my mind," she said and she left saying nothing more.

"I love you," he called after her but she didn't turn.

* * *

The days passed slowly and the nights were cold. He shot game and fished and spent the afternoons gathering wood. At night he felt isolated and lonely. A hundred times he decided to go to the house and each time talked himself out of it. One morning a man on horseback spotted his camp and hailed him. George waved and the man approached. When he dismounted he shook his hand. Looking around the man said, "Looks like you been here a spell."

"A while," he responded.

"Isn't this part of the Allen place?"

"I wouldn't know."

"Well, I don't rightly know either. Hey, you're that Indian fella who got hisself slapped in the pillory back in Williamsburg. Skipper's your name. I recollect 'cause it seemed an odd name for an Indian."

"Yeah, well, small world," George said coldly and made a point of not asking a name in return.

The stranger continued to look at him expecting him to say something else. When the silence got awkward the man said, "Indians!" swung into the saddle and turned the horse's head toward the house.

George said, "Dammit."

All through the day and evening he expected to be ejected from his camp. When he decided to go to sleep he checked the prime in his pistol and attached it to his wrist with a lanyard. The moon had not risen and the fire, which he had not adequately banked, was barely flickering when the sound of a careless footstep jolted him awake. He squawked a somnambulistic outcry, snatched at the lanyard and pointed the pistol toward the sound.

"George, it's me," Mary cried.

He lowered the gun and waited for his heart to slow before he managed to say, "Damn, woman, I nearly shot you."

"What kind of a greeting would that have been?" She dropped the leather bag she was carrying and put her arms around his neck saying, "If the offer is still open, let's go."

He hugged her hard and kissed her equally so. The contact caused an erection to swell in his pant leg. "How long do you figure before they start looking for you?" he whispered in her ear.

She felt the hardness he was thrusting against her loins and grasped his meaning. "There's no time for that. We've got to get away from here right now."

They rode until it was full daylight then found a place in a pine grove where the sun couldn't penetrate. There was nothing for the horse to graze so George tethered him instead of hobbling. The pine needles were as soft as a mattress and the morning air mild and fresh. He removed her dress and paused for a few seconds to admire her perfect body and recollect the joy it had given him years before.

"George, come into me," she murmured a phrase that he would hear in his mind again and again.

Later they slept the sleep of contentment until the light was failing.

* * *

"I hope you don't think I'm going to spend the winter sleeping on the ground," Mary told him.

"Then we will have to go to Potecasi. I don't see any way around it."

"I don't want to see that woman every day."

"Do you have a better idea?"

"What's wrong with Assamoosick?"

"Too close to Chounteroute. Allen is sure to look for you there," he tried to add credibility to his excuse with strong inflection. "Maybe she'll leave on her own when she sees us together."

"You don't know a thing about women, do you?"

Actually he did and he knew it was a foolish argument. "You're just going to have to get used to the idea. We don't have a choice for now."

George, Sr. heard his son's plea and did not take a second to respond, "You're still as worthless as tits on a boar! I've got your sister and her husband to feed and I've been taking care of your first wife because you and her father won't. I'm not about to support your worthless ass and another woman."

In desperation he went to Laura and tried to cajole her into leaving the house only to have her laugh in his face. Then he threatened her with violence but she menaced him with a poker. The exchange escalated to a shoving match. That was when she grabbed the gun from its rack and leveled it on him. He lunged to knock the barrel away from his chest but she was quicker and the ball hit him in the shoulder and passed clear through it. It spun him sideways and he dropped to one knee.

"Now, you get the hell out of here before I reload or my next shot'll blow your fucking balls off."

He took her at her word.

Stumbling along the way to his father's house the pain made him light headed until he staggered off the path and collapsed in the dirt which was the favored shitting spot for Whitey, the dog. The discovery of that reality imbued him with enough strength to crawl as far as the rear stoop where his commotion attracted his mother's attention.

"George, come quick! She shot the boy and she rolled him in dog shit," she called as she pulled him into the kitchen and cut the shirt from him. She had both wounds packed with pigeon down by the time the elder George and Mary Bailey got there.

His father appraised the situation and said, "Now, you're even more worthless."

His ancient and withered grandmother heard what happened and came doddering into the bedroom where they put him to rest. She was hunched and frail but becoming more feisty instead of less, and was considered the matriarch by the Indians of the community to the extent that some gave their children the surname Skipper, per custom, even though they weren't related. When Suntetung informed her of the situation her comment was, "We will have to convene a council to decide what to do with the Oxendine girl. In the mean time George and Mary can stay with me."

John and James were summoned to carry their nephew to Mary's house but when John tried to lift him from under his arms he wailed and cursed and fainted from the pain. Since he was unconscious, James, the bigger of the two, simply threw him over his shoulder and made the transfer to his own old room.

Mary called a council and sent her three sons to summon Silas Oxendine by force if necessary. He came but under protest. Mary began, "Sons and brothers, George and Laura are no longer man and wife. They cannot live together in peace. She must leave his house and promise not to shoot him again. If I weren't a Christian, I would call for flaying her, but we will turn the other cheek if she goes back to her father's house and doesn't cause any more trouble."

Oxendine objected saying, "How'm I goin' feed her? I

ain't got 'nough fur my woman an' me."

Mary contemplated the lout with her rheumy eyes and wondered if God would forgive her if she called for a flaying after all. "Suppose we were to pay you. Say a jug of rum every month. Could you find a way to support her then?"

Oxendine wiped the brown drool that was running from the corner of his mouth and answered, "Well, might be poss'ble in dat case. When does I git de jug?"

"When you get her out of the house—and don't get yourself shot in the process."

He went straight to his daughter and snatched the gun from the rack then he told her, "Git yer things. Dem wild Injuns mean to skin ya alive." She complied very unhappily but there was a look in her eye that a man a little smarter than her father would have found disturbing. Each time the moon was full George, Sr. faithfully took a jug to the Oxendine shanty and inevitably it was gone by the next morning.

CHAPTER FOURTEEN

Lieutenant Governor Alexander Spotswood decided that the only way to permanently resolve the Indian problem was to bring the heathens into the fold and to accomplish this he recruited sixteen-hundred men at arms. They marched to Chounteroute and surrounded the palisade. King Edmonds and James looked through a loophole at the army surrounding them.

James whistled and said, "Did we forget to send the beaver skins?"

"Maybe we better hear what they have to say," the king muttered.

Spotswood and a contingent of officers and interpreters entered through the sally port and were taken to Edmond's house. The pipe was passed with solemnity before Edmonds said to the Lieutenant Governor, "Your numbers are a great flattery considering that we have only thirty warriors."

"Our visit is entirely friendly," Spotswood replied. "We come to extend an offer that will benefit your nation and further unite our two peoples in friendship. It is known that the tribute extracted from you by the treaty of

1677 is a heavy burden. We also know that, as we all do, you desire the best for your sons, therefore, we will forgive the tribute for each and any year that the sons of the chief men attend the new Brafferton School at the College of William and Mary in Williamsburg."

The chief men were stunned and exchanged glances that confirmed all were equally suspicious. No one made any reply so Spotswood continued his spiel, "Naturally, the future of your nation will be enhanced by your sons receiving a Christian education. They will be given skills that will allow them to make their way in the civilized world."

Edmonds wanted to make him stop talking so he interrupted. "This is a question of great importance. We must have time to meet in council before giving you our answer."

"Of course. Allow us to retire so that you may discuss it freely."

When they were gone Wainoak Robin said, "They're not getting my boy." All the men began agreeing and talking at the same time. Edmonds let them yammer boastfully as he thought his way through the matter.

"Brothers," he said when he felt it was time to pull the group together, "we are thirty against that hoard. What makes you think they will take no for an answer?"

The ugly truth of his question brought silence to the assembly.

After a moment James asked rhetorically, "How do we know they won't sell our sons as slaves?"

Edmonds responded, "How could we stop them? Whatever their motive, it is clear they intend to have their way. All we can do is minimize our sorrow."

Sam had been pondering this and offered, "My son has been a disrespectful shit. Maybe some time at school will teach him a lesson."

Edmonds had to smile. Peter laughed and *Cockarouse* Will said, "I'll send a boy. I've got too many mouths to feed."

"Well, bring them then. The sooner we give Spotswood what he came for the sooner he will go away," Edmonds said resignedly.

"What? Two?" Spotswood sputtered when the boys were delivered. Sam's son was belligerent and was dragged with a rope around his neck. Will's boy was younger and cowered at the stranger's feet.

"The rest of us have been cursed with daughters," Edmonds declared sadly.

"This will never do," Spotswood was indignant. "You must find some more boys to send or we will not forgive the tribute."

Edmonds would have tomahawked him on the spot and gotten immense pleasure from it if there weren't sixteen-hundred guns pointed at him. "Brother, we will retire to our wives and do all we can to make more sons so that we can send them to you but only if you keep your word about the tribute. Otherwise the wives will suffer for no gain."

Spotswood glowered but took the two boys and left with his brigade. The chief men congratulated themselves for having gotten rid of him cheaply and celebrated with a pipe and a jug.

Sometime later when the incident with Spotswood was nearly forgotten, except by Sam's and Will's wives, the Indian agents, Thomas Cocke and John Simmons, hailed the women who were the town's outposts. The women in turn raised their voices in the staccato yipping that told the guards at the sally port that friends were approaching. The agents with their two interpreters rode into the palisade and to King Edmonds' house. The king and his wife were seated on the ground with a flat basket of corn and fish between them. Edmonds did not greet the men until he had had his fill.

"Brothers," he said, "greetings. Sit and take some fish and some beer. Wani Kohan will fetch some for us." His woman scowled but went for the beer. "Do you bring news of our sons who are shamefully held hostage by the white-devil, Spotswood?"

"King," Simmons said through the interpreter, Henry Briggs, "your sons are not hostages. They are fed and clothed and receiving the boon of an English education." Edmonds grunted and Simmons continued, "How did you ever convince Spotswood that all the chiefs had only two sons amongst them?"

"It is often assumed by white men who think they are wise in our ways that our women are less fertile than white women. Spotswood's vanity made it easy to convince him that his wisdom was true." The two men smiled at this common misconception.

"King, we bring a message from the Council at Williamsburg—"

"When the Council sends greetings, I reach for my tomahawk," Edmonds interrupted.

Cocke sighed, "Brother, you may need a tomahawk."

Simmons opened a document that he took from his coat pocket. His mouth opened and closed as if the written words were unfamiliar. At last he said simply, "The Council orders that you take in the Meherrin. The Nansemond are to relocate to the Saponie town."

Edmonds stared in disbelief and passed his hand across the bare side of his head, Wani Kohan wailed. The aging warrior king fixed his eyes on Simmons and surprised him by speaking intelligible English, "You are gone mad." Then through Briggs he added, "Will Spotswood send his warriors to conduct the war you are bringing to our town? And when he does, which side will they take? Tell me, did the Council's paper refer to us as the People at the Fork of the River or does it call us snakes?"

Simmons tried to paint the situation in its best light. "The Meherrin have promised to live in peace with their brothers, the Cheroenhaka—"

"Did they say 'Cheroenhaka' or 'Nottoway'?"

Simmons didn't answer and Edmonds added, "Suppose it was in my power to order that the Spanish come to Virginia to live in peace with their English brothers…"

Simmons blanched at the prospect and at Edmonds' acumen. "This may benefit your people, King. The Meherrin bring about twenty warriors to add to your numbers."

He had said it to Briggs but Briggs said to Wynn, "You translate it. He's fit to kill the bloody messenger."

When Edmonds got the translation he replied with heat, "When you drive away the Nansemond warriors the Meherrin will outnumber us. They are dogs and will kill us in our sleep and take our women and sell our children. It took our fathers generations to live in peace with the Nansemond and now you will drive them away and force us to live with dogs."

Simmons took Briggs' concern to heart. He said, "Brother, it is not us who has done this injustice to you. Mr. Cocke and I have your best interest at heart but we are bound to carry the message of the Council."

With a crafty smile and some amusement at their discomfort, Edmonds announced, "I am a reasonable man and I know that you are our friends. My anger is saved for the Meherrin and the Council. You will be my guests tonight and we will celebrate our friendship. Until the feast is prepared you will rest in the longhouse."

To have some fun at their expense Edmonds placed a guard outside the longhouse with orders to keep them confined until after the dancing started. The agents and translators were accustomed to the Cheroenhaka and knew that although generally peaceable they were capable of belligerence and were not unwilling to torture captives. Edmonds kept them in the longhouse until the drumming started then he directed the warriors to dance and had the Englishmen brought to the ceremonial center under guard. Their uneasiness was plain on their faces.

Edmonds rose on their arrival and raised his hands.

"Greetings, friends. Are you ready to join the celebration?" He embraced each of them in turn and offered a jug of rum. Briggs was so relieved his knees nearly buckled.

Cocke had Wynn ask, "Why were we kept under guard?"

Edmonds laughed and took a swig from the jug before he answered. "Brothers, the news you brought made me very unhappy. I was hoping the look on your faces when you thought I might have you flayed would make me laugh, and it did. Now, enjoy the night." He clapped his hands and gestured to someone in the distance. In a moment four girls appeared and began taunting the astonished Englishmen.

When the warriors finished dancing the circle was empty for a time, the tempo of the drumming slowed and the chanting turned low and pulsing. A dozen women materialized from the shadows. Their naked bodies painted black and glistening. The fire light reflected from the curves of their bodies captured the eyes of all the men but the four conflicted white men were awestruck. The girls at their sides fondled them and teased with their hard, nubile breasts. Their ingrained sense of morality was stretched to the breaking point. Edmonds furtively observed them and smiled to himself knowing that it had indeed broken.

The king had a fine breakfast sent to the longhouse but did not call on his guests until they appeared of their own accord. "Brothers," he beamed, "did your night pass with happiness?"

Thomas Cocke replied, "Yes, King, there was much happiness."

"I'm pleased to hear it. Now, what will you do to repay my hospitality?"

Simmons immediately caught Edmond's drift and began stammering while he thought of reasonable responses. "Well, King, we always do everything we can in your best interest."

"Very good, then, get rid of the Meherrin."

"Uh, well, I'm not sure that's within our power to do. The Council as decreed it."

"Do not offend me. Is it not your responsibility to prevent immoral Englishmen from taking advantage of our innocence? Would dishonoring our maidens not be seen badly in Williamsburg? Would it not be wrong for you to stand silent while dogs are sent to defile our home? Would you not like to leave here with your skin still containing your innards?"

"King, what is it you want us to do?"

"Show the Council their madness."

Thomas Cocke said, "We will try."

The moon was not full two times when the troops of Alexander Spotswood herded more than a hundred Meherrin into the palisade at Chounteroute and left with all the full blood Nansemond. Edmonds and the chief men got on their horses and went to Potecasi.

* * *

"Kill 'em," George, Sr. suggested.

"We have to think about the boys at Williamsburg," Edmonds reminded him.

"Well, you could bring the people here."

"And abandon the land to the Meherrin dogs?"

"Was it wise to leave the women behind?"

"The warriors have divided the town and are between the women and the dogs, but without the Nansemond, they are outnumbered. How many men and guns from here will return with us, George?"

"My brothers, Whaley and that worthless son of mine with the bullet hole in him. Maybe there will be some others."

"Hurry, George. We worry about the women. And bring some rum. We're going to need it."

Although they had grown somewhat agrarian three full blood Cheroenhaka living at Potecasi considered themselves warriors and were eager to join their brothers. Eight armed men and a barrel of run were added to the cause. They traversed the distance to Chounteroute in a few hours and arrived before dark. The town was divided by a line starting at the sally port and crossing to the far wall. Warriors sat on opposite sides glaring at each other. With the return of the chief men and the eight newcomers the Cheroenhaka side rejoiced, cheering and howling curses at the Meherrin who no longer had superior numbers. Edmonds bade them to be calm and led his chiefs to the leaders of the Meherrin to try to find some accommodation.

The Meherrin *werrowance* actually looked like a dog. His earlobes were hugely stretched from having worn heavy ear flares for many years to the extent that the holes no longer would hold them. "We are no happier than you, Nottoway," he sneered.

Edmonds was able to dismiss being called a snake by considering that a dog would not know any better. "Brothers," he began magnanimously, "we have this burden forced upon us by the white-devils. They have our sons as hostages and they surround us with so many guns we cannot count them. There is no choice but find a way to live in peace."

Tirehr Skeyu shook his head making his earlobes slap his face. "We cannot live in peace. The blood between us is all bad. You will talk of peace and bury your tomahawks in our skulls while we sleep."

George found that he had a visceral dislike for this man. He stepped forward with his father's best rifle pointed generally at the dog's chest. "We don't need to wait until you're asleep to put a ball through your heart," he growled. The Meherrin warriors raised their guns menacingly.

Edmonds put his hand on George's arm.

"Cheroenhaka will not shed first blood."

A Meherrin directly behind his king said, "When are you going to feed us?" It took the Cheroenhaka contingent off guard. They looked at one another in disbelief.

Finally Robin Scholar said, "Get your own food."

The indisputable impasse and the unreality of the question defused the situation somewhat. The Cheroenhaka chiefs turned their backs and retired to their defensive position between their families and the intruders. George drew a jug off the hogshead and the men smoked while they passed it. "Brothers," he said wiping somebody's spit from the mouth of the jug, "I admit that I cannot see a solution to this problem."

George, Jr. felt the heat of the rum rise in his cheeks. He said, "How do we know the agents made any effort to change the Council's mind? And it seems to me that this is the kind of problem that demands their presence. Maybe we even need to retain a lawyer again."

"He's right," Ned said, "the fools need to see the harm they've done."

Edmonds scratched the bald side of his head. "It would be gratifying to have them here but I fear losing one of our number to go for them."

"Send the boy," George, Sr. said, "if one of those dogs took a shot at him he'd wet his pants."

George quashed his irritation and said, "I don't know where to find them."

Robin Scholar said, "Cocke lives in Surry. He'll know where the others are."

"This is good," Edmonds thought aloud. "His English is best. He'll make them understand."

"Don't be *too* hopeful," his father added, "if he smells a female, he'll forget everything else."

Presumably all the females were downwind for it took only a day and a half to reach Surry and a couple more hours to locate the person of Thomas Cocke, Gentleman.

"Beg your pardon, sir," George said when he found him, "I'm George Skipper of the—"

"I know who you are," Cocke interrupted, "and I suspect I know what you want." Cocke was the most sympathetic toward the Indians of the agents. He was not unwilling to take licentious pleasure in the time he passed in their towns. "What do you think I can do that hasn't already been tried?"

"Try again," George told him frankly. "If a solution isn't found, there will be war."

Cocke took this seriously and after consideration said, "War might be the only solution there is. The winning side gets to keep the town."

"The winning side will want revenge on the cause of the problem. Plus, there's the fate of two young boys being held hostage for the purpose of forcing treaty cooperation."

"Yes, I see what you mean but the Lieutenant Governor and Council are intractable and, with the militia they've raised, they hold all the cards."

"Well, at the very least, we must have someone to mediate between us and the Meherrin dogs. Right now there are no cool heads at Chounteroute. For God's sake, man, get the others and come see for yourselves. It may already be too late."

Simmons was too ill to travel but Edwards and the translators were assembled and went to Chounteroute as quickly as the horses could take them.

"What did I miss?" George asked his father as the agents divided and approached the two kings to see if a meeting could be arranged.

"More of the same. The long eared fox there is spoiling for a fight and Edmonds is trying to keep the rest of us from granting his wish. We're running out of meat because the warriors think if any of them go hunting the dogs will attack."

Cocke and Edwards walked through the sally port to

talk in private. Wynn and Briggs were taking a cup of rum and chatting with the girls. Edmonds approached his chiefs looking solemn. "All is madness," he said to no one in particular.

Days passed without movement. The agents had no suggestions and did nothing better than to keep the two sides separated. Cocke sat next to the Skippers talking with them in English. Suddenly he stopped and looked quizzically at the older man. "Wasn't there once a George Skipper who ran afoul of the law?"

"Perhaps you're thinking of my late father. He was the victim of much calumny."

Cocke smiled and made no response.

George decided he liked the Indian agent and ventured a thought that had been stirring in his mind. "Do you think you could broker a deal that would move one or the other side beyond the wall?"

"What do you mean? Edmonds is adamant that he will never give up the Cheroenhaka homestead."

"Sure and I agree with him but the stalemate will never end until one side is removed from within the fort. Offer them a wager. Single combat. Loser moves outside. If it's us, we'll build another palisade. They could do the same if they had any ambition."

"A curious suggestion," Cocke said looking intrigued. "Shall we put it to the king?"

George called to Edmonds who was sitting with the warriors. He came to them and George explained his proposal.

"This is a very wise idea, George. Ask Cocke to take it to the Meherrin dog."

George, Jr. asked, "Who is the strongest warrior?" He was fairly sure it wasn't him.

Edmonds smiled, "The strongest warriors will not fight. It will be me and the long eared dog. Tell it to Cocke."

Cocke was astounded. "A most curious notion. Is he

certain?"

Edmonds responded to the inquiry, "Take the challenge to the Meherrin dog. We'll see if he's a coward."

Cocke got Edwards and the interpreters and found Tirehr Skeyu. He listened to the proposal without reacting. He told them he would call a council of his chiefs to see if they would abide by the outcome and as he left the place of the meeting he appraised Edmonds carefully.

The two agents loitered with the Cheroenhaka men while the Meherrin held their council. Edwards said to George, Sr., "I assume we're talking about a pistol duel."

George was not familiar with the custom but his son was and replied, "I seriously doubt it." To Edmonds he said, "Tomahawks, right?" Edmonds nodded and he explained it to Edwards whose eyes grew large.

"Good Lord," he said.

Tirehr Skeyu could hardly refuse the challenge, and when his chiefs agreed to accept the outcome, the die was cast. Edmonds immediately removed his beaded doeskin tunic and stepped forward with his tomahawk. He was a sinewy man something over fifty, a bit taller than his adversary who, though younger, appeared slightly dissipated by comparison. Each was equipped with English made steel tomahawks. Tirehr Skeyu's was adorned with eagle feathers, Edmonds' was plain. The Meherrin king crouched slightly and began to circle his opponent but Edmonds stood erect and still with his right arm holding the weapon above his head. Without any warning his arm shot forward had he launched the tomahawk at his enemy. He moved so fast that the spectators didn't have time to worry that if he missed he'd be dead. The blade hit the Meherrin's right eyebrow with a crack and penetrated his brain by the width of two fingers. His knees buckled and he went down on his back without making a sound. The stunned onlookers watched in silence as his twitching limbs grew still and a pool of blood spread under his head.

Edmonds stood oddly still contemplating the corpse without expression then he turned slowly to the Meherrin side of the compound and said in loud voice, "Brothers, take this with you when you leave."

The men crowded Edmonds to offer congratulations. George slapped him on the back and said, "King, let me pour you a drink."

He grinned and said, "I'd like that, George."

* * *

Cocke and Edwards came back to Chounteroute in the spring along with Briggs, Wynn and two strangers. The stranger wore long black square cut coats and long, white, starched collars. Edmonds eyed the strangers warily. Through Wynn he asked the agents, "You bringing more trouble?"

Edwards responded, "King, the Lieutenant Governor sends his greetings and the blessing of the word of God."

"What god?"

"The only true Christian God."

Edmonds scowled. "Who are these men?"

Edwards beamed, "The fine gentlemen are missionaries who will lead you on the path to salvation."

"Take them to the Meherrin and tell them to keep away from my wife," the king said flatly and walked away.

Cocke and Edwards took their charges to the longhouse. They were completely ignored until Watt Bailey's wife got wind of their arrival and took them food. With her assistance they began plying their trade on the unsuspecting. Edmonds sent a messenger to Potecasi to implore George to deliver more rum.

The sound of hymn singing was coming from the longhouse when Edmonds encountered Cocke. Seizing him by the upper arm he asked rhetorically in English, "What more can Spotswood do?"

In August of the next year he got his answer. Simmons arrived looking haggard and he had a nagging cough. "King," he said through Briggs who had become a fixture at Chounteroute, "the Lieutenant Governor sends greetings and extends an invitation to all your chiefs to be his guest in capital."

Edmonds smelled a trap. "We don't want to go."

"It would be a great insult to reject his generous invitation. I'm sure he will offer many fine presents."

"Tell him to keep his presents. All his presents come with hungry mouths."

"I warn you, King, if you anger the Lieutenant Governor there will be trouble."

The chiefs met—less George Skipper who would not set foot in Williamsburg—and after much suspicion was floated around the circle, it was decided that walking into the trap was better than being dragged into it.

At Williamsburg the air was stifling with the tension of an approaching storm in the air. Spotswood received the chiefs in his home and presented them with white *wampum*. "Brothers," he began after the protocol was finished, "you continue to ignore my request to educate your sons. This is your last opportunity to comply with this generous offer. I am willing to permit you to send them to Fort Christiana which is closer to your town."

"You already have two hostages unless you sold them," Sam groused.

Spotswood remained conciliatory, "We have no hostages and we do not sell our brothers' sons into slavery. We simply want to make the benefits of a Christian education available to your offspring. Now, I have reliable information that most of you have sons of school age. They will be delivered immediately."

There was a pause while the chiefs conferred at the end of which they made clear that they had no intention of offering any more sons to the blessing of English schools. Armed men quickly filled the room and the twelve were roughly herded to the stockade where they were chained to the wall. *Cockarouse* Will resisted and was truncheoned insensible. Robin Scholar said, "This is worse than we expected."

"Why am I here?" Sam complained. "The devils already have my son."

"Perhaps we haven't made enough offerings to Otkum," Ned suggested.

"I didn't know Otkum was a white-devil," Peter theorized.

The following morning Spotswood visited the cell with his interpreter to ask if they were ready to cooperate. They remained defiant and heaped upon him every curse their language offered. Wainoak Robin said he wished he could speak English so he had more curses to apply. Spotswood left without comment.

On the second day Edmonds offered a deal. "Suppose we start sending beaver pelts again and even a wolf's skin?"

Again Spotswood left without remark. The twelve chiefs sat in brooding silence.

Peter said suddenly, "I'm hungry. White-devils could at least feed us."

His outburst shattered the stillness and startled Edmond. "Brothers, we must realize that our enemy is strong. We are going to either lose our sons or our lives," he told them.

"Why does he want our sons?" Peter said to the darkness.

Robin Scholar answered, "It can only be madness. English suffer much from madness."

"It is because they limit themselves to only one woman," *Cockarouse* Sam informed them.

"All their habits are maddening."

On the third day without food they capitulated and agreed to offer their sons to be forged on the anvil of Christian education. They had no idea what the truth of it meant. Spotswood made a steeple of his fingers, smiled and said, "Excellent, excellent."

Among the twelve chief men they had eight sons to sacrifice to the cruel plan. The Meherrin fared worse. They sent twelve boys to Fort Christiana to be civilized and Christianized. At Chounteroute the missionaries enforced the policy that anyone found naked in public received ten strokes. Edmonds drowned his sorrows. When the awful news reached George at Potecasi he thanked his lucky stars for the swamp

CHAPTER FIFTEEN

The newly formed Bertie Precinct encompassed Potecasi. James Skipper petitioned for a parcel of land which necessitated loitering in Edenton which was in Chowan. At the end of August he received his grant of six-hundred acres in the Urah Woods which was just south of Potecasi Woods and abutted his late father's land. He had recently taken a girl by the name of Mary Troxell for a wife and hurried back to Potecasi to fetch her and the families to help clear his new land. The group arrived while the surveyor was still blazing trees. Being late summer, there was no time to put crops in the ground so after trees were cleared they went back to Potecasi to spend the winter in comfort.

As seasons passed James planted his crops and built his house. George and Mary shuttled rum to Chounteroute. Auteur Awwa succumbed to his age and was buried next to his old friend, George. Laura vanished from Potecasi which brought much grief to her father as it was no longer seen necessary to supply him with a monthly allowance of rum.

George, Jr. threw himself into rum production with

zeal for although his problem with Laura had apparently vanished he still intended to buy some land outside of the Potecasi settlement to escape the ghosts. Mary was pleased by his industry, at times felt contented, and usually went along to Chounteroute to see her family but she warned, "She'll be back. She'll never leave us in peace."

One morning Mary woke on the wrong side of the bed. "What's wrong," George asked knowing it was a futile question.

"Nothing."

He let it go but her mood did not improve, she stiffened at his touch and answered in monosyllables. "How much longer do I have to endure your silent treatment?" he asked with irritation.

She faced him with indignation and replied, "How much longer do I have to live in sin? I seem to remember you were going to marry me in the church."

A jolt of frustration shook him and he had to wait to answer, "Do you intend to walk into the courthouse where your indenture is recorded, announce that you're Mary Bailey and you would like a marriage license?"

"I should never have let you talk me into running away."

"Why do you say a thing like that at such a hopeful time?"

"Because if I had done what's right, and you waited for me, we could have a Christian wedding."

"We can be married according to our ritual. That's better than nothing."

"It's not the same. My mother taught me different."

"You going to start that again?"

"What's that mean?"

"That's how our problems started in the first place."

"And I suppose you're going to run off and marry somebody else again."

His frustration so tangled his thoughts he was unable to speak until he realized saying nothing was the best thing he could do. He spent the rest of the day weeding the field that was farthest from the house although nearer fields needed weeding more. The weight of his sadness finally oppressed him so badly that he threw his hoe aside and walked to the edge of the bay where he sat on a log and threw stones at bullfrogs until it was too dark to see them. He felt like a helpless child.

* * *

Laura Skipper, nee Oxendine, needed a travelling companion. It proved a small matter to seduce a certain simpleton named Emanuel Chavis and then use promises of more sexual favors to entice him to provide protection for her on a small journey. As had been her custom for years, she first visited one of the full blood Cheroenhaka women and traded for a supply of the root that prevented conception. The thought of being saddled with Emanuel Chavis's bastard made her cringe. The most formidable weapon Chavis owned was a knife so she let him carry her musket which, of course, she had taken from George. The two left Potecasi surreptitiously in the direction of the Chowan Precinct.

* * *

The morning after George sat by the bay contemplating the futility of his existence Mary woke happy again. Baffled as he was, he resumed life as if the incident hadn't happened. A load of spirits was due to be transported to Assamoosick and Chounteroute and Mary expressed excitement about the trip. They left at the end of August on a glorious morning with a pair of hawks circling over head. "That's a good omen," Suntetung told them as they were leaving the settlement.

Mary did not know about Youhanhu and George so he was at liberty to pay his respects to her while at

Assamoosick. "Your woman with the strange colored hair is an improvement over the other," Youhanhu told him.

"Definitely an improvement," he admitted.

"I hear in your voice she might be giving you trouble," she intuited.

"Not much. All women are trouble."

"It's because she is mostly English. You would have better luck with full blooded women."

"They're getting scarce."

"That's why you should have kept me."

Mary saw them talking and grew suspicious. "You make a point of talking to her every time we come here," she accused.

"I talk to a lot of people. She's one of them."

"Do you think she's pretty?"

"Of course she's pretty, but she's got a husband and I have you and that's the end of it."

Naturally it wasn't the end of it. By the time they reached Chounteroute George had broken into a barrel and sulked in silence. Mary went to her parents and George went to smoke with the men. Even though the influence of increasing contact with the English was changing the complexion of the place, Chounteroute was considerably more Indian in nature than Potecasi. Edmonds offered George the services of a maiden which put him in a serious flux.

"King, I cannot thank you enough, but don't dare accept her with Mary here," he confessed.

"Our ways are being taken from us," the king lamented.

* * *

On the way home Mary was still sullen and George was still drinking. "Why don't you stop that? It makes you mean," she harped.

"Why don't you stop being a shrew?"

"So now I'm a shrew?"

"Look, I do everything I can to make you happy and you accuse me of things I didn't do. You're always angry with me. If I wanted other women I would have taken King Edmonds' gift, as it was, I offended him when I refused her."

"But you wanted to."

"What difference does that make? I didn't do it."

She folded her arms and clamped her jaws shut. He uncorked the jug but didn't get it to his mouth when he realized they were surrounded by a group of men pointing guns at them.

"By order of the General Court of the Colony of North Carolina, we are here to arrest the body of one George Skipper, Junior, and apprehend the fugitive, Mary Bailey," the leader recited.

They were manacled and shackled and put in the bed of the wagon. The empty barrels were left by the road. George Allen met them when they crossed into Chowan County and took possession of Mary. He cuffed her on the ear as he pushed her, sobbing quietly, into his carriage. At Edenton George was put into a cell with several other prisoners of many varied complexions. "Something else it's going to take a long time to get out of my head," he muttered to himself.

Mary wrote a letter to her father and persuaded a slave to smuggle it into Allen's outgoing correspondence. When it finally got to him he felt obliged to tell George, Sr. what had happened to his son. "Hell," George told Watt Bailey, "that boy can't do anything right."

It was midwinter and raining when George, Sr. arrived at Edenton. Being his first time to the seat of power and he wondered if he would be arrested and shipped to Virginia, however, boldly he went to the office of the marshal to inquire about his son and his wagon. The wagon was released to him.

"The judge has ordered you held without bond," he

explained through the bars in the door of the cell.

"When's trial?"

"Might be in July."

"I'll be in here near a year by then."

"I'll get you a lawyer," his father told him, "maybe he can do something."

"Much obliged."

The judge was not moved by the motion of Thomas Swann, Esq. George languished in custody although his lot was improved by food his father had provided. "Boy, you're costing me a fortune," he complained before he returned to Potecasi to see to business. Again beset by unwanted thoughts, the gloom and idleness of captivity was fertile terrain for the torment of his guilty memories to the extent he wished he had the means to end his life. Provoking his fellow inmates to murder crossed his mind but, on surveying them again, he decided they were likely to botch the job and thus the minutes dragged until July.

His father had not yet returned from Potecasi on the day he was removed from the cell, marched to the courthouse and put onto a bench behind the attorneys. The case was called and one of the lawyers stood, cleared his throat and began reading:

"I, Thomas Henman, attorney for George Allen, come to prosecute his suit against George Skipper, in custody, etc. of a plea that he, the said defendant, render unto him, the said plaintiff, the sum of five-hundred pounds which the, the said defendant, owes and unjustly detains from him, the said plaintiff. To wit, the thirtieth day of August one-thousand-seven-hundred-twenty-two at the precinct of Chowan for that, to wit, that whereas by an Act of Assembly entitled 'An Act Concerning Servants and Slaves' made and enacted at a General Biennial Assembly, begun and held at the house of Captain Richard Sanderson at Little River, the seventeenth day of November, one-thousand-seven-hundred and fifteen and continued by several adjournments until the nineteenth day of January, one-thousand-seven-hundred and fifteen, amongst divers other things, it is therein and thereby enacted that if any person or persons shall entertain or harbor any runaway servant or slave above one night, he, or they, so offending shall, for every four and twenty hours afterwards, forfeit and pay the sum of ten shillings to the master or mistress of such servant or slave together with all costs, losses and damages which the master or mistress shall sustain by the means of such entertaining or concealment to be recovered in any court of record within this government wherein no essoign protection, injunction or wages of law shall be allowed or admitted of. Nevertheless, the said defendant, not minding or in any manner regarding the said Act, but evilly and maliciously intending to wrong and injure the said plaintiff, the seventeenth day of December in the year of our Lord one-thousand-seven-hundred and nineteen did persuade, delude and take away from the plaintiff's service a servant woman named Mary Bailey, the proper servant of him, the said plaintiff's, and from the said seventeenth day of December in the year one-thousand-seven-hundred and nineteen, at the precinct of Chowan, aforesaid, did entertain and harbor her, the said Mary Bailey, knowing her to be the plaintiff's servant, contrary to and against the meaning, directions and intent of the said Act until the thirtieth day of August, aforesaid, in the year one-thousand-seven-hundred-twenty-two, aforesaid: by reason of which, said harboring and entertaining by the defendant of the plaintiff's said servant from the said seventeenth day of December, one-thousand-seven-hundred an nineteen until the thirtieth day of August, one-thousand-seven-hundred and twenty-two, being nine-hundred eighty-six days: and by force and virtue of the said Act of Assembly, hath accrued to him, the said plaintiff, to recover and have against the defendant the sum of four-hundred-ninety-three pounds and also all such costs losses and damages as he, the said plaintiff, hath sustained by reason of the said harboring and entertaining of the said plaintiff's said servant by the defendant. Wherefore, plaintiff sayth he is damnified and damage hath sustained to the value of five-hundred pounds and therefore he brings this suit, etc."

George's head was spinning as another lawyer rose to say, "Thomas Swann, for the defense. My client pleads not guilty."

The judge, ominous in his huge wig, said, "And hereupon at the motion of the plaintiff, the Marshall is ordered to keep the body of the said defendant in safe custody till he give special security for his appearance at the next court then and there to answer the suit of the said plaintiff till which time the said cause is put in respite. It is also further granted at the plaintiff's motion that a dedimus do issue directed to Captain Henry Harrison, Captain William Browne, Captain John Simmons, Captain Thomas Cocke, gentlemen justices of the peace for the county of Surrey in the Dominion of Virginia, or any two of them, to take the depositions of such evidences as shall be brought before them either by the plaintiff or defendant in the said county, returnable to the next court on the last Tuesday in October next."

Thomas Swann said nothing to George. He was jerked to his feet by the marshal and returned to the cell where the demons returned so he sat in stoic silence and fought them. Maddeningly the phrase he heard the judge say, but which he had no idea what it meant, "dedimus do issue" got stuck in his head and he couldn't stop hearing it over and over again.

George, Sr. returned to Edenton a few days after the hearing and was informed by Swann that the judge had offered 'special security'. On inquiring as to how special it might be, the clerk of court named a sum that exceeded the liquid assets available him. He offered to pledge his land but was reminded that the colony had more than enough land and much preferred cash. Through the bars in the cell door he told his son, "I intend to try to raise it before October. Keep your wits about you and we'll see about getting you out." Wearily he rode home to increase production and look for something to sell.

Nobody came to visit the prisoner after that because the whole family was engaged in the effort to raise money. The elongated isolation wore on George worse than before and increasingly he contemplated the abyss. He began to quarrel with a couple of the more obnoxious inmates and was removed for a night and placed in the stocks. It was hardly a diversion. Despite a great amount of activity the bond money was not raised before the trial date. When it was time to go to Edenton to learn his fate it took two wagons to accommodate the entourage which consisted of Watt Bailey and Mary's mother, Jean and her husband, David Herrin, Suntetung, George, Sr. and his mother, Mary. Thomas Swann had summoned Mary from George Allen's plantation but Allen refused to pay for her expenses so she was forced to petition reimbursement from George. He was feeling defiant the morning of the trial until Swann told him that he was also being sued by the woman he loved. His spirits sank into a dismal funk and then turned into rage when he saw that in the rear of the courtroom staring fixedly to the front was Laura.

Court was called to order and the first piece of business was sending the marshal into the street to find a jury. Twelve stalwarts were finally paraded into the courtroom on the following morning, impaneled and swore their oath. Swann's only defense was that Allen had violated the terms of the indenture by being abusive. It fell on deaf ears. All the jurors had servants and slaves of their own and needed only minutes to return from the deliberation room. The foreman, a certain John Rasberry who may have carried some Indian blood in his veins, rose to deliver the verdict, "We of the jury find ten days and damage five pounds with costs."

"What?" Allen leapt to his feet shouting, "Robbery!"

"Silence!" the judged bellowed. He gave the still

standing foreman an evil glare and said, "Thank you, gentlemen of the jury. Your service is at end." He waited for the twelve to file from the room before continuing. "Wherefore, it is considered that the plaintiff recover and have of the defendant the sum of *ten* pounds and costs, alias execution."

Allen groaned and received the evil glare. The judge cleared his throat and recited, "On the petition of Mary Bailey praying to be allowed for two days attendance and four days coming to and going from court, ordered that the defendant pay her sixteen shillings and eight pence with costs, alias execution."

George, Sr., who had been prepared to settle a judgment of five-hundred pounds, was beside himself with relief. He happily settled with the clerk and counted sixteen shillings, eight pence into Mary's hand while George was taken back to his cell to serve the ten days. Mary returned to Allen's plantation to finish the last year and a half of her indenture. In the street in front of the courthouse Laura and George Allen were seen in an agitated discussion.

The Skipper family remained in Edenton celebrating with the money they didn't have to spend and waiting for George to be released. At night the drumming and chanting heard in their room at the inn made some of the guests very nervous.

CHAPTER SIXTEEN

The Skipper name floating around Edenton pricked the ears of the customs official who was acting as postmaster. He had a letter addressed to George Skipper delivered to the inn where the clan was lodged. George broke the seal and read:

> Oak Grove July 25, 1723
> Berkley County
> South Carolina
>
> Esteemed friend,
> George Skipper, Sr.
> Potecasi
>
> Since the happy time of your visit your nephew and my daughter have been blessed with three more healthy children. Now, in addition to William, Jr. and John there are Benning, Ann and Sarah. But it is my sad duty to report that William, Sr. was stricken by the fever this last winter and succumbed on the second day of Jan'y. Our grief is inconsolable.
> The care of your nieces and nephews need not be a

matter for concern. A fine gentleman of this Country
by name of James Furguson has confided in me that he
intends to ask for the hand of my daughter, Anne,
when a respectable period of mourning is ended. It is
my strong suspicion that she will give him a favorable
response. Whether that be the case or not, you may
rest assured that my grandchildren will not want.
It is the profound hope of all here that someday you
may favor us with another visit.
Till then, sir,
I remain your obedient servant,

Thomas Barker

"This was meant for father," George told his mother.

She patted his hand and assured him, "He won't
mind."

"Cousin William died."

"That's terrible."

"He was the last white Skipper. Well, he left three
sons. I suppose they're not mixed blood. I wonder if we
will ever know them."

Mary studied him curiously. "I doubt I will, but all you
have to do is get on your horse and go introduce yourself."

"Someday. Right now all I want to do is get back to
the farm. There's a world of things fallen behind."

George was released the following morning. His sister
told him, "George, I hope for everyone's sake you can
settle down with a woman who won't get you in trouble."

He let it roll off his back but privately he thought it an
excellent suggestion.

* * *

Laura reappeared at her parents' shabby excuse of a house
and George knew that if he didn't leave Potecasi eventually
he'd kill her. He took his intentions to his father who told
him, "Might be the smartest thing you ever said. I guess if

I was willing to give you money to settle a lawsuit I ought to be willing to give you money for land."

"I only need eighty pounds. I've got the rest."

"No, take the whole two forty. You'll need money to build a house."

"Well, thank you. I'll repay it."

"You don't have to repay it so long as you don't get crazed over some split-tail and find your arse in gaol again."

"I'll try."

It was on the first day of February, 1725 that he received his patent for 120 acres in the Bertie Precinct about thirty miles from Potecasi. He built a fine house with glass in all the windows and a cistern right outside the kitchen door. His grandmother was brought to see it and pronounced it "uppish".

His father asserted, "He's built himself a lure to try to get the redhead back."

He did not respond to that but when his guests had left he sat at his somewhat uppish desk and composed a letter to her wherein he reasoned since neither would be fugitives at the end of her indenture the possibility of a church wedding was realistic. He dispatched a messenger to carry it to the Allen plantation and was careful to keep his name from the outside of the letter.

* * *

A hurricane passed up the coast and the heavy rains flooded Potecasi. It came at a time of upheaval. Hard times fell upon James who was victim of a lingering illness that sapped his strength and prevented him from tending his crops. His brother John helped with the fields and his brother George bought all but forty acres of his land for ten pounds. Wolves killed the dog Whitey which bothered George, Jr. much more than his father. Ancient Mary took to talking in spirit tongues and had to be kept by her son and Suntetung. When the rains came she left her bed jabbering that Quakerhunte and Jesus were together in the sky and she was going to join them then walked outside without anyone noticing, collapsed into the foot deep floodwater and breathed her last. This made Suntetung matriarch and it was a role to which she had been born.

"George," she began, "we will have a have a house grander than the boy's and it will not be in this swamp."

The land that he bought from James had a fine prominence at a bend in the river which suited Suntetung so he set to the task. Some of the more sentient citizens of the Potecasi settlement were willing to work for modest wages but were not to be left unsupervised. George made a camp for himself and the workers but Suntetung preferred the comforts of the Potecasi house. She summoned her sister, Aheeta, who had long since developed woman's breasts and had done a fine job of it.

"She will be your camp wife," Suntetung told George. "She will cook and wash your clothes, but you keep your hands off her."

"*How did I ever get so henpecked?*" he asked himself.

Aheeta had not had the anglicizing effect of contact with the Potecasi clan. "My sister is a selfish fool," she told George on the way to the new house site. "If I am to be your wife then you have to act like a husband."

"Oh, dear," he fretted, "I think you're going to get us both flayed alive."

"Not if you don't tell her."

He didn't have any response to that.

At the camp he found two of his workers sleeping in the whipsaw pit and two others floating on their backs in the river. They were rather rudely put back to work but Aheeta, who arrived wearing only a painted doe skin apron proved to be a serious distraction for the men who were used to the relative modesty displayed by even the full bloods who lived at Potecasi.

George, Jr. appeared one day and when he saw her in

the same costume all he could say was, "My stars."

"Hello, George," she beamed, "how have you been?"

"Not so bad," he replied. "How are you? It's been a long time." When he found his father he said, "You old devil, how did you pull this off?"

"It was your mother's idea."

"I hope you can smell a trap."

"I can but she can't. It's going to be a very long summer."

"Well, why don't you let me take you away from temptation? I've a mind to put a good size still at the new place and I could use your years of experience."

"Where you going to get it?"

"Coppersmith at Edenton, if you'll come along and help explain it to him."

"I wouldn't mind. It's getting risky around here. Tomorrow suit you?"

When he left he told the men that if they went slack Aheeta would be keeping an eye on them and they'd in store for a whipping.

"Don't you worry, boss. We'll be keeping an eye on her too," the self appointed leader of the crew remarked.

George told his son, "I wish your mother wouldn't do me any more favors."

* * *

The coppersmith was called Thomas Spires. He was impressed by the magnitude of the proposed still and agreed to abide by the specifics of the design as outlined by the elder Skipper. His fee was twenty-five pounds, ten shillings which was agreed. Spires promised to complete the project in a fortnight so the two left five pounds in good faith and returned to their respective pursuits.

Aheeta had made corn cakes and baked fish for the workers. She gave some to George when he arrived near dusk after a long day on his horse. He took a whiskey jug from his hiding place and poured a gill for each of them. The workers took theirs to their tents to enjoy it without being in under the critical gaze of their employer. Aheeta took a big swallow and gasped from the burn. "I'm happy you're back," she told him.

"Why's that?" he asked.

"I don't like being alone with them."

"They give you any trouble?"

"No, but I like it better when you're here." She drank some more and putting the cup on the ground took her drum in hand, beat it gently and began to sing.

George felt the fatigue of the ride drain from his limbs as the whiskey did its work. Soon he said, "I'm going to bed, woman. Thank you for dinner." With that he crawled into the tent and pulled off his shirt. Aheeta drained her cup, choked and crawled after him. She slid onto the bearskin beside him and slipped her hand down the front of his trousers. She was already naked and he felt her vaunted breasts against his bare chest and he knew it was hopeless.

"Woman, are you taking the root?" he demanded.

"Sure. If I give light to a bastard with a big nose Suntetung really *will* flay me."

"Oh, you'll pay for that," he smiled and smacked her firm round ass well aware that his life had just gotten very complicated.

* * *

Living alone did not suit George, Jr. Any time he was idle or alone the demons seized him and he relived each degrading thing that had befallen him in the course of his life and the list was getting long. The day approached to collect the still so he resolved to do something that seemed quite logical to him at the time. He would buy a slave and since it was female companionship he craved that part of the decision was obvious. It was a stout investment and after settling for the still he was concerned that the sum of cash he had would limit the quality of his selection. Nevertheless, he hitched his wagon and headed for Edenton.

Thomas Spires was the sort of craftsman who assumed he knew more about what his customers wanted than they did. The most specific specification given him was to encase the condenser coil in a jacket to allow cooling water to flow over it. He omitted that feature.

"Ye don't need it," he insisted.

"Perhaps not, but we asked for it and you agreed to provide it," George reminded him.

"Balderdash! I've made ye a fine piece of equipment that will serve yer evil enterprise just fine. Now, I'll have me money and be done with ye."

"You'll not get a cent until you cover that coil," George told him.

"I'll not lay a hand to it until ye count money onto that table."

"You'll see none of it until you make it the way we ordered it." George felt heat his cheeks and ears flush.

"Fine then. Pay what you owe and for ten pounds more I'll add yer gewgaw."

"You're not getting one farthing more and you will cover that coil," he said inflating his chest and advancing on the man.

Spires opened a drawer under his work bench and produced a pistol as adroitly as he might have a tinner's hammer. "Now, ye sir, will remove yerself from the premises and we will then let the magistrate decide the fate of yer device," he threatened.

George stormed from the place swearing and shaking with rage.

* * *

The morning was stormy and humid with electricity in the

air. After an extravagant breakfast of smoked shad and turtles' eggs he strolled to the waterfront serene in the realization that he now had an extra twenty pounds to invest in the wench of his choice. The market was dank and fetid. It was a short row of arched cloisters with the wares chained to the rear wall. The bucks sat in sullen defiance and the women were huddled together as much as the chains permitted. A few sported loin cloths though most were naked. George tried to coax a girl from the shadows to have a better look but she only clung tighter to the woman beside her.

The men went on the block first and George paced impatiently at the rear of the bidding crowd. Next were able bodied women. He studied them with interest but did not find one that answered all of his requirements. Lastly girls and boys were prodded onto the slightly raised rostrum. Some very small children received no bids at all but competition for nubile girls with their glossy black skin taut over still developing, sharply pointed, breasts got quite brisk. George did not win the first two on which he bid but the next so transfixed him he would not desist. It took nearly every last shilling in his purse but he left with his tall, toothsome acquisition on a tether.

He was told she answered to Willoughby. "Where'd that come from?" he asked in an effort to establish rapport.

She barely spoke English and answered sadly, "Willoughby. I be Willoughby. You's be massa."

"Yes, that's a good beginning. We'll work on verbs later."

The first thing he did once home was to give her a bath which confused and frightened her. She withdrew and cowered until he forced her into the tub then she struck him and bit his hand. By the time he was finished most of the bath water was on the kitchen floor and she sat huddled next to the basin with a towel over her head. He had cuffed her sufficiently to convince her to stop biting but her English was so bad as to make reason and cooperation utterly impossible. He hadn't thought to buy her any clothes in Edenton, in fact he hadn't any money, and he could think of nothing in his rather limited to wardrobe to offer.

"Well, that's not the end of the world," he thought aloud.

He fixed a meal while attempting to show her how to do it which solicited not one glimmer of insight. She did have a healthy appetite, however. He got the idea that a little whiskey might relax her and he certainly needed something to balm his own frustration. She sniffed it and pushed the cup to arm's length.

"Well, waste not, want not," he muttered and drank what she rejected. "Now, look, Willoughby, I didn't buy you to be your servant. You're simply going to have to learn to do things around here."

She stared wide eyed but uttered nothing.

"Let's start with something simple." He took her by the arm which caused her to sharply recoil. He raised his hand threateningly and she relaxed, so taking her arm he pulled her to her feet and guided her outside to the woodpile. He handed her a piece of wood but she stared at it dumbly. He then positioned her arms and laid a couple sticks across them which she accepted. "Come, now," he said coaxing her by the elbow to carry the wood into the kitchen. "That's good. Here now, let's put it in the hearth." He actually put it in the hearth but she smiled as if she had performed a miracle.

"That's better," he told her. "Now, you do it. Go get some more wood." He pushed her gently toward the door. She passed outside and just kept walking. "No, Willoughby, over there. Get some wood from the pile." She still walked with eyes straight ahead. He strode after her and tried to turn her but she resisted so he scooped her in his arms and carried her back to the house. It was then he noticed a strong musky smell. He sniffed her hair and skin and said, "I must have done a poor job of scrubbing you. Let's try it again."

This time she took to the bath as if it were a great luxury and only resisted when he lathered her head and poured a bucket of rinse water over it. She even stood still while he toweled her dry which act frankly, and profoundly, aroused him. "Might as well get some use of you," he said taking her by the arm to his bedroom. "Lay down there."

She sat still and watched him undress uncomprehendingly. "Come on, now," he said making her lie down, "there's got to be something you know how to do." He began the ritual of stroking and nuzzling that had served him so many times in the past but she made no response whatever. So he caressed those amazing breasts that he had bought so dearly. The only result was to incite his urgency. "Look, Willoughby, this is something you're going to have to get used to," he persuaded. "If you relax and cooperate, you will get to like it."

There was no response so he parted her legs and touched her there. She reacted violently to that, turning to her side and drawing her knees into a fetal position. For hours he tried to get her to cooperate, become enthused or simply relent until in a fit of frustration he sated himself by rubbing against that exquisite black hide. She remained rigidly impassive. He lay close by her in the stupor of his release breathing her essence. "Damn, child," he whispered, "you still got that musky smell."

* * *

George lost all patience with the girl and whipped her with a willow switch until he felt better and she began to respond to his orders but she was hopelessly inept at everything she tried. At night he threw some skins on the floor of the tool shed, pushed her into it and barred the door from the outside. After several days of modest improvement he decided to try her in bed again. First he got good and drunk then, with switch in hand, he led her to the bed and began to tell her what to do in a mishmash of English and Cheroenhaka knowing she wouldn't understand anyway.

"*Sat'untatag!* On *ges-satek.* Still like *wahehun,* open *sanseke,* I'm going to touch *ges-t'achanunte owarag.*"

"Skeered," she whimpered.

"I know," said calmly, "but if you relax it will be better for you." He touched her, she jerked but he held her firmly muttering, "*Ges-owarag yowerha.* Very dry." Getting a jar from the shelf he continued, "*Oska-garhusung.* I'll put it on your *owarag* and my *ocherura.*" After applying the boar fat to the quivering girl he aligned himself, lunged and penetrated her forcefully. She shrieked and it took his full weight to keep her from bucking him off of her. When he was finished he lay still, panting and keeping her pinned fast. It gave him a powerful sense of accomplishment and he drifted to deep sleep while she struggled to squirm from under him.

* * *

George needed to tell his father about the trouble with the coppersmith and he was certain that he couldn't leave Willoughby behind. Even if she didn't run he figured the dolt would likely starve to death. Although he had no qualms with letting her run naked around the house, the anglicized part of him felt he had to cover her with something for travelling. Finding two rectangles of burlap he stitched two corners together and draped it over her shoulders. It almost covered her butt.

It was still light enough to inspect the progress of his parents' new house when George and Willoughby arrived. The roof was shingled, the chimney complete and the floor of the kitchen paved with fieldstone. George, Sr. and Aheeta had moved their camp into the kitchen. She greeted them warmly offering water or whiskey. Willoughby accepted water while George took some of each. Then she returned to preparing supper.

"Where'd you get her?" his father asked.

"I bought her in Edenton but it may have been a bad decision. She might be simple in the head."

"I can see you weren't looking at her head when you picked her."

"Maybe I wasn't," he admitted. Then in English asked, "How are you getting on with my aunt?"

"That'd be none of your business and, in return, I'll not ask you anymore questions either."

George got around to the business of the still. "Spires left off the cooling sleeve we told him to make. I refused to give him any money unless he fixed it. Bastard drew a pistol on me and ran me outta the place. I expect he's going to sue us."

The older man looked into the rising darkness and rubbed his jaw. "Suppose he tells the court he knows a couple Indians who are making spirituous liquors without a license and then we get asked what we're doing with it?" he pondered aloud.

"I suppose somebody would take a dim view of our selling it to our *katahtekeh*."

"And when they find out our brothers are in Virginia, somebody up there might remember the name George Skipper was never very welcome. Son, we need make this coppersmith get over being angry at you."

"Maybe you should go to him."

"No, I think we should send a lawyer. For that we'll need hard money. Feel up to making a delivery? I reckon there oughta be enough ready at Potecasi to justify a trip."

"Sure, I'll go see. I ought to pay mother respects anyway."

"You keep your mouth shut about your aunt." He didn't bother to say it in English and Aheeta gave him a look.

Aheeta served the meal first to George, Sr., then to the younger George, then to the black girl whose big eyes shone white in the firelight giving her a look of terror that made it seem as if she might crawl under the fieldstones. Aheeta offered her the meal with no trace condescension and, sensing her fear, tenderly stroked her cheek. "Can't she talk at all?" she asked her nephew.

"She knows a few words of English but she hardly ever says anything."

"That might make her a good woman after all," his father quipped and Aheeta punched his shoulder.

* * *

"How does my new house look?" Suntetung asked her son.

"Beautiful, *ena*. You will live like a queen," he told her.

"And is Aheeta taking care of your father?"

He had practiced for this question all the way from Bertie to Potecasi. "Everything seems fine," was the answer he thought as neutral as possible.

"Who is the black one?"

"My servant. You don't have any clothes you could give her, do you?"

"Oh, dear," she said appraising the girl in a gunnysack who stood behind her son in petrified silence. "Nothing of mine would fit her. I think the only one around here as big as her is that Oxendine bitch. Why are you drawn to such big women?"

George felt his cheeks redden. "I figured I'd get more work out of a big one."

"I know what kind of work you're looking for. You should be ashamed. What happened to the one with hair like fire?"

"I don't think she's coming back. I wrote her a letter but she never answered though I think she's out of bondage."

"Maybe you'll find her at Chounteroute."

"Maybe. Is there anything ready to deliver?"

"You'll have to ask your uncle John."

John had stayed on task and had more than the wagon would hold ready for shipment. "Where'd you get the big black gal?" he asked George.

"Edenton. Want to buy her?"

She was following George so closely wherever he went she put John in mind of a shadow. He inspected her minutely before he replied, "No, but I might rent her for the night."

George could only smile ruefully. "I couldn't take your money," he said. "Layin' with her is not quite as good as sticking it in a knothole."

John pulled his ear while he admired the swell of her hip between the two flaps of burlap. He said, "Now that just don't seem right."

* * *

For a time, as he drove to Assamoosick, George tried to engage Willoughby in conversation with the hope of expanding her vocabulary but he soon tired of her density. When he put her into his sleeping roll that night he didn't even try to arouse her interest but applied a handful of *oska-garhusung* to her *owarag* and relieved himself dispassionately. She remained silently rigid.

He stayed only overnight at Assamoosick for he was beginning to have hope of finding Mary at Chounteroute. He did, however, manage to trade some rum for a dress that fit Willoughby. She seemed ambivalent about it.

The chief men at Chounteroute were overjoyed at his arrival. They unburdened him of his merchandise and immediately partook. George was in no mood to be feted but felt he could not refuse for reasons of good customer relations.

"This batch is a little raw, George" Robin Scholar

observed trying to get his breath.

"Uncle John's been making it while Pa and I been building houses. I don't know how many times he distills it."

Wainoak Robin—a big evil looking Indian with scarification on his cheeks—drawled, "I hope you and your old man get back on the job. This makes my eyes water."

"We will. We're gettin' a new still."

Wainoak Robin passed the jug to King Edmonds and joked, "Here, Edmonds, see if you think we should give some of this to those squatters. It would make it easier to tomahawk them while they were gasping for breath."

"Squatters inside the circle?" George asked.

"Yes, some white-devils built a cabin up stream. We complained to agent Thomas Cocke but I expect we will have to remove them ourselves," Edmonds told him. "Do you want us to send you a message before we attack them?"

With tentative bravado George answered, "Sure."

When the group got enough of the rum into them to stop complaining about its harshness, George nervously sidled next to Watt Bailey and inquired about Mary. Bailey gave him a sidelong glare but finally nodded his head. As soon as he was reasonably able to slip from the group of men he went to Bailey's house where he found her shelling beans. She looked up without smiling or speaking.

"Did you get my letter?" he asked timidly.

She nodded but still didn't speak.

He was wishing he were somewhere else but he persisted. "I never got an answer."

Finally she spoke, "I didn't send one."

"Are you blaming me for your gettin' caught?"

"I don't blame you, George."

"Aren't you even glad to see me?"

"I'm not sure."

"I don't get it. Don't you want to be together?"

She set the bowl of beans on the ground and got to her feet. She looked unblinkingly into his eyes until the urge to flee nearly got the better of him. At last she said, "I done a lot of thinking, George. The last three years changed me somehow."

"What's changed is now we're both free to get married proper."

"Is that what you really want?"

"What I want is you."

"I know you, George. I know you been with other women while I was bound."

"I haven't. I've been building a house for us. At least come see it."

"You swear?"

"Sure I swear. I've been waitin' for you all alone out in the woods."

"I want to believe you but it just don't sound like the George I know."

"Can't a body change? You just said you changed. Does that mean you don't love me anymore?" For the first time he saw emotion in her face. Her chin trembled slightly and, with a rush, she broke and fell against his chest sobbing.

He patted her and when she stopped crying he got her to commit. She said she'd marry him and she was anxious to see the house. They sat and talked their way back to a sense of normalcy. When he felt secure enough, he asked her, "Why did you sue me?"

She laughed. "Well, George Skipper, it was because I needed to eat. That bastard, Allen, wouldn't spend a penny on me. Aren't I worth sixteen shillings?"

"I guess I wouldn't be here if you weren't."

Mary's mother died while she was indentured. When they found her father still drinking with the men his response to the news was, "I figured as much."

"*Akroh*, will you get by if I go away with George?" Mary asked.

Watt was missing a front tooth and he had a habit of spitting through the hole. He spat twice before he replied smiling, "I was getting by since your *ena* died and you got put out. I reckon I can find some old woman to take care of me."

They had switched from English to Cheroenhaka to break the news to Bailey and hearing the announcement, the other men subjected George to much back slapping, jabs and jests. During the buffeting his eyes fell on Willoughby who hadn't moved from the place he had left her. She was petrified of the Indians and was doing the best she could to blend into the shadows. George felt a twinge of fear and would have parted with her for free if somebody would be willing to take her, but Watt knew she had come with him so he was stuck. Eventually Mary noticed her and asked, "Who's the darkie?"

George swallowed hard before he could say, "She's the servant I promised you."

Mary scowled but kept her thoughts to herself. All she said was, "Where's my cat?"

George couldn't wait to couple with a woman who knew what to do and wanted to do it. They left Watt with the men and returned to his house where they had a little something to eat before getting to the business of urgency. When it was over he felt triumphant and Mary felt at peace.

"I've got to get back to Bertie. The Old Man and I have some business to take care of," he told Mary when she woke. She gathered her belongings. He packed Willoughby into the wagon with the furs, hides, tobaccos and empty kegs and, after bidding farewell to Watt and Mary's brother, Watt, they began the journey to their new home.

George, Sr. was collected from his nearly complete house at Holly Bush. They made a stop so Mary could inspect her future quarters then continued to Edenton where lawyer Armstead Jones was retained. He consulted the clerk of court and determined that suit had indeed been filed against George Skipper, Sr. and Jr. in the amount of twenty pounds ten shillings, no mention having been made of the earnest money. The furs and hides were converted to cash. Jones was presented the money plus extra for costs and instructed to settle.

"You haven't been served with a process," the lawyer protested, "why not wait and see if the plaintiff changes his mind? It's always possible he could expire."

George, Sr. was adamant. "No, sir," he insisted, "we are guilty and intend to make it right."

Jones shrugged and settled the matter without his clients showing their faces in the court.

While in town George gave two hundred pounds of tobacco for a marriage license and made good on his promise to Mary in the only church in town.

Jones negotiated with Spires to give possession of the still to the Skippers and in less than a week the parties returned to their respective homes. Mary was enthralled with her new house with its glazed windows and convenient cistern and, to George's amazement, she made progress with Willoughby. For his part, he put the still into operation although his jaws clinched every time he looked at the naked condenser coil.

CHAPTER SEVENTEEN

"You lied to me!" Mary railed when some months later it became obvious Willoughby was with child. Mary was herself in the same situation and George had been filled with contentment that had been a long time coming until the revelation about the slave girl.

"She must have been that way when I bought her," he suggested lamely.

"After all you've done, why should I believe you?" she sobbed.

"Because things are different now."

"How?"

George paused to weigh the relative merits of taking a totalitarian stance or a conciliatory one. He opted for something in the middle. "Because we're married proper now and that's sacred. Anyway, you wait and see what her bastard looks like. It won't look like me," he said knowing he was in need of a miracle but figured delaying his crucifixion was better than confessing on the spot. There was, after all, a slight chance it would favor her side and there was also the chance he might die before it was born.

Mary brooded but became preoccupied with her own

pregnancy and she actually developed a fondness for Willoughby who became more of a pet than a servant.

* * *

George, Sr. brought his wife from Potecasi to Holly Bush to see her completed home. She was thrilled. It was a harmonious fusion of English convenience and Cheroenhaka charm with an enormous hearth, buffalo hides on the floors and ceremonial masks adorning the columns. Aside from the common room with the hearth there was a room George called his study and two bedrooms. Aheeta emerged from one of the bedrooms and greeted her older sister coolly. "I began to think you were not going to join us," she chided.

Suntetung smiled sweetly and said, "I had to come to save my husband. You've let him become a bag of bones."

Aheeta returned the same smile but did not respond and George felt fear quivering between his legs.

* * *

The chief men and their entourage came to Holly Bush at the time of the festival of *Cohonks*. It was a mild winter following a good harvest so the gathering was prepared to revel in plentitude. Before the feast began King Edmonds called a council to address the issue of the squatters.

"Brothers," he began, "our friend Thomas Cocke has returned from the courthouse at the place now called Isle of Wight. His petition to the court for the removal of the squatters on our land was denied. I ask you then what choice remains but to remove them ourselves?"

Watt Bailey never forgot the events of the vision quest he and George attempted in their youth and he was not keen to be involved in any adventure that might obligate him to collect scalps. He rose to address the assembly.

"Brothers, we live in peace with many white-devils. My own wife was one. The problem is not that these people have moved onto our land. The problem is they have not paid for it. Let us make them an offer and if they accept we will profit from it."

Edmonds rose again to speak. "There is wisdom in this but where will it end? Are we to let every white man who wants our land to have it for money?"

George, Sr. was reluctant to get involved in councils but he wanted to make a point. "With money we can buy any land we want and when more settlers come looking for land we can sell for a profit and then buy more land. Look at the fine properties my family has acquired here about. To the white men land is wealth. Should we not prosper from it also?"

Edmonds cocked his head in thought. "This is an interesting idea. Brothers, let us take it to the agents and be guided by their council. Let us now set it aside and celebrate the *cohonks* without those cursed missionaries."

* * *

Thomas Cocke had to reread the document granting the circle and square tracts to the Cheroenhaka before he could answer the chiefs' question. "I am afraid you are forbidden to sell any of your land," he told them.

Robin Scholar shook his head and said aloud to himself, "The white-devils can't do anything without putting a hook in it."

Cocke said matter-of-factly, "We'll just have to start the process of getting it changed."

"While you're doing that, we'll kill the squatters," *Cockarouse* Sam declared.

"Oh, I wish you wouldn't do that. You know how that stirs things up."

"What if we just burn them out?"

Cocke thought for a moment. "Don't tell me when

you do it."

"Fine."

* * *

George, Jr. had discovered that making turpentine was not all that different from making spirituous liquors and it could be sold openly—if not nearly as profitably. The fact that his new property that abutted his uncle James' contained a goodly amount of pitch pine made the enterprise seem divinely preordained. When it was realized that turpentine was a highly effective tool in the task of burning squatters from their homes, the chiefs traded for a barrel. They also traded for a cask of good rum for the celebration to follow the raid.

The warriors stripped to their breechclouts and donned their war paint. They had to post a guard for the missionaries lest they were flogged for their state of undress. They stole to the squatters' farm and waited for dark. Each carried a skin full of turpentine—most of which were leaking badly. It had been decided to only burn the crops to show good will. When the fires attracted the squatters attention and they ran outside to try to quell the flames they were greeted by much hideous howling and a few flaming arrows just so there was no misunderstanding as to whom was responsible.

The town was anxious to start the celebration but they waited for the warriors to return and don their missionary clothes before the cask was tapped and the dancing started. There was plenty of self congratulation among the warriors and they were certain that when their hangovers subsided enough to reconnoiter the squatters' cabin that it would be found abandoned.

It was not to be the case. Ned and Will returned to the site only to find them butchering a hog. "Let's kill 'em and steal the hog," Ned suggested.

"There's four of them and they've all got guns handy.

Let's tell Edmonds and let him decide."

* * *

Willoughby delivered a month before Mary. The infant was clearly not as dark as her but his features were too undeveloped for Mary to condemn George with certainty. When her son arrived she asked, "Do you want to call him George?"

"No," he replied, "I promised my Grandfather there would be a generation free from Georges."

"That's sort of strange. Why did he make you promise that?"

"I don't know but I figure he'll haunt me for sure if I break my promise."

Mary laughed. "What then?"

"I'd like to call him Barnaby."

"Short for Barnabus?"

"I guess."

"That's good, George. A Biblical name is sure to make a better man of him."

George didn't know about that but he was glad she was pleased.

As months passed the two babies' faces took on some definition and, their shading aside, they could have been brothers. In her heart Mary knew they were but the passage of time had blunted her indignation and she found a thousand ways to believe the impossible. Besides, the last thing she wanted to do was raise the boy alone. Besides, George was an Indian and Indians were promiscuous, and besides, she was a slave and, therefore, his property to do with as he pleased. She would pray for forbearance.

"George," she said, "I haven't been to services since long before the baby was born. I want to go to Chounteroute this Sunday."

Inwardly George groaned, but since he was beginning

to hope for forgiveness, he was anxious to indulge her. "Sure. Whatever you want."

"Will you go to meeting with me?"

He would have given a year of his life to take back that last phrase. "No, woman, that's not for me."

"How do you know? You never went."

"I heard plenty of it in school—"

"Just try it once, for me."

"Now, no. I can't."

"What do you mean 'you can't'?"

He drew a deep breath and counted before he said as calmly as possible, "I just can't. I was born a heathen and I intend to stay a heathen, so let it rest."

She pouted but let it go. She'd pray for him when he didn't know it.

They took Willoughby to watch Barnaby while Mary attended the service. The promise of her pulchritudinous bosom was not false. She lactated so abundantly that Mary only nursed for self gratification and that diminishingly. The half breed bastard still had no name. Willoughby hadn't shown any interest in choosing one and no one else much cared.

When the hymn singing started George found the men at Edmonds' house. The King greeted him casually. He had spent the previous evening sampling the latest shipment from Potecasi and it made him think to say, "George, you grow rich at our expense. Should we not tie you to a stake and set a slow fire around it?"

George leaned on one haunch and pulled his pants out of his crack while he thought of a suitable response. "There's two reasons why you can't do that. One is the missionaries would have you crucified but the big reason is you wouldn't get anymore rum."

After everyone stopped laughing Edmonds said, "These missionaries are no laughing matter. They have taken everything of joy from us. I don't know what they will do when they realize they have taken it all. George, you lived among them. Why do they do it?"

"Brother, their God puts them to that same slow fire if they don't do it. They think they have no choice."

Edmonds shook his head slowly. "It's worse than the time Eteshe Ena was queen."

All the men murmured their agreement.

George asked, "Did the squatters leave?"

"Oh, no, that's another blight on our lives. These white-devils are determined. We burned their crops and we steal their pigs but they hang on. You are wise in these things and you think like we do, George. Is killing them the best thing to do?"

Again he had to think. "Killing them will give you satisfaction but you will surely pay a price greater than the game they steal from you or the land they use illegally. It is better to be patient and let Cocke try to do his job. He's a good man—for a white-devil. In my opinion, you would do better to kill the missionaries."

Again there was a murmur of agreement.

Robin Scholar interjected, "That would give us all pleasure but so many of our women have had their minds poisoned by them we would not dare close our eyes."

Another murmur.

"It's bad, George, all very bad." Edmonds looked pained for a moment then added, "We know it is a bad thing to drink rum before the power of the day, but on Sunday, sometimes it's necessary."

* * *

Aheeta would not return to Chounteroute. Suntetung wished she would but did not force the issue while George was of two minds. He had the inkling that now and then he might again sample the forbidden delights of his wife's younger sister but he was fully cognizant of the possibility of ending with his own tomahawk through his skull. He was, however, more preoccupied with the welfare of his daughter, Jean, who had recently lost her husband to pox. They had been living with David Herrin's father, Richard, but with his death Jean and her four young sons and an infant girl were seen as a burden. The older boys, Robert, John, and Tom were just arriving at an age useful around the farm and Willie was a toddler.

When the spring planting was done the Potecasi community was in the habit of uniting to dance and implore higher powers, whether a *quioccos* or Jesus, for a good harvest. Before the festivities started George called his family together and explained his concern for Jean's family.

"Jean is a proud woman and does not want to be a burden to your mother and me but those kids are going to go hungry if we don't do something," he told his son.

George, Jr. scratched his neck under the heavy braid that Mary had plaited for him. "Well, we could try to get her some land," he said.

"You got enough money to buy some for her?"

"No, I was thinking of petitioning for a grant. They won't grant a woman land but I could apply."

"The English are so jealous of land. Why do they give it away sometimes?"

"As I heard it explained, the Lord Proprietors will grant what they consider useless land to get more settlers then they collect taxes from them."

"How long does it take?"

"I don't know. Nothing happens fast in Edenton."

"I suppose we can support her till you get it done. Be better to find her another husband but nobody hereabouts that's worth anything is single."

"With all those little ones most men would think twice."

"Hmm, well, let's let her know what we have in mind—see if she's going to go along with it."

Jean heard the plan and asked, "Some land would be good but where am I going to get a house to live in?"

Suntetung smiled benevolently, "Of course, dear, your men folk will build one for you."

That decided the family retired to the ceremonial area. There was a candle burning on the shrine with a cross and corn and tobacco on the *quioccosan*. George thought, "*I'm not offering any rum…*"

He never brought enough rum to get through the night though he always hoped it would suffice. A new dance started when he realized the jugs were empty so he sauntered into the shadows to refill them. Aheeta noticed him leave and stole after him. He unlocked the door to the shed where he stored his product and sat the jug on the table beneath the tap. She followed him into the shed and wrapped her arms around his middle. "Damn, woman! I might have dropped the jug." He knew immediately it was not his wife.

"Long time, George," she purred.

He had noticed her when she danced and found the red and white circles attractive that she had painted around her nipples. He already had an erection. "Your sister's gonna flay me alive."

"Are you scared?"

"Of course I'm scared. Just let me lock that door."

* * *

George, Jr. was able to get the grant faster than he thought possible. It was six-hundred and fifteen acres bounded by Jean's father-in-law's land and her uncle James'. "Sister, dear," he told her, "It cost me twenty pounds for fees, the lawyer and surveyor. I will deed it to you for that amount."

"Why, George, that's too good to be true. Papa sold that little twenty acres to Mr. Hall for forty-five pounds just before David died." She threw her arms around his neck and hugged him until it felt strange.

"Don't you forget about it, either," he teased. "Now,

all we gotta do is build a house."

Before the house was finished Mary had another son. They decided to name him Benjamin. Somewhere along the way Willoughby's boy acquired the name Toby—no last name—and that same year George, Sr. took sick and died without Suntetung ever catching him with Aheeta. She sold the land at Potecasi that was the refuge of the Cheroenhaka to Edward Goodson who evicted the few stragglers that remained there.

At Chounteroute Watt Bailey, Sr. died.

CHAPTER EIGHTEEN

In the heat of the summer Thomas Cocke and John Simmons arrived at Chounteroute in the company of twenty-one men. Edmonds met him with a look of suspicion. "Are they all missionaries?" he asked with dread in his voice.

Cocke laughed, "No, King, they are prospective customers." He had perfected the Cheroenhaka language and was able to speak directly to his charges.

"What do you mean?"

"I mean I have great news for you. Come, summon all the men. Everyone must hear what I have to say."

Thirteen of the chief men were at Chounteroute. They assembled in the shade of a great, sprawling oak tree to hear Cocke's message. The men who had come with Cocke milled about the town marveling at the novelty of it.

"Brothers," Cocke began quite traditionally, "the document I hold in my hand is the decision of the Council handed down only recently. It allows you to sell any or all of your land to anyone who wants to buy provided no one person buys more than four-hundred acres. You are also free from the obligation to keep Briggs and Wynn. The gentlemen who accompany me are here to select parcels with your permission, of course."

The Indians were dumbstruck. At last Edmonds said, "Brother, we did not think you were capable of bringing good news."

"King, you cut me to the quick."

With the consent of the chief men the mob rode over the countryside choosing parcels. Thomas Cocke was quick to blaze four-hundred prime acres on the river and John Simmons selected two-hundred and seventy-five. His two brothers grabbed four-hundred each and brothers of Henry Briggs claimed prize parcels. After several days of bartering and bickering the most modest tract proposed was sixty-two acres. Cocke and Simmons reckoned that six-thousand and ninety-three acres had been claimed by the prospective buyers. A certain John Allen, gentleman surveyor, was kept busy making plats of the tracts.

To their credit the trustees priced the individual parcels fairly with most selling for sixteen pounds per acre but one choice piece went for twenty-eight pounds per acre. It happen to be the seventh of August, 1735—a fact that meant nothing to the Indians—when the buyers and sellers convened in the home of the justice of the peace for Isle of Wight County which was serving as the courthouse. At the end of the day three-hundred and ninety-six pounds, five shillings and six pence were exchanged for twenty-three tracts of land. James Baker, the clerk of court, took his fees for document preparation and pressed his seal next to the curious marks that the Indians made on the deeds. King Edmonds put the money in his purse.

The next morning the party of Indians rode to Bertie and invested in a hogshead of rum.

* * *

George applied himself to real estate and received two more grants on the Craven side of the river and the following year he was granted another two-hundred acres. His prosperity extended to progeny when Mary presented him a third son whom he named Nathan.

* * *

On a day in early winter the surviving chiefs paid a visit. In front of the blazing hearth they congratulated him for his wealth in land and happy family. Then they explained the reason for their visit. The crops had been poor, there had been no game for years and there was real threat of starvation at Chounteroute and Assamoosick. "We need to sell land quick," Mary's brother, Watt Bailey, told him. "We'd like your help."

"Have you got buyers?"

"We have to run buyers off with guns. Cocke and Edwards negotiated some sales for us. We'd like you to look at them and see if they look right to you."

There were twelve offers to buy parcels in both the Circle and the Square. George didn't find any fault with the prices and he agreed to go with them to complete the deals. He decided to take Barnaby along to give him some exposure to the world. They stopped first at Chounteroute and dispatched messengers to Cocke and Edwards advising of their decision to proceed. George had not seen the Cheroenhaka town for some time. Since Edmonds' death no one had risen to take his place. The chiefs ran the tribe's affairs as a committee and left much undone for lack of agreement. Pox had thinned the numbers and others simply drifted to parts unknown. While waiting to be notified of their date at the courthouse, George tried to liven the place but everyone was hungry and in no mood for dancing.

Since the arrival of the missionaries most everyone had been taught some English and the mode of dress was strictly white-devil, no one carried tomahawks and war paint was forgotten. So much spirit had been sucked from the Cheroenhaka that the Cheraw no longer bothered to attack them. The Meherrin had simply vanished. George found the place depressing.

Barnaby—who was fourteen—did not speak Cheroenhaka, and though he had been to Chounteroute, this was his first time there when he was left to his own devices. Watt Bailey's wife was one of the strangely complexioned sort that some called Portugee without knowing why. She spotted Barnaby one morning whittling a stick and looked at him with curiosity.

"Why, you must be a Skipper boy," she said at last.

He hadn't noticed her and was startled when she spoke. "Yeah. How do you know?" he asked rudely.

"You got the nose," she chuckled.

Barnaby glared but didn't say anything. It was the first time he'd thought about it.

Many days passed before the answer from Cocke arrived. The parties were to meet on the first of January at the justice of peace's house which was still being used for the courthouse. The county had been divided again and was being called Southampton. That fact, and the fact that the day was New Year's, was lost on most of the chiefs. It turned into a long day especially for Barnaby who spent the time in total boredom because it was too cold to play in the river. Eventually twelve parcels were transferred and the indentures signed by Sam, Watt Bailey, Jack Will, John Turner, Frank and George Skipper. George, of course, knew how to sign his name but he made his Indian sign like the rest.

Since no one was acknowledged king the money was divided equally and everyone, save George, went to Fort Christiana to buy food. George took his share and started home with his son.

"They see you at Fort Christiana," he told the boy, "they might keep you."

"Why?"

"It's a peculiarity of the place. They hold Indian boys

prisoner and make 'em go to school and church."

Barnaby felt a lump of fear in his guts. "Then I don't want to be an Indian anymore."

His father chuckled.

* * *

George surveyed his plantation from his front porch. It was the source of great pride but since returning from Chounteroute he had been seized by a deep melancholy that would not release him. The sight of the bare trees across the river and the pale sun on the wet rocks filled him with a despair that felt heavy in his chest. Immobile he stared at his surroundings until the oppressive silence and the chill of the late afternoon drove him into the house. It was quiet inside as well. The children were still playing somewhere in the woods, Willoughby and Mary were sewing. Without speaking he sat by the fire.

"Are you coming down with the gripe?" Mary asked after a time.

"No, why?"

"Not like you to spend a whole day sittin' and starin' at the distance."

"Got a strange feeling, is all."

She gave him a penetrating look that was exclusive to her gender. "Something happen at Chounteroute to upset you?" she asked suspiciously.

He met her eyes and understood the implication of the question, smiled a wan smile and said, "Chounteroute upset me. It's become a sad place."

Mary hadn't been to Chounteroute for several years. "How is it sad?" she asked.

"It's not a Cheroenhaka town anymore." He stopped short of blaming the missionaries to avoid riling her religious sympathies.

"That's too bad. I wonder why Watt stays there. Maybe he should move down here."

"He can come if he wants," he said distractedly. Then he said in the same tone, "I believe I might take a trip."

"Oh, and where to?"

"Nowhere certain. Just to see some new country."

"George Skipper, what is it you really intend to do?" Her voice had an edge to it.

He glared at her and replied with a different edge, "I want to see some new country and I am too old to carry on like you mean."

"You are anything but too old as I have to find out most nights."

Willoughby snickered and George thought he liked her better before she acquired the language. More calmly he offered, "I'll take the boy with me. Will that allay your suspicions?"

"Hmm," was her only answer.

"You gonna make me sit and be quiet all day again in some smelly house?" Barnaby asked when informed of his impending trip.

"I promise it won't be like that again," George assured him.

"Can't Toby come?"

"He has to stay and help the women."

"Why does he always have to work?" Barnaby tried to rescue his friend.

"'Cause he's a slave."

"I feel sorry for him sometimes."

"You'll get over that. Now, get your stuff ready. You're goin' to be sleepin' on the ground for a time."

Mary's suspicions were not entirely allayed. She was not convinced that George was incapable of involving a fourteen year old in some nefarious adventure but she held her peace and told him, "Don't you be gone a long time. I'll worry about Barnaby."

"You won't worry about me?"

"No."

"Well, don't worry about the boy either. He's old

enough to go bear huntin' without a gun."

They rode south and meandered west. The Indian trails were clear and looked well used but there was little sign of white habitation. George's spirits began to lift though he couldn't exactly say why. On an afternoon with rain in the air Indians materialized on the trail behind them. They wore winter robes and paint on their faces. George greeted them in traveling language to find that they had little in common linguistically. He was eventually able to determine by signs and some common words these were sentries and they were approaching their town. These were wilder looking Indians than Barnaby's experience and he was not a little unnerved as one felt his clothes and inspected his musket.

"Don't be scared," his father told him, "but don't let him take it."

"How do I stop him?"

"You point it at him." George signaled for the stranger to stop and he did.

The town was small but orderly and well established. The sentries escorted the pair to the *werrowance* who offered a pipe and inquired about them. He wanted to trade for their guns and knives but took it well to be told that they had no trade goods but would share a little rum. The rain came and they took shelter in the king's house where the women served food. He told George he was called Tansisurie Nipisu—George never did assimilate the name—and his tribe was Catawba. It puzzled him that he couldn't communicate with Barnaby at all and he thought there was something wrong with the boy. George assured him that he wasn't defective but had been only taught to speak the white-devils' language which was a defect to his way of thinking.

Tansisurie Nipisu was greatly pleased with the rum. George gave a little to Barnaby but watered it. At the end of the night the chief sent one of his women to lead the visitors to the longhouse. There were a couple other occupants sitting at the fire. The two put their sleeping gear on a couple beds and joined the people by the fire. A short while later the chief's woman returned with some girls directed them to the guests.

Barnaby had almost no experience with girls and was scared to death when one sat beside him and felt the inside of his leg. He recoiled from her touch which made her giggle and do it again. George laughed at his boy's discomfort and remembered a lesson he had learned from his grandfather.

"Son," he said, "it's time for you to become a man. Take her over there to the bed and let her show you what to do. She's not gonna hurt ya." A little while later he did the same.

They left the Catawbas' town early the next day. On the trail Barnaby was stonily silent. Eventually George couldn't bear it any longer and asked, "What did you think of it?"

His eyes got big and his face looked like red war paint. "Will I ever get to do that again?" he stammered.

His father erupted in laughter. When he could he assured the boy, "You will from time to time and a little more often when you're married, but mind you, you will never do it again if your mother gets wind of this."

The boy looked terrified and felt the fear in his exhausted gonads. He shook his head and said, "No, sir, I won't tell." He fell silent again with a thousand questions in his head that he was afraid to ask.

They stumbled quite accidently onto some white men's camp. Both parties were startled and raise their weapons but George defused the situation. "We're friends," he called.

"You look like Indians," one of the men responded.

"Looks can be deceiving, gentlemen," he said and dismounted to shake hands. "George Skipper's the name and this is my son, Barnaby."

The man shook his hand and introduced the group.

"I'm John Clarke, this is Sam Snead, John Crawford and Tom Moonman. Where you coming from?"

"I've got a farm in Bertie Precinct near the Virginia line. We thought we'd see what the land looked like in these parts."

"Thinking to buy some land are you?"

"Could be. Any available?"

"I do have some land I'm lookin' to sell if you'd care to see it."

The land was good and they shook hands to seal the deal. "There's no county seat in Anson," Clark told him. "We'll have to go to Wilmington to find somebody who can make the papers."

All of them broke camp and rode due east the following morning. Toward nightfall Barnaby asked his father in a low voice, "Are we going to spend the night at the Indian town?"

George had a big smile on his face when he said, "I don't think so this time."

Wilmington impressed George. "Good looking town," he remarked on their arrival. "Little hard to get to with all the rivers."

Clarke agreed, "It's a mite easier to get here by water."

When the formalities were finished Clark conveyed two-hundred acres and George told him, "I'll take the other two hundred when I raise the cash. Be after next harvest I image."

"I'll be happy to do business with you if no one beats you to it." They shook hands and George and Barnaby headed for home.

"Pa, what do want that land for," Barnaby asked.

"I've a mind to move us onto it."

"What's wrong with where we live?"

"There's nothing wrong with it. Just seems like we're getting too many neighbors."

One year later they returned to Anson Precinct and bought Clarke's other two-hundred acres. There was then a courthouse and something of a community but the Catawba town had been decimated by smallpox and was abandoned. Contemplating the dearly remembered, now empty longhouse, Barnaby was crestfallen.

CHAPTER NINETEEN

The injection of money recharged Chounteroute and Sam rose to be de facto king. He was cleaning his gun on a winter morning when a delegation from Williamsburg arrived with a letter addressed to the 'Chief men of the Nottoway Indians'. Sam winced at the sound of the derogatory name but received his visitors politely and asked to have it read. It seemed a certain George Washington, Colonel Virginia Militia, wanted to recruit the warriors of the 'Nottoway Nation' to assist in the capture of Fort Duquesne. Sam was puzzled by the request, delegations from Williamsburg being usually the portent of doom, this was unsettling.

"Leave the letter. We will convene a council and send you our decision," he told the messengers.

The council convened at George's house. "We like to come here," Watt Bailey admitted. "My sister is a good cook."

"You like Mary's cooking better or George's rum?" Sam chided.

George read the letter and asked the group, "Do any of you know this George Washington?"

Sam answered, "No, but Governour Dinwiddie's man said he is a Colonel in the militia and a brave warrior."

"And where is this Fort Duquesne?"

"They say it's in a place called Pennsylvania."

"Some say the French can be trusted more than the English."

George considered that momentarily. "I doubt it. One white-devil is the same as the next," he said laughing. "How many warriors do we have now?"

"Maybe twenty-five—"

Barnaby, sitting with the chiefs, interrupted, "I'll go!"

His mother turned from the hearth where she was fixing supper and smacked him square on the ear with a heavy wooden spoon. "You get that idea outta your head," she told him bringing laughter from the crowd.

"Well, why not?" George said. "If the warriors want to fight we should let them. Maybe they'll come back with some nice red coats and French scalps. They can demand soldiers' pay and you can insist this Washington send you presents."

John Turner said, "Maybe he can get rid of the missionaries."

Will watched Willoughby putting food on the big table. He said to George quietly in Cheroenhaka, "Why don't you let me have that slave of yours tonight?"

"Because you're my friend, Will."

George left with the chiefs in the morning because they had more offers to buy land. Barnaby, on being invited to go along, said he's rather take a 'whupping'.

While George was at Jerusalem, where the new courthouse was, Benjamin ran into the house in a panic. "There's wild Indians coming," he said between gasps. "I seen 'em sneakin' across the river."

Mary looked curiously at him and reminded, "We're Indians, dear. Show me where they are." She looked through the window where he pointed. "Oh, my, they do look like trouble. Get the guns and bar the door and shutters."

Four decidedly un-anglicized Indians with faces painted all red were creeping up the hill. When they saw the shutters slam closed they sprinted to the house and tried to force the door. Mary and her three sons took defensive positions with muskets pointed at the door should it fail. Toby was ready to reload and Willoughby hid under the table. There was glass breaking and pounding on a shutter and all the guns turned to it.

Barnaby, as the oldest free male, assumed command of the situation. "If we can't run 'em off, they'll burn us out."

"What do we do?" Ben asked his brother.

His mother answered, "We throw the door open and when they come through don't you dare miss. Willoughby, you get behind that door and pull it open fast. Come on, girl, git!"

She crawled across the room on hands and knees, lifted the bar and pulling the door open hid behind it. All they could see through the doorway was tree tops and blue sky. Then two confused looking Indians appeared in the opening trying to see into the darkness. Three shots exploded simultaneously and both were knocked backwards off their feet. Barnaby was first to grab another gun from Toby and ran to the door. Mary hadn't fired and followed her son. They saw the other two warriors backing away from the porch and shot at them, missing, but putting them to flight. Ben and Nathan were then at the porch rail and fired missing again but the pair kept running until they were deep into the woods.

"See if they're dead," Mary told Barnaby. Reluctantly he went to the bodies and saw that one had two holes in his chest and was thoroughly dead. The other had been hit in the head and was still breathing.

"Should we finish him?" Nathan asked in a shaky voice.

Mary's heart was pounding but she managed to tell them what to do. "No, drag them both down to the river and throw 'em in the deep part where the current's strong. Take his tomahawk away in case he wakes up."

"Can we scalp 'em?" Ben asked.

"I'll tan your hide if you do," Mary said in a convincing tone. "Nat and Toby, you go along with the guns in case those other two try to sneak back."

"This sort of thing hasn't happened in a great long while," George said when he got home and heard the story. "Any idea who they were."

"They looked like the warriors in the old days before the missionaries," Mary told him. "I'm sure they were heathens."

George didn't rise to that. "Well, I'm proud of you boys for taking care of your mother," he told the three who threatened to burst with pride all over Willoughby's clean floor.

The next thing that got George in an uproar was the tax collector. He appeared on the day George was repairing the glass that the Indian had smashed. "I'm busy," he told the tall skinny stranger with an enlarged adam's apple.

"Sir," he said, "I am an authorized agent of the colony and I do not intend to be dismissed by the likes of you. The governor's records indicate that you have never paid quit rents."

"What's that?" George feigned ignorance.

"Taxes, sir—that you owe for the land."

"Never heard of such a thing." He quit fussing with the pitch around the glass and reached for his gun that was leaning against the wall. He only leaned on it but he scowled menacingly at the gentleman in clean shirt and silk stockings with a pistol in his belt.

"Do not attempt to intimidate me, sir. If you do it will not go well for you. Now, I intend to collect what is due his Lordship. You have four-hundred acres therefore you owe sixteen pounds. Let's have it and no foolishness. I can accept tobacco or hard currency."

"Sir, I have neither. How would like a nice barrel of pitch?"

"Certainly not. Tobacco which you must deliver or hard currency which I can accept."

"You will find neither of those commodities here."

"In that case I will have to arrest you." He drew the pistol from his belt and cocked it. "Come along," he said, his adam's apple bobbing up and down his overly long skinny neck. "Leave your weapon."

The door opened and the three boys stepped onto the porch with their muskets leveled. George slowly pointed his at the man and said, "We will have to continue this conversation later as you are about to leave."

"You'll not hear the end of this, sir. Do you know that you are threatening the sheriff?"

"Well, I suspected as much. Now, you remove yourself from this property before one of these boys does something we'll all regret."

His sputtering could be heard all the way to the ford.

"You boys shouldn't have done that but I'm proud of you nonetheless."

Mary appeared in the door. "Don't encourage them. This kind of thing just causes trouble. Why don't you just pay the taxes and keep the peace?"

"I just don't feel like I get my money's worth from paying taxes," he said and went back to the window.

* * *

A messenger came to tell George that the chiefs had offers to sell more land and ask would he kindly join them. Barnaby expressed interest in going to Chounteroute but after the incident with the marauding Indians George insisted he stay to help protect his mother. "You didn't want to go with me before. Why so interested now?"

He debated giving an evasive answer but settled on the truth. "I need a woman."

His father chuckled, "Well, that's a better reason than most but you watch out for trouble here and when I get home you can go by yourself."

The warriors were back at Chounteroute and George didn't see any red coats. "What happened at Fort Duquesne?" he asked Robin Scholar who had been part of the war party.

"As you said, George, all white-devils are the same. We marched to the fort to kill the French and were shot at by Virginians. Then Washington was afraid to attack the fort because there were so many of them. Then the French Indians ran away and then there were more of us than them so the French burned their own fort and went down the river before we knew they were gone. This Washington may be a *cockarouse* but he's a foolish warrior and he didn't pay us."

"Not even coats?"

"No, but *he* wears very fine clothes."

"Not even scalps?"

"Not many. We killed a couple of scouts."

"We'll see Cocke at the courthouse and ask him to see about the pay."

"Cocke is dead and so is Edwards."

"Have they been replaced?"

"We don't know."

"If not maybe we can petition for replacements more favorable to our cause."

"You think like a white-devil, George."

"It's in the blood. But even so, the boys and I had a problem with the sheriff and I think we'll be moving to my new land in Anson.

* * *

"Brothers," George said after he examined the offers, "these men mean to steal your land."

"What good is it to us?" Sam replied. "All the game is

gone. Without the pay for the warriors helping Washington fight the French we have nothing to buy food with and there is nothing in the fields."

"And what will you buy with this? You are selling more land than my tract in Anson and you won't even get eight pounds."

"We are very hungry, George. We have no choice."

The chiefs assembled at the new town called Jerusalem and made a camp by the river while George went to have a talk with one of the new agents, an indifferent sort of man called Ethelred Taylor. "Sir," he began, "I perceive that you are being highly pernicious."

"What is the meaning such language?"

He dropped the purchase offers on the table asking, "Do you intend to approve these sales?"

"The chiefs approve them. Why should I object?"

"Because they are a crime, sir. Eighteen shillings, nine pence for seventy-two acres! This Henry Blow's own brother paid sixteen pounds per acre when Edmonds was king."

"Times have changed. The land west of the mountains is so plentiful that these little parcels are being bought more as a courtesy to your people than an actual investment in property. Do you want the money or not?"

George saw that this was going nowhere. "Well, then as a *courtesy*, do you suppose you might speak to one Colonel Washington on behalf of the warriors who accompanied him in a recent raid on the French fort in the matter of payment?"

"I have to object to your tone. I happen to know that the Virginians who participated in that foray have not been paid either, but I feel it my duty to send a letter to Governour Dinwiddie concerning this matter."

"Thank you, and I apologize for the tone but I still think you're turning a blind eye to robbery. If I were to see it happen again, I might be compelled to bring the matter to the attention of the Assembly."

Taylor cocked one eyebrow and scowled with the other but he did not reply.

The death of the previous trustees and the appointment of the new threw the procedure into a flap and the clerk was driven to circuitous and interminable language to perfect the indentures. George didn't even try to read them. He just made his Indian sign and reflected that the time it would take him to read them was worth more than the pound that was his share and which he did not even accept.

* * *

One of the tenants at the Bertie community was a black man who had a black wife when he arrived and shortly thereafter he took an Indian wife as well. His progeny were manifold. George approached the aging gentleman when he was ready to move south. "Mr. Quick," he said after a cordial greeting, "do you think any of your boys would be interested in some work for pay?"

The elder Quick was a large man with a daunting presence in spite of his years. "I reckon I'd box their ears if they don't," he answered. "What sorta work ya got?"

"I'm moving my brood to a new piece of land south of here," George explained, "and I need the parcel cleared, a house built and some crops in the ground."

Quick fixed a rheumy eye on George and smiled with what teeth he had. "You goin' a need more 'an a few hands."

"As I recall, Mr. Quick, you got more than a few sons and a great hoard of grandsons."

"It might be so. Jus' might be so," he laughed gently. "When ya gonna leave?"

"Believe I'll be ready come a fortnight."

"Come by here when ya leave. I'll have some boys for ya." Then he started chuckling and couldn't bring himself to stop.

When George saw the caravan that had assembled to follow him to Anson he worried that he should have been more specific as to how much help he wanted. The families of Solomon, Benjamin and Burris Quick amounted to twenty-one people. They exhibited the most diverse spectrum of skin tones he had ever seen. Before they departed the elder Quick pulled on George's arm and said in his ear, "Now, if any 'em ain't workin', ya take da cat to theys backs."

An image of trying to subdue the mountainous Burris Quick for a whipping flashed through his mind. George sighed and began the journey south.

The industry of the Quick clan was a remarkable sight. They established a camp and divided labor according to talent. Game was shot, fish were trapped and preserved by the women as the girls gathered tubers and wild fruit, all the while the stout males began the task of clearing, planting and house building. Old man Quick had been a stern taskmaster who countenanced no slack in his family, which trait was instilled in his offspring. There was another trait instilled in Quick offspring. It was larceny. A cow appeared in the camp one day. When George inquired as to its provenance, Burris muttered something to the effect that his son, Izzy, had found it. George ignored it.

Before it was midsummer George knew he didn't have sufficient cash to pay all the Quicks in his employ. Actually he knew from the start but he wanted to get as much labor as he could before confronting the issue. Calling the three heads of the families together he broke the news and asked what they would do. Solomon answered for the three, "We figured as much. Hard money be scarce. Why doan you lets us have 'nough land to live on? We all needs land more 'an money anyways."

George supposed that it would be no worse than it had been having them next door at Bertie so he agreed to let them squat for a year for their labor and after that, if they stayed, to pay rent.

* * *

Temperance Quick was on the light side of dusky. She also was blessed with great luminous eyes, a full, sensuous mouth and a highly appealing pair of hips, all of which drove Barnaby to paroxysms of backwardness. He contrived opportunities to find her alone only to be unable to force anything coherent across his lips. She would look at him queerly and giggle. He would just smile and nod and get away as fast as he could. All through the summer he mooned over her but failed to harness the flight reflex that seized him each time he tried to make his approach. When the feel of the air had a touch of autumn George made the boys accompany him to Holly Bush to harvest the crops he had left in the fields, especially the sorghum. With Ben and Nate driving wagons, he sidled his horse next to Barnaby's and gave him the talk.

"If you plan to get anywhere with that girl you gotta get some ballocks."

"I didn't know anybody knew," he said feeling his cheeks flush.

"Damn fool. Everybody knows, including her."

"What do I do?"

"Boy, you're like teats on a boar. All you got to do is say hello. After that the great difficulty is to get a woman to shut up."

"You think she likes me?"

"Lordy, if I hadn't watched you being born I would never believe you were a son of mine. She wants it as much as you do. With nothing but cousins around she's getting tired of having to outrun 'em."

Barnaby spent the harvest time rehearsing for when he next saw Temperance. The occasion was the celebration George threw on their return from Holly Bush with the harvest. Barnaby saw her with the women finishing the food preparations. He half filled a cup from the cask of rum tapped for the festivities and drained it. His father saw this and shook his head. "Get your arse over there, boy," and he encouraged him with the side of his foot. As Barnaby was propelled toward the girl his father muttered, "Teats on a boar…"

"Hello, Temperance, it's good to see you."

She tilted her head and smiled a one sided smile. "Why, Barnabus Skipper, I did not know y'all possessed the gift o' speech."

Her mother overheard and said, "You two run along. We're almost done here now."

Temperance seized the moment. "Now, that I know you can talk, tell me how was your trip home?"

"It was good but this is home now."

"That's right. I keep forgetting what with all changes and everything I get homesick sometimes."

"Really?"

"Well, I don't have any friends here like back home."

"I'll be your friend." His new found boldness startled him.

"I don't know anything about you other than you're the quiet type," she said and took his hand. "Why don't you take me walkin' by the river and we can see if we do wanna be friends."

A chill of fear ran perilously close to his groin but he took her hand and they walked to the river where he abruptly tried to kiss her.

She resisted saying, "Is that why you wanna be friends?"

Crestfallen and trembling he said, "I just thought you'd like it too."

She knew then that she had him and said, "Maybe I would like it. I guess if ya was a goodun you'd try agin."

He presumed he was a 'goodun' and he did try again employing all the scant art that the Catawba girl had shown him some years earlier. When he reached under her dress she emitted a sort of moan and a sigh and he pressed to lay her on the ground but she pushed him away saying, "Not yet. We's has to git back or they gonna miss us."

Suddenly fearful again he became apologetic and stepped back. "All right, but did I do something wrong?"

"No, ya silly ass, you did somethin' right, an' that's why we have to git back afore you do somethin' else an we's git caught. We's gonna has to do a heap o' work on you." She shook her head and tossed her wavy hair as she took his hand again.

Barnaby was flustered, disappointed, confused, ecstatic, anxious and hopeful for the remainder of the evening. He spent as much time as he could next to Temperance and he found that his father's prediction that she was more than capable of keeping the conversation moving was on the mark. Later in the evening when the revelers were showing signs of fatigue she said to him, "I don't think anybody'll miss us now if we was to go walkin' agin."

When it was over she told him, "I bin waitin' on you to git some courage all summer long."

CHAPTER TWENTY

Barnaby asked Temperance to marry him. His father asked, "Why you buyin' the cow when you're gettin' the milk for free?" Mary punched him.

She said, "It's about time you stopped your heathen fornication and let the girl be an honest woman."

The couple went to the Anson Courthouse to get a license. They were told the fee was fifteen pounds. Barnaby was dumbstruck by the amount. "I didn't bring that much," he shamefacedly admitted. "I thought it was supposed to be twenty shillings."

"It went up." The clerk, a certain John Frohock who was also clerk of Rowan County, turned back to what he had been writing.

Temperance looked troubled. "Don't worry," he assured her, "I'll get it and we'll come back."

Barnaby asked his father for the money and was answered with an explosion. "That crooked bastard! The marriage license fee did not jump to fifteen pounds. I didn't think you buying the cow was going to bankrupt the family. If my mother was still alive, she'd marry—"

"George," Mary interrupted, "you give them the

money. I'll not have them living in sin under my roof."

George grudgingly gave the money cursing the missionaries under his breath. Barnaby and Temperance went back to the courthouse, paid the fee and were told to wait. Some great while later they were handed a quarto with the clerk's seal.

"Thank ye," Barnabus said politely to Frohock and squinted to decipher the handwriting. He shook his head and turned back to the clerk. "This says refused."

"Quite. She is very clearly a mulatto and you appear to be white. We will have no mixed marriages in this county."

Temperance gasped and started to cry. Barnaby said, "Why, you evil bastard. Give me back the money."

"The fee must be paid whether the decision is favorable or not."

"You knew this before you took the money. Why didn't you tell us?"

"It is not my decision. It is the magistrate's. I only prepare the document," Frohock said dismissing him.

"That's dishonest, Frohock. You haven't heard the end of this." he said angrily but the clerk only smirked. Then he heard Temperance crying and turned to her. "Don't worry. We'll get married in another county."

When George heard what had happened he was sharing a dram with John Clark who remarked, "They are a corrupt bunch. Made me pay tax on my land twice because I wasn't smart enough to get a receipt the first time."

George was seething about the fifteen pounds but remained calm for the benefit of his guest. He said, "I moved down here to get away from His Majesty's dirty minions but more keep arriving every day."

"Some folk talk about setting things aright," Clark said.

Barnaby was still shaking in his anger. "Like what?" he asked.

"Raising our own militia to stand up for our rights. By

force if necessary."

"You can count me in."

George pulled on the hair that was tied at the nape of his neck and said, "I might join such a group myself if I was asked."

Mary grudgingly relaxed her proscription against sin under the roof and Temperance moved into the house taking the Skipper name.

* * *

The Cheroenhaka sent a small delegation to invite George to participate in the sale of more land. He needed a change of scenery so he gladly accepted and returned to Chounteroute with Robin Scholar's brother, Robert, Jack Will, Richard Turner's grandson, John, and Tom Step.

"George, my brother," Sam greeted his arrival, "how are things at your new home?"

"Pretty fair although in that country we have much trouble with the colonial authorities."

"Well, that will always be. They are a troublesome race."

It was a blustery day in January when the land sales were registered with the recorder, and the chimney in the courthouse wasn't drawing well. Ten sales took place in the smoky room with the chiefs getting good prices. George took his share this time and before leaving Jerusalem used a little of it to buy a jug of Old Monongahela for the celebration that night.

Because of the foul weather the chiefs retired to the longhouse to smoke and drink. Sam took a swallow of the whiskey and said, "George, we miss your rum since you went to Anson."

"At least you weren't false enough to say you missed me."

"Oh, sometime we miss you, but we always miss the rum. Maybe we should move to Anson."

"There is still plenty of good land there," George assured him while noticing some women entered with their supper.

Sam sighed, "There are so few of us left we don't need much land. Every year some die of smallpox and most of the boys who went to Fort Christiana never came back, but the good of being so few is that the missionaries have lost interest in us and went away."

George started to say, "See, there's a little good in—", but his jaw dropped and he fell silent when he saw Laura Oxendine setting a platter of sturgeon stakes in the center of the circle of men. He felt the sensation of falling in the pit of his stomach. She had aged very well and he was seized by a sudden and curious attraction.

Sam chuckled at his reaction. "Oh, I forgot to warn you that your first wife was living here."

"Hello, George. It's good to see you after so many years," Laura said without guile.

"Hello to you," he replied timorously. "What brought you here?"

"I needed a place to live and Sam was good enough to let me stay."

"She carries her load," Sam said. "She's a damn good cook."

"I recall as much."

"Maybe we can talk later, George," she said and withdrew with the other women. "Save me a little of your whiskey."

When she was gone George said to Sam, "You don't let her have a gun do you?"

The local chiefs retired to their respective houses leaving George alone in the longhouse. He was banking the fire for the night when Laura entered with a long wool cloak drawn around her. George's first thought was that she might have a gun under it.

"So how have you been?" she asked.

"Well, since the bullet hole healed, I've been just fine."

"You had it coming, but I'm glad I didn't take my second shot."

"And how have you been?"

"Since I came to Chounteroute I've been happy."

"That's good."

"I hear you have some sons."

"Three."

"And how is the redhead?"

"She's fine."

"Did you save any of that whiskey?"

"The men killed it, but I've got my travelling flask." He took it from his bag and offered it to her.

She took a long draught and asked, "Can I sit down?"

He nodded and they sat on the skins close to the fire. "So, did you remarry?" he asked.

"No, you gave me my fill of that."

"How long have you been here?"

"A few years. I put myself out and when the indenture was over I just wandered back here and decided to stay. They say you got rich."

"I got a lot of land. Never have a lot of money."

"How old are the boys?"

"Twenty-three, nineteen and seventeen."

"They as bad as you?"

"Probably."

"It's the Skipper blood."

"You might be right"

She opened her cloak and was naked beneath it. "You want to do it for old time's sake?"

He thought she looked damned good. Her breasts were still full, hips not gone to fat, and her belly not distended. "But you shot me," he stammered.

"No need to take it personal. You had it comin'." She moved toward him saying, "Don't try to act like you don't want it. I know you too well."

He reached a tentative hand to cup her breast, he felt its weight and his self-command was gone.

Laura's technique had somewhat slowed with maturity but was no less enthusiastic. From the same process of maturation George's staying power had increased exponentially. Mutually spent, she lay next to him and murmured, "I knew there had to be a reason I didn't shoot your balls off."

The sky was clear in the morning but the air was still cool. The town knew about Laura's conquest, but to the Indian way of thinking, such things weren't gossip worthy. Sam remarked, "Since the missionaries left it's good to see things getting back to normal."

George bade his farewells and rode south but not toward Anson. He paid a call at Urah woods, visited his uncle James who was frail and senile and being attended by his youngest son, George. He checked his acreage for squatters, finding none, and crossing the river turned south toward Edenton. There he paid the printer to strike a few handbills offering his Bertie and Chowan tracts for sale which he tacked to various bulletin boards.

He wandered toward Wilmington where he intended to post a few more of the bills. The weather improved steadily and the oaks and evergreens of the coastal groves were fairer than the winter barrenness of the inland forests. Remembering the tryst with Laura imbued him with a self satisfied contentment he had found missing for a time. Mary's response to his advances had come to lack reciprocal enthusiasm. There was no longing for Laura in his musings, only a sense of fulfillment that seemed somehow to vanquish a demon—perhaps the demon of being shot by Laura or maybe it was just the demon of fading potency.

He found the Holly Shelter Road and began to ride past well established plantations seated along the west side of North East Cape Fear River. When he came to Castle Hayne the plantations were on the east side and he found he was passing through fields of wheat, corn, tobacco and indigo. There followed The Hermitage, Rocky Run, Rook

Hill, Nesse's Creek, Fair Fields, Sans Souci, and after fording Smith Creek, Hilton was the last before entering Wilmington. The place had grown since he had seen it when he bought the land from John Clarke back in forty-nine. Approaching from the north he noticed a familiar scent on the air so he turned toward the river where there had been built a broad new wharf with a schooner tied alongside that bore the name Mary. A building of utilitarian façade stood well back from the wharf. It bore a sign engraved with bold letters announcing 'Richard Rundle, Distiller'.

George approached the still house intent on sharing a little professional camaraderie with the proprietor and perhaps coming away with a tip or two on improving his product, and replenishing his traveling stock, but the place was locked, seemingly deserted. With a shrug he rode back to Front Street and turned south toward the center of town. He advanced all the way to the dock before finding a living soul of whom he might inquire as to the sepulchral nature of the place.

The person was a Negro, presumably a slave. He doffed his hat before answering, "Why, is Sunday, suh."

"Oh, yes, of course. Might you direct me to an inn?"

George obtained a bed and meal in an inn with the unlikely name, Flounder. The other patrons, both of them, were disinclined to break the Sabbath with libation and were equally disinclined to engage a heathen in conversation. He wished he were spending the night in an Indian town. On the morrow he posted his handbills and determined to investigate the still house on his way out of town.

The sides of the building were thrown open and the workers were visible from without, most being slaves. George dismounted and hitched his horse. He approached the nearest white man and raised his hand. "Good morning, sir. Would the proprietor be around at the moment?"

The man pulled on his braces and eyed the stranger coolly. "The *proprietress* would be in her house at this hour. And what would be the nature of your business?"

George found the man a bit impertinent but responded politely, "I have no business with the *proprietress*. I am a passerby who happens to also be a distiller and I had hoped to be gratified by making the acquaintance of a fellow of my trade."

"Harrumph," harrumphed the white whiskered foreman. "If you call at the house to rear of the still house, the lady may decide to receive you." He took a handkerchief from his hip pocket and wiped the sweat from his forehead and walked away.

George was glad to be rid of him, and fetching his horse, walked to the indicated house. A Negro sat on the steps of the verandah and rose when he approached the house. "Kin I hep ya, suh?" he asked.

"Yes, I was hoping to have a word with the proprietor of the distillery. Would he be available?"

"Massa done be dead, suh, an Missus be takin' her brekfus."

George was feeling like this was becoming more trouble than it was worth. He contemplated the slave for a time before deciding what to say. "I wouldn't want to interrupt her breakfast," he said after a pause and began to leave.

"What is it, Sam?" a woman's voice called from inside.

"Vis'tor, ma'am," the slave turned his head toward the open window to reply.

The door opened and a woman came onto the verandah. She was a fine looking specimen with an exceedingly ample bosom, clear blue eyes set in a fair face with a wide mouth and high soft cheekbones. Her hair was wavy auburn colored and tied at the nape with a black velvet ribbon. She wore a light cotton dress of robin's egg blue that had lace at the collar and cuffs. It fit her form well and he was overcome with desire to see what was beneath it. He reckoned she might be ten years his junior. "How can I help you, sir?" she asked.

George was trying to not gawk but he was determined to imprint her image in his mind. "Begging your pardon, madam, I did not intend to disturb you. I was only interested in making the acquaintance of a fellow distiller before I left the area."

She descended the steps with her hand extended. "I am Lucretia Rundle," she said. "Widow Lucretia Rundle."

George took the extended hand saying, "George Skipper of Anson District. Pleased to make your acquaintance and I offer my condolences for your loss." The woman's magnetism was disorienting.

She eyed him as minutely as he was inspecting her. "My husband has been gone a year. My mourning is over. You say you're a distiller."

"Planter and distiller, madam. My distillery is a small operation. No comparison to what I saw through the open doors when I passed your still house. May I ask what you produce?"

"You may. We produce strictly gin."

"Gin. I can't say I've ever tasted that spirit. I make mostly rum and a small amount of whiskey. Is there a chance you would favor me with a tour of your operation? I'm curious as to what might be different in the way gin is made. Of course I insist that you return to breakfast first."

"I am quite finished with breakfast and would be pleased to show off my late husband's pride and joy—may he rest in peace. There is one difference in the making of gin from other spirits. I expect that you will find it interesting." She began walking and inquired, "What brings you to Wilmington, Mr. Skipper?"

"I have a mind to sell some land in the Craven and Bertie Precincts where I have been on other business and I thought to pass through Wilmington on the way to Anson for the purpose of posting some advertisements."

"Other business? You seem to have a great many

interests."

"More land transactions. I have a partnership interest in some Indian land."

"Indian. I thought perhaps you might be an Indian. How fascinating that is."

"Well, I'm glad you don't think I'm going to cleave your skull and collect your scalp."

"You aren't are you?"

"I'll try to avoid those urges although your lovely hair would make good addition to my collection," told her grinning.

"Mr. Skipper, I hope you're pulling my leg."

"Guilty. I missed the initiation into collecting scalps while I was away at school," he lied. "And it would please me to be addressed as George if you don't find that improper."

"I do not and you may call me Lucretia. I prefer it to Lucy which my departed husband insisted on calling me."

They arrived at the still and George owned that he had never beheld such a device. His simple retort and condenser would seem like a washtub next to the gin still. It consisted of four separate components of beautifully wrought copper. He stood in awe trying to understand how it worked. Finally he turned, meeting her eyes, and said, "My stars. What a thing of beauty."

Lucretia was smiling at his reaction. She pointed to a small chamber supported by tubes between the boiler and the condenser. "This is what's different in the process of making gin," she told him. "We pass the vapor through botanicals in this basket. They give the gin its flavor."

"I have never heard tell of such a thing. What are the botanicals?"

"Now, that is a trade secret," she said with a laugh.

"Well, then I surely have to acquire a bit of gin to see what this secret business is all about. Perhaps you'd sell me small amount to keep me company on the trail."

"But you might not like it and you would curse my

memory."

"How could I fail to appreciate something that comes from this remarkable contrivance and produced by your lovely hands?"

"At least you must have a sample. It is a wee bit early in the day, but if you would like to return to the house, I have some at a more suitable temperature. You know, gin was invented by the Dutch as a medicine. Fortunately the English discovered it's true worth." She showed him to the parlor and called for Sam who quickly left to fetch the gin.

While they waited she said, "I never met an Indian socially before. I don't know exactly what I expected but certainly not a landed gentleman planter and distiller."

"I learned the trade from my grandfather. He was an Englishman who thought the prohibition against selling whiskey to the Indians was barbarous so he built a still in the village and made it for them."

"My goodness, didn't the authorities object?"

"Yes, they did so he bought some land deep in a swamp and moved his operation where they couldn't find him."

The gin arrived and Sam served it to them in dainty glasses. George found it cool and fragrant. "My stars," he repeated, "it's like love in a glass."

Lucretia burst out laughing. "You're an interesting creature, George. Are all Indians so expressive?"

He thought before answering and while he thought he admired her lovely face and enticing body. Finally he said, "Why yes, many Indians are quite loquacious and full of wit."

"Please do tell what it's like in an Indian town."

At first he was struck with a melancholy sense of loss but he looked at his hostess and was inspired to pique her interest. "Before the soldiers forced us to send our boys to school at Fort Christiana and made our enemies move in with us, we led an idyllic life. We provided for our families, observed our festivals and rituals, and defended ourselves from enemies exactly like the white race except we were free from the hypocritical dichotomy of the white men's laws."

She knitted her brow at such a ponderous pronouncement in criticism of her race. While composing a rejoinder she refilled the glasses. "Do Indians not have laws?" was what she decided to ask.

"Absolutely, and they have strict justice, but they do not punish people for pursuing their natural urges."

"Meaning what?"

He hesitated weighing the risk of offending her with testing her moral waters and finally said, "We don't put people into the stocks for—for, shall we say, carnality. I hope that doesn't offend."

She didn't blink. "I'm a widow, George, not a debutant."

Hope rose. He took a sip of gin while wondering if she was sending a signal. He had no experience with a woman who was not at least aware of Indian mores. Fear of making an erroneous assumption kept him from attempting familiarity. He could see himself being dragged to the Wilmington jail by a posse of indignant white-devils. Still, the conquest of a woman raised white had a powerful appeal and, being a year into widowhood, she might even be craving the services of a noble savage.

His silence while he pondered turning his tale toward the salacious became tense. She broke the spell. "Do tell about the ceremonies."

"Well, the biggest ceremony is the Green Corn Dance. It must be performed before the corn can be harvested. All the tribes in the area meet at the ceremonial center where they purify themselves for a couple days. The medicine men prepare a secret potion which brings visions to the dancers and erases all the animosities of the previous year."

"What happens when all the animosities are gone?"

He had momentarily succeeded in quashing his libidinousness but the image of Mary on her knees after his first and only Green Corn Dance brought it back forcefully. He labored again to judge how truthfully he should answer. "There is love and forgiveness," he finally said.

"That must be a miraculous potion. What is in it?"

"Only the shamans know."

"Pity. It sounds like something we need more of," she said not making eye contact as she refilled the glasses. George tried to read her nuance but saw the posse in his mind's eye instead.

He took a big swallow of gin that burned his throat. He thought it might embolden him and he wondered if she were capable of drinking enough to loosen her inhibitions. *"Dammit,"* he thought, *"maybe she doesn't have inhibitions."* The lull became awkward again and he said, "You might be right." Wishing he had some right then, he added, "But it's only made once a year."

"Then perhaps it's like syllabub which we only make at Christmas," she offered frivolously.

"It has a powerful awful flavor and is so potent you only hold it your mouth for a time then spit it out."

"My goodness. What are these visions like?"

"At first it's like having blinders removed. Then it becomes sort of like receiving commandments from the Great Spirit."

She gazed at him with wide eyes and breathed, "Fascinating." He knew that if he were younger he'd have an erection to hide. "And what does the Great Spirit command?"

"Oh—" he thought how to respond while he scratched his chin, "to make peace with our enemies and learn to live with the white-devils."

She laughed and said, "Does that mean I'm a white-devil?"

His confidence spiked. He smiled deviously and fixed

her gaze with his. "I haven't seen any sign of devilment."

"Well, and you won't."

The wind left his sails.

"Lucretia, I feel as though I've taken up too much of your day," he said hoping the threat of leaving would force her hand if there were a hand to be forced.

"Oh," she said, "perhaps you're expected. How thoughtless of me to keep you."

"*Shit!*" he thought, "*why did I say that?*" He grasped for ways to dither. "No, nobody expects me but I'm sure you must have things that require your attention."

"Well, do take the rest of this gin for your journey. It's my gift to you for sharing your fascinating tales."

He was thinking of a different sort of gift but he resigned himself to being an artless fool and went to get his flask from the saddlebag. "I will never forget the pleasure of this interlude," he tried once more to get her to insist he linger but she did not rise to it. She offered her hand to shake which he took and covered with his left. "Thank you, Lucretia, for your hospitality."

"Safe journey, George," she said brightly.

He forced himself to smile, turn, and he plodded from the room feeling like he was leaving a funeral. On the road west self hatred vied with the empty feeling of lost opportunity. He thought, "*I 'm like teats on a boar.*"

CHAPTER TWENTY-ONE

It was four years before a messenger beckoned George back to Virginia to sell more Cheroenhaka parcels. Yellow fever had taken many lives in the dwindling town notably Sam and Laura Oxendine. George was eldest remaining chief, there being only Jack Will, Robbin Scholar and a young William Pearch besides. The reservation land was crisscrossed with new roads and the woods were full of surveyors carving it into parcels. George agreed with others that the land should all be sold as it was worthless to the Indians and might as well be converted to money.

A local lawyer by name of Miles Carey had made a fair offer on a parcel that was larger than the four-hundred acres allowed to any single buyer, furthermore, he wanted credit. The current trustees, gents Joseph Gray, Howell Edmunds and William Taylor, lobbied the Assembly on behalf of Miles Carey and the Indians were equally in favor of modifying the earlier decree. The result was a protracted sojourn in the moribund community that had an emotionally debilitating effect on George's spirits. Added to his panoply of demons was the castigation he still heaped upon himself for having so ineptly handled his attraction to Lucretia Rundle who he considered to have been his last chance for a dalliance.

Having nothing to do, he went to Potecasi to see his sister. Jean had not remarried. She had assumed the role of matriarch as her mother and grandmother had done although her tenure was distinctly anglicized. "Damn them, there's going to be bloodshed if they don't change their ways," she raged as soon as the formalities of greetings were finished. "The sheriff comes 'round here collecting taxes and he wants land tax and head tax. I say 'damn you, we're Indians. We don't pay head tax.' And he says when it comes to taxes we're as white as he is."

"It's as bad in Anson," George told her. "They've gone so far as to burn out some families who couldn't pay the tax even though they'd paid tax less than a year earlier. There's a tax when you buy there's a tax when you sell and there's a tax for doing nothing. You're right about the bloodshed. It's got to come. There's talk in Anson about forming a militia."

"Well, you stay out of it. I don't have another brother."

"Don't worry about me. I'm a peaceful Indian," he said but they both knew he was being disingenuous.

His uncle, James, was still in the realm of the living but didn't recognize him. Cousin George was ready to bear arms against the provincial authority. "The sheriff's been here. He wants me to tithe for Pa. Can you imagine that? The poor old man's not worth twenty-five pounds anymore."

George went to inspect his properties in Bertie and Craven expecting to find the buildings torched. When they weren't he decided they must have reasoned they couldn't terrorize a man when he wasn't there. He returned to Chounteroute and chafed until September when the third transaction was finally perfected. Much hostility was aroused in the courthouse by the onerous fees demanded by the clerk but of course they were paid.

George took his share of the remainder of the proceeds and rode hard for Anson.

* * *

Sheriff James Medlock found George in a testy discussion with Nathan about the proper shape of a barrel stave. "I'm sheriff of —" he began to say.

George was rankled by the interruption. "I know who you are. What do you want?"

"None of your cheek, man. I'm here to collect your lawful taxes."

"What taxes?"

"Capitation and tithables. I can see you, how many servants do you have?"

"See here, I'm an Indian. Indians don't pay taxes to the English King."

"If you chose to live off of a reservation you become one of His Majesty's subjects. Now, how many servants?"

"I don't have any servants."

"Oh, then who is this boy making barrels for you?"

"He's my son."

"Do you pay him a wage?"

"Of course not."

"Then he's a servant and I noted a Negress feeding the chickens when I came 'round the house, that's two. I'll brook no more insolence, Skipper. I know you have two more sons and a young nigger. That's five plus you, and if there's any argument, I will come back with a few regulars to investigate persistent rumors that you are making whiskey without a license."

"That nonsense again? I suspect you know that your predecessor also investigated that rumor and went away with his tail between his legs. I make turpentine."

"Skipper, I know you're making whiskey and when I prove it I am going to confiscate this property to pay your fine. Now, you will pay the head taxes or I am going to open that barrel and take a whiff of your turpentine."

The barrel on wagon was full of rum. He had brought it from his clandestine still house to mingle it with barrels of turpentine that were ready to be taken to the port, the rum, of course, going elsewhere. George seethed. "I'll get the money from the house."

Medlock pulled a pistol from inside his coat, pointed it at Nathan and said, "I'll wait here with the boy just in case you're thinking of bringing a gun with the money."

"You'll get your taxes and I'll get a receipt."

"Your remittance will be in my ledger."

"And where will that ledger be when you come back next month to collect again? Write a receipt or I'll come back with three guns and we'll see how many shots are in that pistol. Now, how much per head?"

"Twenty-five pounds. That's a total of one-hundred and twenty-five."

George felt a hammer blow to his diaphragm as if there had been a thunder clap. He stared at Medlock, mouth open and would have grabbed him by the throat if he didn't have a gun in his hand. He clamped his jaw shut and glared before finally turning and walking to the house. He came back with a double handful of coins and gestured to pour them in the sheriff's hands. Medlock was obliged to stick the pistol in belt to receive the cascade of coins with both hands. When George dumped the assorted *pistoles* and sovereigns from his hands he punched Medlock squarely on the end of his nose and Barnaby and Benjamin stepped around the corner with muskets leveled.

The man staggered but did not fall. His nose began to bleed profusely and he staunched it with the sleeve of his coat. George stepped back to give the two a clear shot if Medlock gave them a reason to fire. "Now that's only fair," he said. "If you're going to bleed us you ought to bleed a little yourself. So pick up your blood money and leave us in peace."

Mary was furious. "How many times are we going to

have to move because you threaten to shoot the sheriff?"

"I paid the tax this time so we're not going anywhere."

"You know he'll be back to arrest you."

"If he arrests me he'll have a fight on his hands."

"Then the boys will get arrested too."

"It won't just be the boys. I'm going to meeting tonight over at Clarkes place. There's a Quaker fella going to talk about the Regulators."

"What's that?" Mary's tirade subsided a little.

"A militia aimed at regulating things around here."

"You're just gonna make more trouble," she said but she knew she could not win this argument.

* * *

Harman Husband came from Orange County to speak to the men assembled at John Clarkes'. He was a member of the Assembly but a preacher by trade and his speech sounded more like a sermon than a call to arms. In fact he made it clear he was a dyed in the wool pacifist but he urged the men of Anson to present a united front of opposition to corruption in local government. The crowd was enthusiastic to everything he said except peaceful resistance. There was also a great deal of indignation about the 'palace' governor Tryon was having built in New Bern.

George and Barnaby, Mary forbade her younger sons to attend, listened to their neighbors' complaints. "When I couldn't pay the quit rent in hard money they sued me in New Bern," William Bart ranted. "It cost me more to go there to defend myself than the quit rent."

Steven Piecock maintained heatedly, "The money Medlock collects never gets to New Bern. He and Hutchins and Frohock divide it amongst themselves."

Barnaby was getting swept into the passions of the moment. He rose and shouted, "Frohock wanted so much for a marriage license I've been obliged to live in sin."

Some in the room gasped and some laughed. George shook his head.

Husband addressed him directly, "Son, in the Society of Friends we do not think it necessary to have the secular government sanctify marriage. Simply repeat thine vows in front of pious witnesses and the Lord will sanctify the union."

Barnaby sat and whispered to his father, "You'll back me up when I tell mother that, won't you?"

"If you'd known that before I could have saved my fifteen pounds."

There were near forty men in the barn. They agreed by voice vote to act in unison when a member claimed official abuse and they agreed to heed the call to action from other Regulator groups in the Province. After Husband left they agreed to arrive armed.

* * *

Barnabus was often rankled by his father's condescension. He farmed a plot apart from George's, and from its produce saved some money, but George made him pay rent, told him what to do and not to do. So he decided to buy a piece of land of his own. He found a fine parcel of bottom land that abutted the new road to Wilmington and Brunswick, had it surveyed, paid the patent fee and the clerk's fee although he was loathe to give more money to Frohock.

The property was a few miles from George's house. He left at first light by himself in the wagon with his axe intending to clear a home site. It was a balmy morning and the dew was still on the ground when he hitched the horse to a sapling. He felled a couple trees and cut them into manageable lengths intending to take them home to the sawpit there to make them into floor planks. Before he levered the first into the wagon sheriff Medlock served him with a process.

"Cease and desist," he demanded with a smile that revealed the gap in his teeth.

Barnaby looked uncomprehendingly at the paper in his hand. "What's this?"

"You are trespassing and preparing to steal the lumber of the lawful owner of this property."

"I'm the lawful owner of this property."

"You are quite mistaken. This property has been granted to Mr. Edmund Fanning, gent of Orange County."

Medlock had approached with his pistol in hand. Barnabus looked from the process to the pistol and shook with impotent rage. "I bought and paid for this land. I've got a deed to prove it."

"Your deed is defective. Now leave before I arrest you for the damage you've done to Mr. Fanning's timber." He gestured toward the wagon with the pistol.

He threw the axe into the wagon and put his boot on the step. "So how long has this Fanning owned this tract?"

"I'm told it's been several years."

"So where are his improvements? You can't keep a grant without improving it."

"They're here somewhere. You don't need to worry it. Get moving."

* * *

"We need to call a Regulator meeting," Barnaby insisted.

"There's already a meeting scheduled this month," George told him. "You'll still be fit to be tied by then."

"So now what am I going to do?"

"I reckon you're gonna do what you've been doing."

"I been getting a little tired of being your tenant and letting you tell me what I can do and what I can't."

"Boy, that's no way to talk to your father."

"I don't see why you don't just give that piece of land and let me do what I want with it."

"Because I believe that a man has to make his own way but I'll sell it to you."

Barnaby sighed, "What do you want?"

He also agreed to sell him eight horses so they went to the little log courthouse to make it legal. "Coming here's a waste of time and money," Barnaby groused. "Nothing this thieving bastard does is legal."

George actually agreed but felt that right was on his side. "How much you gonna extort from us today, Frohock?" he asked the clerk of court.

"Fifteen pounds for each entry."

"Is that the only number you know, Frohock?" Barnaby asked sarcastically.

"I also know twenty-five. Which do you prefer?"

"We'll take fifteen," George said. "Here's what we want to do: I'm selling fifty acres of land that does not belong to Edmund Fanning to my boy here. Also eight horses. You think you can handle that?"

"Watch your tongue, Skipper, or the fee just might go up."

"You already named your price, now start writin'. We'll stay here to make sure you do it right."

Frohock was sufficiently greedy to endure their abuse to get the fees. "Now," he said after collecting the thirty pounds, "you must pay for the stamps. Five pounds each document."

"We don't want stamps."

"It's an act of Parliament. Without the stamps the documents are worthless."

"Frohock, you're a lying bastard."

"Do you want the documents or not?"

On leaving the courthouse they met their neighbor Elija Clarke. "Have you heard what they did in Wilmington?" he asked.

"No, but I expect you're about to tell us," George replied.

"They had a riot in opposition to the Stamp Act."

"We just heard of the Stamp Act? But don't rightly know what it is."

"Oh, it's a new tax. We don't see it much out here 'cause we don't see much that's imported from England but now you gotta pay for a tax stamp on damn near everything. I heared there's been more protests in Boston and Philadelphia. Important people like Doctor Franklin gettin' involved. What you two doin' here anyway?"

Barnaby answered, "We're making a contribution to that shit, Frohock."

Elija chuckled. "See you at the meetin'."

Before they mounted their horses George handed the deed and the bill of sale to his son. "There. Do you feel like a man now?" he said. Barnabus did not dignify the remark with a response.

* * *

A Regulator meeting at the home of John Snor drew over a hundred men. The news of the day was the rumor that John Frohock had sold his clerkship to a stranger from Connecticut called Sam Spencer for 195 pounds.

"Frohock must have thought things were getting' a little too hot for him sell out so cheap," Tom Mason said to George.

"I'll wager you're right. He's still clerk in Orange though, so he can apply himself full time to skinning the poor folk over there."

"It'd be a shame to let him get out of the county without a least putting some stripes on him," Mason opined.

"That's a mighty appealing thought, Tom."

"You got anything to do after the meeting?"

"Nothin' important."

"I'll bet we can find few more boys who might like to join us," Mason said and moved though the crowd.

The Regulators' bylaws banned spirits at the meetings.

George didn't remember being consulted about that but he took a jug later to the gathering at Anson courthouse. It would have been enough to arouse the passions of a dozen men, however, forty answered the call so no one got more than a swallow and some were passed an empty jug.

Frohock had a house not far from the courthouse that he used when in the county. It was known that he was usually alone as he kept his family at his primary residence in Hillsborough. The mob surrounded the house while a few used a log as a battering ram to break the door then they rushed to the bedroom and threw a gunny sack over Frohock's head. They carried him into the woods behind the house and tied his arms around a gum tree. There had been much argument as to who would lay on the lashes. In the end lots were drawn but after the winner administered twenty good strokes Barnaby was handed the whip as payment for the marriage license incident. Nobody spoke so he couldn't know their voices. In the end they left him tied to the tree with the bag on his head. It took him most of the next day to get loose.

* * *

The following year Governor Tryon passed through Anson via the new road on an inspection tour of the Cherokee border. The Anson farmers had never seen an entourage of the like of this. The governor rode in a coach and six with bewigged postilions in red livery heavily festooned with gold braid and wearing tri-corn hats sporting white ostrich feathers. An honor guard preceded him, a regiment of regular militia followed and a baggage train came after that.

John Clarke elbowed George in the ribs as they watched the spectacle pass. "And you thought they built the road to make it easier for you to carry turpentine to the port."

All George could say was, "My stars."

The spectacle might have seemed amusing despite the obvious waste of public money and had the troops not commandeered a total of sixty head of cattle from several of the Regulators' farms.

Samuel Spencer recouped his 195 pounds investment in his first month as clerk of court. A lawyer named Anthony Hutchins gained equal notoriety as his and Sheriff Medlock's legal advisor. Talk at the Regulator meetings grew increasingly inflammatory until Colonel Bryan, a man of some military experience, was invited to speak. He quite calmly told the crowd that the time for action had come and that they were to follow him to the Anson Courthouse. By the time he reached it he had eight-hundred outraged farmers behind him. Court happened to be in session when the mob arrived. Not fifty of them could fit into the place. The rest, including George who was feeling his age, confined themselves to shouting and brandishing guns. Those who crowded inside pulled the justices from the bench and danced a jig upon it while the others beat the clerk and the lawyers insensible. They were disappointed to find the sheriff absent. Shortly thereafter Medlock resigned his position and left the county. His replacement was William Picket who attempted to keep a low profile.

John Snor got the idea to petition Governor Tryon for redress. Most thought it futile but none were opposed to trying. Snor with John Ryle and Sam Gaylord appointed themselves to compose the document. They listed seven grievances and offered seventeen remedies, the last of which was the appointment of 'Doctor Benjamin Franklin, or some other known patriot,' to represent their interests at the court of St. James. Ninety-nine Regulators put their names to it including George, whose eyes were failing and couldn't read it, and Barnaby. The governor did not respond.

Mary died suddenly which grieved the family deeply. She hadn't been ill she simply seemed to reach the end of her life force. Her influence over Benjamin and Nathan was stronger than over Barnaby and she had gotten them to promise to stay away from Regulator meetings. With her passing they felt free to join the fray with an intensity aiming to recoup lost time.

"Boys," George said to them having confronted his own mortality in the death of Mary, "my bones are creaking too loud to fight a battle but it's comin' and I'll need you three to cover my share of the fightin'."

The following year there was an even more violent riot a Hillsborough but it commenced without the knowledge of the Anson Regulators. Fanning was beaten blind in one eye, his house burned, anyone found in the courthouse got a thrashing, a few miscreants shit on the justices' bench and somebody exhumed a slave's carcass that was well along the process of rotting and left it on the lawyers' bar. Whether it was the shit or the carcass was never known but something moved the Assembly to appropriate the money necessary for the governor to raise a militia and it also gave him power to declare rioting to be treasonous and therefore punishable by being hanged, drawn and quartered. Though it was a matter of little concern to the bellicose Regulators of Anson, the Assembly also saw fit to expel the pacifist, Harman Husband, and throw him into jail.

* * *

Thursday morning May 16, 1771, George woke with a stiff neck from sleeping on the ground. "Pa, you should've stayed home," Benjamin told him.

"I ain't gonna miss this," he groaned. "I want to make sure you do me proud."

The Regulators were camped between Salisbury Road and Alamance Creek on the plantation of Michael Holt who was not happy about it. He was a Captain in the regular militia who had developed an abiding dislike for

Regulators when they beat the daylights out of him during the Hillsborough riot. The Skippers were unaware of the irony of their choice of campsites as there was no organized communication. They were not even aware that roughly two-thousand Regulators had joined the field.

Barnaby was trying to make coffee but burnt his fingers and spilled it. "You're still like teats on a boar," his father grumbled.

"You figure we're gonna fight today or just present petitions and talk?" Benjamin said to no one in particular.

"Probably talk," George said brusquely. The pain in his neck was not relenting.

"Won't be much of a fight if there's many like that Parsons. He only brought twelve balls," Ben said.

"Old fool," George muttered.

"Hey," Barnaby said, "some of 'em are movin'."

"I didn't hear an order," Nathan remarked.

"Those young idiots are having a wrestling match," Ben pointed to two boys rolling on the ground.

George got creakily to his feet using his rifle as a crutch. "You're not gonna hear orders. There's nobody to give 'em. Let's move forward and see what's goin' on."

They passed through a woods with bands of Regulators on all sides. The crush of men in the trees made it hard to keep moving and stay out of the mire to their right. The crowd forced them to stop in sight of a clearing. Nathan climbed a little dogwood and said, "I see Tryon's men. Two big lines of them and they got cannon and cavalry."

Somebody nearby called to him, "Do you see Captain Montgomery?"

"What's he look like?"

"I don't know," the man called back.

"Do you see anybody talkin'?" Barnaby asked him.

"Wait! There's somebody comin' forward with a piece of paper. Looks like he's readin' it out loud." A few moments later he added, "Whatever he said he's done and gone back to the lines. Look out. I'm comin' down.

We're movin' forward again."

They moved more laterally than forward. "At least we're on dry ground," Ben noted. His attention was attracted by a commotion and shrieking. "What's that?"

Two men were tied to trees and each was being whipped. George pushed his way toward the beatings. "Who are they?" he asked the crowd.

"Prisoners," a grinning man replied.

"Why you damned fools," he shouted, "do you want them doin' the same when they take you prisoner?" The two wielding the bullwhips did not pay attention but some in the crowd murmured agreement and moved away.

The four kept pushing through the crowd until they were near enough to the edge of the field to hear a few men with a modicum of military experience trying to bring a little order to the mob. They were having mixed success. A group of unarmed fools were prancing toward the orderly lines of militia with their shirts open beating their chests and taunting the soldiers to shoot.

"Just as soon be rid of the jackasses," George spat.

A mounted man in farmers' clothes broke from the center of the militia's line and galloped toward them. Tryon could be seen where the horseman had just quitted talking to another in ordinary clothes. His gestures were sharply animated and the civilian began to walk toward the Regulators. Tryon roughly grabbed the gun from a soldier and fired at the man's back. They could see the exit wound explode through his chest and he fell to his knees and then onto his face. The body did not even twitch.

The man on horseback reached the Regulators' line when he heard the shot. He turned sharply to the sound, stared in shock and shouted, "That's Robert Thompson!"

Tryon could be seen talking excitedly to a man in officers' uniform who disappeared into the ranks to reappear shortly with a white flag. The Regulators let him cross half the space between them before they opened fire. He threw the flag and himself headlong to the ground then rolled and scrambled stumbling to his feet and began running. Absurdly the buttons of his breeches had popped and he began to lose them.

Somebody shouted, "Fire and be damned!"

George couldn't see well enough to know why everybody was laughing. "The damned fool lost his breeches," Ben told him. "He was bare assed by time he reached the lines."

"That's what saved his life—"

The first artillery volley prevented him from finishing his witticism. The shells fell short and the second volley went over their head shattering branches in the trees. Fire was returned and the battle began in earnest. Captain Montgomery had organized a company to charge the artillery. They detached from the left side and crossed the intervening space so quickly that the militiamen withdrew. Two brawny farm boys grabbed a small field piece and wheeled it at a run back to the Regulator line but no one thought to grab the ammunition.

Before Montgomery's band reached the shelter of the woods again a shell landed in their midst fragmenting most of them including the Captain. A chaotic retreat began led principally by those who neglected to mold enough balls the previous evening. Regulators climbed over those still attempting to advance who assumed they were being routed and turned as well.

George was buffeted by the tidal mass of men trying to avoid the incoming fire. His crotchety hips not letting him keep pace with panicked younger men. His three sons were still at the front firing. They watched as some light horse surrounded a small group of Regulators who had apparently been specifically targeted and were quickly captured. Firing from the trees was becoming sporadic and the ranks of militia were advancing steadily.

"I'd say the game's up," Barnaby told his brothers.

"We looked like a bunch of damned fools," Nathan said and punched the ground.

"We look like a bunch of damned farmers," Barnaby corrected.

"I thought we'd at least make a showing." Ben shook his head.

"We're going to be dead damned fools if we don't move," Nathan reminded them and they quickly joined the retreat.

Barnaby looked at the men around them then asked, "Hey, where's the old man?"

"I didn't see him after we started shooting," Nathan said.

"He probably started moving back when the shooting started because he couldn't see," Ben reasoned.

"Well, keep your eyes peeled for him."

A volley landed quite a bit ahead of them and they heard men shouting and moaning. "Isn't anybody helping the wounded?" Ben asked as he looked at writhing bodies.

"We can come back when the shelling is over," Barnaby told him. "There'll be a truce."

"We gotta find the old man," Nathan insisted. "He might be wounded."

"How you gonna find him?" Barnaby shouted. "I can't see for the smoke."

That made Ben think. "Smell that?" he asked.

"What?"

"That's not powder, that's wood smoke. The woods is on fire."

"Which way is it coming from?"

Nathan pointed to his left saying, "I can see flames through there." He turned around to look backward. "The fire's all around! They deliberately set it all around."

"Damn Tryon! Now, we really gotta find the old man."

Barnabus took charge. "Nate, you go see if he's in the camp. Come back and tell us. Ben and I'll start checkin' bodies."

Nathan found the camp not only empty but gone. He

started back to the woods to be met by his brothers coming toward him. "Too much smoke," Ben told him, "couldn't see or breathe."

"There's wounded in there. What are we goin' to do about 'em?"

"Not a damn thing we can do. They're getting roasted alive. The old man too if he's in there."

George was in there. The concussion of an exploding shell stunned him and knocked him down. Fleeing Regulators trampled over him with one big hobnail boot shattering his hip. He lay where he fell cursing at the top of his lungs, but nobody heard him, until he succumbed to the smoke. He was already dead before the flames reached him.

EPILOGUE

JUNE 19, 1771

HILLSBOROUGH

On the day of the battle Tryon hanged a simpleton named James Few at the campground. Few didn't know why he was even there. Twelve Regulators were captured and held for trial. Of the twelve Regulators tried all were found guilty of treason. Tryon pardoned six, the others being sentenced to be hung, drawn and quartered although they were simply hung. Gunsmith, James Pugh, probably dropped more militiamen at Alamance than any other Regulator. He spoke with the noose around his neck famously saying, "The blood that we have shed will be as good seed sown in good ground, which soon will reap a hundred fold."

Four years later, in the good ground of Lexington and Concord, other patriots reaped the hundred fold.

# # #

AUTHOR'S NOTES

Although this is a work of fiction most characters and events are taken from the historical record—all of the Skipper males and some of the females are. Of course conversation and daily occurrences are inventions as is George's use of rum to ingratiate himself with the Cheroenhaka—it was probably just his native charm. He really did have an Indian wife called Mary, Francis and John both had wives named Ann. The record gives Francis' wife as being "colored". George did acquire the land at Potecasi in 1668. In fact all of the land transactions—except Barnaby's defective deed—are taken from colonial records and all of the court cases are based on fact including Mary Bailey's sixteen shilling judgment. The recitation of the case is verbatim from the court record.

The passenger list of the Three Brothers has survived and I confess that no Skippers are on it, and it sailed at a later date, but the coincidence of the ship's name and family folklore of three brothers immigrating to the New World was irresistible.

The Cheroenhaka place names are authentic as are most of their troubles with the Colonial Government and the settlers. The chiefs were deceitfully imprisoned by Spotswood and incredibly the Nansemond were removed and the Meherrin were forced on the Cheroenhaka. All of the Cheroenhaka chief men, including George Skipper, are historical figures. Even Hairy Belly has a little veracity, the historical record in another time and place mentions a woman named Nancy Furbelow.

Because of the length of time that the name George Skipper occurs in the historical record I have assumed that there must have been three generations of them. In fact there may have been four. George and Barnaby signing the Anson Regulator petition is true although there is no proof of them participating in the Battle of Alamance—but how could they have resisted? The description of the battle is taken from internet sources which verify the roasting of the wounded.

The legend of Uttamussack and the pawcorance is supposedly true although it's hard to imagine that it buzzed like a bee—more likely the Indians were buzzing. The well organized Indian massacre is true as is the removal from Tamahiton to Assamoosick for reasons of encroachment. The description of the town of Chounteroute is based on a description made at a later time. Cheroenhaka warriors were enlisted by George Washington during the French and Indian War and apparently never paid.

Concerning etymology, effort was made to avoid putting modern words into the mouths of characters who could not have known them. If the dialog does not sound authentic for the period it is because I don't believe ordinary people spoke in the archaic manner of the writing of some early chroniclers. In reading, for example, the Autobiography of Benjamin Franklin and The History and Present State of Virginia by Robert Beverly, both written in the eighteen century, one finds the language surprisingly modern. I have made an intentional effort to evolve the speech of proper Englishmen to the speech of back country farmers. Indians have been given broken English at times but speak correctly when they use their own language. Lawyers and judges always talk funny.

Carolina Bays are a common geological feature in the area where this story is set. They are elliptical ponds all oriented in the same general direction and are theorized to have been formed by a prehistoric meteor strike. The Bays will assume a larger role in the subsequent telling of the history of the Skipper family in the Carolinas which was originally spelled Carolana. I apologize to any Skipper descendants who may be scandalized by my irreverent and bawdy character developments.

Glossary of Cheroenhaka Words

Aheeta = Sun
Akroh = Father
Asunta = Darkness
Auteur = Fire
Awwa = Water
Cheer = Dog
Cheeta = Bird
Darsunke = Tongue
Dekanee = Two
Deeshu = Star
Ena = Mother
Eniha = Man
Eteshe = Chief
Gahuntee = Black
Garhusung = Boar
Genheke = Summer
Ges = You, your
Hahenu = Thunder
Howerac = Hair
Huse = Wolf
Katahtekeh = Brother
Kohan = Shad
Newisha = Little
Ocherura = Stick
Ohunwitstag = Wing
Oska = Fat
Oranakewn = Forest
Owarag = Lips
Owheryakun = White
Otkum = Devil
Quakerhunte = Creator
Queru = Rabbit
Sanseke = Leg
Sariyoka = Running
Satek = Back
Sat'untatag = You listen
Shautaroswache = Spring
Sunhe = Heart
Suntetung = Morning

T'achanunte = Happy
Teerheer = King
Unke = Belly
Wani = Silver
Wahehun = Dead body
Youhanhu = Light
Yowerha = Dry

Glossary of other Indian Words

Cockarouse = Brave man
Cohonks = Winter
Huskanawing = Rite of passage to become a shaman
Mahkwa = Bear
Niminisisan = Hair
Okeepenauk = A tuber
Pawcorance = Legendary crystal altar at Uttamussack
Quioccos = Idol
Quioccosan = Altar
Quiocosine = Cemetery
Tsenacomoco = Territory of Virginia
Uttamussack = Sacred place name
Werrowance = Chief

FAMILY TRAITS

Made in the USA
Charleston, SC
13 September 2013